THE BATTLE OF T

$\mathcal{T}$ALIESIN'S MANTLE

Armour

Taliesin's Mantle: Battle of the Trees II

© Anne Hamilton 2022
Published by Armour Books
P. O. Box 492, Corinda QLD 4075

Cover Images: markedman80, Getty Images; morrbyte, Deposit Photos; svyatoslavlipik, Deposit Photos; fotoatelie, Canstockphoto
Chapter music images: Beckon Creative; Viktoria.1703; Greg Rosenke; Gleen Art; SeaDesignCORP, Etsy; davector, Creative Fabrica
Celtic tree image: zhevelev, Depositphotos
Interior Design and Typeset by Beckon Creative

ISBN: 978-1-925380-50-7

 A catalogue record for this book is available from the National Library of Australia

Note: Australian spelling and grammar conventions are used throughout this book.

THE BATTLE OF THE TREES II

TALIESIN'S MANTLE

ANNE HAMILTON

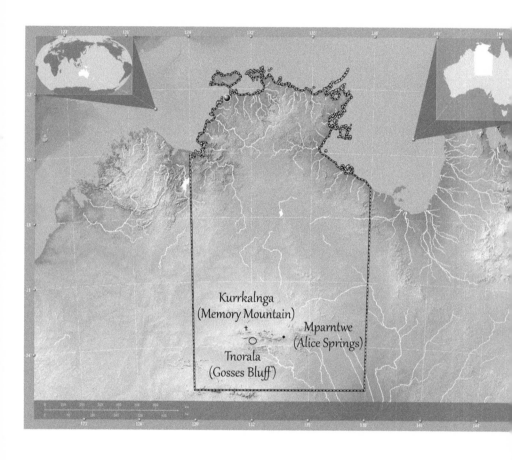

Prelude

'GAWAIN! DOWNSTAIRS IMMEDIATELY. We have a guest.'

Gawain jerked in his chair, startled. He'd been so engrossed in his project he hadn't registered another presence in the room. Clicking far too late on the privacy tab, he noticed his father's scowl reflected in the computer monitor.

'Yes, sir.' He swivelled to face his father as the screen flickered and a new viewing pane opened. *Did he see? Ohpleasepleaseplease don't let him have realised.* 'Coming right now.'

His father's face had assumed its hatchet look. Gawain knew not to hesitate. He left the computer without a backward glance and followed his father out the door. The light switched off automatically behind them.

Has he found out? *Oh, Ican'tIcan'tIcan't go to military school…*

Even before he reached the top step, his fear shifted focus. In front of the alcove where his mother's gold-flecked antique vase was showcased stood a marine at full attention, assault rifle across his chest. Another was stationed at the foot of the stairs. And a third barred the doorway into his father's private study.

Whatwhatwhat? Gawain took a deep breath and forced himself into an inner mental calm. *Who on earth are these guys? Why are they here?*

The marine in front of the study stood aside as his father pressed the handplate that registered his genetic code. *This is serious. I haven't been allowed inside for at least five years.* The door slid open, whisper quiet.

Gawain followed his father in. The room was as cold as a tomb and shadowed in a twilight gloom. *Why's the environmental programming turned off?* He stopped, disturbed as the door-bolt shot home behind him. The floor-to-ceiling wall of books that had awed him as a child was gone and a gigantic world map had taken its place. On it, a green column of light branched like the limbs of a tree, sending tumbling leaf-shapes across the globe. *Message-interceptor.*

'Sso thiss iss your sson.' The voice had a reptilian hiss. 'The right age, yess…'

Gawain was so glad the shadows hid his jerk of unease. His eyes, still adjusting to the murky light, just made out his father's chair swivelling to face them.

A gargantuan figure was seated in it, regarding them with an amused smirk. '…but that doess not imply aptitude for the tassk.'

Gawain's father sounded almost fawning. 'He's far more intelligent than he looks.'

'Sso, good. He'll need to be.'

Gawain peered at the giant, trying to make out his features. *Surely his eyes aren't yellow? The pupils can't be slits.*

'Come closser, boy. Closser.'

No-no-no. Unexplained terror gripped Gawain. His feet remained rooted to the spot. He almost stumbled as his father pushed him forward.

Slime enclosed his hand. 'Let me explain your asssignment, boy.'

Don'tthrowupdon'tthrowupdon't... Gawain clenched his stomach tight as nausea threatened.

'America needss you, boy. On your sshoulderss resstss the fate of the free world. Your father iss confident you are up to thiss misssion and, make no misstake, it will require both a clever mind, a ssturdy will and unquesstioned loyalty...'

Thiscan'tbehappening. It's a bad scene from a rotten movie. I'm being asked to be a spy?

'Boy, you will be ssent to a sspecial ssummer sschool for young sscientisstss and musst find and befriend twinss named Reece and Holly. They may be ussing other namess.'

Summer? Whatarelief. Morethanhalfayear away. But science? Badbadbad but infinitely better than the military academy. 'I'll do my best, sir.'

'Your orderss are ssimply to watch them. You will leave for Ausstralia tomorrow.'

Gawain gulped. *Australia? Halfway around the world? Not summer here but summer downunder? Tomorrow? But it's not even the end of October.*

The slimy hand squeezed his palm so tightly that pain shot through it, sharp as a piercing stiletto. He gasped, then froze, holding his breath. The pain subsided, before spiking again.

'Give him the glasssess.'

His hand throbbing, Gawain was pulled around by his father. A pair of wire-rimmed spectacles was perched on his nose. 'Gawain, you don't need to concern yourself with reporting in.

These glasses will do that for you. They're indestructible and will see everything you see. Just concentrate on finding the twins and insinuating yourself into their lives. You're good at making friends, son. That's why you've been selected for this assignment. It's vital to our national security.'

Gawain knew a response was expected from him. 'Yes, sir.'

He felt a pat on his shoulder; the first he could remember in years. The door opened automatically as his father sent him upstairs. 'Do me proud, son.'

They were the most terrifying words his father had ever uttered.

The marines on the stairwell saluted as he passed.

1

GAWAIN STARED OUT HIS WINDOW, watching a silhouette skitter up a tree and scamper from branch to branch. *Australia?* A chipmunk paused in the gnarled fork of a tree, an acorn clutched in its paws. *Kangaroos, desert, g'day mate.* He shook his head. *The end of the earth.* He'd been forbidden to tell his friends where he was going. *No contact.* One of the marines had taken his cellphone and another had confiscated his computer.

Downunder. The country where there should be signs, 'Here be dragons.' So close to the edge of the world there was a danger of falling off.

He rubbed his palm, trying to erase the pain. The chipmunk, with a shiver, disappeared into the darkening air.

His door slammed. He jerked in fright. *Who's deactivated my privacy locks?*

He turned just as his little sister jumped onto his bed and thrust something into his rucksack. 'Gawain,' she pleaded, her face teary.

'No.' He ignored her choking tone. 'I don't care what it is, Angie. The answer is *no*.' He plunged his hand into the rucksack, pulling out a pair of socks and a mass of coppery curls and spangled satin. It was Angie's favourite doll.

'No?' Angie folded her arms. 'Good!' A gold lamé glove drooped through the crook of her elbow. Its fingers were too big for the hand inside it. 'I knew the President wouldn't say I had to leave Princess Emma behind.'

Gawain, about to hand Princess Emma back, hesitated. *Behind?* His suspicions surged. 'You're *not* coming to Australia.' He meant it as a question but it came out like an accusation.

'Am so.' Angie's tone was vehement. 'Gawain, how would the President even know about Princess Emma?'

'Don't know, sparrow.' Gawain rubbed his aching palm. *What on earth was anyone thinking by sending Angie with him on a spy mission?*

The door opened. A tall blonde woman in a steel-grey suit came in. Her eyes were hidden behind mirror glasses. Without a word, she put her hand out for the doll. Angie squealed and tried to rescue Princess Emma but the woman took it and shoved it, head first, into her suit pocket.

'Angelina, how many times do I have to explain?' The woman's lips thinned in disapproval. 'Anything with an anti-theft device is out. You cannot take this with you.'

She's coming as Angie's babysitter? Wait a moment... as mine?

The woman changed tactics and tried a winning smile. 'I know it's asking a lot from someone only eight years old...'

'I'm *nine*.' Angie pouted and took an aggressive stance.

'Pardon me for asking, ma'am...' Gawain stared at the face reflected in the woman's glasses, alarmed at how timid and mouse-like he looked. '...but can't you take the identification chip out?'

'Young man...' The woman's smile broadened. '...you are fortunate to have parents who care enough about you to have chip-coded everything you own and lodged the numbers with the National Security Register. So, if anybody steals your property, if you misplace something or even if you get lost hiking, the NSR can get a position trace in seconds. The location fix is so accurate it can pinpoint an object to within...' She held up a glossy red fingernail. '...this much. The width of a finger.' She straightened so she towered over Gawain. 'Do you get the picture?'

You don't need to patronise me. 'You didn't answer my question. Can't you take the chip out?'

'Your father has access to the latest prototype chips.' The woman was clearly trying not to sound exasperated. 'Princess Emma has smartdust that's been absorbed into her structure.' Her lips curled. 'I'd like to be able to say only the good guys work for the NSR but we can never be too sure, can we? Do you understand what it means to be able to pinpoint the location of something so accurately?'

Gawain couldn't believe what she was implying. 'Someone who wanted revenge on my dad could shoot at us from space with a laser beam?'

'Nothing so melodramatic.' She folded her arms. 'Only happens in movies.'

Gawain was struck by the irony of her stance and expression: almost exactly the same as Angie's.

'I'm here to protect you, Gawain. I'm here to keep you both safe.' She put out her hand. 'Thania Hale, at your service.'

Gawain ignored her outstretched arm.

Her mouth twisted. 'Gawain, if you want to help your country, just do as I say. If you'd explain that to Angelina, too, I'd be immensely grateful.' She stood there a moment longer before turning on an elegant heel and heading for the door. 'Packed and ready in ten minutes. Both of you.'

Gawain, trying to push his sense of desolation aside, returned to the window.

'Let's go spy on her.' Angie tugged at his shirt. 'We've got to rescue Princess Emma.' She tugged again.

'Stop!' Gawain fixed his gaze on her gold lamé glove. 'This isn't a game, sparrow. There are stormtroopers outside and we've got to be ready to go or we'll be in trouble.'

'Don't care.' Angie glared at him. 'Don't want to go.' She reached into her pocket and pulled out a glossy black stone. 'I've been saving this, Gawain. Remember what you said? It's true, isn't it?'

He blinked. The iron meteorite he'd given her for her birthday. *What did I say? She hadn't understood 'meteorite', so I said 'falling star'. As in when-you-wish-upon-a-star kind of star. Oh, shoot. Wishes.*

'Three wishes, you said.' She rubbed the meteorite with a look of dreamy reverence. 'I want Princess Emma. I don't want to go to Australia. I'm saving the third wish for later.'

How do I get out of this one? She'll be crushed. 'Great wishes.' Gawain sighed, gentling his voice. 'But you might want to try again when your wishing star wakes up. It looks like it's gone to sleep.'

Angie held up the stone to check.

A hand swooped down from nowhere and scooped it from her fingers. Miss Hale tossed it out the door to one of the marines, ignoring Angie's howls of rage.

'Ready in five minutes, young man.' She snarled at Gawain. 'And if you know what's good for you, don't keep me waiting.'

Gawain didn't move. Angie was screaming. 'She's tooked Princess Emma!' She'd reverted to hysterical babytalk. 'And now she's took my wishing star as well.' She raced to the door and roared. 'It don't have a code-chip. Why can't I have it?'

'Four and a half minutes.' Miss Hale's voice was imperturbable. So imperturbable it was annoying.

Angie was in meltdown.

How do I calm her? A long-forgotten memory flashed to the forefront of his thoughts. *It's not a sleeping star, but Angie will love it.* He ran to his wardrobe, flung it open, and began throwing clothes, shoes, games in every direction.

Angie continued screaming.

At the very back of the bottom drawer, he found his box of earth treasures. Pulling out the battered container, Gawain lifted the lid. *Where's that fossil from Morocco?* He picked up an old playing card, brushed aside a peacock feather, pulled out a pink nautilus shell and a prickly pine cone. *Wherewherewhere?*

'Gawain!' Miss Hale's voice was edged with ice.

'Gawain!' It was his father.

'Coming, sir!' Gawain realised he didn't have time to search the clutter.

'Calm your sister down!' His father sounded furious.

Do I take that as permission to bring my earth treasures—and my other treasures—with me? He thrust the playing card, the feather, the shell and the pine cone back in the box. Darting to his desk, he popped the secret drawer and retrieved the hidden nano-jot. Slapping its sticky side under his armpit, he grabbed his rucksack and the box of earth treasures and hurtled out the door.

Downunder. With Angie. Sorry, Australia. You're not going to know what's hit you.

2

GAWAIN HAD MANAGED TO CALM Angie down on the way to the airport. It was easier than he thought it would be. They clambered out of the armoured Hummer and headed for the terminal's automatic doors.

Gawain stopped right in the middle of them, unable to believe his eyes. Clustered around the reservation desks and book-in counters were a dozen red-haired freckled boys wearing the same jeans and plaid flannel shirt as he was. Next to each boy was a small blonde girl in a pink top and check skirt. And on one hand of every girl—*just one hand, of course*—was a floppy gold glove.

The sight of Angie and himself all but cloned over and over was daunting enough, but it was as nothing to the vision of a dozen 'Miss Hales' in mirror glasses, accompanied by a dozen pairs of burly security men. *What on earth?*

Miss Hale led the way. Pulling out his passport and visa, he followed her to the first-class counter. 'Thank you, Gawain.' The attendant's mouth dipped in a curious smile, before even looking at his documents. 'I'll need Angelina's passport and visa, too.'

Is she a mind-reader? Like, this is seriously spooky. 'How do you know our names?'

The attendant's full wattage smile became, if possible, even brighter. 'Every boy and girl flying out of Hopkins International this evening is Gawain and Angelina. You're the ninth Gawain through this desk alone in the last half hour.' She winked as she placed his open passport on a scanner. 'Put your hand on the ID plate, please. You may feel a slight tingle, but please don't move it or the DNA match may need to be redone.'

Miss Hale almost yanked Gawain's arm off as he was about to rest it on the plate. 'I'm invoking the privacy amendment.'

'So this is the real Gawain Aishdene?' The attendant's fixed smile didn't falter. 'Please understand that, without a DNA match, these children need to undergo a deep tissue security scan.'

Uh...oh. Nano-jot.

Miss Hale's lips disappeared in a thin line, but the attendant ignored her and focussed on Gawain. 'For security purposes, I am required to ask if you packed your own bag.'

'Y...yes.' Gawain's hand prickled with fire.

'Are you carrying anything for someone not travelling on the plane?'

'No.'

'Good.' The attendant handed him a boarding pass. 'Enjoy your holiday in Switzerland. Your flight leaves from Gate 4.'

'*Switz*erland?' Gawain squealed. 'But there's a mistake, we're...' He broke off as Miss Hale pinched his arm. She pulled him aside as Angie went to the counter to answer the same questions. 'What's going on?'

'We've had to make contingency plans and lay a number of false trails.' Miss Hale's tone was placating. 'Gawain, I understand how stressful this must be, but I'm on your side. Really.' She held out her hand. 'Peace?'

Fuming, Gawain ignored it. *How can I do this spy thing when everyone's doing all they can to draw attention to me? Angie and I will be a viral sensation on the internet in no time.*

Angie's golden glove tugged at his sleeve. 'How come we're going to Swizzleland?'

Gawain didn't answer. He grabbed her hand and pulled her across the departure lounge. His thoughts were so agitated he hardly heard her counting.

'Fourteen, fifteen… seventeen… twenty-one.' Her gold finger bobbed up and down. 'There's twenty-one of us, Gawain.'

'I think you've counted some of them twice.' He joined the queue for the scanner arch and put his rucksack on the roller.

'Don't think so.' Angie placed her pink satchel just behind his. 'I think I missed some.'

'Gate 4.' Miss Hale had no luggage. She was waiting for them as they picked up their packs on the far side of the arch. 'Final boarding call's just been announced.'

'What about the deep tissue scan for concealable weapons?' Gawain asked.

'Officious woman.' Miss Hale glanced over her shoulder. 'You don't fit the profile of a terrorist, Gawain. Suicide bombers don't normally travel with their eight-year-old sisters, for one thing.'

'Nine!' Angie snapped.

Not normally. Gawain sighed and looked for Gate 4. He spotted three Gawains—one eating a donut, another sipping a soda, and the third gazing agape at an ancient tree spreading up through a network of structural girders to the roof. There wasn't a scampering, chattering chipmunk in sight. Instead a pearl-scaled dragon slithered through the leafy lower branches flicking its ruby tongue. *Cool hologram.*

'Twenty-six,' Angie announced.

'You're just picking numbers out of the air.' His gaze was drawn by the dragon's snout swivelling towards him. *There's something not quite right about that hologram.* 'By my count, it's…' Its sloe-black eyes transfixed him. '…twent…'

He never finished the word. By the time he saw the flash, it was too late. He felt himself twisting, felt his body propelled backwards. There was no sound. He fell against Miss Hale as he thudded to the floor, realising his right shoulder had bloomed into a spray of blood.

He saw Miss Hale grab Angie and pull her down, watched the walls of the airport begin to spin. There was a moment of silence, then screaming, then long crimson fingernails in front of his face. *One of them's badly chipped.*

Moments later, Angie wavered in front of his eyes. 'Get down!' His voice was hoarse as he yelled and reached to yank her down. He fell back, groaning, as an arc of agony lanced across his right shoulder.

Angie shook her head, as if his behaviour was distinctly odd. 'He did know about Princess Emma.'

'Wha…?' Gawain's head reeled.

'The President.' Angie's blonde curls bobbed as she nodded with conviction. 'He did know about Princess Emma.'

The President? 'We've gotta get—' He stopped, becoming aware of his surroundings. He was lying across a row of padded seats, his head propped against a hill of pillows, his shoulder wrapped in a medicated bandage. 'Where are we?'

It was obvious he was in a plane. But there was no one else in it except Angie. A full-length curtain half-covered a logo on the cabin wall in front of him. Gawain recognised the design at once: the Great Seal of the President of the United States.

'Yes. You're in Air Force One.' With a dramatic flourish, Miss Hale emerged from behind the curtain.

'Air Force One?!' Gawain jerked up so fast a shaft of pain went right through his shoulder. He shook as he fell back on the pillows. 'The President's own plane?'

'He's not using it at the moment, so we've borrowed it.'

'You borrowed it?' Gawain's eyes narrowed. 'Just like that?'

'Just like that.'

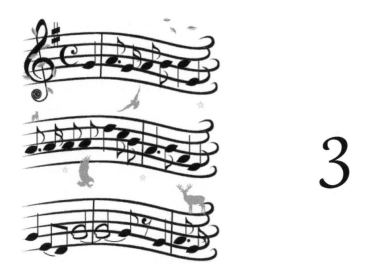

3

MISS HALE PERCHED ON AN ARMREST facing Gawain. 'I'm sorry, Gawain.' She winced as she glanced at his shoulder.

'Sorry?!' The taut band around Gawain's frightened thoughts snapped. 'I've been shot! That's bad. But it could be worse. Some poor pretend Gawain could be dead.'

Miss Hale's eyebrows lifted. 'You're a strange kid, Gawain. Most boys your age wouldn't think for a moment about anyone else in danger, let alone first.'

Her mirror glasses were broken. A corner was missing and the frames were no longer straight. Gawain heaved a deep sigh. 'You saved my life?'

'Just doing my job.'

'Thanks.'

Miss Hale's face was flushed. 'I'm not doing it very well. We didn't anticipate an attempt on your life. Our worst-case scenario was a kidnap attempt. So we simply worked to make you and Angelina impossible to identify...'

Kidnap? I'm supposed to be joining a summer school for young scientists. No one knows I'm a spy, so why would anyone want to abduct me?

'...but it looks as if we've misjudged the opposition. Badly.' Miss Hale paused. 'Whoever that opposition is... I don't know how they penetrated your disguise either.'

There was a momentary silence.

'They didn't know who we was.' Angie glared at Miss Hale. 'We didn't have nothing on us what could've been traced. So there's only one way they could of done it.'

Gawain stared at Angie. She wasn't half as okay as she looked. This wasn't the baby talk of hysteria or the cutiepie speech she used to wheedle her own way, it was the bad grammar of I'm-so-scared-I-can't-think-straight. It hadn't happened since he'd sorted out the Benessford twins for her.

'Oh?' Miss Hale's raised eyebrows were visible high above the rim of her broken glasses. 'So what's that?'

'Them's identified you.'

She might be scared, but she might be right too. 'I bet your gun's coded.' His mouth twitched in a momentary sneer. 'They didn't trace us, they traced *you*.'

Miss Hale began to protest but Angie pounced. 'They wasn't trying to kill Gawain. It was a kidnap what went wrong.'

'What could either of you possibly know...' Miss Hale's voice rose in strident scorn. '...that my very worried colleagues don't?'

Angie matched her, scorn for scorn. 'The kidnappers was a bad shot. They was shooting at you, not Gawain.'

Miss Hale looked up, as the throb of the engines starting up hummed through the cabin. 'Put your seat-belts on, both of you. Would you like help, Gawain?'

Gawain shook his head. Moving his pillows awkwardly, he strapped himself in. Angie, her tongue poked out of the side of her mouth with the effort, also insisted on doing it herself.

'Well now...' Miss Hale moved from the armrest to a seat and put on her own belt. '...neither of you is stupid it seems. So, tell me, why've you been pretending?'

'Why are we going to Swizzleland?' Angie countered.

'We're not. It's a false trail.' She smiled, the curve of her lips at odds with the frown of her forehead.

A moment later, with a smooth thrum of its engines, the plane began its straight vertical ascent. The moon was rising over the lake, as the upwards thrust changed smoothly to horizontal flight. From the window, Gawain could see the plane's reflection in the water as it skimmed across the glimmering surface. A blur of shoreline, then a patchwork grid of lights sped by below. Seconds later, the plane was soaring over the wild cataracts at the lake's end where the river went hurtling down on its way to the sea.

'How long before we get to Australia?' Angie peered out her window.

'A few hours,' Miss Hale said. 'There won't be any stopover.'

'How long will you be with us?' Gawain wondered how on earth he was going to befriend anyone with someone as intimidating as Miss Hale looking over his shoulder—his very painful shoulder—the whole time.

'Although I'm your guardian for the duration of the school, I will by no means be glued to your side. I'll be watching your back, of course. But apart from checking occasionally to see you're keeping up with the special work programmes your teachers back here have set you, I don't expect we'll have any interaction to speak of.'

Gawain stifled a sigh of relief. *So what's she here for? Oh dumbdumbdumb, Gawain. You're her cover story. You're Hale's excuse to be at this school.*

'Don't think it's going to be all fun and games.' Miss Hale shook her head. 'I believe, Gawain, that your history teacher has given you a research assignment on the 20th century.'

'I thought I'd finally left President Kennedy and the Cuban Missile Crisis behind.'

'I'm bored,' Angie announced.

Gawain curled his upper lip at her. 'You get to fly in the President's own plane every day? You're in a hypersonic vertical-lift sub-orbital superjet and you're bored?'

'I don't have Princess Emma to share it with.' Angie's smile was sweet but he detected the lurking venom. 'You haven't been good company, Gawain, even when you're awake. More interested in cubic missiles than anythink like rescuing damsels in distress.'

Gawain thought of reminding her he'd been shot and was in pain. Only he wasn't in pain. As long as he kept still, he felt almost normal. A little shaky, true, but quite alert. He wondered what drugs he'd been given. He wondered how long he'd been unconscious. He turned to Miss Hale. 'How come we're in Air Force One? You can't have whistled it up at a moment's notice, just because I got shot.'

Miss Hale shrugged. 'As a matter of fact, it was always Eyes' intention to take you to Australia this way.'

Eyes? Who on earth are Eyes?

'A normal trip would have involved three airport transfers and a long helicopter flight,' Miss Hale went on. 'The school is in quite a remote location.'

And you want to make an impression on the school trustees. A bigbigbig impression.

'I'm bored.' Angie's face was a picture of depression. 'Without

Princess Emma there's no-one to play with.' She brightened so quickly Gawain knew to be alarmed. 'Can I visit the cockpit?'

Miss Hale considered this for several seconds. 'I'll go ask.' She unclipped her seat-belt and walked forward.

As she disappeared behind the grey curtain, Gawain turned to Angie. 'You little schemer.'

Angie grinned. 'Wanna go forward too?'

'What if they don't let us?'

'I have the finest line of tantrums in the whole of Ohio.' Angie released her seat-belt. 'Ask dad. Ask mom.' Her grin faded. 'Besides, I want to meet the President's pilot. Don't you?'

Gawain pointed to his rucksack. 'Hand that over, will you, sparrow? If you'd only restrained your boredom for half a minute, I'd have given you the present I've...'

'You've rescued Princess Emma?!' Angie jumped up and down with excitement. 'Oh, I knew you'd find a way, Gawain. I knew it... you're the bestest...'

Gawain looked up as the curtain was jerked aside. Miss Hale strode out and swiped the pack just as Angie picked it up. 'So that's how the opposition found us. Very clever to try to make me believe it was my codes they located.' She wrenched the zipper open to look for secret pockets. 'You made me feel a fool...' She found the battered wooden box inside. 'What's this?'

Gawain held up a hand in feeble surrender. 'Your stormtroopers checked and okayed it. I asked first.'

Miss Hale flipped the lid up and stared at the contents.

'They're my earth treasures.' Gawain knew he shouldn't feel embarrassed but he found himself flushing. 'It's just stuff I collected when I was younger. I stopped when I was eight—right about Angie's age.'

'I'm *nine*,' Angie asserted, her teeth gritted.

'I kind of outgrew collecting.' Gawain watched Miss Hale pull out the shell. 'That's a nautilus. It hasn't a tag. None of this stuff does. They're all found things.' He recalled his father's comment on the nautilus. 'If you put it to your ear, you'll hear the sound of the sea no matter where you are.' It was a private memory, secret and precious from the time when his father was a safe harbour, not a barbed-wire barrier.

'Give it to me.' Angie took the shell from Miss Hale and placed it against her ear.

'It's really just the echo of your own pulsebeat,' Gawain said. 'But it does sound like waves on a shore, doesn't it?'

'No.' Angie, the shell pressed hard against her ear, seemed puzzled. 'It sounds like someone calling for help. Help me, Reece... the tree, Reece...'

Reece? The name of one of the twins he was supposed to find? 'Don't be silly.'

'I'm *not* being silly...' Angie's face screwed up. 'Who's Reece?'

'This doesn't look like something you picked up on a beach.' Miss Hale ignored Angie and held up a stone.

'That's an ammonite fossil. It's the present I was going to give Angie to replace her wishing star.'

'Does it have three wishes?' Angie asked.

'Yep. But it works like Santa. Depends on whether you're naughty or nice.'

'That is an unworthy falsehood, Sir Gawain.' Angie folded her arms. 'Princess Emma would be ashamed to hear you'd tried to pressure me with such a base manipulation.'

Where'd she hear that? Sometimes I wonder if she's really eight years old.

'Ammonite?' Miss Hale sounded puzzled as she turned the

fossil over.

'It's a prehistoric shellfish. I got it in Morocco when Nana took me for a holiday. She dropped in one day and whispered, "Come with me to the Casbah, Gawain," and I thought she meant a new ice cream parlour.'

Gawain saw Miss Hale's expression change, as if she were seeing the box of treasures in a new light. *Has she guessed?* Did she realise each carefully-collected item was a memory of a rare happy moment from his childhood?

'A shellfish?' One red-painted fingernail traced the ribbed outline of the fossil imbedded in the grainy rock. 'Looks like a ram's horn to me.'

'Yes, it's a sacred stone in some ancient religions because it looks like the spiral of a horn. The shepherd who sold it told me the horn will come alive and blow a warning when great danger threatens.'

'*Sold* it?'

'There's no tag on it.' Gawain felt flustered. His palm stabbed with pain once more. 'No chip. No registration.'

'Why not? It's valuable, isn't it?'

'Because...' Gawain hesitated. '...I never told anyone about it before. It was my secret.' He thought of the old sunworn shepherd in his wind-whirled cloak, telling him all about the stone—science on one hand, mystery on the other—remembering his lisping, broken English and the way he'd patted him on the head, took his half dollar and told him to hold onto the stone until he could interpret its message. And full of expectation, he'd waited for months for writing to appear on it. He'd checked it each day and, at last, disappointed beyond measure, realised he'd been conned. But it was impossible to explain this complex tangle of hope and disillusionment. He could still recall the Berber shepherd dancing down a palm-lined track, flapping dusty white sleeves like wings, and crooning, '*I'm a little sharva all alone, wish I could work by mobile phone...*' before vanishing between one blink and the next.

Angie looked into the box and turned appealing eyes on him. 'Can I have all of this stuff, Gawain?'

'No. You can have the ammonite, but the rest is mine.' He scowled. 'Don't try it,' he warned, seeing her face crumble. 'If you start bawling, you won't even get the ammonite. No blackmailing, sparrow.'

Angie looked crushed, but she didn't kick and scream. But she did get that look in her eye that meant she was planning mayhem.

'Tell you what, young lady...' Miss Hale's tone was placating in a clear attempt to quieten any over-reaction from Angie. 'Why don't you start your own collection?'

'What with?' Angie sniffed. 'A hammonite?'

Miss Hale reached into her pocket. 'Gawain's got a lot of top stuff in the box.' She held out her closed fist. 'Really top stuff.' Opening her hand, she revealed the meteorite she'd swiped a few hours back. 'But even he doesn't have a sleeping star.' Dropping the stone into Angie's outstretched glove, she smiled. 'How about we check out the cockpit?'

With a whoop, Angie jumped up. Gawain attempted to follow her, but Miss Hale stopped him. 'You need to rest, young man. Get some sleep. You've been shot, you know.'

I

THE BOY HUGGED HIS KNEES as he sat on the stone steps and stared out across the snow-mantled courtyard. Firelight glowed in the hall behind him, but he preferred the frosty night to the carousing inside. As the twilight deepened, he began to shiver as, one by one, snowflakes began to appear, slowly covering the trampled patches lying deep on the centuries-old tiles. Pulling his furs closer, he watched the stars rising over the ice-cloaked peaks on the horizon.

As coarse laughter and raucous calls continued to drift out from the hall, an eerie blue shadow glided across the snow. The shadow—branched and divided into long arms and mysterious tapered fingers—seemed like a monstrous walking tree.

Hounds rushed from the hall, barking. The boy pounced on them, but it was only after a vigorous tussle they obeyed his grunts to sit. Even so, they growled, only falling silent as a dark man materialised from the blue shadow.

He was riding a stag, its coat as pale and white as the distant snow-clad mountains, its eyes deep pools, its antlers reflecting the torchlight of the hall like fire-tongued branches. The Wild Man wore a twig crown hung with moss, berries and lichen. His leggings were of birch bark and a cloak of rough skins slid from his bare, dusky shoulders.

The boy stared at the berries dangling in tangled strands of the man's hair.

'Twinkle, twinkle, little star... how I wonder...' the Wild Man sang. 'I know what yer thinkin', dog-boy.' He winked. 'But there ain't no magic 'bout mulberries in winter. If they was growin' in the sea, it'd be different.'

The boy blinked, trying to remember what 'sea' was. The image that appeared in his mind couldn't be right. Nothing could grow in such a tireless swirl of water. He strained to think, frowning at the horizon where stars glittered like swordpoints.

The Wild Man followed his gaze. 'Stars?' He climbed off the stag. 'They're making ya anxious, eh? Nah, they're a good sign, dog-boy, not an evil omen. Surely ya remember stars? It's only been a coupla years since they were last visible. Now they're back, it means the heavens are clearin' and this deadly winter's comin' ta an end.'

Inside the hall, the noise grew louder.

'C'mon,' said the Wild Man, 'bring the dogs and let's give the king a real reason ta make merry.'

4

GAWAIN SIPPED COFFEE BETWEEN BITES of a cinnamon-dusted pastry scroll. He'd woken to daylight in the window and thought he'd been unconscious for ages.

'Only a few hours.' Miss Hale had corrected his mistake. 'Night is very short flying at high speed into the west.'

'Just what the pilot said,' Angie agreed.

'Had any sleep?' Gawain asked.

Angie rolled her eyes.

Stupid question, huh? Gawain pulled out his history assignment before she started campaigning for his box of earth treasures. He was sure it was coming. *Thompson hates me.* COMPARE AND CONTRAST THE CUBAN MISSILE CRISIS WITH THE REACTION TO HITLER'S ANNEXATION OF AUSTRIA. *He's got to be joking.*

'Five minutes to destination.' The voice of the pilot echoed through the aircraft. 'Prepare for touchdown: fasten seatbelts.'

Touchdown? Sounds like a rocket. 'We're there? Already?'

'This isn't Snail Force One.' Miss Hale reached for Angie's seatbelt. 'Buckle up.'

Gawain felt his stomach tightening. *Australia. A world away. No going back. G'day, mate. Here be dragons.* He tried to calm a rising sense of panic. *A summer school of genius teenage nerds. How am I ever going to fit in?* He closed his eyes. *Howhowhow?*

The plane rapidly decelerated to landing speed, pushing him deep into the padded seats. Pain stabbed at his shoulder as a line of hills—a long mustard-coloured caterpillar—flashed past the window. It was followed by a ring of mountains jutting from a red-dust plain. The plane banked again, flew over the mountains and, moments later, long before Gawain expected its final descent, landed vertically with only the slightest of bumps.

Gawain peered out the window. *Is that a school? More like a derelict ranch.*

'You two stay here…' Miss Hale checked her gun. 'I'll investigate where the reception committee is.'

A parade of dark-clad men and women passed by his seat from the rear. *The stormtroopers have been here all the time.* The cabin door whooshed open. Miss Hale whipped off her glasses as they fogged instantly from the heat.

From Gawain's angle, all he could see was a flat horizon: ochre plains dotted with low scrub; sun-seared grass struggling for survival in red sand; a pale, almost milk-white sky. An eerie silence.

'This isn't right.' Angie pouted. 'You're trying to trick us.'

'Get back!' Miss Hale's voice was an icy contrast to the heat outside.

'Sparrow!' Gawain left his seat to grab her golden-gloved hand. 'Stay with me.'

'But this isn't Oz…' Angie's lip quivered. 'There's no yellow brick road.'

Is that how Hale calmed her down?

A titter of laughter came from one of the black-clad squad. Miss Hale turned with a savage glare.

'I wanna go home.' Angie began to blubber dangerously. 'I wanna…'

'Come here, sparrow.' Gawain guided her to a window near the door. 'There's a good view from here.'

Angie's face was screwed up. 'No scarecrow, no tin man, no Wicked Witch of the West?'

Gawain shook his head. 'No Toto, no flying monkeys, no Emerald City either. Sometimes people call Australia "Oz" but it isn't really. You're okay about it, aren't you?'

'I wouldn't of come if I'd known the truth.' Angie pressed her nose to the window. 'Mom tricked me.'

Mom told her Australia was Oz? Gawain felt a sudden, splitting headache and a burning in his hand.

From around the side of the building a figure appeared. *The biggest…* Gawain hesitated, unsure if he could even think the description without being racist. The biggest, blackest man he'd ever seen strode towards the plane, followed by a massive dog.

White with red-tipped ears, the dog's eyes appeared to glow like fire-embers. 'Back, Retro.' The giant looked up at Miss Hale through his glinting, red-tinted glasses.

The colour of blood. Let's get out of here. It might not be Oz, but it's somewhere badbadbad.

The giant waved at Miss Hale. 'Don't be afraid!' He was clearly aware of the effect he had.

Don't be afraid? Of the biggest, ugliest, blackest, most sinister-looking red-eyed man I've ever seen in my entire life? With the biggest, ugliest, whitest, most sinister-looking red-eyed dog in existence? Gawain wouldn't have been in the least surprised in fact to see Red Glasses pluck Miss Hale from her perch, mutter 'fie fi fo fum' and swallow her whole.

'You mob lost?' the giant asked.

'Who are you?' Miss Hale demanded.

The huge dog barked at her ferociously. 'Quieten down, Retro,' the giant admonished. 'There's no threat here.' He beamed at Miss Hale with a gap-toothed grin. 'Advisable, ma'am, to put your weapons down.' His smile widened. 'Makes Retro nervous, y'see. While you're at it, could you call off your tactical mob? In the interest of Retro's nervous condition, of course.'

He's laughing at us.

'Who *are* you?' Miss Hale made no move to disarm.

'Me? My mob call me "Uri". Uri Messenger. I'm the janitor.' His smile thinned. The dog barked, shaking its huge head. 'That's what I think, too, Retro,' the giant agreed.

'Mister Messenger...' Miss Hale straightened herself. 'We seem to have been given slightly incorrect GPS coordinates. Is there a school in this vicinity?'

'School?'

Miss Hale hesitated. 'A private academy... or a military college?'

The giant shook his head.

'I see.' Miss Hale took out her phone.

'Sorry I can't help you mob.' The giant shrugged as she brought up a satellite map. 'All I know of round here is a secret facility catering for highly nerdy and mostly idealistic teen geniuses.'

Miss Hale's head snapped up.

Retro growled and thumped the giant's knee with his tail before she could say a word.

'Oh. Sorry, Retro.' The giant pulled down one side of his blood-red glasses with a massive sand-dusted finger and winked at Gawain. 'Retro's a grammar nazi. That would be genii, not geniuses.'

He is so laughing at us. Gawain felt an almost irrepressible impulse to join in. As he spluttered, Miss Hale clicked her fingers for silence.

Her back became ramrod stiff. 'Who is in charge here?'

'At the moment I am. The genii are all out on an orientation tour.' The giant's gap-toothed grin was back. 'I'll rustle up the jeep and take Gawain and Angie out to join them. The bus has only been gone ten minutes.' He strode off, the massive white dog frisking at his heels. Light winked from his blood-red glasses as he threw a glance over his shoulder at Miss Hale. 'You're late, you know.'

He knew who we were all along. And he put Hale in her place. Something within Gawain couldn't help feeling exultant. He carefully compressed his lips so no trace of emotion showed.

Moments later, an engine roared and a dragontail of dust emerged from the nearest shed. A jeep hurtled out and slewed around in a tight curve to stop just outside the open hatch of the aircraft.

'Rightio,' the giant hollered, waving to Miss Hale. 'Throw the little kidlets down. I'll catch 'em.'

'Yay!' Angie was all eagerness. 'I'll jump.'

Miss Hale grabbed her by the wrist. 'You will *not!*' Her voice was scathing. 'We've got steps.' Her mouth was a thin sneering line. 'Chain that dog.'

'What for?' The giant's voice dropped to a pretend whisper. 'I wouldn't want him to hear me say this, but Retro's as meek as a lamb. Unless he senses danger. Or unless it's a matter of grammar.'

Gawain couldn't resist it. 'Peace, Retro. We comes in peaces.'

Retro growled. His teeth bared in a vicious snarl.

Miss Hale's upper lip curled. 'You want me to believe that mongrel really understands?'

'Don't be like that, ma'am. Retro's got a sensitive personality. He likes to be liked.'

Retro's growling increased in volume.

'Well,' said Gawain. 'I come in peace. But I can't vouch for anyone else.'

Retro's growl ceased and he wagged his tail.

'You've won a friend, Gawain Greyhawk.' The giant nodded in obvious approval. *And you too, Angharad Goldenhand. Still as risk-eager as ever, I see.*

Gawain stared. He felt himself paling, his hand tingling—not with the usual burning stab but with cool refreshment. His mind had been full of harpsong and the rustling of wings—and he'd heard a voice inside his head calling Angie by a different name. *The giant's voice.* He turned to her and realised, by the shock on her face, she'd heard it too. *But did anyone else?*

Miss Hale clicked her fingers at the nearest member of her squad. 'Unload the all-terrain vehicle.' She turned to the giant. 'You may be our escort, Mister Messenger. Gawain, Angelina and I will follow you in the ATV.'

'Please call me "Uri", Nathania. We don't stand on ceremony here.'

The look of shock on Miss Hale's face said it all. 'Thania is my name—but only my *friends* have the right to use it, *Mister* Messenger.'

Gawain realised she was livid. She'd never anticipated a school janitor at the end of the earth taking liberties with her name. Her repressed rage kept everyone quiet as the steps were lowered and the ATV unloaded. Only an occasional woof from Retro broke the silence. As the automated steps unfolded, Uri moved the jeep forward.

A pair of stormtroopers descended the steps and waited at the bottom, assault rifles at the ready. Gawain watched Uri move closer and lower his red glasses to look them over with obvious disbelief. For just a moment his eyes were unshielded—strange, unearthly eyes. They had no white. The irises were dark, the pupils wide, like slitted bars. *Sheep eyes... or dragon's. Like the hologram at the airport.*

Gawain, unsure of what he'd seen, shook his head as Uri tilted his glasses back into place. He followed Miss Hale and Angie down the steps, stunned by the blast of heat as he left the plane. *What's the ground temperature? Must be over a hundred.* Two guards were behind him, carrying his rucksack and Angie's pink satchel.

Retro loped round the steps to them. Up close, the dog was even bigger than it seemed in the jeep. It stood higher than Angie. With a joyous slurp, it licked her face. She giggled and flung her arms around it. 'Can I ride with Retro? Pleasepleasepleaseplease*please*, Miss Hale. Pleasepleasepleaseplease*please*. I'll be gooder than anything.'

Retro snarled.

Grinning, she patted his neck. 'Just testing, Retro.' She put her mouth to his ear. 'Miss Hale does not believe you understand the finer points of grammar.' She batted her eyelids at Miss Hale. '*Please.* I won't be out of your sight for a single moment.'

Gawain could see Miss Hale was tempted. He decided to sway the decision. 'Thompson, my teacher—you know, the guy who hates my guts and expects me to produce some insightful report on the Cuban Missile Crisis—says this: a principle is worth fighting for. But not much else. Not if you lose the respect and cooperation of people in the process.'

Miss Hale wiped beads of sweat from her forehead, then directed the guards to mount the outside of the ATV. 'You two ride shotgun.' She turned to Gawain with a smile. 'Retro is undoubtedly quite capable of protecting you and Angelina in the jeep.'

Gawain smiled back. *A small win is still a win.*

He was in the jeep before Miss Hale could change her mind. Angie clambered in the back with Retro.

With a rev of the engine, Uri took off along the dirt track in a roar of dust. 'We'll soon catch the bus up.'

Grateful for the wind in his face, Gawain threw his head back and took a deep breath. Free. *Sort of. Don't have to worry about my father sending me to military school. Just have to find two kids named Reece and Holly.*

His shoulder began to ache, his hand twitched with stabbing pain. *Mistake. Hale's got the medication patches.* Glancing behind him, he was surprised to see the ATV was slipping further and further back.

Uri jerked a thumb. 'Wanna lose 'em?'

'They got our stuff.' Gawain thought of his rucksack and Angie's satchel.

Uri shook his head. 'Nah. While Retro was distracting that mob with his impeccable grammatical correctness, I got your bags.' He grinned. 'And all your medication.'

Gawain realised he should be feeling untold fear. He was alone with his sister in the middle of a desert at the end of the earth, with the strangest man in the universe—a man with dragon-sheep eyes and blood-red glasses. He looked Uri up and down, noting the frayed jeans and the leather jacket with its logo *White Stag Security*.

He nodded. 'Let's do it, Uri.'

The jeep jumped as it accelerated down the track, leaving the ATV a diminishing speck far behind them.

5

'SLAP THIS ON YOURSELVES.' Uri handed Gawain a tube of sunscreen. 'Wouldn't want you getting heatstroke, Greyhawk.'

'What'd I do to deserve a tribal name?' *Does just arriving qualify?*

'Well, I can hardly call you "Taliesin", can I? Not after all the trouble you've gone to.'

Gawain felt a tingle pass up his entire body from his toes to his head. He froze. *If he knows, then my father must. I'm deaddeaddead.*

'Does Retro need sunscreen?' Angie asked as Uri took the tube from Gawain's nerveless fingers and handed it to her.

'Not really.' Uri shook his massive head. 'But he'd like the attention. Dab some behind his ears.'

'Like perfume?'

'Yep.' Uri pointed to the cluster of hills in front of them. Stark, solitary and treeless, the strange formation seemed to float like an umber-painted island, its base disappearing in a heat shimmer and its top brooding above the featureless plain. 'Tnorala. The bus will be somewhere here.' He stopped the jeep.

Several seconds passed before Gawain realised his dazed, panicked thoughts weren't responsible for the blurry look of the hills. They were hovering in a heat haze.

'What's Tnorala?' Angie squirted the sunscreen.

'Most maps label it "Gosses Bluff". It's not any ordinary ring of hills—it's all that's left of the central uplift of an impact crater. A comet crashed there.'

Angie's expression was calculating. 'Comets are like meteorites, right? So there'd be more than three wishes there. Maybe three billion. Or three trillion.'

Uri's red glasses winked in the light. 'In some places the Dreaming came down to earth as a stone.' He indicated the hills, silent and eerie. 'Of all of those places, Tnorala is one of the most mysterious. The people hereabouts tell of dancing starwomen who dropped a baby's cradle. The child fell to earth and the cradle overturned. Tnorala is the upturned cradle and the baby is still underneath.'

Angie frowned. 'Is it okay?'

Uri ignored the question. 'On the other side of the world, they saw the baby falling and made a song about it. The tune's long gone, but the words haven't been lost.' His voice assumed a low, rocking lilt. 'Hushabye baby on the treetops…'

'When the wind blows the cradle will rock.' Angie leaned against Retro. 'When the bough breaks the cradle will fall, and down will come baby, cradle and all.'

'The song of Hu Gadarn.' Uri sighed. The air was motionless now they were no longer moving but, even so, Gawain was sure he could hear the creaking of branches, faint and far-off, along with the skirling of leaves high in a treetop.

'Hu Gadarn,' Uri's harpvoice sang, distant and full of regret. 'Once my friend. Once, before the world began. See how the mighty have fallen.' 'Hu brought horse-riding to the people of the north, the blue-painted

Celts.' Uri's cheery smile belied the heartache of the song. He turned to Gawain. 'Are you okay there? I can choose another lullaby, if you need one.'

He told the story to calm me down? Gawain was conscious of his heart's erratic thudding.

'I didn't mean to frighten you, Greyhawk. Your secret is still safe. However if I was you, I'd—' Uri broke off as Retro's massive paws thumped down on his shoulders with a vicious snarl.

Gawain froze. Angie jumped.

Uri slapped his forehead with an open palm. 'Sorry, Retro. Sorry. Yes, of course, that would be subjunctive case I should've been using.' He paused. 'If I *were* you...' Retro released his paws and slurped the back of Uri's head. Uri turned to pat him. 'However if I *were* you, Greyhawk, I wouldn't be tempted to access any of my digital caches while I'm here.'

He knows about the nano-jot?

'Gawain...' Angie folded her arms. 'What he means is: leave the spy stuff to Hale.'

Uri flexed his eyebrows. 'While you've got those glasses on, you need to be very careful. That thing in your hand is apt to make you reckless and forgetful.'

Thing in my hand? I don't have anything in my hand. Unless an incredible, burning itch counts. 'What about the glasses right now? Won't they be recording your warning?'

Uri laughed and started up the engine once more. 'This isn't the first school out here, you know. And this isn't your average jeep. Last year, the kids had to invent and install a wide-spectrum communications blocker. The year before that, it was radar invisibility.'

Gawain felt as if his stomach had lurched upwards to his mouth, then fallen towards his knees. He wanted to throw up. *What am I*

doing here? I'll be exposed in two seconds. I gottagotta get outta here.
'Could you turn around, please Mister Messenger?'

'I could.' Uri pointed along a cross-trail. 'But there are their tracks.'
The jeep cornered on just two wheels as it lurched into a narrower,
bumpier road. Stunted scrub grew in the middle of stony path.

Whose side are you on? Gawain couldn't see any sign of bus
tracks. *I don't think anyone's been up this trail in a century.* Then he
noticed a dustcloud up ahead. It was close to a small pyramid-
shaped hill well outside the Bluff.

Half a minute later the dust had settled and a small cream-
coloured bus became visible. Uri tooted to attract attention.
'Fortunately, the supernerds didn't disable the horn when they were
installing the communication blockade.'

Retro bounded from the jeep the moment it stopped. He loped
around the bus and rubbed against the back of a girl. She laughed
and turned to hug the huge white hound.

She looks like she belongs in the cast of a steampunk movie. Gawain
was cautious as he left the jeep.

A couple of kids stood next to a tall, gesticulating woman. 'The
magnetic and gravitational anomalies throughout this area are the
result of the cosmic impact. This natural feature, the pyramidal hill
called "The Wizard of Oz", is the last remnant of the centre's outer
rim. All the rest has eroded away.'

'It *is* Oz!' Angie's expression was caught between delight and
disbelief. She threw up her hands and squealed. 'We made it!'

The woman didn't even glance in her direction. She was
clearly in full lecture mode. 'Take a close look, students. Put your
observation skills to work. See if you can find any shattercones—
either here or later inside the crater.' Her nod was crisp and
dismissive. 'Remember: half an hour only for field exploration.
Take a hat, water and sunblock.'

Waving the students off, she turned to Uri. Her look became relaxed and friendly. 'They haven't stopped grumbling since I told them we weren't going to explore the Bluff via Google Maps—because there's no power for their phones or books.' She smiled in welcome. 'These are our latecomers, I take it? Gawain and Angelina Aishdene.' She held out her hand to Gawain. 'We've never had a music mastermind on camp before. I'm looking forward to seeing what you have to contribute.'

Gawain's stomach lurched once more. *Musicmusicmusic. How'd they know? I'm deaddeaddead.*

Uri shook his head. 'Meg, his musical talent is a secret.'

A frown creased Angie's brow. 'It is?'

Uri dropped down beside her. 'Yup. And if you don't want me to tell everyone about what you did to the Benessf…'

Angie's hands went up in surrender. 'I promise. I won't say a word.' She crossed her hands over her heart. 'Not a single word.'

'Emrys!' The teacher called out to a student stooping over a rust-coloured rock.

The boy straightened and sauntered back. 'Yeah, Ms Gunn?'

'This is Gawain Aishdene. Make him welcome and bring him up to date on what's expected on this tour.'

'G'day.' Emrys shoved his hands in the pockets of his shorts. 'C'mon, Wayne, lots to do and not much time to do it.'

'It's *Gawain*.' *Let the bullying begin.*

Emrys looked him up and down. 'You a Yank, Speckly Boy?'

Give as good as you get. 'What gave it away, Bumblebrains?'

'Accent.' Emrys headed towards the bus and vaulted inside. He was back seconds later with a water bottle and floppy hat. 'You'll need these, *Gay*wain. I'm frying in this heat and I was born in this country.'

'You're Australian, Bumblebrains?' Gawain wasn't sure why he was surprised.

'Nup. I'm a Welsh lord, Speckly Boy. Unlike you, I had to buy my way onto this camp.'

Is he serious? Gawain couldn't tell from the tone whether Emrys was being sarcastic or not. He flipped the hat onto his head and wondered if he should ask Uri for some painkillers to go with the water. 'Lead on, Macduff. As they say.'

'Wrong part of the Island of the Mighty. I can see geography is not your strong point, *Gay*wain. Wales is in the west of Britain. Scotland, on the other hand, where Macduff comes from, is in the north.' Emrys hollered across the scrub-dotted plain as he strode off. 'Vasily! Time to meet your mortal enemy. Come one, come all, gather round and meet *Gay*wain.'

He's nuts. Stark, raving nuts.

Gawain followed him as three figures ambled towards them from different points of the compass. He could tell by the tilt of their heads they were all appraising him. His stomach lurched again but he lifted his chin, trying to look casual and unconcerned.

'Listen up, everyone. I have brought us a new nerd for our collection. It answers to Gawain…' Miraculously Emrys got his name correct. '…but you may call it "Speckly Boy". He's okay. Despite his appalling sense of geography. You'll probably have to explain to him where the Russian Federation is, Vasily. And I'm sure he's never even heard of Indonesia, Cardea.'

With a jolt Gawain realised Emrys had put him through a test. And somehow, even though he'd reacted badly to the hazing, he'd passed. He tried to concentrate as Emrys introduced them. Vasily from Russia; blond hair and wary grey eyes; looked twenty-ish. Cardea from Indonesia; brown eyes; otherwise invisible in her flowing white burqa. Cerylen from Australia; top hat and eyecup straight from a steampunk drama; light-up-the-world smile.

This is all? Hale can check the backgrounds of everyone here in seconds. 'Where is everyone?'

'Hong Kong.' Vasily flipped a draggle of blond hair back from his sweat-stained forehead and adjusted his hat. 'Most of the school, they were to rendezvous there and then catch a charter flight in.'

'But apparently one of our illustrious number is from Guatemala and he didn't get the right vaccination shots before leaving.' Emrys shook his head. 'Looks like he might be a carrier of xantika virus. So everyone's in quarantine in Hong Kong for at least seven days.'

'Everyone except us.' Cerylen's dazzling smile disappeared as she sighed.

This sounds like a set-up. Me, four other teenagers... and my kid sister. How do we get outta this trap—whatever it is?

'Time's a'wasting.' Cerylen flapped a sheet of paper in front of Cardea's burqa. 'It's up to you and me, sister, to find a power source.'

What? Surely the school has power.

Without explaining, Cerylen and Cardea headed off. Cerylen read from the sheet as they went. 'Shattercones form a record of the moment of impact from a cosmic projectile. When the comet crashed, the ground liquefied and a shockwave passed through the molten rock. The imprint of this shockwave remained when the rocks cooled and hardened. It is visible as a design known as "mare's tail stone" or "angelwings".'

Paper. How archaic. 'Can't we use tablets here?'

Emrys sighed. 'Our first priority is to find a way to power our computers, tablets and books. Ms Gunn told us that whatever method we come up with has to take into account the magnetic and electrical anomalies of this crater.'

'Bonding exercise.' Vasily scowled. 'A clever way to ensure we work as a team to create a power source.'

Gawain couldn't believe his ears. *No computer, no internet… no world. Trapped—and no way to call for help.*

6

AS SOON AS THE ATV ARRIVED, two stormtroopers jumped out and headed for the jeep. Gawain watched Uri saunter across to them as one slid under the side while the other lifted the hood. 'You mob looking for anything special? Like what makes a clapped-out old jeep go faster'n one o' them there ATVs o' yours.'

Retro swivelled, baring his fangs in a silent snarl. Uri blew him an air kiss. 'Faster than one of *those* ATVs of yours.'

Miss Hale scowled. 'Over three hundred students were invited to attend this school. Seventy passed the entry test. Forty-nine were selected. Where are they?'

'Nathania, Nathania.' Uri tutted. 'Manners, please! Even here in the uncultured Outback, we observe the niceties. In fact, they're so much more important here than in the wilds of civilisation. There are impressionable children watching and, with so few adults present, your status as a role model is significantly enhanced.' His broken-tooth smile flashed and his eyebrows waggled.

Gawain pressed his lips together trying to stop a bubble of laughter escaping. Uri's takedown was so skilfully done Miss Hale had no comeback. *What could she say to 'you're a big bad example to the little kiddies'?* Her mouth was pinched, as if she were trying to suck a lemon.

'Ms Gunn…' Uri produced a sweeping regency bow. 'May I introduce Miss Hale? Miss Hale, it's my pleasure to acquaint you with Ms Gunn.'

The two women glowered at each other.

Another flourishing bow from Uri and, a moment later, he was at Gawain's side. Gawain blinked, unsure how he'd got there. He hoisted Angie on Retro's back and, linking elbows with Emrys on one side and Gawain on the other, they strolled towards the Bluff. Behind him, Gawain could hear Ms Gunn making some convoluted explanation about the missing students. 'Charter flight', 'custom clearances', 'vaccination consent' and 'engine trouble' drifted across to him.

'Yes, milord, it's your call. And yes, I can get rid of them, if you wish.'

Gawain realised Uri was talking to Emrys. *He forrealreallyis a Welsh lord? It wasn't a joke? And how did I miss the start of the conversation?*

Emrys had a pensive look as he gazed up at the ochre-and-umber streaked ring of Gosses Bluff. He blew out his cheeks. 'Short-term gain for long-term pain? Commander Hale and her goons are trouble but, if we got rid of them, there'd be twice as many of them next day.' He sounded tired.

Commander? Like how come everybody knows more than I do?

'Come around this way a little.' Uri followed the line of a low ridge, gesturing for them to keep up. 'From over here we can view the harvest, boys.'

'Harvest?' *In the desert? How on earth...?* Gawain stifled a gasp as he reached the end of the ridge and scanned the horizon. In front of them, as far as the eye could see, was a massive array of solar collection panels.

'It's a light farm.' Emrys raised his arms. 'They're harvesting solar energy.'

'But what for?' Gawain was awed.

'It's sold to the world grid.' Uri nodded to himself. 'Ireland. Taiwan. Kashmir. The big customer, though, is California. Huge energy requirements, boys. Not to mention a state legislature paranoid about black-outs after they lost that lawsuit a decade back. Now they pay top dollar for power from anywhere they can get it— here, the Sahara, the hydro-electric schemes in the Andes, the wind farms off the west coast of New Zealand, the wave generators of Norway, the solar towers of the Gobi Desert. They're not keen to put all their eggs in one energy basket.'

Emrys glanced from Uri to the solar array and back again. His mouth puckered. 'We don't need much. They'd hardly notice if we siphoned some off.'

'What do you mean you don't need much?' Uri stared. 'I thought you were building a time machine.'

A time machine? Like, for real?

'The priority, Uri, is to power the computers, tablets and books.' The pucker moved from one side of Emrys' mouth to the other. 'Seems too easy, somehow. Too convenient.' He turned to Gawain. 'What do you think, Speckly Boy?'

'Siphoning energy seems somewhat like stealing.'

Roars of deep laughter rumbled up from Uri's belly as he thumped his thigh. Retro, attracted by the sound of hilarity, raced up, Angie still on his back. He danced around the three of them in a whirl of tail-chasing.

Gawain felt himself flushing with embarrassment.

'You know...' Uri's red glasses winked like Christmas lights. '...when Jib said Greyhawk was coming, I thought, *yay! Just what this place needs—the voice of moral conscience.*'

'Retro!' Emrys shouted. 'Stop!' He grabbed Retro's collar as he slewed to glare at Uri. 'That is so insulting.' He poked the White Stag badge on Uri's shirt. 'What on either earth makes you think I'm a thief?'

I don't. I know you better than that. Uri's lilting harpsong voice whispered inside Gawain's head. A gentle waft of wind tickled his hair. *I think you're a killer.*

Emrys threw back his head and a slow, lazy smile traced its way across his lips. A twinkle appeared in his eyes.

He is even nuttier than I thought. I'm at camp with a homicidal maniac. Can I go home now, Miss Hale? I'll take Angie and you can stay here. I don't believe there is any Reece or Holly. I don't know what's going on but everything I've been told so far is a lie.

Emrys reached out to tickle Retro behind the ears. Angie stared, transfixed, at his right hand. 'You've got one glove! Just like me.' She seemed thrilled.

Gawain stared. The glove was unobtrusive. Unless the angle was right, it was barely visible. Emrys' hand looked perfectly normal. Only as he moved his arm would a mesh of silver show, then vanish again.

'An invisible silver glove.' Angie's voice throbbed with raw desire.

Emrys didn't seem to notice it. 'Who owns that land?' He pointed to the panel array. 'Who do we talk to, so we can *buy* some solar power?'

Uri raised his chin. 'It's tribal land, belonging to the Western Arrente people. Kulpitarra is the nearest community. But they don't own this set-up.'

'They're well paid.' Miss Hale made her way up the ridge, her shoes clacking across the stones in quick-march time.

'I didn't say they weren't.' Uri's voice was mild. But it held a clear undertone of accusation.

Miss Hale stared at him. The tension was palpable.

Test of wills. Gawain wondered who'd break first. And what it was about. Their gazes were locked for half a minute when Ms Gunn rolled up with Cerylen, Cardea and Vasily. She seemed rattled. 'Gather round, students.' She shot a glance at Uri and Miss Hale. 'Yes, gather round.' She pointed towards the regimented shadows of the solar array. 'The crater. Well, yes, you were supposed to discover its secrets for yourselves, but…'

She pointed up to the ochre ring of the Bluff. 'You'll find electrical and magnetic anomalies all through this area. They are the result of a comet crashing to earth here and making a huge crater. See the ring of Tnorala? Well, it isn't the crater itself, even though it looks like it—it's just the central uplift.'

Her glance at Miss Hale was swift and wary. 'The central uplift. Of course you're wondering what that is.'

No, actually I'm wondering why you're suddenly so nervous when ten minutes ago you could've eaten Hale and her stormtroopers for breakfast.

'The central uplift is like the bump you get on your head when you're hit by a golf ball. It's the place where the comet actually crashed. The rocks melted, splashed up, then cooled in a solid lump. Of course the crater was all around the lump, but it's all been eroded now. As you can see—' She waved her arms in an erratic roll. '—as flat as a pancake. All that's left is the central Bluff, and all that's left of it is just a ring.'

'So that means we're in the crater now.' Emrys sounded almost bored.

Ms Gunn nodded. 'As far as you can see in any direction, milord. See those hills way, way over? Once upon a time they were the edge of the crater.'

They'd be a half hour's drive away. Maybe an hour. Gawain decided to help the conversation along. 'It must've been one mighty big comet, ma'am.'

Ms Gunn sounded almost grateful for his contribution as she shook her head. 'This isn't a particularly big crater, Gawain. Not like Chicxulub, in Mexico: where the comet that killed the dinosaurs hit. Still, it's got plenty of magnetic and electrical anomalies.'

Gawain took a deep breath. *If I had a suspicious mind, which I didn't used to have before today, I'd wonder why everyone is so desperate for us to know about the magnetic and electrical anomalies. What are they hiding?*

A sudden, blood-chilling yell caused him to jump with fright. 'Eh, you mob!' With graceful leaps, a group of young men appeared on the ridge near Uri and Miss Hale.

His hand spasming with sudden pain, Gawain gasped and retreated a step. He eyed the feathered spear the leader was holding in one hand. In the other, a strange contrast, was a GPS tracker. The whole party was dressed in red loincloths and decorated in heavy white paint.

It's welcome-to-country! Fantastic! We're going to get a haka! Wait—maybe that's New Zealand?

A click sounded behind him. It took Gawain a moment to register it was a safety catch being unclipped.

Before he could shout a warning, a shot rang out.

7

GAWAIN STOOD THERE, BLINKING. The young men had all thrown themselves to the ground. The bullet must have whizzed over them.

Why are people shooting around me? Twice in one day is insanity. He checked his right shoulder. *Bandage slipped; wound re-opened.*

He turned, realising Retro was on top of the trigger-happy stormtrooper, his claws in the guy's upper arms and shins, the guy's weapon in his mouth. The other stormtroopers were clearly unsure whether to point their guns at Retro or the newcomers.

'Hold this, Greyhawk.' Uri dropped a pebble into Gawain's hand. Extending his arm, he pulled the leader of the aboriginal contingent to his feet. 'G'day, Jed. What you mob hunting?'

Retro clicked his tongue and grimaced but his concentration was all on the stormtrooper.

Jed examined his GPS tracker with a scowl. 'Broken.'

'These lovely gentlemen will replace it with the latest version, Jed. One that'll work in space; underwater; in a blizzard forty degrees below.'

'We get them kinda problems here all the time.' Jed's voice dripped sarcasm.

Retro's growl rose in tone until Uri held up a restraining finger. 'I'm sure they'll even rustle up one that takes account of the electrical and magnetic abnormalities around here.'

Please. Gawain wanted to roll his eyes. *Asifwecouldforget.*

'One that takes account o' the gravitational fluct-u-a-tions?' Jed let the word roll off his tongue with slow emphasis.

Miss Hale seemed to come out of a daze. 'What are these people doing here? They're trespassing.'

'Don't tell me.' Jed folded his arms over his spear. 'The government's passed legislation that means ya can trespass on yer own land?' Behind him, the group of young men were rising to their feet.

'It's not your land. It was legally requisitioned.'

Jed laughed so much he almost lost his footing. 'Government-person, Tnorala is our Dreaming. It has *not* been requisitioned. The fact we are paid royalties fer the use o' the space above and below the surface does not confer ownership on the users.' His smile disappeared. 'If ya'd like ta check the precise wording o' the document, it can be arranged.'

'Jed, ignore Miss Hale. I'm going to recommend she be sent for classes in basic manners. This is the second time in just a few minutes she's failed in elementary courtesy.' Uri flicked a glance over the stormtroopers. 'Retro, please hop off Agent McKenzie. You've made your point.'

With a huge dribbling slurp straight up McKenzie's face, Retro loped over to the group of aboriginal boys. Their tentative grins became broad and cheesy as Retro took his stand beside them.

'We gotta problem, boss man.' Jed unfolded his arms and thumped his spear. 'Spirit bird.'

'You know that white man got no Dreaming.' Uri patted Gawain's left shoulder as Retro growled. 'Please explain for the benefit of my American colleague here.'

'There's this spirit bird hangin' round.' Jed frowned. 'Hard ta describe. Haven't seen it.'

'How do you sense it then?' Emrys seemed genuinely fascinated.

'We heard it. Came this way, flying over Tnorala headed toward Ntaria. High up, singing its song. Ya can't mistake that song: *I'm a little sharva, hey you mob, ya wanna join me in a job?*'

'Sharva?' Cerylen clapped a hand to her mouth. 'You sure?'

Sharva? Gawain stared at her. *She's met the sharva too? Is it a bird?* He clenched the pebble Uri had given him. *The tighter he held it, the less his palm burned. I thought it was a Berber shepherd but I guess it can appear however it wants.*

'Yep, I'm sure.' Jed looked Cerylen up and down. 'Nice eyecup, kid. What magnification?'

'Up to nine thousand.'

'Deadly.' Envy oozed from Jed's voice. 'Polarising? Automatic focus?'

'Of course.' Cerylen nodded. 'I'm Cerylen Morgan, by the way.'

'Hi, Cherry. Pleased ta meet ya.' Jed shook hands with her.

She gestured towards Emrys. 'This is my brother, Emrys Rhystyllen…'

They're related? Twins? No, different surnames.

'…and Vasily Arkipov, Cardea Sushila, and…'

Gawain put out his left hand. 'Gawain Aishdene.'

Jed retreated a step. 'Gwion gwion.' A ferocious glare distorted his features. 'First a spirit bird, then gwion gwion.'

Gawain took the hint from Jed's reaction. *Quick, clarify this.* 'That'd be Gawain. Not Gwion.'

'Laajmorro one-arm, Wanjina people.' Jed poked a finger at Gawain's bandaged arm.

'Oww! What'd you do *that* for?'

Jed pointed at Gawain's hair. 'Fire-head.' At his face. 'Sky-eyes. Lion-skin.'

'Speckly Boy.' Emrys stepped to Gawain's side. 'I hate to be the bearer of bad news, buddy, but unbelievably I think your freckles, blue eyes and the present incapacitation of your right arm fulfil certain mythological descriptors around here. Keep your mouth shut while we figure out if this turn of events is good or bad.'

'Bad,' Uri announced. 'Wanjina people come from the other side of the Tanami Desert. We're talking tribal enemies here.'

'Gwion gwion... gwion gwion...' The young men began chanting, their feet stamping the ground.

'Spirit bird.' Jed's head was rocking. 'Blood-painter.'

'Gawain, get back to the ATV.' Miss Hale's order rang out. She pulled him aside just as Jed's spear sliced through the leg of his jeans. It slashed the edge of his shoe and thudded into the ground next to him.

Shouting followed, and pushing. Miss Hale's gun was out and the stormtroopers all trained their weapons on Jed. Gawain found himself hustled to the ATV and thrust inside.

Uri was at Miss Hale's window in an instant.

'You irresponsible moron,' she snarled.

You don't need to rub it in. I know I am. People tell me so all the time. He wondered if he should tell her his leg was bleeding.

'If you'd a single braincell…' Miss Hale shouted through the window, '…you wouldn't have risked the boy's life bringing him out with savages on the loose.'

She's not talking to me? 'It wasn't Uri's fault.'

'Agent Hale…' Uri's glasses had darkened like wine. '…if you hadn't pulled Gawain aside, he wouldn't now be bleeding in more than one place.'

'He's injured?' Miss Hale leaned to stare at Gawain's jeans, soaked in blood.

'It's just a flesh wound.' *At least I hope so.*

Uri glanced at him with a curious expression. 'Commander, Gawain was injured because you interfered. These people are *not* savages. They have their rules, their laws, their customs. Which means there's always a warning shot. *You* made the mistake of pulling Gawain into the path of that warning shot.'

Gawain felt light-headed. *Blood loss.*

'Hi!' It was Emrys. He yanked the door open. 'Buddy, congratulations! I'm impressed. This is a story to dine out on for the rest of your life. Don't know how you did it. But you turned welcome-to-country into a death threat in under two minutes flat.' He produced a sudden grin for Miss Hale. 'Can Speckly Boy go back in the bus with us?'

Miss Hale took a deep breath. Gawain could see her hesitancy.

'We've got a first-class first-rate first-world first-aid kit.' Emrys raised his hands and smiled in reassurance. Light danced for a fraction of a second from the silver-mesh glove. 'And my sister's just completed her basic medical certificate.'

'We'll be right behind you.'

'Thanks, Agent Hale,' Emrys said. 'You're a sweetie.'

That's overdoing it.

Emrys waved. 'I don't care what anyone says about you.'

Compliment one moment, insult the next. He's totally nuts—I so like him.

Gawain slipped out of the ATV into the desert heat. He was grateful for Emrys' intervention but too exhausted to say so. He was also grateful when Emrys took him by the elbow and steered him in a straight line. He felt himself relax. His hand, long clasped tight on Uri's pebble, finally dropped open. The pebble fell to the ground.

'What's this?' Emrys stooped down to pick it up.

'Nothing. Just Uri's idea of a souvenir, I think.'

'Strange choice.' Emrys was silent a moment. 'A bullet.'

8

GAWAIN TRIED NOT TO THINK about the implications as Emrys handed the bullet to him. *It wasn't a pebble.* The shot hadn't whizzed over Jed and his friends at all. Somehow Uri had caught the bullet in passing. And nobody noticed. *What is he? And where is he?*

The jeep revved up beside the bus driver's door. 'See y'all back at the homestead.' Uri waved to Ms Gunn and sped off, Retro in the back seat.

At the side door of the bus, Vasily leaned down to pull Gawain up the steps.

As he sank, feeling dizzy, into the nearest seat, Angie slid in beside him. 'Can I try them?'

Huh? It took Gawain a few seconds to understand, and more to react when she snatched his glasses. 'Sparrow, give them back.'

Angie's face screwed up as she peered through the lenses. 'Can't see a think.' She gave them to Cardea.

'Not my style.' Cardea was quick to hand them on.

It's some weird pass-the-speccies game.

Cerylen held them up for inspection. Gawain was fascinated by her eyecup swivelling, stopping, focussing.

'Interesting.' Cerylen's lens began to protrude in slow, regular clicks. 'Most ingenious.' The lens retracted.

'Gawain wants them back.' Angie tapped her on the back.

Cerylen bolted upright with a scream, flailing her hands and knocking the glasses against the seat in front.

Gawain froze.

'Sorry, sorry. I didn't mean...' Angie cringed against him as the bus jerked to a halt.

'What's up?' Ms Gunn opened the partition shielding her from the bus occupants. Cerylen's shriek had been so piercing she'd even heard it through her safety booth. 'A snake? Goanna?'

Emrys waved at her. 'Nothing to worry about, Ms Gunn. Cerylen just hates being touched. Especially on the back.' He smiled at Angie. 'Still, let that be a warning to you, chickadee.'

Cerylen shuddered, visibly pulled herself together and looked at the glasses in her hands. 'Oh, so sorry, Gawain. I've cracked them.'

Impossible. Aren't they indestructible? He took them from her and found a tiny hole in the left lens, so perfectly round it looked like a miniscule bullet had penetrated it. A spiderweb tracery radiated out from the hole.

Vasily took the glasses and held them up to the light. He flicked one corner with his index finger. The spiderweb crackled right across from one lens to the other. 'Busted.'

Emrys snatched the glasses from Vasily. 'Definitely busted.' Sliding open the window, he tossed out the glasses.

A collective sigh of relief echoed through the bus.

'Did you just toss some litter into the desert, Emrys Rhystyllen?' Ms Gunn demanded as the bus slowed to a crawl.

'I was recycling,' Emrys called. 'A sand product back to the sand.'

Ms Gunn glared and then, very slowly, very deliberately, winked. 'I'm glad you were considering the environment.'

Gawain took a deep breath as the bus sped off. *They knew. Everyone knew they were spy glasses. It was an act. Cerylen's taking the blame for the 'accident', but she couldn't have just knocked...*

His thoughts were interrupted as Jed wriggled down the aisle on his stomach. 'Are we safe from prying eyes now?' He held up a flask of water to Gawain. 'Sorry about the spear, Gwion.'

'What are you doing down there?' Gawain raised the flask and sipped the water.

'I'm joinin' this camp.' Jed tucked himself up against the seat opposite Gawain. 'My mob has always had the right ta participate in the supernerd camp. It's in the fine print o' the documentation when our land was forcibly rented fer purposes above and below. But none o' us ever had the incentive before.'

His language skills have dramatically improved. 'Why?'

'Put two and two together, Gwion. The sharva wants us ta join it in a job. And logically the job must have something ta do with you mob. So we're in. But we don't wanna appear too eager.'

'So that's what that act back there was for.' Emrys gave him the thumbs-up.

'Nah.' Jed shook his head.

'Scare tactics.' Vasily grinned. 'The stormtroopers will think twice about being out at night, roaming around in the dark.'

Jed nodded. 'Those bullyboys ya got spying on ya are a major pest. Surveillance glasses, Gwion—didn't ya know?'

'Yeah, I did.' Gawain sniffed. 'But between being shot at and getting speared, I've been the centre of attention all day. Opportunities to quietly dispose of said glasses haven't presented themselves.'

Emrys parked his chin on Gawain's good shoulder. 'That actually sounds like the truth. What's your specialty again?'

'Music. What's yours?'

'Interstitial time. The infinitesimal gap between one second and the next.'

Cerylen reached back to tap her brother on the shoulder. 'We've never considered the possibility music could widen that gap.'

Jed wagged his finger at Gawain. 'Have some more water, Gwion. Yer lookin' white.'

'It's my natural skin colour.'

'Yer tendin' more ta the blueish white than the pinkish white. In't that right, Cherry? Make us all happy by havin' some water, Gwion.'

'*Gawain*. Stop calling me Gwion.' He turned from Jed to push Emrys' chin off his shoulder and give him a close-quarter glower. 'You're the one who's supposed to be Welsh, not me.'

'You hit your head, Speckly Boy? The gwion gwion spirit is from the other side of the desert, not the other side of the world.'

'Yup.' Jed clapped his hands together. 'Gwion gwion's the name o' spirit ancestors from way over the border, up the northwest. Ever heard o' the Wanjina? The rock paintings in the Kimberleys with the ghoulish faces, the huge eyes, the strange haloes? The gwion gwion are part o' that Dreaming.'

'Might be so,' Gawain said. 'But Gwion also happens to be another name for the great sixth century Welsh poet, Taliesin.'

'He's correct.' Cerylen sounded surprised. 'Not just a musical genius but an expert on Welsh legends?'

I don't want her thinking that. 'I just know about Taliesin being another name for Gwion because "gwion" used to be my chatroom identity. Gawain was already taken. Some people then guessed my real name was Taliesin. But it's not.'

'Taliesin? And yer a muso?' Jed's forehead creased as he looked Gawain up and down. His mouth fell open. 'Yer kiddin' me!' He threw up his hands and high-fived himself. 'Yer *Taliesin's Mantle*? I've died and gone ta heaven.' He looked around the group, searching each blank face in turn. 'None o' ya know who *Taliesin's Mantle* is? I can't believe it! Yer all ignorant savages.'

'Spit it out, Jed,' Emrys said.

'Like, the most totally deadly freeweb band in the world. In my humble opinion. Some people slam freeweb as coarse and raw, but *Taliesin's Mantle* has mastered a throbbin' pulse o' ancient power.' Jed pointed a finger at Vasily. 'Don't roll ya eyes, barbarian. I might be quotin' a majorly biased five-star review—but it's still true. Listen ta the songs and ya can feel the trees walkin' and the landscape speakin'.'

'Trees walking?' Vasily looked dubious. 'Landscape speaking?'

'And songlines wakin'.' Jed folded his arms, his brows furrowing in a dare-you-to-contradict-me scowl.

Gawain swallowed a painful gulp. '*Taliesin's Mantle* is a secret. Please. Don't call me Gwion, don't call me Taliesin. Don't mention freeweb.'

'But...' Jed's scowl disappeared into a baffled frown.

'I don't want my father finding out. He'll send me to a military academy if I don't...' He broke off, unable to finish.

'Ya don't want ya mob ta know either?' Jed leaned forward, staring, as if considering an impossibility.

Either? An image of Uri saying, *That thing in your hand is apt to make you reckless and forgetful,* surfaced in Gawain's memory. 'Jed? Not Jedidiah Harris? Who sent those mind-blowing didgeridoo tracks?'

'Welsh heroes.' Jed swivelled to Cerylen. The change of topic was abrupt and suspicious. 'Cherry, sorry. We cut in on ya and didn't let ya explain 'bout Taliesin.'

Are we letting him get away with that? Is the subject of didgeridoos taboo?

Cerylen pressed her lips together before answering. 'Not much to tell. Gwion's the Welsh poet who wrote a riddle poem, *Hanes Taliesin*. That means "The Tale of Taliesin". Some people believe it contains a secret key to the hidden name of the tree godling worshipped in oak forests by the druids.' She shrugged. 'If it's Welsh heroes you're wanting, my little brother is the one to ask. He was brought up on them—Merlin especially.'

Emrys sighed. 'And being of a more scientific bent than my big sister here, I have carefully examined the mythological evidence and come to a less-than-legendary conclusion. I think the untarnished truth is...'

'Un*varn*ished,' Cerylen interrupted.

Emrys winked. 'The un*vanq*uished truth is that, a century or two before Edmund Halley figured out that a particular comet came back every seventy-five years or so, Gwion realised exactly the same thing. What's more, he gathered the legends people had woven around various different sightings and worked out the different names the comet had been given on each appearance. Somewhat ironic that we're here at an impact crater, discussing mythological cometary incarnations.'

'I've seen the whole *Merlin* series on Heroflix, and it kinda all made sense except those last coupla words.' Jed folded his arms again.

Vasily frowned. 'I lost him long before then.'

'People made up legends about Halley's Comet,' Emrys explained. 'The tales of Taliesin, King Arthur and Merlin, Sir

Kay and a host of other gods and heroes as well. Welsh, English, European, take your pick. Anywhere in the world.'

Jed scratched his head and looked through the bus windows to the purple-shadowed Bluff. 'Ya sayin' the starmaidens o'Tnorala belong ta this comet?'

'More than possible. But, like the Californian legislature and their energy purchases, I don't want to put all my delusions in the one basket.'

'*Con*clusions.' There was a hint of sharpness in Cerylen's voice. 'Jed, you haven't explained what gwion gwion means to you. It's not to do with a crater, is it?'

'Mebbe, now I consider it. Stacks o' impact craters in the Kimberleys. And those Wanjina sure look like they come from another planet.'

'Are Wanjina one-armed?' Gawain asked.

'No, just Laaj-morro. He's a warrior from the Milky Way...'

'Doesn't this prove my point?' Emrys raised his hand and the silvermesh glove stayed visible for several seconds. 'From the Milky Way. From the stars. Just like Taliesin—whose original country was the "region of the summer stars". The myths about one-armed gods are really about comets.'

Don't buy it. 'So? They're myths. They're not real.'

'Not *real*? That doesn't make sense,' Cerylen said. 'We're all myth.'

Whatwhatwhat?

'No.' Emrys shook his head before Gawain could voice his protest. 'We're not *all* myth, sis. However, the line between the mythical and the real is like the gap in interstitial time: so small you wouldn't notice it even when you're looking straight at it.'

'And the meeting o' myth here is deadly ta the max,' Jed mused. 'You're Gawain and Gwion and Taliesin. You don't paint, eh? The gwion gwion is a spirit bird who taught the people of the

Kimberleys ta paint on rocky overhangs an' cave walls. It used its own blood ta do it. That's why it's called a blood-painter.'

Vasily cocked a pale eyebrow. 'If you really thought Gawain was your spirit bird ancestor, why did you attack him? Are not your ancestors sacred? Do you not reverence them with songlines and Dreamings?'

Jed put his fingers together in a bird beak and pointed it at Vasily. 'Gwion gwion's not an ancestor from here—it's from up the Kimberleys, over the Tanami Desert; it belongs ta a different tribe entirely. That makes it the enemy—what you mob would prob'ly call a "demon". Spirit ancestors never leave their tribal localities unless there's war afoot.'

This is ridiculous. These guys aren't supernerds. They're nutters. Mixing mythologies and cultures and suggesting their invented tangle is fact. His palm itched—a ferocious, burning irritation that began to consume all his attention. He knew his shoulder wound needed attention again but it was a minor thing compared to the stabbing pain in his hand. *I hope we reach wherever we're going soon.* He closed his eyes, and leaned back against the headrest.

As he drifted into unconsciousness, he heard a soft exchange between the others. 'I cannot believe you trust him.' Vasily sounded mystified.

'Admitting to the spy glasses is a good sign.' That was Emrys. 'He could be giving us all the inflammation he knows.'

'*Inform*ation,' Cerylen corrected with a sigh.

'It proves nothing.' Cardea spoke up. 'We all have something to hide. The spy glasses aren't the real problem when it comes to Gawain. That seed growing in his hand is.'

INTERSTITIAL

II

'HUSH BABI BYE AR GOPAON Y COED...' A faint melody drifted down from the sky, as the snow and stars danced together in a shimmer of luminous white. The words of the song were unfamiliar to the dog-boy but the tune... the tune... He struggled to remember.

Hushabye baby on the treetops...

The snow whirled up to the stars and, together, they flowed along the river of time, through the branches of the Tree. Its leaves flickered with the ebb and flow of the light, their soft susurration a faint lullaby sent forth to the ages. High on its topmost branch was a cradle and, in it, a white stag stood, tall and watchful.

A tumultuous roar from the feasting hall shattered the dog-boy's vision. The huddle of hounds at his feet was dislodged as the Wild Man pulled him up and said, 'Don't tell me. The high king's made another proclamation—lemme guess: *none may sip and none may sup until a marvel be unveiled before mine sovereign eyes.* No wonder they're pounding the table in there.' He patted the white stag.

The dog-boy stared, trying to work out if the stag in his vision was the same as the one in front of him.

The Wild Man sighed. 'His head's swellin'. In another age, it'd be totalitarian dictatorship.'

The dog-boy tugged at the man's furred sleeve and tried to speak. But only a muffled gurgle came out.

'Ya think my stag will pass fer a wonder?' A flurry of snow swirled around the Wild Man. 'Nah, I doubt it.'

The dog-boy hurried at the man's heels, the hounds dashing past them both into the hall. There was almost a collision as the Wild Man stopped on the threshold. At the far end sat the king, his face abstracted. Around him the hungry and thirsty boredom of his liegemen had turned to riotous cruelty. In the middle, fastened by a long chain to one of the support pillars, was a prisoner. Half-naked and covered in bruises and blood, he held his head down as the liegemen took bets while throwing mead horns and bones at him.

'So this is the spy the king has summoned me ta question?' Wild Man stared. 'The one found half-drowned in the king's weir who gives his name in riddles?'

A cheer erupted as a throw caught the prisoner's ear. The dog-boy tugged at the Wild Man's sleeve.

'Yer sorry fer the prisoner, aren't ya?' he asked. 'Even if he is a sea wolf from the dragonships o' the Northmen. I'll do what I can…'

Throwing off the boy's hold, he strode into the hall. A hush fell over the assembly as he stepped in front of the captive. 'Hvað nefna?'

The prisoner didn't respond. But he raised his head.

The dog-boy felt uneasy as the prisoner's gaze turned from the Wild Man to him. A feather-touch brushed against his mind—a half-formed question—and instantly withdrew. The man's look was disconcerting—not cowed or beaten, but cool and appraising.

'Don't know Norse, eh?' The Wild Man folded his arms. 'Or do ya?'

'Mae'n siarard rhydyllau,' the king called out. 'Wyt ti'n gallu darganfod o ble mae'n dod?'

'Nothing but riddles?' the Wild Man laughed. 'Yeah, but I doubt he knows how many mulberry trees grow in the sea.' Although he raised his voice, he didn't even glance towards the king. 'Anyone'd think I was a riddlemaster the way ya go on.'

The captive stared at the Wild Man's twig crown with its scattering of mulberries. 'Mer... *lin?*'

For a moment the Wild Man was obviously disconcerted. 'Don't even think it! They'll be expectin' magic on tap. I've enough problems.'

But the prisoner, continuing to stare, began to chant in a hoarse voice. 'The man in the wilderness asked of me, *"How many mulberry trees grow in the sea?"* and I answered him as best I could, *"As many fine fishes as swim in the wood."*'

Silence fell in the hall.

The Wild Man and the captive locked gazes.

'Now it so happens the English ya speakin' doesn't exist fer over a thousand years,' the Wild Man stated.

The dog-boy blinked. Tried to process what the Wild Man meant. Failed. He stared at the prisoner.

The man's eyes were flecked with smoky whorls of starlight that spun, slowly and sedately, like the shimmering wheel of a galaxy. The dog-boy felt himself being drawn into them, then beyond them, into the deeps of time. And there, at its heart, he saw again the Tree.

He gasped. Stars were caught in its branches, like glittering fruit. He turned to run. Panic arose within him. The Tree was calling, summoning him to the sylvan throne. He glanced behind and saw it shuddering. A shadow with eight thin legs fell from it...

He screamed in terror.

9

GAWAIN JOLTED INTO CONSCIOUSNESS when Angie jumped on the bed. 'You get all the inciting accidents, Gawain.'

He shook his head, struggling into wakefulness. *How'd I get into bed?* His right shoulder had been rebandaged, the bottom of one jean-leg had been cut off and a medi-pack applied. He felt no pain, just an incredible drowsiness. And immense hunger. 'Is it dinner-time?'

'You missed it.' Angie's golden glove was covered with crumbs and flopping over her elbow. 'And breakfast and lunch and dinner and supper and breakfast and lunch and dinner and...'

'I've been out more than two days?'

Angie grinned. 'Mom's rung. But I didn't tell her you got shot. Or speared. I said you were out learning about magnetic and gravitational anomalies. That shut her up. I told her we were having fun and making new friends. And I told her I want a steampunk eyecup. And I told her I want a dog just like Retro. And she said

I could, if I find out what breed he is. And she says to give you a huggy huggy and a kissy kissy, so pretend I have, willya, Gawain, when she calls back?'

Gawain shuddered. 'Your restraint is truly appreciated, sparrow.' He felt light-headed, his thoughts flitting and unable to connect. *I wonder if sharvas are listed in the telephone directory. My spy glasses are out in the desert. The dog must respond to a secret signal when there's a grammar mistake. Someone's finally cracked my secret identity. Maybe I can bribe him with a song.*

'I've been exploring, Gawain. This place is *old*.'

Gawain propped himself up with the pillow. He was able to see out the lace-curtained window to a cluster of sprawling sheds. Next to them was a water tank and rusty windmill turning lazily. *Too slow to power our devices.* He looked around the room. And blinked in disbelief. Real wood panelling. *Trees died for this. Maybe whole forests.* No climate control—not even something as archaic as air-conditioning. There was a tiny wall fan. It wasn't moving. 'Old—as in out of the Dark Ages?'

'Pretty much.' Angie's voice became muffled as she wriggled down under his bed. 'But Cherry is making us all evaporative coolers. She says it's the first priority.'

We've flown through a time bubble and we're back in the twentieth century—or the nineteenth. 'I thought that was powering our tablets and computers.'

'Vasily's fixed that. Mom wouldn't have got through, if he hadn't of rigged up a power source.'

'How?'

'Dunno... aha! I knew it! And I knew it again! And again!' Angie crawled out from under the bed with three tiny silver buttons in her hand. Her scowl was furious as she pulled out Gawain's box of earth treasures. She opened it and dropped the buttons in. Gawain could see there were already more than a dozen in there just like it.

'What's going on?'

'We're keeping them here until we decide what to do with them,' Angie said.

We? Who is 'we'?

Angie pulled a nautilus shell from the box, then put it back and removed a card. A green giant was pictured on it. 'Gawain, you're way too old for this stuff. So can I have it all?'

'Are you kidding? No!'

'Why not?'

He couldn't think of a good reason. 'Because that's the Green Knight, that's why. A magician at one of mom's parties gave it to me because it goes with my name.'

'I knew you were "*Sir*" Gawain.' Angie blew him a kiss. 'A courteous knight would say "yes" to a lady.'

'In that case, I'll probably agree to share when Cerylen asks me.'

'I meant *me!*' Angie stomped on the floorboards. 'I'm the lady.'

Gawain ignored her. 'When you were a teeny tiny baby, mom had a huge party for some senator's election campaign and she hired a magician to entertain the guests. He had just asked for a volunteer to take off his head when Mom saw me watching and told me to go straight to bed. But the magician heard her call me "Gawain" and so he insisted I had to be the one to use the sword.'

'You chopped somebody's head off?' Angie was agog and horrified, both at once.

Gawain leaned back on the pillow. In his mind's eye, he could see the lazy, blinking eyes of the illusionist, his green velvet jacket, his top hat. The glittering sword with its razor-sharp edge. His mother's ashen face.

With sudden, almost electric insight, he realised why she'd never let him near another of her parties. Until this moment, he'd always thought she'd been angry at him. But he realised she never again wanted to choose between being a good hostess and a good mother.

'The magician told everyone that, in the story of King Arthur where the Green Knight appears, it was Sir Gawain who lopped off the Green Knight's head and so it had to be me help him with the trick.'

'You chopped somebody's head off?' Angie repeated, her eyes huge with astonishment.

'I sure did.' Gawain couldn't help but grin. 'And he walked around with it under his arm for the rest of the party. It was so cool.' He laughed, recalling the expressions of the guests who didn't know where to look: at the vacant space above the conjurer's neck or at the head itself tucked neatly under his arm. He had only been as tall as the man's waist at the time, so he'd spent the rest of the evening chatting to the head. It was a glorious time. He'd drunk a glass of champagne, thinking it was pink lemonade, then wobbled around the garden where they'd sung silly songs to the man in the moon. One of the most ridiculous popped like a bursting bubble into his memory. '*I'm a little sharva, lost my head, and my pal Gawain should be in bed.*'

Gawain felt a tingle pass up his spine. *Sharva? Like why didn't I remember before now?*

Angie sniffed as she brought a bee trapped in amber out of the box. A grey hawk's feather. The bullet Uri had caught. Two teeth glued to a tiny blue card. 'These yours?'

'The tooth fairy didn't want them. Rejects.' He remembered the violent argument between his mother and grandmother when she discovered he'd lost two of his front teeth and neither of his parents had noticed. Now that he came to consider it, that was the week he'd been whisked off to the Casbah.

'What are the silver buttons?'

'Surveillance listening devices that the security goons keep planting everywhere. You're lucky you're not sharing with one of the stormtroopers. That was Witchiepoo's first idea.'

She means Hale.

'Gawain...' Angie tilted her head. 'Who's Angharad Goldenhand?'

'I dunno. Why?'

'Just...' Angie hesitated as she stared at her golden glove. 'Oh, nothing.' She sighed. 'I wish Princess Emma was here.' Putting her hand in her pocket, she brought the meteorite out. 'It's still asleep. Just when I have some serious wishing to do.'

Angie turned to examine a picture on the wall above his bedside table. 'He's naked,' she giggled.

Gawain twisted his head. 'It's a famous picture by Leonardo da Vinci. *The Ideal Man.*'

'You don't look like that.'

'I'm not ideal.'

'Princess Emma thinks you are.'

'No, you can't have my earth treasures.'

'Princess Emma likes consistency in her men.'

'Oh yeah?' *She's gotta have a soap opera addiction. Does mom know?* 'So how come you never told me that before?'

'I haven't told you lots of things.'

Gawain closed his eyes, too tired to spar any longer. Then he snapped to attention. Miss Hale's stiletto voice echoed down the corridor. 'That dog's a monster. Remove it: understand? Fix the surveillance. And find the source of the problem. Look into projects from previous schools. There must be a reason why the mindshadow pulses aren't working on the kids.'

Mindshadow pulses? Like in mind control?

Footsteps headed their way. The door opened. 'Oh, Gawain.' Miss Hale's tone oozed honey. 'You're awake at last. Hungry?'

'Starving,' Gawain admitted. 'Angie was about to get me a sandwich.'

Angie frowned, looking baffled.

Get outta here, sis. Take the box of earth treasures with you before she spots the bugs.

Angie got the message. But instead of leaving, she slammed down the top of the box.

Miss Hale moved towards her. 'Angelina, what have you got there?'

Angie produced a sudden pout. 'Gawain should learn to share. You'd think from his reaction to my perfectly reasonable request that I was gonna steal his most precious possessions.'

Gawain could tell from Miss Hale's expression she wasn't falling for Angie's line. Her hand was out and her lips formed a thin, grim curve.

'There you are, Angie!' Cerylen rushed in, holding a tray of sandwiches. 'I saved these for you before the ravenous hordes wolfed the entire lot...' She stopped, her lips curving into a tentative smile, her eyecup swivelling. 'You're awake, Gawain. How wonderful. Want an egg-and-lettuce sanger?'

Sanger? Gawain was under the distinct impression Cerylen was the cavalry sent to rescue them. He had no idea what a sanger was but he beamed at her and inspected the tray. It had more than sandwiches. There were pineapple slices, grapes and a strawberry muffin. *My favouritefavouritefavourite. How'd she know? And how to help her cavalry charge achieve its purpose?* 'I hear you're constructing an evaporative cooler.'

Her smile became dazzling. 'It's nothing fancy. Really very simple.' She sat on the edge of his bed. 'We all hope you'll be able to join us soon, Gawain. We're going into town tomorrow. Shopping. I want some magnolia nail polish, Vasily wants a nuclear reactor and Emrys wants a cyclotron. However Miss Hale has persuaded us to be less ambitious and settle for solar converters. Haven't you, Miss Hale?'

As far as Gawain could tell, Angie had fished all the silver bugs from the box while Miss Hale was distracted by Cerylen. He ate the strawberry muffin, watching Miss Hale as she struggled to divide her attention between the three of them. *She probably wishes she had eyes in the back of her head.* Then, half way through an egg-and-lettuce sandwich, he realised. *She* does *have eyes in the back of her head. I bet those mirrored glasses record what's going on behind her as well as in front.*

Miss Hale didn't answer Cerylen's question. She turned to Angie, grabbed her fist and prised open her fingers. She spilled the surveillance bugs into her own palm and then left, without a word.

Gawain looked at Angie, then at Cerylen. Silence. He didn't dare break it.

Angie was shaking with rage. 'Cherry, we've got to get rid of her.'

'How?' Cerylen's voice was a throaty whisper.

Gawain pointed his finger. 'Angie, you have to behave perfectly. Model citizen. Obedience without question. You've gotta get rid of the attitude, sis. You've gotta stop acting like one of mom's bitchy friends, three years old one minute, thirty the next.'

Angie took a deep breath. 'I don't know how, but I'll do it.'

'Just don't *over*do it, 'kay?'

'Can I be cute?' Angie didn't wait for an answer. She hurtled out the open door. 'I've got to save Retro.'

Gawain dropped his head to his chest. 'Was there something ambiguous about the instruction to "behave perfectly"?'

Cerylen shook her head. Her voice was low, soft, breathy. 'She's great. I don't know what we'd do without her to run interference for all of us.'

Run interference? It dawned on Gawain he'd been sent to Australia to be a spy—which meant there were kids here with secrets. Truly world-shaking, perhaps world-shattering, secrets. And Angie was on their side.

Maybe that made it easier. If she was trusted by them, she'd learn things to pass on. It wouldn't occur to her not to.

He steadied himself and stood up.

Flashpoint of agony. His palm began to spasm.

10

'HE'S HERE!' AT LEAST EMRYS seemed genuinely thrilled to see him. 'Hey, welcome to consciousness, buddy. I thought we were going to have to get out a mental detector to be sure you were okay.'

'*Metal* detector,' Cerylen corrected, leading Gawain into the work studio.

Emrys winked. 'That too, sis. But it'd be for Angie and her bug collection.'

Bug collection? I guess he means the tiny silver surveillance devices. Gawain didn't respond to the banter. He concentrated on putting one foot in front of the other. The pain in his hand had diminished but he didn't dare clasp the one Emrys was holding out. It was all he could do to tack a smile on his face. He hoped he didn't look as shaky as he felt.

'Here, have a seat.' Emrys swung a computer chair around and rolled it over to him in a single swift action.

Obviously I do look that shaky. Grateful, he sat down.

'Have a biscuit.' Emrys held out a plate. 'Cookie, I mean. I believe Angie helped make them but they're not half bad.'

Left hand forward. Open fingers. Pick up cookie. Place in mouth.

It was like turning on a switch in his brain. The moment the cookie hit his tongue, he felt himself become more alert.

No one else had even turned from their tablets. They were all so absorbed in their private projects that his return was a non-event for them. Vasily had earphones on as he looked at a screen of code. He could only see the back of Cardea's burqa as she gazed at an online newspaper headline: Terrorists attack Ohio terminal. Video footage of all the Angies and Gawains wandering around Hopkins International Airport was already up.

'You're wall-to-wall on the internet,' Emrys said. 'Conspiracy theorists are having a field day. A tree gunned you down, y'know.'

A tree? 'I saw a dragon. A hologram. White skin, black eyes, red tongue.'

'No one's spotted that. At least, if they have, no one has mentioned it. There's a few screen captures of a strange shadow. Looks like a horse with eight legs. But no dragon. Hologram or otherwise.'

Did I imagine it? Gawain sighed. *What were you thinking, Miss Hale? Even if I wasn't shot, didn't you see this publicity coming? A couple of dozen Angies and Gawains, all in identical outfits. You gotta wonder about the intelligence of our intelligence operatives.*

Cerylen folded her arms. 'If I didn't know better, I'd think Witchiepoo was deliberately trying to draw attention to you and Angie.'

Deliberately? It wasn't a plan that back-fired?

'Now, that'd be absurd, sis.' Emrys looked her straight in the eye. 'That would mean she was a double agent.' His voice became slower and more emphatic. 'That... would... mean... we... couldn't... trust... her.'

Not trust her? That doesn't compute. She's supposed to be protecting me. Well, protecting me is her excuse for being here but I still think it's genuine. He rolled his chair closer to the screen, smiling in apology as he intruded on Cardea's personal space. 'Okay if I look over your shoulder?'

She said nothing. Just waved a hand. As he was wondering if the gesture meant 'yes' or 'no', it dawned on him her skin was the wrong colour. *That's because it's not her skin. It's Jed's.* He stared. *What's he doing under that burqa?* Two and two finally clicked together. *The stormtroopers don't know he's here. He's managed to hide himself for a couple of days, despite their surveillance bugs. So where's Cardea?* Gawain drew a deep breath. *How's she keeping hidden? Who's she with?*

Jed clicked the privacy tab on the computer and a crackle of digital lightning sounded from the device. Gawain winked back at him: it was the beginning of *Thunder Angels*, the most popular download *Taliesin's Mantle* had ever produced.

I really have to find something to bribe him with. If my father finds out, I'm deaddeaddead... He took another deep breath. *Two things to consider about this situation: one, the stormtroopers are so lax they may as well be amateurs and, two, this place is crawling with so many secrets it's enough to make me really anxious. These guys are all worse than I am!*

'Cookie!' Emrys shoved a biscuit towards his mouth. The silver mesh hand winked momentarily. 'Open up, buster!'

'I can feed myself.'

'Prove it.'

Gawain took the cookie and had munched half of it before he realised Emrys was ordering him around like a two-year-old. Worse, he was obeying without question. 'Are you always this dictatorial?'

'I am *not* a dictator, buster. I am an aristocrat.'

'*Auto*crat, you mean.' Cerylen thumped his upper arm.

'That too, sis.'

'He's just inherited a castle in the Welsh marches.' Cerylen held up her hands as if she'd just explained everything about her brother's attitude.

'Yep, I've got affluenza.'

Cerylen's eyecup rotated with a click. 'This is going to be a bad pun on influenza, isn't it?'

Emrys grinned. 'Of course. Affluenza is enough wealth to make you sick.'

The eyecup swivelled back. 'We couldn't have afforded to come to this school normally.' Cerylen exhaled a long sighing breath. 'But it hasn't turned out anything like we thought.'

'It's a strange place.' Gawain started on the other half of the cookie.

'We've been to much stranger.' Emrys tapped his fingers on the back of Gawain's chair.

Vasily held up his hand—one by one, his fingers performed a silent countdown. 'We have exclusion.' He pumped his fist. 'Since they are all out chasing Retro, I estimate we have ten minutes, perhaps less.' He swung around on his chair. So did Jed.

Exclusion? Of what?

Emrys flicked his ear to get his attention. 'So, Gawain: who exactly are you spying for?'

The question was so unexpected, so direct that Gawain nearly choked on his half-eaten cookie.

'It can't be Miss Hale.' Emrys took his burning hand and rested it on his silver glove. 'Because she is clearly trying to make you famous, not keep you hidden.'

The pain levels in his hand dropped so fast Gawain felt his whole body relax. 'It was a mistake in strategy. An attempt to confuse the bad guys that blew up in her face.'

'Yeah, right.' Vasily folded his arms. 'So, just who are the bad guys?'

'I have no idea.' Faced with a wall of disbelief, Gawain crumbled. 'I was minding my own business, trying to keep my secret identity secret—because my dad will send me to a military academy if he ever finds out about my music—when this...' He paused. *How to describe a yellow-eyed giant with a slimy skin and hissing voice?* '...strange man turned up at our house. He told me I had to come to this summer camp and find some twins named Reece and Holly. That the fate of the free world depended on it.' Gawain shrugged. 'Obviously he got his facts wrong.' Cos there's only us.'

Silence.

'What was his name?' Cerylen asked.

'I didn't get introduced.'

'What did he look like?'

'It was dark... I couldn't see him very well.' Gawain shook his head. 'Oh, okay, I know how this is going to sound but...' He hesitated. '...he kinda looked like an alien. He was huge. And he had yellow eyes and a slimy skin and a hissing voice.'

Cerylen exchanged a horrified glance with Emrys.

'But... like I said, it was dark... and he might have...' Gawain couldn't believe his own stupidity. *Ludicrous. How could I have said the guy was an alien?* He tried to retrieve his lapse into absurdity. '...well, you know, he might have had jaundice. That turns the whites of your eyes yellow. And if he wasn't feeling well, that would account for the scratchy way he talked.'

'Who are you trying to convince?' Vasily asked. 'Yourself or us?'

With a sudden lurch and flap of the burqa, Jed reached for his keyboard and hit the 'alt' key. For no apparent reason Gawain could discern, he began tapping it.

'Sounds like an A flat,' Gawain said. 'Key of A flat minor is a great choice for death metal. Not really my styl...' He broke off as he noticed the faintest of shadows on the wall outside the studio. Two figures: one short and slender, the other as tall as a giant. *How long have they been listening in?* He pointed to the door with his left hand, leaving his right still resting on Emrys' glove.

Emrys turned and straight away raised his voice. 'So what *is* your style, Gawain?'

'Tone shapes.' *No point in concealing it.* 'Tone shapes of natural phenomena. *Thunder Angels* is my most popular download. *Midnight Dew* is gaining, though. So is *Snow Riders*. It's a fusion of dreamy and tinkly with Japanese bells. *Wind Hooves* isn't doing so well. It's got far better production values than *Thunder Angels* but the most of the comments say it's just a pale copy of it; trying to cash in on the popularity of *Angels*. Which is stupid because how can I cash in when they're both on freeweb?'

'What are you working on now?'

Gawain felt momentarily shy. '*Galactic Tree* is the provisional title. It's more from a...' He hesitated. *Should I admit to the visions? The dog-boy and the Wild Man? The stag and the mulberries-that-grow-in-the-sea?* '...dream than inspiration from nature. I get this picture in my mind's eye of a tree glowing with starfruit whose branches weave in and out through the cracks in the continuum between time and eternity.'

Emrys patted his hand. 'There aren't *cracks* in any continuum. They're interstitial gaps.'

As he let go of Gawain's hand, pain flooded back. Gawain gasped as his fingers locked into a claw. He bit his lip and tried to school his face into an expressionless mask. Emrys stared at his face for a few seconds before looking down at his paralysed hand. An alarm sounded.

'Exclusion not operat…' Vasily broke off as, with a balletic leap, Angie bounded into the room.

'Gawain, you gotta stop incomplete comparisons.'

Huh?

Miss Hale followed her in. The shadows on the outside wall didn't move.

'Incomplete comparisons of what?' Gawain tried not to think of the pain in his palm.

'Well, like what I said to Retro.' Angie flung out her arms. 'I told him he is faster, stronger, cleverer. And he growled so much I thought he was gonna eat me. But Uri said it was because I didn't finish the comparison. Retro would be complimented to be told he's faster, stronger and cleverer than a lion but insulted if I meant an earthworm.' She clapped her hands together above her head. 'And that means you've gotta stop saying things like "sweet as".'

'I don't say that.'

'Yes, you do.'

Gawain didn't want to argue. 'Okay, I promise not to do it anymore.'

'You know, Gawain, you're such a sweetiepie when you even give it half a try.'

Gawain wondered why Angie was overdoing the praise. *Is it for Miss Hale's benefit?* He was impressed by her sweet, meltingly sincere expression.

'I'm going to tell Retro too that you're just like the Finchy man. I could have given him the wrong idea about your grammatical inaccuracies.'

'The Finchy man?' Curiosity edged Miss Hale's voice.

'You know,' Angie said. 'The ideal one.' She put out her hands as if she were about to do a star jump to demonstrate the correct pose.

'Leonardo da Vinci,' Gawain interpreted. *I really should nominate you for an Oscar, sparrow. I don't have the slightest clue what you're up to but Witchiepoo Hale won't see through this act in a million years. Even I half believe that you're batty as.*

Then he noticed the glint in Cerylen's eye and the tiny movement of her eyecup. *She knows, sis. You aren't deceiving* her *one little bit.*

Angie thrust her hand into her pocket and drew out her wishing star. 'It's still sleeping.' She stared at it with intensity. 'I think it's got knocked unconscious. Just like you, Gawain. It hasn't twinkled once.'

'It's a meteorite!' Emrys exclaimed. 'Cool specimen! Looks like iron, not stone.' He bent down so he was Angie's height. 'You know, chickadee, a loving sister would give a meteorite as nice and chunky as that to her brother.'

'He's got enough earth treasures! He's got a hammonite, a nautilus shell, a hawk's feather, a bullet, a Green…'

Emrys held up a finger to shush her. 'He's also got a very very sore hand. And if he could hold that meteorite, I'm sure it would help him a lot.'

Right. Sure. As if. Gawain winced. *Ow! Is that an incomplete comparison?*

Angie's pout was almost a snarl. 'Here!' she snapped and threw the meteorite.

He reacted by instinct, catching it on the full toss. A lance of pain shot up his right arm. And then, nothing.

The pain was gone. Instantly.

Gawain glanced at Miss Hale, wondering what she would say. But she seemed caught in a stupefied daze.

He looked beyond her to the shadows on the wall in the outside corridor. The figures were still there. A moment later, huge wings sprouted from behind the shoulders of the giant.

Then, in a silent, luminous flash, both figures vanished from sight.

INTERSTITIAL

III

THE IMMENSITY OF THE FALL was almost too much to comprehend. The dog-boy shook with the terror of the memory, the shock of dropping out of the flux of time and plunging downdowndown everandforeverdown. *There was a stag too. A stag that... tried to save me? Or kill me?*

With the utmost difficulty, he tore his gaze away from the prisoner's eyes. Instead he found himself staring at the man's hands. There was an entire finger missing: the ring-finger.

'A'i denuydd yw e?' the king asked. In the stillness, his question echoed with unnatural loudness.

'Is he a druid?' The Wild Man repeated the king's question, shaking his dusky head in bemusement at the prisoner. Then his expression changed to a glare. 'Just who are ya?'

The captive shifted himself. He was in obvious pain. His eyes were empty, misted and withdrawn. It was so long before he answered the dog-boy wondered if he had lost consciousness. But finally, he did answer, his voice, at first a rasp, slowly swelling with power:

'I am a hart with antlers tall
I am a cliff where eagles call
I am a star on heaven's stair
I am the thief of the silver chair
I am the kettle's steamy kiss
I am a metal mist-wreathed fist
I am a shell, asleep in stone
I am the song within the bone
I am a lion crouched on an arch
I am a lance for battle's march
I am a fort, set by the sea
I am a word that's yet to be.
I am the magi, lost in time,
I trod the path of ancient rhyme,
mistaking starlight for the star—
forgetting how apart they are.'

The Wild Man was staring. 'Like I said, ya speak perfect English from a thousand years in the future. So I gotta ask ya: ever met a devil named Aanundus?'

Aanundus. The dog-boy couldn't think how he knew the name or quite what 'devil' meant. *Is it the same as 'alien'?*

The startled look in the captive's eyes seemed to be all the answer the Wild Man needed. 'Tell me. What's ya name?'

'Ta...' began the prisoner. A mead horn hit the flaggings, spilling a vile-smelling froth across his face. '...lliii...' His reply was drowned in a nauseated splutter. '...ze...'

'Teli...?' the king called out. 'Beth mae e'n dweud? Teli... ze...? Talyizan?'

Taliesin. The name was a flame in his mind... a roaring fire. Another Taliesin in another time... in another age...

'Of course!' The Wild Man turned, clapping the dog-boy on the back. The flicker of memory was gone in a jolt. 'Taliesin!' The Wild Man grinned. 'What a deadly kinda switch!' With a flourish, he bowed to the king. 'Ya wish fer a marvel, my lord?' Pointing to the captive, he raised his voice. 'This poor kid is Taliesin, the greatest bard the world'll ever know...' He paused, adding under his breath, 'At least until a guy called Shakespeare turns up.'

At this there was a sudden furore of calls—'Gallwn fwyta! Gallwn fwyta!'—and drumming demands for mead.

The Wild Man signed to the king and sent the dog-boy to fetch the warder who guarded the keys to the captive's chains. Straining, he could just make out the conversation between the Wild Man and the captive.

'They understand you?' the prisoner asked.

'Not a word.' The Wild Man sounded cheerful. 'Not a single word. Ya really think any o' them speak a solitary syllable of third-millennium English?' He laughed. 'Nah! The kingsmen have had enough an' decided I was tellin' 'em the feast could begin.' He smiled at the prisoner. 'Improvise,' he advised. 'It's the only way. The men'll love ya, at least as long as there's food an' drink around. Especially drink.'

'I've been here long enough to know their moods.'

'I'm sure ya have.' The Wild Man nodded. 'Tell me, can ya sing?'

'I can get by. I can even play the harp. Though I'm not quite sure what the current fashion is.'

'Ya play the harp? Deadly!' The Wild Man's smile widened. 'Oh, they'll utterly adore ya here.' He paused, his smile fading. 'By the way, in case ya haven't already realised it, Taliesin, this is the sixth century.'

11

GAWAIN FELT SO RESTED when he woke, he was tempted to luxuriate in bed all day. His hand still clasped the meteorite. Flexing his fingers, he closed them over it once more, thinking about the previous afternoon.

He'd eaten cheese-and-pickle sandwiches. He'd watched Cerylen rig up an evaporative cooler. He'd listened to a podcast on the use of sound frequency to shatter glass, make bridges vibrate and demolish skyscrapers. He'd talked to Emrys about opening the gate between time and eternity using a similar sound principle. He hadn't understood even one percent of the conversation. He'd watched Jed leave to go to the bathroom and seen the same burqa come back with Cardea inside. *Don't like it. Is she really so religious or is it just a super-convenient disguise?*

He'd been troubled as he helped Angie and Ms Gunn make spaghetti bolognaise for dinner. Then he'd crashed straight afterwards.

Now he was ready to take on the world.

His door banged open.

'Gawain!'

He groaned and looked at the ceiling as Angie jumped on to the bed next to him. 'Kissy kissy. Huggy huggy.' Her grin was feral. 'Mom rang again. You owe me.'

'What for?'

'Mom's getting you music lessons for your birthday.'

'*What*?!' He bolted up, in real terror.

'You know mom. Her latest trophy friend is the lead violinist of the Boston Symphony Orchestra. They thought you'd look good with a bowtie and harp.'

'Is this a bad joke?'

'You owe me big time, Gawain. I told her I knew you well enough to know you couldn't imagine anything more horrifying than music lessons. Which is obviously true from your reaction. I also told her you didn't have the discipline for a harp. Which is probably untrue.' Angie's sigh was long and exaggerated. 'It was tough to convince her, Gawain. I had to pull out the trumpet card.'

'That would be *trump* card.'

'That too.'

'You're starting to sound like Emrys. You're spending too much time with him.'

'Am not. You haven't asked about my trump card. I said dad would be real mad if mom encouraged you in something so frivolous. So she agreed to drop the idea.'

Gawain blew her a kiss.

He lay back in relief. Angie plopped herself beside him. 'Look!' She held out her hand. Over a dozen silver surveillance bugs sat in her palm. 'Retro helped me find them. That's why Witchiepoo doesn't like him.'

Gawain took one button and whistled. 'Good morning, Miss Hale.' He held out the button to Angie. 'Step on it.'

Angie's eyes lit up. With great glee, she took off one shoe, sat down on the floor, and pounded the button as if it were a cockroach. Then she reached for another. She was on her sixth kill when Emrys sauntered in.

'Rise and shine, bro. We're heading into town to stock up on supplies. The charter plane was bringing them in but it won't be arriving for another few days. So Ms Gunn is taking us out to do the hunter-gatherer thing. Are you up to it, buster?'

'Sure.' *No way I'm staying here with the goons.* 'You better come too, sparrow.'

'I don't wanna.'

'I owe you a big favour. You don't want a new doll?'

'A new doll?!' Angie was affronted. 'How would you feel if you was in Princess Emma's shoes and heard I'd got a new doll?'

Gawain curled his lip. 'There are many things I'm capable of, sparrow, but putting myself in Princess Emma's teensy pink shoes isn't one of them.'

Angie sneered back. 'I gotta protect Retro.'

Cerylen poked her head around the door. 'Retro's waiting in the bus.'

'Then I'm coming too!'

'Ms Gunn is leaving in fifteen minutes.' Cerylen's smile was back to super-sweet super-dazzling. 'So everyone's got to be ready. Hot pancakes are on now if you want breakfast.'

Seconds later, Gawain was alone. He was up in an instant, searching his rucksack for fresh jeans. He found underwear, socks, school tie. *What're my leather shoes doing here? Where are my spare jeans? I can't go like a hillbilly.* He looked down at the jeans he was wearing with one cut-off leg and the bandage below it.

Ten minutes later, he'd persuaded Cerylen to cut off the other leg of the jeans. They both wolfed down pancakes, and made the bus with a minute to spare. Ms Gunn was in the driver's booth, revving the engine and Uri was sprawled across two seats, his red glasses looking like stained glass in a church window. Retro was on the floor at the back; Emrys and Vasily were deep in conversation; it was impossible to tell from the averted burqa whether it was Jed or Cardea next to Angie.

Miss Hale had her foot on the side steps—her mirrored glasses were gone and she wore a tinted wraparound bluescreen. *Maybe it was a mistake to let Angie loose on the surveillance bugs.*

'Heigh ho, the Witch is dead—which old witch? The Wicked Witch!' Angie's voice was shrill as she struck up the munchkins' song from *The Wizard of Oz*. 'Heigh ho, the Wicked Witch is dead!' She danced down the aisle to Retro. 'Come on, Gawain! Sing with me.'

Gawain couldn't think of anything worse. Retro, however, began a wavering, mournful croon. Vasily and Emrys both put their hands over their ears.

'I'll see you in town. Be right behind you all the way.' Miss Hale slammed the side door shut and marched back to the ATV.

'Phew!' Angie wiped her brow. 'Thanks, Retro.'

The huge dog purred at her.

'Thanks, Angie!' Jed wriggled out from under the seat behind Retro. 'I'm glad I don't hafta squeeze into this hidey hole all the way.'

If he has a perfect right to be on camp, why does he go through this elaborate routine?

Jed settled on the floor.

'Does Ms Gunn know you're here?' Gawain asked in a whisper.

Jed shrugged.

Does that mean yes or no?

The bus was off. It headed down the sandy track towards the Bluff, past low flat scrub and sere grass, veering to skirt the escarpment ring. It passed close to the hill Gawain remembered was called 'The Wizard of Oz'. Obviously Angie remembered too. 'We're off to see the Wizard, the wonderful Wizard of Oz.' Her voice was warm and melodious, a complete contrast to her previous shrill tones.

'Since I can't get you a doll, what about red shoes?' Gawain asked her. 'You need them if you're going to be Dorothy in the eternal fight against the forces of Witchiepoo and her minions.'

'In the book of *The Wizard of Oz*, Dorothy's shoes are silver, not red.'

She's read the book? 'Silver, then.'

The quiet murmur of Emrys and Vasily as they chatted together, the soft voices of Cardea and Cerylen, the gentle humming of Jed as he joined in Angie's song combined to form a lullaby background to Gawain's thoughts.

Hushabye baby on the treetops... When the wind blows the cradle will rock. Uri's harpsong voice was inside his head once more. *Go to sleep, Greyhawk. It's a long trip.*

The bus reached bitumen where a signpost indicated Mparntwe via Ntaria to the right, and Mparntwe via Yapalpe to the left.

The land of unpronounceable names. 'Here be dragons' territory. Wait—Ntaria? Didn't Jed say the sharva was headed that way? 'Uri, are we going via Ntaria?'

The giant's red glasses winked. 'Sure!' He tapped the driver's security booth. 'Take us past Hermannsburg, Meg. The kidlets wanna see it.'

They sped along a road no wider than the vehicle, the sunburnt plains stretching before them and the mountains closing in on either side. An hour passed.

'Palm Valley.' Emrys pointed to a sign indicating a turnoff ahead. 'Is there really an oasis out here?'

Ms Gunn nodded. 'With a unique species of palm tree, found nowhere else on the planet. It's also got an impact crater.'

'Is there a rock-a-bye starbaby too?' Angie bounced with excitement. 'Did it fall out of the palm tree? Are there any wishes in the shatterstones?'

'Shatter*cones*,' Gawain corrected.

Angie's eyes narrowed into a calculating look. Gawain sucked in an uneven breath, recognising her expression. It was a precursor to the finest line of tantrums in all of Ohio. *She wants to go to Palm Valley and nothing's going to stop her.* He was wondering how to prevent the tantrum when, up ahead, he glimpsed a flatbed roaring down the narrow road towards them—*traffic.*

'Ute coming,' Ms Gunn called, swerving the bus at the last moment. *To the wrong side.* Gawain yelped, blood pounding in his ears, expecting an instant collision.

'We drive on the left here.' Uri's voice was quiet, soothing, calming. Settle down, Angharad Goldenhand. You wouldn't want Retro to think you're less than adorable, would you? He pointed to a cluster of ancient buildings, dusty and wilted in the heat. 'Hermannsburg. A famous art centre. Just an hour now into town.'

Gawain's wild heartbeat slowed. He turned to look out the window and take in the passing scenery—the stark rust-hued mountain chains like the backbones of dinosaurs, the dry river beds like ribbons of sand in a pavement of rocks, the white gums towering majestically towards the brilliantly blue sky. He rubbed his eyes, yawned and, with a shock, woke up as the bus stopped at a traffic light. *I'm sleeping way too much. It's not normal.*

'Doctor first,' Uri said.

Ms Gunn turned the bus into a back street and parked it outside a suburban medical centre.

'Come on, Gawain.' Uri adjusted his red glasses as he opened the side door.

'Huh? Me?'

'Yeah, you. We're not too sure about Eyes' medical ministrations, so Ms Gunn'd like to get you checked.'

'I'm okay.'

'She'd still like to know what they've pumped into you.'

Gawain was reluctant but he took Uri's massive hand and stepped out of the bus. The heat hit him straight away. He turned to watch Miss Hale step out from the airconditioning of the ATV to join him. Her bluescreen instantly fogged.

Nice to know she doesn't learn from experience. She whipped the bluescreen off as Uri headed up the path to the surgery.

He opened the door and vanished for a few seconds before appearing again. 'The doctor's been called to an accident at the boat races. We can wait here, but it'd be much faster if we nip down to the river and catch him there.'

Miss Hale scowled. 'Gawain doesn't need a doctor.'

'At the end of the day,' Ms Gunn said, 'the school is responsible for his health, not you. It's in the application form.'

'We didn't sign an application form.'

Gawain noticed her bluescreen flickering in a rapid sequence of pulses. *She's got an information feed inside those glasses.*

'Well, since that's mandatory, it's so convenient you're here today.' Ms Gunn's smile was smug. 'You can leave right away. There are daily international flights. Alice Springs airport is just down the road. We'd be happy to show you.'

'A signed application form will be messaged to you in the next five minutes.' Miss Hale's tone was brisk and efficient. 'It was simply an oversight.'

Uri opened the side door to the bus to usher Gawain back inside. 'We're going to the races!'

'Yay!' Angie threw up her hands.

Gawain shook his head.

'You'll love it,' Uri told him. 'The Henley-on-Todd Regatta is the biggest event on the annual calendar.' His broken teeth were revealed by a wide easy grin. 'There was rain last month so the races were cancelled because the river was running with water. Now it's dry, so the Regatta's on again.'

Vasily was clearly baffled. 'I do not understand. The boat race was cancelled because the river contained water?'

Uri closed the door. 'It's the world's only *dry* river boat race.'

The bus started up and, a minute later, they were on the bridge across the Todd River. Its riverbed was dry and parched. But, as if to make up for the lack of water, there were flags, banners and striped stalls everywhere. A dozen boats were lined up on the sand: wooden dingys, aluminium tinnys, long canoes, a baby catamaran, even a fully-rigged pirate ship sporting wheels. People were milling around the stalls, under the trees, near the boats.

We'll never find the doctor.

'Stop!' Uri pointed to a Red Cross banner.

Ms Gunn slammed on the brakes. 'I'll find a place to park then we'll meet you at the Red Cross tent.' She waved Uri and Gawain out.

They had taken no more than a dozen paces towards the tent when a squint-eyed pirate with an upraised cutlass and a miniature treasure chest appeared in front of them. 'Pieces-of-eight, pieces-of-eight. Stop right there, me hearties, and hand over eight buckeroochies.'

The cutlass was antique plastic. The treasure chest was antique plastic. Gawain looked at Uri. 'I think he wants antique plastic money.'

The pirate peered at him. 'Arrr... that'd be an American accent, wouldn't it be?'

Gawain nodded.

'Arrr... wouldn't know somebody name of Gawain Ashton, would you?'

Gawain froze. *Here I am at the end of the world and a fake pirate knows a name so close to my own, it can't possibly be coincidence.*

12

'WHY?' MISS HALE PUSHED GAWAIN aside as she barked her question at the pirate.

Oww! I didn't need a doctor until you did that.

The pirate drove his plastic cutlass into the sand. Opening the treasure chest, he handed Gawain a map. 'Now what was it?' He scratched his black bandana. 'Yep, that's it: *I'm a little sharva, ducking spies, while Gawain's the subject of all eyes.*'

'Who gave this to you?' Miss Hale swiped the map.

The pirate shrugged. 'A guy with purple hair and blue moustache, wearing a white safari jacket embroidered with cherries. Yellow tie too. Promised the Red Cross eight thousand dollars if I delivered it. So I've been out looking for Gawain.' He stooped to retrieve his plastic cutlass.

Uri nodded. 'A lot to pay for delivery, unless you take into account this is the big charity event of the year.'

'Arrr...' the pirate agreed. 'Lots of peeps playing practical jokes.

Lots of peeps doing crazy things. All part of the fun and games.' He grinned. 'Reminds me, I've a race to interrupt.' With a cry of 'yo ho ho, pieces-of-eight, pieces-of-eight!' he set off through the crowd.

Miss Hale turned to Gawain in accusation. 'Those savages used the same word the other day. *Sharva*. What does it mean?'

Savages! That's my friend Jed you're talking about. 'How would I know?' He looked at the map in her hands. *I'm the subject of all eyes? Or Eyes?*

'Gawain!' Angie was trudging towards him across the sand. Two of Hale's minions, decked out with their own bluescreens, accompanied her. Retro was gambolling in front of them. 'We can buy stuff here.' Angie produced her melt-a-heart-of-stone smile for Miss Hale. 'I've seen some silver sandals. Can I try them on while you're at the doctor?'

Miss Hale was apparently immune to cuteness of any kind. 'No, you can't.' She passed the map to one of the minions. 'We're leaving. We'll find a doctor somewhere else.'

Angie began to wheedle. 'But you...'

She was cut off by an echoing yell: 'Yee—*haaaar!*'

A massive red-bearded bare-chested man wearing a horned helmet sprang towards her, scooped her up, hoisted her over his shoulder and ran off through the crowd. While the first minion bent to retrieve the map that the second had dropped in the sand, Miss Hale whipped out her gun.

Uri's reactions were lightning-swift. *'No!'* He slammed her arm down and the bullet hit the sand. 'It's only a viking raid! We don't have an immunity sticker.'

Miss Hale disentangled herself and dodged past him. 'After them!' She set off in pursuit of the hollering viking, the minions following. Retro sent the first of them sprawling in the sand, while Miss Hale and the second agent found the crowd parting to allow police to descend from all points of the compass. They were intercepted before they'd run more than twenty paces.

'Oh dearie dearie me.' Uri caught up with Miss Hale, just as an officer disarmed her. 'You're gonna have some explaining to do, ma'am. This isn't America, y'know.'

Miss Hale blinked... and frowned.

Gawain watched dozens of people turn to stare at her, more in curiosity than alarm. *Don't they know what a gunshot is? Of course they do. Maybe they thought it was part of the fun and games?* It took him a moment to register that the gun laws in Australia were vastly different from those in the United States.

The same thought obviously occurred to Miss Hale. Momentary anxiety showed on her face. Reaching for her I.D., she cleared her throat. 'Sheriff...'

'Sergeant,' a burly policeman corrected.

'While you're making friends with the local constabulary...' Uri's broken-toothed grin was so broad Gawain knew he was loving the situation. '...Gawain and I will go ransom Angie.'

'Ransom?' Miss Hale whirled to face him.

'We'll be at the viking longship when you've sorted everything out.' Uri's smile faded. 'Assuming you do sort it out, of course. Do pick up the solar converters for us, won't you?'

Gawain allowed Uri to escort him away. He threw a fleeting glance at the burly sergeant who stared back, his expression grim and frustrated as if he were powerless to act.

I know how he feels. Since the moment Uri had slammed Miss Hale's gun down, the music of rushing wings had raised goosebumps on Gawain's flesh. Little shivers were still running up and down his spine every few seconds. *Something strange is going on. That cop didn't want us to go. We're important witnesses.*

Uri's strolling gait slowed. 'Angie will be upset if we rescue her too quickly.'

'She will?' The threnody of wingbeats in Gawain's blood began to quieten.

'Would you want to be interrupted while you were eating ice-cream?' Uri jerked a thumb towards Miss Hale. 'I tried to tell her. All the local charities are represented here, and the rules are simple: if a kid without an immunity sticker is taken by a buccaneer, you ransom them at the pirate ship, if it's a viking, you find them at the longship, and if it's aliens, they'll be at the spaceship.'

'I could get abducted by little green men?'

'Don't get your hopes up. They tend to go for the little 'uns. You're a bit big to hoist over just anyone's shoulder.'

But not yours. Gawain felt a sudden shiver, despite the noonday heat. He glanced sideways at Uri's crimson glasses. 'How long will Miss Hale be?'

'Quite a while, I suspect. It's a privilege to bear arms in Australia—not a right, as it is in America. There'll be extra problems if she doesn't have her passport on her, not to mention a current visa. Then there's those surveillance bluescreens: they're a serious breach of the privacy laws. And of course there's the possibility of espionage. Commander Hale is a foreign agent in a friendly country, but I doubt the foreign power she represents has notified the authorities here of her presence—so this seemingly-innocent babysitting job might hide a more sinister agenda.'

She could be days! Gawain was surprised at the exultant surge of delight rising within him.

'I'm afraid that's too much to hope for.'

Did he hear my thoughts? Or just guess them?

'Still she may be several hours,' Uri went on. 'These are local cops, not Federal police. They don't have the resources to check her cover story straight away.'

Cover story? Gawain glanced at Uri. *You don't trust her either.*

The sense of freedom was still intoxicating. They wandered for a time, following Retro past the vendors' stalls to the river bank.

Uri's eyebrows curved into a single line. 'Either he wants a better view of the races or he's found the scent of something interesting.'

Retro woofed. A moment later, with a faint whoosh that sent a frisson up Gawain's back, a man jumped from a tree. Ripples of emerald light pulsed around him as he landed beside them. 'Don't be afraid.' The man was even taller than Uri. He had golden skin, hooded eyes and long black hair, and was wearing an azure silk jacket. His red glasses were the same shade as Uri's.

How could I have missed him? Gawain peered upwards into the sparse foliage of the gum tree.

'Jib!' Uri greeted the Chinese man with delight. 'What took you so long?'

'The bypass around Persia is grid-locked; the queue's at a standstill.' Jib waved at Gawain. 'You know, I bet he was all snarky about being courteous and polite. And here he is—introductions forgotten.'

'But, Jib, you already know Gawain.' Uri shook his head as Jib rolled his eyes.

He does?

'However, Gawain, I have been remiss not to think of you. This is my illustrious and historically renowned colleague, Jib.'

'*Historically renowned.* That has a delectable ring to it. *Illustrious.* I wonder if I should get a calling card with that on.' He waggled a long glossy fingernail at Uri. 'Your problem wasn't easy to solve. It took a while to track Vasily down. He's an orphan named after a distant relative, Vasili Arkipov. Commander Nathania Hale on the other hand is named after great-great-great-great-great uncle Nathan.'

It took Gawain less than a second to make the connection. 'She's related to Nathan Hale? *The* Nathan Hale? The guy who said, "I regret I have but one life to give for my country" when he was about to be hanged?'

'The very same,' Jib agreed. 'The Nathan Hale who gave his life for the cause of American independence.'

Explains why she's a spy.

Jib's smile was slow and inscrutable. 'The original Vasili Arkipov is, of course, a very different kind of war hero.'

Uri's mouth twisted. 'I know that look, Jib. You've consulted the scrolls of summoning.'

Jib nodded. 'Destiny's children are about to collide. It's about the choice between loyalty and faithfulness. There's a perilous and subtle distinction between the two and, on it, the fate of the world will hang.'

Not again. Just what Yellow Eyes said.

'The reckless patriotism of the Hales meets the disciplined bravery of the Arkipovs. It'd be interesting to watch, but I must fly. Zài jiàn, comrade.' He nodded at Uri. 'You did get the message about Mike's meeting the day after tomorrow?'

Uri nodded.

Jib turned to Gawain. 'You need to do something about your hand—soon, real soon. Don't leave it too long.' He stepped behind the gum tree.

'My hand?' Gawain looked around the tree to ask for clarification. Jib had disappeared. He looked upwards, but no one was there either. *I'm dreaming. Maybe I'm still in Ohio and none of this is happening.*

Uri was smiling. 'That's a relief. Only a prophecy to do with Vasily and Miss Hale. I thought it was more serious.'

ONLY *a prophecy? Jib didn't mention prophecy. Unless scrolls of summoning are prophecy.*

Retro woofed. And woofed again.

'You're right, boy,' Uri said. 'It *is* high-time we rescued Angie.'

13

GAWAIN COULDN'T BELIEVE IT. Jib's disappearance was startling enough but the boat race was one long hallucination.

On the firing signal, the competitors hoisted their boats to their thighs and raced to the finish line. The sandy riverbed was the least of the hindrances. A battalion of blue-skinned aliens, armed with the meanest greenest weapons Gawain had ever seen, immobilised contestants with water jets from their high-powered backpacks. Once an entire boat was down, the aliens escorted their prisoners to a spaceship.

Just past this rocket with its noisy corralled hostages Gawain found the longship. Angie wasn't at all happy to be rescued. She had ice cream on her shirt, a can of lemonade in her hand, and she was chatting to several fellow captives as if she'd known them all her life. 'Gawain! I don't hafta be ramsummed if I don't wanna, do I?'

'If you want silver shoes, you do.'

Retro slurped her face.

'Okay, Retro, just for you.'

Uri guided them past the stalls to the Flying Doctor's tent. Gawain felt sore, awkward and confused as he tried to explain his injuries to a nurse.

'Let me get this right... Wayne, is it? You've been shot, then speared.' She looked at Uri to confirm this story, then told them to wait on folding metal chairs while she called a doctor.

The doctor took Gawain inside the tent, examined the leg injury, pronounced it 'superficial', cleaned and re-bandaged it, then turned to Gawain's shoulder. After a moment, she asked him to lie down while she examined him with a hand-held internal imaging device. She looked at the screen for so long Gawain began to imagine the worst.

'Are you going to amputate?'

'Of course not. All the same I've never seen pain dampeners like these.' The doctor looked him in the eye. 'What're you doing with military-issue combat-injury pain alleviators?'

Gawain smiled, unsure what to say.

The doctor sighed and set about re-bandaging his shoulder. 'It seems to be healing nicely... all the same, I want to see you again in a week.' She raised an eyebrow. 'I'll re-use the pain-dampeners, if it's all the same to you.'

Angie wandered in, a smudge of mustard on her lips, silver sandals on her feet. 'Uri says you should drink this.' She gave him a bottle of water. 'Else you'll get deerhide rations.'

'Dehydration,' the doctor corrected.

'How much do we owe?' Gawain asked.

She shrugged. 'Tricky. Do you have a Medicare Number? All the same I need to ask your guardian some questions. Don't worry. This procedure's all the same with everyone.'

They went out to the reception area where the nurse was talking to Uri.

'Sure, we can deliver it.' Uri slipped a packet into his pocket. 'At the turn-off to Ikuntji?'

'I got you a present.' Angie handed him a book, distracting him. It was so old and discoloured that pages were falling out of it.

'It's real paper.' Angie was obviously proud of herself. 'Not an e-book.'

'*Sir Gawain and the Green Knight!* Where on earth did you find it, sis?' Scents of vanilla and nutmeg wafted up from the paper.

'There's a historical re-enactment stall just over there with ancient technology. It's got an internet café and a bookshop. The man there said he could get me a story about Angharad Goldenhand. He said it would take a week.' She turned her most appealing smile on him. 'Can we come back then?'

'You'll have to ask Uri.' He glanced back to see Doctor All-The-Same and Uri deep in conversation.

Angie took his hand. 'Come and see, Gawain. I asked Mr Sharmika if he had any books suitable for my best brother Gawain and...'

'I'm your only brother.'

'Are you sure?'

'What's that mean?'

Angie ignored him. 'Mr Sharmika asked if I wanted the story where Gawain marries the ugliest woman in the world to save King Arthur's butt, or the one where Gawain is the last person to speak to Merlin when he gets trapped inside the enchanted tree, or the one where the Green Giant's head gets chopped off. I really wanted the one where Gawain marries the ugliest woman in the whole wide world but I knew you'd want the Green Giant.'

The re-enactment tent was cool and dark with internet booths along a wall. A flap at the far end led to an Aladdin's Cave of old books and second-hand wares. Glancing to the side, he saw Emrys and Vasily sitting at one internet station and Jed and Cardea at another.

His hand began to itch. *I should've asked the doctor. How did I forget? After what Jib said? I better go back.*

'Where's Mister Sharmika?' Angie asked the sales assistant.

'Pardon?'

'Mister Sharmika. He said he could get me a book about Angharad Goldenhand.' She held up her glove as if it explained everything.

'You're mistaken, dear. There's no one here by that name.'

'But he sold me this…' Angie grabbed the book from Gawain. 'He was standing right where you are.'

'Was he?' The woman looked startled.

Gawain was relieved to know Angie was seeing things too. *Maybe it's the heat. I'll just get her settled then go back to the doctor.* 'Would you have any more books like it?'

'Arthurian legend is over there.' The woman pointed inside the Aladdin's Cave.

Gawain headed to the far side and almost ran into an elderly Japanese man with round metal spectacles. 'Konichiwa.' The man bowed, then took a white and gold paper parasol from the left sleeve of his grey silk kimono and twirled it above his head. From his right sleeve, he pulled out a small box. He opened it on his palm and revealed a tiny doll, rotating on a mirrored platform. Gawain recognised the melody chiming from the music box at once. It was the sharva's tune.

It's the sharva!? The Japanese gentleman's smile was enigmatic as the parasol began to spin even faster. Gawain glanced with alarm at the woman behind the desk.

'Cone of silence.' The man's accent was gone. 'She can't hear us now, and neither can Angie's wallet.'

Angie pulled the wallet out, scowling. 'But I cleaned the bugs out before we came. How can they be back already?'

'Are you the sharva?' Gawain asked.

The Japanese man blinked behind his glasses. 'Would you like me to be?'

Gawain was wary. 'That's beside the point.'

The man scowled. His clothes took on the appearance of feathers, his legs became thin bony sticks. 'You're right. It's quite beside the point. But you don't have to rub it in. After all I've done for you! Lost my head and what do I get? *"Beside the point."* Is that grateful, I ask you? I track you down to that dingy oasis to save you from a deadly scorpion and what do I get? Dismissed as an irrelevancy.'

'Scorpion? What scorpion?' Gawain asked, flummoxed. 'I thought you wanted to sell me an ammonite.'

'Good! At least you realised that.' The sharva's outrage turned to glee. 'There wasn't a scorpion, actually. But if there had been, I'd have rescued you. So I hope you're grateful for having been saved from a death worse than fate.'

Gawain didn't know what to say.

'Sharmika! It *is* you!' Cerylen rose up like a sunrise from behind a bookcase, her eyecup swivelling, her face luminous with delight.

'You've met my sharva?' Gawain was incredulous. *She knows my sharva by name?*

'*My* sharva? Ooooh!' The sharva held its wings to its heart.

Cerylen kicked its spindly legs. 'Sharmika! You haven't changed at all!' Her smile became dazzling. 'Is Tamizel here?'

'Of course not.' Sharmika's feathers fluttered. 'He simply sent me to help you.'

'How wonderful! But how did he know where to find us? Or that we're going to rescue him from the Storm-Tree?'

'Rescue?' Sharmika twirled the parasol faster. 'That's impossible. That's why it's me and not him. This is about warning. Aanundus is after you. All of you.'

'We know.' Cerylen's smile disappeared. 'Gawain told us.'

I did? I don't even know who Aanunwhatever is. Wait... wasn't that the name in the vision with the dog-boy?

Cerylen's eyecup rotated. 'We can't figure out how he knew we'd be at this school.'

'He doesn't—at least not for sure.' Sharmika's feathers shook. 'The school is a lure—an annual bait-the-hook-and-throw-out-the-line and hope you'll fall for it. Every year he's been waiting for either you or Reece to turn up.'

Reece? She knows Reece? Gawain took a deep breath. *Of course she does.*

'And every year,' Sharmika said, 'Aanundus sends a spy—or two—to the school to report back to him. Vasily was one of last year's recruits.'

'Vasily!' Cerylen jerked around to the internet booth where Emrys was sitting, his head close to Vasily's. 'We've trusted him... far *too* much.'

Sharmika patted Cerylen on the head. 'Calm down, lollykins. Vasily is a double agent. I've turned him. He's on our side.'

Cerylen's eyes widened. '*You* were at the school last year?'

Sharmika rolled its eyes. 'I knew you'd turn up sooner or later but not exactly *when.*'

'I lost the map.' Gawain felt he had to admit the truth. 'Miss Hale has it.'

'Not to worry. Any clue is enough. Any ammonite. Any playing card.' Sharmika grinned at Angie. 'Any Finchy man!'

Angie's eyes glowed. 'It's Vinci. But you know what I said, even though you weren't there. So you're a genie. We get three wishes, don't we?'

'Oh, goody!' Sharmika's wingtips fluttered. 'That means one for each of you. Three wishes and three of you. The perfect equation.'

'I don't understand.' Gawain shushed Angie as she tried to interrupt. 'Aren't any of the things you gave me special?'

'Nope. They're not different clues, Gawain. They all point to the one thing.'

'Clues to what?' A crease had appeared above Cerylen's nose. 'Why isn't Tamizel sending clues to Reece or me?'

'Besides the fact it's too dangerous, neither of you write music.' The sharva turned to Gawain. 'I've told you the same thing every time, Gawain—over and over again. But obviously you haven't got it yet. Despite my best efforts, Sharmika the sharva is a complete failure.' He adopted a tragic stance.

Angie was perplexed. 'You're Mister Sharmika but you're a genie too. So why can't I have the book on Angharad Goldenhand right away?'

Gawain shushed her again. 'Mister Sharmika, please just tell us what the clues mean.'

'I'm afraid I'm just the messenger.' Sharmika waggled his shoulders, then folded his wings together. 'Not the interpreter.' The parasol began to float.

Angie stared open-mouthed, but Gawain refused to be distracted. '*Please*,' he begged.

Sharmika scowled for a moment, then brightened. 'First I was a taxi service...' It blew a kiss at Cerylen. '...then I was a messenger. An interpreter is really a step up the ladder, I suppose.' Next moment the sharva was attired in a striped waistcoat, ghostly thumbs in ghostly pockets. 'Step right up, step right up, ladies and gentleman.' Its tone was hectoring. 'Let's put our thinking hats on.' A white bowler appeared on Angie's head, a green one on Gawain's and a golden top hat on Cerylen's. Its own was multi-coloured with a silver whirligig on top. 'Righto...' It pointed a long claw at Gawain. 'What did I say at Serpent Mound?'

Angie took her bowler off. 'I want a red hat. I want the hat of feelings.'

'You've already expressed far too many.' Sharmika didn't shift its gaze from Gawain. 'Well, young man?'

Gawain was unable to take his eyes off the silver whirligig. 'Serpent Mound? That's a crater in Ohio. Not as big as the crater here at Gosses Bluff, though.' He raised his hands in a helpless gesture. 'Did we meet at Serpent Mound?'

'Did we meet at Serpent Mound?' Sharmika's eyes rolled and its tongue quivered. 'You've forgotten what I told you about Jed?'

Jed? But I didn't know Jed until a few days ago.

Shaking its head, the sharva lowered its beak to inspect Gawain's hand. 'Why am I not surprised?'

14

'ARE YOU LOOKING FOR something special?' The sales assistant's voice floated in under the parasol, reverberating as if it were trapped in an echo chamber.

Gawain slewed and tacked on a bright smile. Behind him he could hear the muted rustle of paper as the parasol folded. Glancing over his shoulder he could see that the sharva was gone, along with the Japanese gentleman.

There was only Angie and Cerylen, still wearing the hats the sharva had given them. Angie clutched some books and Cerylen held a music box. 'We'll have these.' Cerylen took out her wallet and pushed Angie towards the sales counter.

Gawain headed straight for the internet booths just as Uri entered the tent and pitched Vasily and Emrys out of their seats. 'Come along, you mob. Time to help Ms Gunn with the groceries.'

As Emrys picked himself up, Gawain glimpsed some of the sheaf of printouts next to the computer. Gwion Gwion.

Taliesin and the Welsh Bards. Tribal Customs in Central Australia. *Is he checking on me?* His palm started itching furiously again. It had become bright red. Gawain stared at it. *I wanted to ask Uri something about this. What was it?* He glanced back at Emrys as he folded the printouts and stuffed them in his jeans pocket.

Uri directed them outside and up the bank of the dry river. They followed Retro's barking down a side street towards a supermarket. There was the bus—and Ms Gunn at the side door, busily stocking a cooler box with the help of Cardea. Jed was loading meat into chilly bags. Grateful he wasn't expected to lift any trays of vegetables or bottles of water to the luggage compartment, Gawain took a seat in the bus. As he watched the others work, he considered the situation.

Vasily is a spy. A turncoat. Well, maybe that's harsh. Anyway, he's... he's... like me. And, come to think of it, so is Emrys with that strange glove of his. Is it hiding something gone wrong with the palm of his hand? And Jed... imagine having to come all the way to the end of the world to find the one person who can expose the secret of Taliesin's Mantle. And what did the sharva tell me about him? How could it have known, years ago, that I was going to meet him one day? As for Cardea... who knows what she looks like behind that burqa? Well, maybe Jed does. Or maybe not.

He took a deep breath. *So many mysteries.* Gawain was so wrapped in his thoughts he only just registered when the others finished loading the groceries. One by one they jumped into the bus. Ms Gunn set off with a roar of the engine.

'We're going back via Glen Helen... the doctor asked us to drop something off to one of the communities out that way.' Uri turned to smile from the front passenger seat. His glasses had taken on a wine-coloured tint. 'It's not just a better road for most of the trip, you can see the Sleeping Lady too.'

There was no sign of Miss Hale or her ATV. Gawain wondered if the choice of route was more about keeping it that way than doing a favour for the doctor.

The drive was quiet.

Gawain noticed Cerylen's head nodding and slumping, her golden top hat sliding askew. *She's falling asleep.* Jed was on the floor, his head against Retro's flank. He was snoring.

Angie had her white bowler over her face and was mumbling into it. *I'm not gonna ask.*

Emrys and Vasily just stared out the window. Gawain's hand stopped itching. Just a dull ache persisted across his fingers.

He had a million questions. Well, maybe not a million. But a dozen. *Who is Tamizel? Why does he need rescue? What is the Storm-Tree? Did I really meet the sharva at Serpent Mound? What did it tell me? What's wrong with my hand? And why can't I remember to ask anyone about it?* He fidgeted with the meteorite, glad that he'd found it in his pocket. As long as he kept holding it, the pain in his hand was bearable. *If this school is an annual set-up to track down Reece and Holly, then the staggering cost must justify their importance. So what does creepy Yellow-Eyes guy want with them? And is he Aanundus? How long will the police detain Miss Hale?*

Gawain had no idea how to break the stifling silence. Then he remembered what Jib had said. Something about the scrolls of summoning and Vasily being named after a war hero. 'Hey, Vasily. Isn't there some hero in your country goes by your name?'

Vasily turned and blinked. 'You know about Vasili Arkipov?' His voice sounded incredulous.

'Not much. That's why I'm asking.'

'You have heard of the Cuban Missile Crisis?'

Gawain felt his lower jaw drop. *What kind of coincidence is this?* 'I have a history assignment I'm supposed to complete while I'm here. It's on Hitler and the Cuban Missile Crisis.'

Vasily's eyebrows came together in a disbelieving expression. 'What alternate universe are you living in? Hitler was dead for almost two decades before the Cuban Missile Crisis.'

'I know that. I have to compare and contrast Hitler's annexation of Austria with the Cuban Missile Crisis.'

Uri's red glasses winked as he glanced over his shoulder. 'Easy,' he said. 'It's about timing. One event is exactly the same length of time from the start of the twentieth century as the other is from the end of it. To the very day.'

'A nice piece of trivia but I think Thompson will want more than that in the compare-and-contrast stakes.'

'Trivia? The dates are very significant. Hitler chose the first, believing in its occult power. He wanted to possess the holy lance held in the Imperial Treasury in Vienna. An ancient spear that was said to confer invincibility in battle.'

Vasily rolled his eyes. 'He actually believed some old relics would allow him to take Moscow? Did he not know Montgomery's first rule of war?' He turned to Gawain. 'Your teacher must hate you, Speckly Boy. Is it personal or does he inflict this kind of thing on the entire class?'

Gawain shrugged. 'Help me out. What does your namesake have to do with the Cuban Missile Crisis?'

Vasily shrugged. 'Very well. I will enlighten you. Vasili Arkipov was the deputy commander of a Soviet nuclear submarine on patrol off the shores of Cuba on 27 October 1962. His vessel was in international waters but a group of eleven American destroyers began launching depth charges, trying to force it to the surface. The captain of the submarine believed World War III had broken out and wanted to launch a nuclear torpedo in retaliation. Had he done so, a war of mutual annihilation between the two great superpowers of the day would have occurred. Arkipov alone argued against the firing of the torpedo. Some historians have said he saved the world from destruction. They maintain the incident brought the world so close to the brink of nuclear war it was probably the most dangerous moment in all of human history.'

'Wow!' Emrys had turned around to listen and was clearly impressed. 'The world needs more heroes like that.'

'Heroes?' Vasily shrugged. 'What the world needs is decent people, making the right decisions for the right reasons.' His voice was tight with subdued passion.

'That was awesome. You sounded just like an academic treatise,' Gawain said. 'I would never have found such a completely different perspective. Can I do an interview? Thompson loves audio files that feature oral history.'

Vasily produced a tight smile. 'That is actually the condensed summary of my presentation. I also have a five-minute and a ten-minute version. When you have been to as many schools as I have, no one notices if it is the same speech a dozen times over.'

Emrys poked him on the shoulder. 'What exactly is your supernerd speciality, Vasily?'

The smile became broader. 'There is an old Russian proverb: *doveryay, no proveryay*. It means: "trust but verify." My speciality is using trust as a currency and making friends easily. People do not think to verify my story as much as they should. As much as I verify theirs.'

Trust as a currency? Gawain didn't know what to think. *Was Vasily trying to get them to trust him by actually admitting to the possibility his story needs checking? Was it doublethink?*

'The ability to trade in trust is another benefit of attending so many different schools,' Vasily went on. 'Of course, I lose the friends just as easily, which is not a benefit—at least, that is my view of it. Though my spy masters think differently.'

Emrys began coughing so much that Gawain thought he was choking.

Vasily shook his head and grinned at Emrys. 'No need to act surprised, Lord Rhystyllyn. I know you know. So what is the point of not admitting all this?'

'I d...didn't, actually,' Emrys spluttered. He sounded rueful. 'And I should know better than to trust anyone without checking.'

'I knew about Vasily,' Gawain admitted, nodding at Emrys before turning to the blonde Russian. 'But how did you know that I know? How'd I give myself away?'

'You did not.' Vasily's grin broadened until it was almost irritating. 'You and I simply have a mutual acquaintance.'

'We do?' *Like, we do? How can I check this? How can I verify it?*

'Yes, we do. In fact, that acquaintance was the one who told you about me. He has been giving you messages for years. However you seem to have an inordinate talent for losing them, from what I am told.'

The sharva! Gawain blinked and wondered if he'd said the word aloud. *Vasily knows the sharva!*

'Loath as I am to interrupt this ever so interesting confession,' Uri said, 'I'd like you to notice some geography.' The bus was coming over a high pass and Uri pointed to a mountain draped in blue and misty purple. 'Mount Sonder. Her ancient name is Rwetyepme, the Sleeping Lady.'

As Gawain looked at the soft curves of the heat-hazed mountain, a shimmer of light rippled the curtain of cloud beyond it. From the highest reaches of the sky, rainbow colours floated down. Strange. Gawain fixed his gaze on it, trying to work out what caused it.

Even as the sun began to set, swathing the landscape in indigo shadows and the sky in tints of red-gold, the rainbow didn't fade. It narrowed into a bright and vibrant shaft, like a spear out of heaven.

The bus drove on. Just past Glen Helen resort, the bitumen ended and the smooth ride was over. The bus bumped and juddered along the unsealed track. 'I thought you said this was a better road,' Emrys called to Uri.

'For most of the way.'

The last rays of the sun had disappeared when they stopped at a bend in the road, headlights beaming out into the darkness. The only other light was the rainbow lance, high up, far off in the distance. The more Gawain looked at it, the more the hairs on the back of his neck rose.

He realised that Emrys was also staring far too intently at the swirl of red, blue and green.

Jed moved to the front of the bus. 'Why're we stopped?' he asked Uri.

'Got some medication for someone at Ikuntji,' Ms Gunn answered him. 'They're supposed to be here at the junction, waiting for us.'

'Mebbe we could just go along the turnoff a bit and meet 'em en route?' Jed's voice sounded far too eager to Gawain.

Uri turned a quizzical smile on him.

Ms Gunn raised an eyebrow. 'You wouldn't happen to have an ulterior motive, would you, Jedidiah Harris?'

Jed held his hand to his heart. But his attempt at an innocent look wasn't working and he obviously knew it. 'I've never seen Kurrkalnga at night,' he confessed. 'They got a singalong, ya know.'

Ms Gunn exchanged a glance with Uri. 'Why not?' she asked. 'Cultural experiences are supposed to be an integral part of the school's programming.'

'We'll scare Agent Hale half to death if we're not back by midnight.'

'Good.'

'Meg!' Uri grinned. 'I didn't know you were like that.'

'I could do with a whole day without Hale and her minions. Pity we don't have Cinderella on board. It'd be just perfect if she was on a time budget and this coach turned into a pumpkin at midnight.'

'Well, now. Bus-to-pumpkin.' Uri's gap-toothed grin widened as he turned. 'Rightio, listen up, you supernerds! Any of you mob into mineral-vegetable transformation?'

INTERSTITIAL

IV

'GWALCH*MAI!*' THE SHOUT CROSSED the trickling beck, echoed against crags covered in ice as hard as iron, then swept back past the dog-boy into the grey misted vales far below. 'Gwalch*mai—ar frys!*'

The dog-boy plodded through the snow, ignoring the call. *Don't get distracted by some giggling servant girl.* He shook the snow out of his hair. His thoughts flickered, like ever-moving flames, fragmenting and re-forming. His head ached. His memory had been improving for days but, as it did, strange images spun through his mind: *a tree as tall as heaven, a dragon's tail trying to capture a tumbling sword, a leaping stag falling through stars, a circle of stones, firelight in a castle, a jumble of dogs, a king's feast and all around a torrent of incomprehensible words.*

Struggling to speak. No sound coming from his mouth, no matter how hard he tried.

The flames of thought were coalescing. *Yrien. I belong to the court of King Yrien and it's my job to care for the dogs.* He frowned, staring at the snow drifts. *So why am I out here?*

'*Gwalchmai!*' There was such urgency in the servant girl's voice that he looked back over his shoulder. She was pointing down the valley to a line of horsemen cresting the brow of a hill.

The dog-boy didn't hesitate. He ran.

'*Helwch ef!*' one of the horsemen yelled.

The dog-boy splashed across the freezing beck, soaking his leggings and rough boots. He was already a dozen strides into the woods when he heard the girl's squeal. *Mistake. I'll leave footprints.* He turned back to the beck, and quietly moved up its winding course. Steep overhanging snowbanks closed in around him, and he crouched beneath them, listening to the shouts and exclamations. *They'll know I'm in the water by now, but they'll follow it downstream. They'll expect me to run to Yrien, to head for the court.*

It was the most coherent thought he'd had in days and he knew it. *That's what fear does to you.*

He closed his eyes, and held his breath, praying. He pulled an edge of fur across his mouth, covering his misty breath in case it betrayed him. Waiting five minutes, he moved on, his feet frozen. Another five minutes passed and he reached the ice-slick stones of the high ford. He was tempted to leave the beck.

There's a road nearby. But he couldn't remember how he knew, so he decided against it. Upstream the beck fell more steeply from the moors; trees crowded closer, their ice needles chiming as he brushed against overhanging branches.

When the trees gave out, the stream was exposed to view from a stretch of ancient road. He hurried on, hearing voices. The rattle of hooves on the streambed was followed by the whipcrack of breaking ice, a wild splattering of water, scattered shouts and curses. Along with the pounding dread of his own heart, he felt an elemental fury. *I hate him, hatehimhatehimhatehim. I hate Arthur so much I'd cheer if he died.*

The dog-boy paused. *Arthur? Who's Arthur?*

Realising he was no match for the horses, he turned to face the hunters. A white stag stood at the water's edge. As it lowered its head to the water, he noticed something caught in its seven tines. A golden strand with plump, purple mulberries hung around its neck. *Mulberries.* His thoughts began to float. *Mulberry trees come from China which won't be discovered for another eight centuries...*

The ponies clattered around the bend, churning up the ice. The stag bounded up the snow-crusted bank and dashed away. The ponies crashed after it.

The dog-boy stood still for an entire minute, hardly able to believe his luck. *They didn't even see me.* Echoes of the pursuit died away, until the only sound he could hear was the trickle of the beck. It would be a long chase—the black ponies were as hardy, as sure-footed, and as swift as the stag.

He hesitated. *I could go back to Yrien's court.* He thought of the firelit hall and the warm tumble of the dogs he was charged to keep. *Or I could go up the fells*—his teeth chattered at the very thought of it. He was still standing, indecisive, when a gleam caught his eye. It was the golden strand of mulberries. *They're growing.* He looked closer. *They're growing on this strand.* He closed his eyes. *But mulberries grow on trees, not on gold.* For a moment panic returned. *Is this a different time or a different world?*

Picking up the mulberries, he looped them around his neck. The bank was slippery with ice and he was concentrating on climbing it, when he felt warm air at the back of his neck. He could smell a pungent horsiness. Startled, he turned...

A willow-green ghostly snout, an impossible neck. *Ettin.* Another word pulled up from the deep fathoms of lost memory. *Chasing... up a golden stair...* The ghostly creature opened its terrifying mouth to blow on him. *It's just playing with me like a cat would play with a mouse.*

He skidded on a patch of hard-packed ice and fell. Looking up, he saw three of the horse-giants. Picking himself up, he ran. They shrieked as they blew along behind him, their misty bodies tattering into shreds. Their legs were wisps, strangely separate from their bodies.

They're not even trying: they're still playing with me.

The dog-boy stumbled, then slid into a hollow. Almost unbalancing again, he careened up the far side, only to find the crest hid a steep bank. He flailed, just stopping himself from falling over the edge. Below him, Arthur's troop was returning to the beck. He flung himself back, hoping they hadn't seen him.

They must have lost the stag. But they couldn't possibly lose my trail—not now. He felt warmth on his neck and, closing his eyes, prayed. *Let it be quick.* Seconds ticked by but nothing happened. He opened his eyes. The ettins had flowed over him, blowing away his tracks in the process. He heard the horses screaming, and the terrified shouts of Arthur's men. *Are the ettins on my side?*

He trudged on, realising that he no longer needed to rush. An exultant joy bubbled within. The ettins were behind him, like his very own trusted dog pack, gusting away the evidence of his passing. The golden strand of mulberries was looped around his neck. The way ahead was clear. *I'm safe.* The dog-boy realised it was the first time he'd felt that way in months.

If only I could remember who Arthur is.

He headed up the snow-encrusted hillside.

15

THE LIGHT, HIGH IN THE SKY, was visible from the bus window all the way along the track. It split into a triplet beam, each line of colour twisting and spinning into a writhing serpent—coiled and plaited, red over blue over green. Sometimes it pulsed and, when it did, Gawain's hand would tense and the pain intensify.

He glanced ahead from time to time, looking for headlights that would indicate a vehicle was coming to meet them. But there was no one else on the road. The bus had bumped along the dark track for over half an hour before Gawain noticed a glow in the distance. At first he thought the moon was cresting the horizon, but it was too small.

'That's Kurrkalnga.' Jed pointed at the glow through the front windscreen. 'Where heaven meets earth.'

'It is a cross.' Vasily expelled a long breath. 'Like on the top of a church.'

As the bus moved closer, Gawain could see that Vasily was right. It was a bright, illuminated cross, high on a hill.

'Is this a religious gathering?' Vasily sounded both wary and dubious as he turned to Jed.

'The whole o' life is a sacred assembly.' Jed folded his arms and pouted. 'Here at Memory Mountain we just make it consciously so.' He turned to Gawain. 'This ain't gonna be yer kinda music, Speckly Boy.'

'My taste is much wider than you'd suspect.'

Jed's pout turned to a grin. 'So's mine.'

Even before the bus pulled into the dim and flickering light of a carpark by the roadside, Gawain could hear singing. He couldn't make out the words. Still, he recognised the flow and cadence of a hymn.

'If ya take off yer shoes when ya get out, Speckly Boy, ya'll be able to feel the way the song soaks into the land. Heals it.'

As Gawain pushed off his shoes his thoughts flitted back to the shattercones with their record of vibration in the rocks of Tnorala. The witness throughout the ages to the comet's moment of impact was the land itself—still shocked, still locked in pain. *Songs that heal... wow! Could I shape that kind of music? Songs that heal trauma and abuse and suffering?*

With great care not to use his sore hand, he pulled his socks off.

Retro pushed past Jed as the door slid open and leapt to the ground. 'Stay with your master,' Uri said.

Huh? Isn't Uri his master?

Retro gave a low growl but remained by the bus door as Angie, Cerylen and Cardea stepped out into the darkness.

Gawain followed them, stopping to watch Uri weave his way through a crowd of people, some standing, some sitting in the sand, some kneeling. There was a campfire to one side, providing just enough light to see by. Retro guided Emrys past it.

Gawain closed his eyes and allowed the swell of music to flood over him. Despite Jed's words, he couldn't feel anything through his feet. And he didn't understand a single word. But it didn't matter. The music was speaking of love and peace, blessing and grace. His heart drank in the dreaming within the song. His hand, tense and cramped, relaxed as the soothing sounds ebbed and flowed. A touch, light as a fluttering petal, moved down his arm.

Opening his eyes, he realised Cardea was beside him. Uri was near the campfire, talking to one of the singers, obviously asking about the packet of medication visible in his hands.

Jed moved to Cardea's side and, together, they started humming. One note, held impossibly long, began to open up, to bloom and flower. Gawain sensed it at first, hanging in the air, and then—incredulous, disbelieving—he saw it, a living thing twirling and dancing, grief and joy entwined in its heart. It rose in the air, high, high, higher—all the way to the cross. Kissing its light, the note continued its upward journey, dancing far beyond the cross towards the coloured serpent trailing across the stars in its skin of red and blue-green. The note became an arrow, striking at the sinuous head. Then it was gone. The sky went dark, starless.

As it did, Emrys leaned forward to shake Cerylen. 'Quick, sis, wake up! Wake up! Look!'

Gawain blinked. *What? How'd I get back in the bus? What happened? How'd we all get here? Did I just imagine joining a corroboree that was singing hymns of praise instead of ancient chants?* He glanced up at the clock at the front of the bus. *It's after midnight. Somehow I've lost five hours.*

'Wake up, sis!' Emrys insisted. 'Look! Is that what I think it is? I've been watching it for hours and I'm sure it's part of the tachyon decelerator phenomenon.'

Cerylen seemed groggy as she peered back through the bus window at the spear of light. Her eyecup turned into a telescope.

Uri turned to regard them both. 'The locals would call it a rainbow serpent.'

Emrys folded his arms. 'Yes, of course anyone would describe it as a rainbow serpent. But what is it *really*, Uri? Scientifically, I mean.'

'Google has some explanation about jet contrails I don't believe either.'

Gawain wasn't sure how, he was aware in a flash of insight, that Uri knew exactly what the shimmering lightshaft was. *Why's he being so evasive?*

'You might also, should you have a mystical bent,' Uri went on, 'consider it to be the spiritual counterpart of the holy lance I mentioned a few hours back that Herr Hitler was so keen to get his mittens on.'

'Uri...' Emrys reached forward and tapped the *White Stag Security* logo on Uri's shirt. 'Don't do this. You're messing with my mind. This is a scientific problem, nothing more.'

'You know better than that, Time-killer.'

Time-killer!? What's that mean? Gawain wondered if Uri would correct him if he made up some scientific mumbo-jumbo. 'It's a sort of aurora...' He tried to sound as authoritative as possible. 'The kind you get in the wake of a large meteorite. An ionisation trail caused by the interaction between cosmic radiation and a disturbed magnetic field.'

'If there's going to be a meteorite impact over there,' Emrys said, 'we need to duck. We're east of it and it's big enough to send tektites hurtling down on us...'

He sounded respectful of Gawain's scientific fairytale. *Far too respectful.* Gawain didn't say a word. He couldn't shift his gaze away from the rainbow lance. His eyes felt locked into position.

And, in looking at it so intently, he felt utterly utterly overwhelmed. *The spear in the leg. The gunshot at the airport. The school with only seven students. The sharva. What was it the sharva had said about meeting me at Serpent Mound? Did Vasily know? The only weird thing I remember from there was that Indian chief who sold me a starmap. But I think I've lost it. Still, if every clue is the same clue, does that even matter?*

It was too hard to think about; all too bizarre. *And it's not about me.* His mind returned to the moment he'd left his father's office. *Do me proud, son.*

Sudden terror seized him. *What on earth are you up to, dad?*

16

AS SOON AS THE BUS had reached the homestead, everyone had been ordered to bed. Gawain had tried to protest but Vasily's wink and 'Catch you later,' convinced him not to make a fuss.

He woke late in the afternoon. *Songs that heal trauma and abuse and suffering.* It was the first thought in his mind as he opened his eyes. *Songs that bring heaven down to earth.*

Angie came through his room on one of her regular checks. 'You're awake!' she said. 'Ms Gunn gave me a job to do. I'm an official bug-collector.'

Ms Gunn wants you out of her hair. He decided that keeping her out of everyone else's way too was a good idea, but after just a minute, she insisted on going to the bathroom. It took him almost half an hour to realise it was just a ruse to scour every room in the house for hidden listening devices. Her dedication to the job surprised him. She had no compunction whatsoever about where she looked. No surveillance bug was safe from her seek-and-destroy missions.

Gawain knew he should head to the kitchen for a very late breakfast but his hand had started to throb again and he felt too woozy to get up. So he picked up the meteorite, clutched it in his hand and lay back down, trying to read *Sir Gawain and the Green Knight*. It was a poem and would have been heavy enough going even without Angie's regular squeals of 'Die! Die! Die!' Her warcry was invariably followed by a pounding with the 'magic silver stomping sandals', culminating in an exultant whoop.

Once he noticed she always returned to his room for the kill, Gawain realised that what she really wanted was praise. So he was happy enough to put his book down from time to time and draw a five-pointed star on Angie's golden glove: her personal kill score. The stars were wobbly because he didn't dare stop clutching the meteorite: it was the only way to subdue the pain. 'I think you've got them all,' he suggested, when he couldn't take her noisy death-scenes any longer. 'Nine is a good tally.'

'Privacy's at stake, Gawain.' Her glower was stern and appraising. 'You're too complacent.'

I wonder where she heard that? 'You're doing just great then. Don't let your brother interfere.'

He didn't know he'd fallen back asleep until he woke up with a jerk. Angie was wearing a firebird costume and humming to herself as she sat on the floor and carved a triangle eye into a pumpkin. 'Ms Gunn said I could get one ready for Halloween.'

Halloween already? Gawain stared at the carving knife in her hand. It was huge, sharp and dangerous. He guessed Angie had been underfoot. 'Did you ask permission to take that knife?'

Angie scowled. 'Did I need to?'

'Hand it over.'

Her scowl deepened. Then she smiled. 'I'm finished anyway.' She held up the pumpkin. The mouth was lopsided and the eyes askew but it was a creditable job.

Putting the pumpkin and the knife on the bed beside him, she folded her arms. 'Time for another security check. Who knows if Witchiepoo's bugs have been replaced? You, Sir Ideal Knight, have been sleeping on the job!' She crawled under the bed and scrambled out to check behind Leonardo's print. Gawain lay back and patted the pumpkin as she opened the tallboy wardrobe. She ran her finger back and forward over a knot in the woodwork inside it, then put her eye to it.

'Found another one?' Gawain asked as she knocked on the back wall.

With a shushing motion, Angie beckoned him over. 'I think there's a way into Narnia.' She was shaking with excitement. 'It isn't Oz, after all!'

Too many fairytales and fantasy books. Gawain knew she'd keep on until he inspected her find. He hopped off the bed but stopped to look out the window. Night was falling again: the western horizon was streaked with tangerine and russet. The first stars had appeared too, blazing coldfire from deep heaven and ancient time. They seemed like diamond-hard implacable watchers, not the irrepressible pixie eyes he remembered twinkling back home in Ohio. Sadness engulfed him. *I feel so scared, not even the stars are to be trusted.*

Then he heard a movement, saw a silhouette. The smell of the barbecue Uri and Ms Gunn were preparing began to waft in. His mouth began to water.

His attention returned to Angie as she tugged at his shirt. Without a word, she pointed at the knot in the back of the wardrobe and made a pushing motion.

'You want me to…?'

'Shh!' Angie put her finger to her mouth and glared.

Gawain leaned towards her. 'Push on it?' he breathed into her ear. Angie nodded.

The things I do… He went to the tallboy and pressed the knot with his right fist. *…to humour…* The wall slid back so abruptly he nearly lost his balance. A dark cavity was revealed.

Gawain stared in disbelief. Angie darted in.

'Sis! It's dange…' He realised he'd never stop her. Narnia, Oz, Wonderland… a thousand fairytales had to be dancing in her mind. But she simply reached in and picked up a long, dim shape from the back.

It was a sword.

Silver-grey cloudripples wavered along its glowing blade. Its ornate hilt was patterned with scrollwork and indecipherable writing. It was so heavy Angie could hardly lift it. Gawain reached to help her, then took it from her with his left hand. *It looks just like the sword I used to cut the magician's head off.*

He flexed his fingers around the hilt, feeling its weight, letting his grip slide to a comfortable position. He held it vertical, aware of the pain it caused across his shoulders. Still grasping the meteorite, he touched the edge of the sword with his thumb. *Razor-sharp.* He let it drop to a horizontal position, allowed it to rotate in his hand. Moving to stand on the balls of his feet, he raised it over his head. The pain across his shoulders was severe, but he didn't care. He aimed a practice strike at the Finchy man —

— and the sword burst into flames.

As golden tongues of fire licked along the edges of the blade, Angie squealed and fell. Gawain tried to quell a rising sense of panic. He found he couldn't drop the sword. He felt the heat and his hand flared with a burning spike so painful he thought he'd die.

All around him, he could hear voices, singing and talking. Wings rustling, beating wildly.

'It is awake!'

'It stirs; it remembers itself!'

'Who has it?'

'A boy!'

'That cannot be.'

'Unless it is sleeping, humans cannot touch it and live.'

'He is unharmed.'

'Check the scrolls of destiny.'

Help. Gawain wanted to scream, but his voice didn't work either. *Helphelphelphelphelp.* Tears sparked in his eyes.

The door opened. 'Hey, Speckly Boy...' Emrys froze. The flames on the sword leapt towards him, swirling around his body in a whoosh of celebrations. 'Holly!' he shouted as jets of coloured fireworks exploded back over Gawain. 'Hurry, Holly! Hurry! Quickl*yyyyyy!*' A conflagration roared up to the ceiling.

Seconds later, Cerylen arrived, her top hat askew, her eyecup gyrating. She pirouetted around Emrys in a balletic move and leapt over Angie. The moment she touched the sword, the flames died. It fell from Gawain's hands, ripping off skin as it dropped to the floor.

How'd she do that? Gawain was stunned. *And how on earth did Emrys know she could do it?*

She picked up the sword and folded her arms over it as she squinted at Emrys. He coughed and spluttered, using the wall to hold himself up. 'Dinner time.' Her voice was cool and dispassionate. 'Ms Gunn expects us at the barbecue in five minutes.'

What? It took him a moment to register. *Emrys called her 'Holly'.* And another moment to register a second fact: Vasily, Cardea and Jed were all in the doorway. They'd seen everything.

'We need to set the table for dinner.' Vasily nudged Cardea. 'Let's go. We've got our work cut out for us.'

Emrys rubbed his forehead. The silver-mesh glove flickered in and out of visibility.

'I think I need one of those.' Gawain, still in shock, pointed to Emrys' hand.

'No, you don't.' Cerylen's eyecup swivelled to focus on each of his palms in turn. 'You need two.'

17

'WE'LL TALK LATER.' EMRYS PUSHED himself away from the wall. 'Come on, everyone. We'll draw suspicion, if we're not careful.'

Angie followed him out, carrying the pumpkin. Jed picked up the knife and nodded at Cerylen. They both left.

Gawain still felt a slight shaking through his entire body. *Move slow. Use wall for support.* He made it out the door, down the hallway, to the dining area. Uri was there, collecting plates and cutlery.

Gawain held out his hands, revealing the inflamed area in one palm and the peeled skin on the other. 'Have you got anything that can help this?'

As Uri turned, his eyes seemed like whitefire behind the blood-red glasses. Gawain felt himself engulfed by harpsong. *You've left it too late,* a voice sounded inside his head. *You should have done something as soon as you knew. You've known ever since you met Hu Gadarn that something was wrong. The only possibility other than amputation...*

Gawain felt a tidal wave of fear rising inside him.

...is for you to destroy the sylvan throne. Yes, the Tree within must be put to the axe.' 'Here,' Uri said, out loud. 'That hand looks nasty. I'll check in the first aid kit. There's sure to be some gel.'

Gawain didn't even see him move. The first aid kit was just there, in the blink of an eye, and Uri was treating his wounds so gently, and talking so matter-of-factly about the trip back from Alice Springs, Gawain felt better all over. *I feel safe near Uri, but I'm not sure I should.*

Uri picked up the plates and cutlery with one massive hand and, with the other, guided Gawain to the barbecue area. Emrys and Jed were talking about the multi-coloured ribbon of light they'd seen in the sky near Memory Mountain.

'Rainbow serpent, mate.' Jed was insistent. 'Clear as the freckles on Speckly Boy's nose.'

'As a matter of fact, I'm with Speckly Boy on this.' Emrys took a plate from the top of the pile Uri had put down. 'Ionisation trail of a meteor, that's what you said, wasn't it, Gawain?'

'Rainbow serpents can fit your scientific framework.' Jed was grinning. 'There's a rainbow serpent legend associated with Kandimalal, the crater at Wolfe Creek, up over the Tanami. The Lawn Hill crater at Boodjamulla has one too. There's even a town in New Zealand that means *"the footsteps of the rainbow god"* with impact evidence right next door.'

'Impact evidence?' Emrys held up a forked sausage. 'Jed, you're holding out on us, mate. What kinda terminology is "impact evidence"? You got a secret bent for hard science, don't ya?'

Jed blew a raspberry at him. 'Mate, I'm here ta protect Tnorala from the likes o'... well, not you mob. Witchiepoo and her minions, who'll no doubt be back before mornin'. In fact, I'm surprised there's no one left here on guard. She didn't take all o' her stormtroopers ta town. I don't like what I'm startin' ta suspect.'

Gawain felt his whole body clenching. *He's right. Where are the stormtroopers?*

'Angie's doin' a deadly job stompin' those bugs, but I'm kinda wondering if they're replacing 'em just ta make us believe stompin' works. They gotta have better surveillance than they're makin' out.' Jed stabbed a lamb chop, flipped it onto his plate and scowled at Emrys. 'I'm thinking o' using Retro ta track their movements. He's yer dog, in't he? Not Uri's?' He loaded the chop with onion and sauce. 'And he's special. Like that three-headed dog, Cerebus, that guards the Underworld?'

Emrys favoured him with a long stare before forking half a sausage into his mouth. 'Jed, I said it before and I say it again. You're holding out on us, mate. I don't know any indigenous bloke who'd be willing to talk about the legends of another tribe. But, for you, no worries. You talk about Wolfe Creek, up over the Tanami which, unless I imagined it, you pointed out was enemy territory. Your mob don't talk about that mob's Dreaming. Then there's Lawn Hill, over near the Isa. Again, mate, your mob don't talk about them mob or their Dreaming.'

Retro growled and pounced at Emrys.

'Your mob don't talk about *those* mob.' Emrys patted Retro, before turning back to Jed. 'Then, kia ora bro, you know obscure facts about Aotearoa, the land of the great white kiwi—New Zealand. And now Greek mythology.'

'Heroflix.' Jed winked. 'Ya were expectin' somethin' more dastardly an' suspicious?'

Emrys rolled his eyes. 'If it's Heroflix, how come you think Retro's *Greek*? Why don't you know the *Celtic* underworld was guarded by huge white dogs with red eyes and red-tipped ears?'

Jed blinked. 'Musta missed that show. Wasn't in any *Merlin* episode.' He turned to stare at Retro's red eyes and red-tipped ears. Gawain followed his gaze.

Retro growled. His white fur spiked. A frisson of unease tingled its way up Gawain's spine. *A guard dog of the underworld?*

Uri sauntered over. 'Milord, it's time for the washing up.'

'*Washing up?*' Emrys grimaced and threw up a hand in obvious horror. 'Again?'

Uri nodded. 'Cerylen said you two have some long-term agreement about washing up. You'll be taking each of her rostered spots.'

'*Long-term?*' Emrys' sigh was deep and heavy as he slumped back in his chair. 'Forever, she means. Okay, lead me to it.'

Gawain's palm started to ache again. *Destroy the sylvan throne. The Tree within must be put to the axe.* He watched Emrys follow Uri to the industrial sinks.

Cardea came to sit on one side of him while Cerylen moved to occupy the seat her brother had vacated. 'So.' Her eyecup swivelled back and forward. 'How'd you do that with the sword?'

'That was my question.' Gawain stared at her. He folded his arms. 'How did you do that with the sword?'

She glared right back. 'It's *my* sword.' She shrugged. 'Sort of, anyway. Tamizel got me to retrieve it from the Lake. I've had some authority over it ever since.'

'Who's Tamizel?'

'He's an alien.'

'With yellow eyes?'

'So you've met Aanundus. What did he offer you?'

'A handshake. You didn't answer my question.'

'About Tamizel having yellow eyes? No, he doesn't. His eyes are never the same colour twice. Well, maybe they are, but I never noticed.' Cerylen seemed to be thawing towards him. 'He's trapped in the Storm-Tree and Reece and I are going to get him out.'

'What was the sword doing in my cupboard?'

Cerylen glared. 'That was the next question I was about to ask you.'

Gawain took a deep breath. 'Where'd you think it was?'

'Half the continent away in another cupboard.'

'I see.' Gawain winced. 'Emrys—he's Reece, isn't he?'

Cerylen nodded. 'Emrys is the name on his birth certificate, though everyone calls him Reece.' She sniffed. 'Everyone but his biological father, that is. And to keep him on side, because we wouldn't be here without his financial assistance and the kind of leverage only the aristocracy can wield, I'm making sure I address my twisted twin as "Emrys, Lord Rhystyllen" at every available opportunity.'

Twin? Yellow Eyes was right. 'So, I'm guessing this makes you Holly, not Cerylen?'

'Take your pick.' She shrugged. 'My gran calls me Celyren, which is Welsh for *Holly*; my mum calls me Holly; my dad calls me Cerylen, which is Welsh for *beloved*; my brother calls me sis or Hol; and my biological father calls me Lady Rhystyllen. And as you've probably noticed, Jed calls me Cherry.'

'Which one does Tamizel call you?'

The dazzling smile was back. 'Good question. I'm not sure now he's given up on Lady Death.'

Lady Death? Is she making this up? 'What're you doing here? At this school, I mean?'

'Reece and I want to invent a time machine. Well, not exactly. We want to find a way of accessing interstitial time—to open the gap between one moment and the next and step into the space continuum between time and eternity.'

Like that *made sense.*

Vasily strolled over and pulled up a chair next to Cardea's. 'Okay, Speckly Boy.' His voice was a whisper. 'How did you get that sword to explode?'

'Don't know.' Gawain shrugged. 'Why not ask her?' He pointed to Cerylen. 'It's hers.'

'Are you really on our side, Vasily?' Cerylen's tone was back to frigid.

Vasily frowned. 'Last year I was recruited to attend this school as a spy,' he admitted. 'I was ordered to identify some twins named Reece and Holly. I have come back this year to discover who the puppeteer is.'

'Puppeteer?' Gawain asked.

'The one who controls my spy masters. All I have is the codename "Eyes".'

'Eyes?' Gawain asked. 'Miss Hale used that name.' *Maybe Uri did too.*

Vasily folded his arms. 'I am sure she knows.'

Angie came skipping over. She'd added a tiara to the star-spangled firebird costume. *How'd she pack an entire Halloween costume undetected?*

She dropped a handful of silver bugs in front of Gawain. 'These were all in our room! I cleaned up just before we left, but look!'

So there are stormtroopers still around. I hope Jed's wrong about the bugs.

Angie pouted. 'I've had to take retaliatory action, dearest brother, and I trust you will support me in the war against Witchiepoo.'

Retaliatory action? 'What've you done?'

'Frozen undies! I've hidden Witchiepoo's unmentionables in a very secret location.' She scooped the bugs onto the floor and began to pound them viciously. Vasily flicked one that escaped back into her clutches.

Gawain took a deep breath. *Frozen undies?* 'This is going to backfire seriously.'

Angie shook her head. 'No. It's my plan the stormtroopers all think I'm a spiteful brat; but I'm really a scheming munchkin with an agenda of my own.'

'Where do you get this megalomaniac sort of stuff? It'll be a world takeover next.'

'Gawain, you're stupid. You should be thanking me. Very soon, everyone will think anything what goes missing round here will be my fault even if it isn't. So I reckon I'm helping you all. I'm as clever as a supernerdy teenage genius, you know.'

Don't roll your eyes. 'You just called me "stupid".'

Angie raised her golden glove, ignoring him. 'You know, the trauma of dad's absence for work has been very bad for me. I'm manifesting serious disruptive behaviour as a consequence, don't you think?'

No, I don't think. 'Where'd you get that from?'

'A tv show. Except the little girl didn't have an absent dad, it was her mom who disappeared. She wore one white glove with pearls all over it that her mom had on on her wedding day. And then if anyone tried to take it from her, she went feral.'

'Oh.' *When did she start to believe she'd lost dad?* Gawain had never understood before the sudden appearance of the golden glove. *Was it the same time I did?*

'Did your mother wear that glove on her wedding day?' Cerylen's voice was soft and understanding.

'No. On her first date with dad.' She held out the glove to Gawain.

'Once upon a time,' Cerylen whispered, 'there was a man named Merlin. My brother's named after him. Merlin got the reputation for being wild, forgetful and magical, and for vanishing over long periods without a trace. But there was nothing really mysterious about him except for the fact he lived backwards in time and popped out of the interstices every so often.'

Angie's eyes grew big with wonder. Her glove was still out, unmoving.

'If your dad is anything like my dad,' Cerylen went on, 'he's probably got a fair bit of Merlin in him. Emrys and I had to sit our dad down and explain it wasn't a good thing to keep a Merlin locked inside. It's no good living backwards. It's no good being imprisoned by the past, Angie. I don't know how you've been hurt but I know this: don't excuse your father or your mother. Forgive them. Don't live backwards in time. It doesn't just hurt you, it hurts everyone around you.'

Angie was still holding her arm out to Gawain. 'Draw more stars on it.' She handed him a pen. 'I killed seventeen.'

Gawain was silent as he penned stars all the way up Angie's glove. *Don't live backwards in time.*

'Thanks for your advice,' Angie said to Cerylen.

When Gawain had finished drawing the stars, he looked up at Cerylen. 'How are you going to power your time machine? You'll need stupendous amounts of energy.'

She waved an arm. 'We've got a huge solar array out there.'

Vasily's lips twisted. 'It would not be enough. And even if it were, how would you hide your cyclotron? I doubt if you could sneak into CERN in Switzerland and borrow theirs.' His sneer widened. 'So you would need to secretly develop one of your own. It would have to be a couple of kilometres in diameter at least to build up enough energy to power any time device.'

'Are you offering to be our construction manager? I think I could convince Reece to finance the project.'

Vasily laughed. 'Not a chance. Too risky. Keeping it secret would be almost impossible. Even if you did, the moment you switched it on the whole world would know. The magnetic and gravitational anomalies would give it away instantly.'

Unless... Gawain took a deep breath. *...unlessunlessunless you put it where there are pre-existing anomalies. Like...*

Cerylen must have realised at the same moment. 'No one would ever suspect if you put it in a circular structure where anomalies had already been found.' She pointed in the direction of Tnorala. 'The Bluff—it's the perfect hiding place.' Her eyecup swivelled. 'And the solar array is ideal as a power source. All we'd need is Jed's okay.'

Vasily rocked on his chair, his eyes growing wide. 'You are too late, *malyshka*.' His face drained of colour. 'It must have already been done. I always wondered why Eyes chose *this* place for the school.'

Angie poked Gawain's hand. He yelped in agony. 'Should we be running for it, Gawain?' she asked, as he gasped and jerked.

He trembled in pain, unable to answer.

'They are here somewhere.' Vasily's chair tipped dangerously. 'There must be a hidden base. That is where the stormtroopers have disappeared.'

Of course. How else would they be replacing the surveillance bugs Angie was pulverising? Gawain closed his eyes, trying to contain the shaking.

A feather-light touch brushed his skin and the throbbing subsided. He opened his eyes. Cardea was stroking the back of his hand with the meteorite and staring at him far too intently. 'Thank you,' he rasped.

'Take it.' She handed it to him.

As he closed his fist over it, the pain vanished. 'How'd you know?'

'I saw you holding it on the bus.'

She's watching me? 'Creepy yellow-eyed alien guy—I think he poisoned me.'

Vasily leaned over to inspect Gawain's fist. 'Let me see, Speckly Boy.'
Gawain was wary as he opened his hand.

Vasily frowned. 'Subcutaneous tracking device. Injected into your palm. You should not ever have felt more than a slight tingle at the handshake.' His frown deepened. 'Your body is rejecting it. And it is defending itself.' He paused. 'We had better call for help.'

'Help?' Cerylen's eyecup swivelled towards him. 'Out here?'

Vasily folded his arms. 'Out *here*? You have been to Alpha Centauri and got help there. What makes you think this here is too far?'

Alpha Centauri? You're kidding me!

'How do you know I've been to Alpha Centauri?' Cerylen's hands went to her hips.

Vasily winked. 'Back in a minute, *malyshka.*'

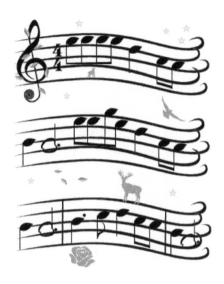

18

TRUE TO HIS WORD VASILY was back a minute later. Cardea gave up the chair next to Gawain and Vasily slid into it, unfolding a thin laptop and pressing the fingerprint recognition panel. A password box appeared.

moon~rose, he typed.

Archaic. Gawain pressed his lips together. *And easily hacked. Why isn't he using triple security of iris, voice and DNA recognition?*

A deep blue rose with midnight-dark petals flickered onto the screen. 'I've missed you, Sily,' the rose said. 'Where've you been?'

'Busy.' Vasily sat back with a sigh. 'Eygul: meet Gawain, Cerylen and Cardea. I am allowing them to ask you questions. Please treat them with the same respect that you—no, erase that. Please treat them with *much more* respect than you treat me.'

The petals of the rose quivered like lips. 'Oh, Sily, you're my friend. How could you possibly believe I don't treat you with the utmost reverence?'

'It calls you "Silly"?' Cardea asked.

'I'm not an "it".' The rose sounded cantankerous. 'And Sily's just short for Vasily. He's adorable, don't you think?'

'Cut it, Eygul. Gawain, you have got a question.'

'I do?'

'Yes. About the subcutaneous tracking device in your palm.'

'Oh.' Gawain held up his hand. 'Yeah.' He sniffed. 'What can I do about this?'

'Serious infection. A fig poultice to draw the septic build-up plus a frankincense rub to cleanse the wound would probably do the trick.'

Gawain was dubious. 'Sounds positively medieval.'

'Really?' Electric blue edges flickered on the rose's petals. 'What century is this again, Sily?'

'Twenty-first.'

'Oops.' The petals fluttered. 'Laser. No, not advisable. Might interfere with the inbuilt pulse and trigger the anti-removal programming. Vacuum surgery might have the same effect. Looks like the self-destruct mechanism is set to kill mode.'

Kill mode? Did dad know Yellow Eyes was doing this?

'Kill?' Cerylen folded her arms. 'So we can't remove it? What about reducing the pain? Or stopping the device reporting back to base?' She paused. 'Safely?'

The rose folded up, then unfolded. Faint words appeared and vanished on the blue petals. Accessing: mi6, mossad, asio, cia.

Cardea jumped up. 'I need to talk to Uri.'

What? Gawain only just registered her departure, his gaze locked on the list of international security and intelligence agencies. The screen froze as 'iii' appeared.

'Eygul.' Vasily's voice had a frantic edge. 'Exit before Eyes trace you.'

Eyes? Of course. They'd be 'iii'. Wonder what it stands for.

'Eygul! I have told you not...'

'Stop shouting, Sily! I'm *not* deaf. I have the answer: iridium. Even trace amounts would help.'

'What's iridium?' Gawain asked.

'Iridium is a silvery metal, similar to platinum. It has strong corrosion resistance at high temperatures and is one of the rarest elements in the earth's crust. When a laser pulse is directed at iridium, an unusual form of oxygen is produced. This oxygen is poisonous to cancer cells but not to ordinary human tissue.'

Cancer? This thing in my hand is giving me cancer? So I die slowly if I keep it and I die quickly if I try to remove it!

'Meteorites,' Eygul went on, 'have a greater percentage of iridium than terrestrial rocks.'

Cerylen's to-die-for smile was back. 'Of course! Meteorites!'

Iridium is in meteorites. Gawain didn't know he was holding his breath until he let it go. 'So that's why my hand's okay when I'm holding one.' *Such a simple solution. Except I don't want to spend the rest of my life with a meteorite in my hand.* He frowned. *Did Emrys know about the iridium when he told Angie to give me the meteorite?*

'I think I can do it.' Cerylen nodded to herself. 'Should be relatively easy to make you a glove.'

Gawain's jaw dropped a fraction, realising the implications. 'You made the one Emrys is wearing?'

'Of course.' She pointed to her eyecup. 'This isn't a steampunk fashion accessory. Well, not *just* that. It's a jeweller's magnifier. My dad made it specially for me—my *dad*, not my biological father. He also made me a tiny, tiny craft hook so I could crochet the glove out of the thinnest of spun metal. He helped Emrys and me spin the metal too.'

'It's insanely fabulous.' Gawain smiled. '*Deadly*, as Jed would say. I'd be forever grateful if you could make me one. But I'm hoping there'll be another solution and you won't need to.'

'What kind of metal is in milord Emrys' glove?' Vasily asked. 'Meteoric iron with high iridium content?'

'Not exactly.' Cerylen's state was cool and appraising. For a moment that seemed like all she was going to say, but then she added: 'Swordmetal.'

Swordmetal? Like in a certain sword that burst into flames when I touched it?

'Sily,' the rose sniffed. 'I hate to interrupt but I took a quick look around while I was back-dooring into Eyes to find out about subcutaneous tracking devices.'

Vasily's teeth gritted. 'You know my orders, Eygul, yet you completely disregard every risk…'

'Sily, you know Holly has a higher authorisation than you do. And she asked for help.'

Vasily rolled his eyes and sighed.

Gawain watched the eyecup swivel as a thoughtful pout appear on Cerylen's lips. *How had the computer program recognised Holly? She'd been introduced as* 'Cerylen'.

A schematic diagram appeared on the screen—a map with a circular formation in the centre labelled Tnorala. As the contrast deepened into high definition, an image flashed into his mind. *The map from Serpent Mound. The map I'd forgotten even existed. The map I was handed by the sharva in another impact crater in another hemisphere.* 'Reminds me of Serpent Mound,' he breathed.

'Overlay or split screen?' Eygul asked.

Gawain shook his head. 'Sorry. I didn't mean I wanted a map of Serpent Mound. I was thinking of something else.'

'And I wasn't thinking of giving you a map of it,' Eygul said. 'I was thinking of showing you the map you were given there that you've so obviously lost.'

Whatwhatwhat? How does Eygul know that?

'Who are you?' Cerylen took a step forward, her voice alive with suspicion.

Absolutely. Who are you?

'Oh, Holly, Holly, Holly—haven't we been through this before?'

'Are you…?'

'Eygul,' Vasily cut in. 'Are you pulling a live feed from the Eyes surveillance systems?'

'Of course. Despite your myriad distractions, that's what I've been attempting to explain to you.'

'I ordered you out of there.' Vasily groaned. 'But since you are in the system anyway, I have two questions. These three shining dots here on the map. And that group of moving shadows there.'

'The shadows appear to be your stormtroopers in an underground base.' A red circle appeared on the screen to highlight their position. 'But I think you already guessed that was the case. As for the dazzling dots, I've been listening in on their conversation and I have deduced that their names are Uri, Ravi and Mike. Ravi and Mike arrived without any discernible transport device just as the washing up finished. They are currently with Reece, Cardea and Jed and they are singing. My preliminary data about their nature is contradictory and therefore inconclusive.'

Reece? How does he know that? Not just Cerylen's real name but Emrys' as well?

'What do you mean "contradictory"?' Vasily demanded.

'I'm not sure they're human. Whether they are friendly or unfriendly is uncertain. Would you like visuals?' Before anyone answered, the map disappeared and the glowing dots faded into a close-up of three men all wearing blood-red glasses. Retro was at their feet, clearly content with Uri's vigorous patting. Jed and Emrys were looking on as Cardea leaned against Uri, her burqa right next to his ear. *She's starting to seriously scare me.*

'Are we going to wait for Jib?' Uri asked.

A deep, resonant voice sounded from the shadows. 'There is an invitation to attend to, first.'

Gawain watched the men turn, in perfect unison, as Angie came towards them. She'd added a necklace to her firebird costume and was holding the pumpkin she'd carved. A tealight glowed inside it. He heard a rustle, soft and indefinable, like wings fluttering, and Uri's harpsong voice inside his head. *'Don't be afraid, Greyhawk.'* His ears, however, heard something entirely different coming from the screen: 'Why are you doing this, Angharad Goldenhand?'

Angie's smile was wide. 'Look what I made.'

Taking the pumpkin, Mike blew out the candle. He handed it to Ravi. In the blink of an eye, it was smashed.

Whatthe…?

A gasping intake of breath came from Angie. Gawain could see tears glistening in her eyes. Her mouth was open, ready to scream. Emrys and Jed looked startled but Cardea nestled closer to Uri. 'Thank you,' she whispered.

'You!' Angie screeched, whirling on her in accusation. 'You told them to wreck it?'

Cardea's burqa quivered. Gawain felt as if millions of eyes had swivelled to her and an innumerable crowd had drawn breath, waiting for a reply.

'She asked.' It was Uri who spoke.

'It was necessary,' Mike added. 'Your attention-seeking has crossed a dangerous boundary, Angharad Goldenhand.'

'Necessary?' Jed asked.

'Yes.' Uri kept his gaze on Angie as he nodded.

'Why?' Jed demanded. 'I believe ya, but I still wanna know why.'

'The Dark has no hands.'

An unnatural oppressive stillness seemed to descend. Gawain felt as if he were outside, next to Angie, not inside watching Eygul's transmissions. He glanced up and, above them all, a monstrous smoky shadow loomed, a head and a limbless torso, peering down from the pulsing sky. Gawain, terrified, felt the shadow's weight, impossibly heavy, as it tried to reach him.

'And because the Dark has no hands,' Uri went on, 'it cannot open doors.'

Cardea looked upwards, trembling. 'Some people say that evil doesn't exist, but that's because they haven't met it face to face.'

Gawain realised she could see the monstrous shadow, perhaps had sensed it long before anyone else had.

'And though evil isn't human, it can't operate unless it has a human to do its work for it,' Uri said. 'You left the door open, Angie, and a light on inside the house—'

'It was only a pumpkin,' Angie breathed.

'It was an invitation,' Uri corrected.

'To the Darkness,' Ravi added.

'A ghost fence,' Mike said, 'doesn't keep the Dark away—it's an attraction.'

A ghost fence? Gawain's gaze was captured by the smoky limbless shadow as its edges tightened. He could feel its relentless pressure, sense the constant search for an opening, a weakness.

Mike turned to Jed and Emrys. 'Long ago, it wasn't pumpkins and turnips used to make ghost fences on the night of the dead—it was skulls.' His gaze shifted to Angie. 'It wouldn't have mattered that you didn't intend to leave a gate open or issue an invitation.'

'They're not ordinary gates you're talking about, are they?' Angie's voice had a shake in it.

'No, not to you.'

'But to you?' Emrys pointed a finger at Mike.

'Feelings,' Uri sighed. 'They're worse than weight. Far worse. But we are willing to suffer all the wounds of feeling and all of gravity's pain to help you lock the gate you've opened.'

'Me?' Emrys demanded.

Gawain frowned. *What an odd remark. Gravity doesn't hurt. Not unless you fall. Or perhaps if you aren't used to it.* He stared in dawning realisation, at their odd glasses, their odd eyes, their exceptional tallness. *What are they? Where in the universe do they come from?*

Wet roses scented the air. A flash of light passed through the room. On the screen, a shimmering column crystallised into robes of azure silk and golden tassels. Jib waved his hands in front of Mike. 'Where were you?' His words were accusing even if his tone was neutral.

Jed and Emrys both took a step back as Mike looked up.

'Another gridlock at the Persian bypass, Jib?'

'I risked the direct route, thinking you'd be there to cover me.' Jib shook his jet-black locks. 'I've come with a warning that the children's invitation has been accepted. Nine hostiles incoming, a myriad cubits out, heading from the summer stars region, moving at flank speed.'

Uri jumped up. 'You're right. There'll be a perimeter breach in under ten minutes.' He glanced at Mike, then at Ravi. 'How far can we push the boundaries in what we can reveal?'

Neither of them answered.

Invitation? Did they mean Angie's pumpkin? What hostiles?

Eygul's screen flickered back to the map overview. Zooming further and further out, it highlighted a fuzzy patch just crossing the coast of Western Australia. 'Wow! These guys are good to pick up that so far out. On radar it looks like a rain cloud. But it's moving far too fast.'

Uri was already running. 'Round up the kids, Meg,' he shouted. 'Nine hornets. Coming in north by north-west.'

Come, Gawain. The harpsong was back in Gawain's mind. Find your earth treasures quickly. We need them. Hurry.

Gawain was up in an instant. He had taken just half a dozen steps when Angie hurtled through the door and slammed into him. The box of earth treasures fell from her hands and spilled onto the ground. *How'd she get that so fast?*

'It's my fault, isn't it? And we need to give Jib the hammonite.' Angie's voice was husky. 'Is it okay? You got to be the one to give permission. Mike said so. He said it's got to be you.'

Gawain nodded. Jib could have the whole box as far as he was concerned. *I want to wake up home in Ohio.* He turned and, to his surprise, Jib was right behind him. Reaching out with a long elegant finger, Jib's hand seemed to dissolve into the stone as he pulled the ammonite out of its stone matrix. It glowed with a pearl-and-gold sheen, looking as if it had reverted to the original shell before it had become a fossil.

That's impossible. It can't reverse.

Jib kept pulling, allowing the ammonite to become unnaturally long. It was forming a spiral curve like a ram's horn. He raised his arm high above his head as the twists and bends grew longer. Then, in the blink of an eye, he was gone.

Gawain turned, startled, feeling himself drawn into a strange, otherworldly trance. Looking up, he spotted Jib on the roof—a flat silhouette against the fading glow of sunset, an immense winding horn in his hands. He raised the horn to his mouth. A single deep groan, a sound ancient and primeval, seemed to be born out of the earth. Gawain felt fear race along his limbs, felt his bowels loosen, felt his feet turn to wax. *I think my soul's quaking.* His hands were trembling. *Today's the day the sharva spoke of… when the ammonite comes alive and blows a warning.*

He sensed the sound of the horn moving out—over and across the landscape. 'Melt,' it said. 'Hide. Let the rocks cover you.' The sound began to wane in intensity, but Gawain knew it wouldn't really go away. *The echo of it will never leave this land.*

Jed appeared in the doorway. 'The songlines are shuddering. The Dreaming is unravelling. Or perhaps remaking itself.'

'Five minutes,' Uri called. 'Incoming hornets.'

Gawain fought himself free of the trance. 'Angie! Quick! Get the sword!' *We've got to hide it. That's what they're here for. The sword. That's what I'm really supposed to find. Not Reece and Holly—but the sword.*

Angie ran. Half a minute later, she was back, the sword in her hand. It was no longer milky with mist-shimmer, but alight with silverfire.

She skidded up to Gawain. He'd hardly touched it before it burst into golden tongues of flame. 'No!' He beat frantically at it with the back of his hand. 'No*nonononononono*!'

Cardea ran up with a wet tea-towel.

'Stop it!' Even as Gawain screamed, the firelight died. The sword went dark and cool.

Cardea's towel wasn't needed. 'It obeys your commands!'

Does it? Gawain couldn't help sounding fearful. 'I don't want it to.' He stared at the weapon.

'We can't stay here!' Reece called. 'Uri, where can we hide?'

'I thought you'd never ask.' Uri pointed towards the Bluff.

'Isn't that where their base is?' Cerylen asked.

'They don't know everything there is to know about Tnorala,' Uri said. 'Do they, Jed?'

Jed hesitated only a moment. 'There's a Dreaming that speaks o' the coming o' Fire-head Sky-eyes Lion-skin. We are instructed ta shelter him only if the songlines have moved.' His gaze flicked between Uri and Gawain. 'Have the songlines moved, Uwriy'el Mal'ak?'

'Clever child,' Uri said. 'So you've worked out who we are. Yes, Jedidiah Harris, Beloved of the Mighty, the songlines have moved. Ever so slightly.' He tilted his red glasses and winked.

Gawain couldn't understand their conversation. All he knew was that they were running out of time. On the western horizon, silhouetted by sunset glow, a flight of jets appeared. There were, as Jib had said, nine of them. A tail of flame showed behind each of them as, one by one, they activated thruster deceleration.

Hornet gunships, Gawain realised in astonishment, recognising the shape of the sharply tapered forward cannons even at a distance. The distant flubber of whirring blades became audible as, deceleration complete, the ships converted from jet to 'copter.

Uri picked Angie up and dumped her on Retro's back. Turning slowly around the rest of the group, he stopped at Vasily and pointed. A moment later, Vasily was whooshed up behind Angie, his laptop still under one arm. A surprised squeak was the only sound he made as Uri ordered: 'Hold on tight. Keep her safe.' Then, patting Retro on the flank, he yelled: 'Off, Retro! To Tnorala!' He turned back to Mike and Ravi. 'Whatever authorisations you have from the Most High, use them.'

Mike nodded. 'You know what is limiting our response. Without those permissions, we cannot attack.' He vanished. But his voice lingered in the air. 'Still, we can attempt a decoy. I will go with Meg in the bus. Ravi will take the jeep.'

'Come with me, all of you!' Uri plucked Cardea from the ground and hoisted her on his left shoulder. His arm reached for

Cerylen and, in an instant, she was in the crook of his right arm, being carried like a baby.

Retro was loping steadily, despite the burden on his back. Gawain followed, dragging the sword. His leg was aching and his shoulder soon began to throb. Reece stuck by his side. 'You don't have to wait for me.'

Reece snorted. 'You might just need a helping hand.'

Gawain was grateful. Night was falling and it was becoming harder to keep Retro in sight through the scrub. Sand and grass clumps made a difficult, uneven surface, slowing up their movement.

Uri was striding behind them, the girls tucked in his massive arms. His glasses had become black as the sky darkened and the first stars appeared.

'What's Jed doing?' Gawain could see that Jed was trailing well behind Uri. Someone was with him. It looked like Cerylen, but that was impossible. She was under Uri's arm.

'He's destroying our trail.' Uri didn't even glance back. 'And his own.'

The sound of the gunships was like rumbling thunder. Their spotlights swept the plain as they roared towards the homestead. Behind him, the sound of the approaching gunships reached a crescendo. Suddenly, there was a whoosh and, immediately after, an explosion. Instinctively Gawain turned back. *Did we fire on them?*

'They've destroyed the jeep,' Uri said.

'What about Ravi?'

No answer.

The sound of thunder diminished as, one by one, the gunships landed. Gawain's leg was on fire. He didn't know if he could continue.

Suddenly, a shoulder was under his arm, helping him move. 'You can make it,' Reece whispered.

The night was shadowy and soon he lost all sense of time. He felt as if he'd fallen into a nightmare.

HIGH ON THE FELLS, next to a frozen tarn, the dog-boy stumbled across an old sheep-fold. Part of the front wall had fallen down, but most was still intact. The dog-boy crawled into a corner away from the snowdrift and sat against the wall.

He'd remembered who Arthur was. And as far as he could work out, he hadn't done anything to him. Yet Arthur hated him. It was unfathomable. *Why does he even notice me? He's the King of the Britons and I'm nobody.* The dog-boy sighed. He was cold and hungry, and the mulberries looked luscious. *But they're magic.*

The softest noise interrupted his thoughts: a clip of hooves moving in slow, stealthy steps. He leaned towards the tumbledown doorway, ready to pounce...

It was only a sheep. Its eyes looked familiar. *Uri had eyes like a sheep.* He tilted his head. *Who's Uri?*

The sheep edged forward, its gaze fixed on the mulberries. Stumbling in its footsteps came a lamb. *What a terrible spring to be a mother.*

The ewe dared to come close enough to snatch at the mulberry leaves. It jumped back when the dog-boy plucked a single half-frozen berry, then held it out to the tiny lamb. The sheep butted his hand away, before snatching at the leaves again. The dog-boy held them above his head, before trying to feed the lamb once more. But the ewe turned vicious, biting his hand. The dog-boy yelped. '*I don't want to hurt your baby, I'm just trying to feed it,*' was what he wanted to say. But only a rustling crackle emerged from his mouth.

An idea darted into his mind—a possibility remaining long enough in his thoughts for him to grasp it. *My speech centre's been affected. That's what's happened. Probably a blow to the head.*

The lamb tottered forward, its tiny eyes beseeching. The dog-boy held out fingers stained with juice, and the mother let him pick it up. Plucking the last few berries from the loop, he sat down on the stones of the partly-broken entrance and began to feed it. As it snuggled into his furs, the dog-boy shook his head. *Don't get any ideas, lambchop. I'm not your mom.*

He was about to stand up when a shout of triumph echoed down the slope towards him. It was Arthur himself—black clothes, black cloak, black horse, black hair tied back by a thong—*he's dressed for a hunt.*

Arthur raised his sword and the black horse took a step forward. The dog-boy began to scramble for cover. As he did, the landscape began to ripple. The black horse took another step forward and the white snow disappeared in a green haze of grass. The horse stepped forward again and the grey gloaming sky was broken by a spear of light as the sun appeared, warm and dazzling in a wide expanse of blue. Another step and the frozen tarn became a shimmering stretch of water. Another step and the ice-clad branches of the trees were transformed by verdant foliage and glistening fruit. Another step and the ewe next to the dog-boy became a bleating herd of sheep, surrounded by frisking lambs. Another step and a giant club appeared in the dog-boy's hands. The lamb he'd been holding curled around his neck and baa-ed placidly.

Arthur's face passed through wonderment to alarm, then terror. He tried to pull his horse back but the starving animal was oblivious to his commands, heading for the grass near the dog-boy's feet. Arthur leapt from the horse and raised his sword. 'Who are you?' he screamed.

The dog-boy's first startled thought was: *doesn't he recognise me?* and his second: *I can understand him! Finally! He's speaking my language!*

'I am the Knight of Summer Day.'

The dog-boy looked around for the source of the voice, but could see no one.

'What are you doing here?' Arthur's eyes never wavered from the dog-boy's face.

'I am tending my flocks.' And those flocks weren't just sheep anymore either—there were cattle and deer too, hares scampering, pigs rootling, goats romping. Birdsong carolled out of the trees.

'This is *my* realm.' Arthur raised his sword.

That'll be Excalibur. The dog-boy felt mesmerised. His eyes were drawn by the serpentine patterns of its scrollwork. *Wait. I recognise that pattern. It's the sword of the... the sword of the...* He couldn't remember the word, but he remembered holding the sword while the blade burnt and the air around him murmured. *Just like the air is speaking now.*

'You threaten me in my own domain, Winter King?' the air asked.

'Ah!' Arthur cried. 'So it is you who denies us Summer! You who keep us in this accursed Winter! Even if we found the Grail of Redemption, you would still toy with us, would you not?' A warm breeze blew, tugging at Arthur's hair. 'I shall overcome your baleful magicks! I shall find the Hallows of Kingship. With them I shall restore the land. See? I have the Sword already!'

'*You stole it?*' The air sounded incredulous.

The dog-boy was dumbfounded. *Stole it? Hold on, didn't he pull it from a stone?* He frowned. *It's the sword of the…* And then the memory came, astonishing and terrifying, in a sudden wild rush. *It's the sword of the cherubim, the whirling blade of the hosts of fire, and it brought me here to this time. It can take me home.*

He almost gasped.

'I am the King,' Arthur thundered. 'The land is mine. Everything in it is mine.'

You stole the sword from me! The dog-boy felt the realisation hit him. *You're a thief and I can expose you! That's why you hate me.*

'Acknowledge me as your king,' Arthur roared. 'Bow before me, Knight of Summer Day.'

'*Indeed, I will not, King of the Wasteland. Indeed, I take your kingship from you…*'

Arthur stepped back, his face paling.

He'll throw the sword in the lake, and then I'll never find it. The dog-boy felt a surge of despair just as he heard a voice in his head.

When on earth are you going to get a move on, dog-boy? How much longer do you expect me to hold him here? A moment later there was a whistling intake of breath. *The sword is yours? You brought it here? Out of the hands of Aanundus!* A soft gasp. *Oh, by the Tree, this is Merlin's speech pattern—the one that doesn't exist for more than a thousand years. Who are you?*

I don't know.

Don't know, Gwalchmai?

Why do you call me 'Gwalchmai'? Doesn't that mean, 'Come here, you idiot'?

It means Hawk of May. It's the name of the prince of Lothian. And if you're not that unlucky dolt, who are you?

First, who are you?

Guinevere's serving girl saw the hunt chasing you and said you were in trouble.

As Arthur's courage returned, he stepped forward, raising Excalibur for a killing blow. The dog-boy felt himself thrust aside. He fell backwards out of himself—or at least a giant version of himself sitting on a rock and yawning at Arthur. '...but I shall return your kingdom to you, if you answer my riddle,' he saw himself say amiably. 'I shall give you time to think it over, of course. This isn't a blood sport. Not on my part anyway.'

Arthur stopped.

The dog-boy could almost see his thinking. *A riddle wasn't a bad deal. It wasn't a big deal either*—the dog-boy realised Arthur was probably calculating how much of a riddlemaster the Wild Man was. Besides, he was probably also figuring a riddle might just buy enough time to work out a way to vanquish this shapeshifting giant-magician-of-a-dog-boy. *I am a vicious brute who, after all, has challenged the high king and deserves to die.*

The dog-boy felt a sort of kick inside his head. Stop trying to analyse Arthur's thoughts—just get out of here.

But you didn't answer my question. Who are you?

That's not important. Go west. Into Inglewood.

'Riddle?' Arthur asked at last. 'What riddle would you have me answer, Knight of Summer Day?'

The kick inside the dog-boy's head was harder this time.

Where's Inglewood?

Giantsgrove. The Wraithwood. Is that the name you know it by? The vale of fire and ghosts, phantom lights and monsters. Arthur's not going to search there.

The dog-boy had no idea. Ghosts and monsters and phantom lights didn't sound good but he scrambled up. The voices gusted after him on a warming breeze.

'It's an age-old riddle, whose answer would prove you wise enough to retain your kingship. The realm lies in the balance. If you cannot answer wisely, your kingdom is forfeit.'

'If...' Arthur began.

'Yes, if,' the voice agreed.

If. The tree. Strange disconnected words came to the dog-boy's mind. *The tree of If. The tree in me. The sylvan throne that must be put to the axe.*

Another gust of wind, skirling with snow this time, hid Arthur from the dog-boy's sight. In the blink of an eye, everywhere was snow, deep snow, as far as he could see. He turned to look back, watching his footsteps being rubbed out one by one. *The ettins.*

In the distance, Arthur and the voice still parried one another.

'You delay, Knight of Summer Day.' So Arthur had figured out what tactic the voice was employing. 'Your riddle?' he demanded.

'It is the most challenging of all, Winter King—but under the circumstances the choice of difficulty is warranted.' The voice faded as the dog-boy reached a copse of ice-encrusted hagthorns but the riddle came to him as a fading whisper: 'What do women want most?'

19

ONLY AN OCCASIONAL SMALL EXPLOSION as the jeep crackled and burned disturbed the silence. The gunships were fanning out across the landscape, their searchlights racing ahead of them. There was another explosion, the bus this time.

Mike. Gawain refused to think. His shoulder had begun to ache relentlessly again, but he gripped the sword with grim determination and followed Retro's distant form.

'Down!' Uri yelled without warning. He dropped Cardea and Cerylen to the ground and pushed them flat to the sand. They crawled forward.

Reece pulled Gawain into the nearest scanty bush as a gunship zoomed overhead. The full intensity of its searchlights seared his eyeballs. Uri took his hand and lifted him up. *Courage, Greyhawk.* He could see Cerylen heading for the Bluff. *Where's Cardea?*

'I wish I had red glasses,' Gawain said as the lights strobed in front of his eyes.

'They have advantages,' Uri agreed.

'Are they like Miss Hale's screens?'

'No, they are simply for corrective vision.'

'Really?' Reece sounded dubious.

So we can see with heaven's eyes, Time-killer.

Before Gawain could ask what that meant, a loud baying echoed from behind them. 'Hunting dogs,' Uri said. 'They've certainly come prepared.'

'Have they found our trail?'

Uri nodded. 'But don't worry.'

Gawain knew he should have been surprised to find Cardea had come back, but he wasn't. *Are you here for Uri? Or for me?* He could see Angie, Vasily and Retro not far ahead. *Where's Cerylen?* Looming above them were the high circular walls of Tnorala. *I didn't realise we'd come this far.* His feet crunched on flat rocks as he looked back towards the homestead. It was lit up by sparks floating skywards from the burning jeep. *Ravi. I'm so sorry, so sorry, so sorry. Mike. So so sorry.*

What about, Greyhawk?

It was Ravi's voice. Not full of harpsong as Uri's was, but a circling flute-skirl that rose and fell in melodic waves. *We need authorisation, Greyhawk.*

You're not to inform him, Raphay'el. Uri's voice was a crash of stern rebuke. *The offer must be voluntary.* Without warning, he pushed Cardea to one side and yelled. 'Down, Retro!'

Retro's limbs star-spread, thumping Vasily sideways. A laser beam spat down from the stars, hitting the exact spot where he had been standing.

Gawain jumped as the ground exploded in gobbets of hot, liquid rock.

He felt a rising sense of panic as he clutched the sword. *Miss Hale. She laughed at me. She said they wouldn't fire at us from space. Was she lying? Or just wrong? How'd they find us? What are they locked on to?*

And he knew. *It's me.*

He looked down at his hand. *They're using me to herd everyone into a trap. And get the sword. Jed was right. Those bugs still worked when they were pulverised. They knew the moment I found the sword.* The baying of the hunting dogs seemed preternaturally loud. *We can't outrun them.* Gawain felt himself beginning to shake with fear as he realised what he'd have to do to save the others. *I've got to leave.*

'You know the truth,' Uri said.

'I've got to go.' Gawain held out the sword. 'You take this and I'll lead them away. Don't follow me.'

Uri stared at the sword. He took off his glasses. Time itself seemed to stop, as the sound of fluttering wings became almost deafening.

'Choice,' Cardea whispered up at him.

Uri locked gazes with Gawain. Ɍaphay'el, Ɱiyka'el, Ǥabriy'el, what do Ɉ do?

Ƭhis cannot be happening. It was Ravi.

Ƕow can the test be for us and not for them? Mike sounded unnerved.

What do Ɉ do? Uri grabbed Gawain's wrist. 'I hope I'm going to be able to explain this.'

'What?'

'Why we're not taking the sword.' We're not, are we, Ɱiyka'el? When we've waited millennia for its voluntary relinquishment.

'*You* put it in the wardrobe.' Gawain was suddenly sure of it.

'Holly asked me to keep it safe. And since it's safer with *you* than anyone else, I just transferred it from her wardrobe to your wardrobe.'

Another laser bolt spat down from the sky. Gawain felt its searing heat spearing down so close behind him that it grazed his heels.

'They're trying to get us to move.' Cardea's voice was strangely soothing. 'Another choice.'

Dust was on his tongue, his eyes were blinded with grit and tears.

Reece strode to confront Uri. 'In all this time, I never realised *you* owned the sword. And, technically, you could've taken it back any time.'

'Holly said to guard it,' Uri pointed out. 'And we cannot steal. Even if it was stolen from us. It must be voluntarily relinquished.'

It's not a normal sword if Uri's people owned it. Gawain felt a sudden urge to laugh at the absurdity of the thought. *Normal sword? When it bursts into flame each time I touch it?*

Jed padded back to them, Cerylen with him. His arm was around her back. *And she isn't screaming.*

'Witchiepoo's behind us,' he said. 'Ravi says they've got a fix on Speckly Boy. And tracking devices capable o' registering body heat. And hunting dogs, just in case their technology spits the dummy. Which it does regularly round here. Magnetic and gravitational anomalies, ya know.' His grin was so broad it was visible even in the darkness. 'What's the plan, Uwriy'el Mal'ak?'

'That depends on you, Jedidiah Harris. The Mal'akim have chosen. Now it falls to you.'

The grin became a scowl. 'Falls ta me? If Gawain wasn't *Taliesin's Mantle*, I'd probably leave ya all out here fer Witchiepoo. And ya know it. How many years did it take ya and yer mob ta arrange exactly this choice at exactly this moment, Uwriy'el Mal'ak?'

You overestimate us, Beloved of the Mighty.

'Do I?'

'We don't manipulate, you know that.'

'Don't kid yerselfs.' Jed grabbed Reece's elbow with one hand and Cerylen's wrist with the other and dragged them both towards the Bluff. 'Well, c'mon then!'

20

URI LIFTED GAWAIN FROM THE GROUND and slung him over his shoulder. Cardea trotted by their side. Dust was all around. Spotlights were angling back and forward not far behind them. Yet somehow, as Uri headed out through the scrub, the distance from their pursuit began increasing, not decreasing.

Jed, Cerylen and Reece reached the shingle at the base of the Bluff. They were visible only as faint ghostly shapes against the dark rise of Tnorala. 'Follow me.' Jed gestured towards a clump of shadows. Gawain realised it was Angie and Vasily, along with Retro.

Cardea caught up with Jed and pulled his hand away from Cerylen. 'All the significant choices are currently yours,' she said to him. 'And you're distracted.'

Is she jealous?

But Retro was growling in a curious undertone at Cerylen.

'Cherry's with me.' Jed scowled at both Cardea and Retro, before turning to Uri. 'I don't s'pose ya could fuzz up the bad guys' heat-seeking technology fer a coupla minutes?'

'I thought you'd never ask.'

Jed frowned. 'Second time ya've said that. Do we hafta ask specifically fer everything we want?'

'Pretty much.'

'I see. Okay, then while ya're at it, can ya confuse the dogs?'

Uri nodded, putting Gawain down.

Jed moved forward a dozen paces. Taking Cerylen by the hand, he disappeared deeper into the shadows. Gawain could hear his voice echoing. 'Lemme show ya how it works, Cherry. If ever ya need to hide…'

A terrifying shadow—like an enormous bee—or an eight-legged flying horse—flitted across the screen of Gawain's mind.

Retro vanished after Jed and Celyren, followed by Angie, Vasily and Cardea.

Shadows won't help—not when they can lock onto the implant in my hand. He staggered forward, realising they were in a crevice. Keeping the sword down, he took a careful step, his eyes straining to pick out any shape ahead of him. To his surprise, he heard a sliding sound behind him, like heavy steel rolling and locking in place.

'Arlte.' As Jed spoke, lights flickered.

'We're safe.' Uri gestured behind them to a metal door. 'It's a genetically-coded lock.'

Genetically-coded? And it just so happens Jed can override it?

'Where are we?' Vasily asked.

'In the service tunnel for the cyclotron.' Uri gestured at the rock-hewn walls.

'Cyclotron?' Reece craned his head to see the end of the tunnel. 'As in nuclear accelerator ring? Like, in essential operational requirement of a time machine?'

'Don't worry,' Uri said. 'It's not in operation.'

They headed into a small storage room. Jed and Vasily moved the dusty table, making plenty of space to congregate. Angie signalled Gawain, mouthing something he couldn't make out. 'What is it?' he asked after she'd screwed up her nose at him for the third time.

'Thank you, Jed,' she stage-whispered.

Gawain flushed and turned to Jed. *How could I forget?* Even as he opened his mouth, so did everyone else. It became a chorus of gratitude: *thank you, thankyou, thanks, thanks, Jed.*

Jed scuffed the floor in embarrassment. 'Nuttin', really.' He glanced at Gawain. 'I was thinkin' whether it was okay ta show ya what's here, anyway.'

'What d'you think, sis?' Emrys turned to Celyren, spreading his arms wide. 'Enough power here to widen the gap so we can see into interstitial time?'

Celyren nodded. 'It's primitive but we should be still able to cut into the skin of time even so.'

'*Primitive?*' Emrys, frowning, took a step forward. 'What d'you mean by *that*? Skin of time? Where'd you get that idea?'

Uri stared at Celyren. 'Move back, milord.' His voice sharp and sudden. 'You too, Jed.'

Both of them froze into immobility.

Mocking laughter echoed from behind them. A sibilant whisper drifted into the room. 'Sso, at lasst, after sso long, Uwriy'el!'

Gawain felt his heart stop and his body freeze. It was the voice of Yellow Eyes—*what had the sharva called him?*—Aanundus.

'Hu Gadarn.' Uri's glasses shifted colour as he scanned floors, walls, ceiling. His voice was wary, uncertain. 'Where are you?'

A deep almost-melodramatic sigh rippled through the air. 'I wass beginning to think you'd never get here, Uwriy'el. Have you enjoyed your yearss of baby-ssitting? Or hass it been tediouss? No doubt you've been frusstrated attempting to help thesse doltissh children. But I commend you on finally getting them all jusst where I want them.'

'It's been interesting. Getting their permission to help has often been difficult.'

'Uwriy'el, Uwriy'el!' The voice tutted. 'I don't believe you're allowed to reveal that. That'ss presssing the boundariess of legality, ssurely? Am I detecting the tiniesst hint of a rebelliouss sstreak at long lasst?'

'It's a trick.' Jed thrust out his lower lip. 'Some sort o' projection. No one can actually be in here. They can't override the system.'

The voice laughed. 'Missster Harriss. How good of you to come. It'ss not a trick. Actually, it'ss a trap. A sset-up. We've been trying for yearss to get into the sservice tunnel, but ass you know, no one can accesss the entry excccept ssomeone with your sskin code. We've been waiting for you. Jusst as your people put monitorss up to find a way in when the cccyclotron wass being built, sso we put up monitorss to find out who had locked the sservice doorss and how to unlock them.'

The squeeze on Gawain's heart was sudden and terrifying. *That's why Aanundus wanted* me *here. The story about looking for Reece and Holly was a way to hide a deeper truth. He knew Jed would want to impress Taliesin's Mantle... and show me the secrets of Tnorala.*

Jed looked completely unimpressed as he shrugged. 'You're not fooling me.'

'You think I'm jusst a dissembodied voiccce, Missster Harriss?' Down the tunnel stepped a figure so tall its head was bent to avoid the ceiling. Gawain stared at the yellow eyes, the oily cadaver-coloured skin, the wide and feral smile, and knew Jed was absolutely and totally wrong. This wasn't a projection. Behind the figure, to its left, Miss Hale was standing, her face blank and impassive, her gun held to the head of a shape struggling in the grasp of one of the black-garbed squad. It looked like Cerylen.

But that's impossible. She's next to Jed.

The golden top hat was gone but the struggling, grunting figure had an eyecup—and, more significantly, a feisty attitude.

A faint smile thinned Aanundus' lips. 'It wass difficult to find a disstraction ssufficient to deflect your attention, Uwriy'el. You kept protecting the children and disperssing the mindsshadow pulssess, didn't you? Sstill, we decccided a high moral dilemma, like retaking the ssword, would draw your eyess from a ssubstitution for Holly.'

Substitution for Holly? That's Cerylen he means.

The figure next to Jed twirled into a coquettish bow.

Huh? If that's not Cerylen, who is it?

The fighting, kicking form in the stormtrooper's grasp managed to get her mouth free. 'Reece, it's Hollë. They've—' Her words were cut off.

Hol-lay? Was that what she said?

'Hollë hass joined forces with me,' Aanundus revealed, smirking. 'Yes, the Hive Queen is now an ally. Oh, we each fought for ssupremacccy for a while but realissed eventually how sstupid it wass to fight each other.'

Reece sighed. 'And here I was, hoping Hollë would have trapped you in one of her webs and kept you for a snack.'

'No chance.' The doppelgänger at Jed's side wrinkled its nose. 'He tastes positively disgusting.'

'Cherry!' Jed stepped back in disbelief, his voice full of stunned betrayal.

'Handss up. Or the girl diess.' Aanundus backhanded Cerylen and the trooper holding her almost fell over. 'Sstop it!' he hissed at her. 'Or one by one, your friendss will be eliminated. Sstarting with the little one.'

Angie! Gawain felt instant panic, but Cerylen had already stopped struggling.

'You can't kill her,' Reece shouted. 'She's the real Holly and she's the guardian of the sword. You need her.' He raised his hands anyway.

Gawain rested the sword against his thigh and raised his hands as well. *What can we do? What? We need help. But where can help come from?*

'You think I need her? How naïve, Reecce. I thought you'd have given me credit for more intelligenccce by now. I've been waiting sso long to ssee you again.' A flash of light spat out from somewhere near Aanundus' chest and, a moment later, Gawain felt a thud near his feet.

He glanced down. A hand in a silver glove was on the ground. He blinked… and glanced up. One of Reece's hands was missing.

For a moment, Gawain couldn't process what that meant. But as Reece crumpled to the floor, Cerylen's double picked up the silver hand. With a bright laugh, Hollë sauntered towards Aanundus. 'Got it.' Her voice was full of raw desire. 'We have the glove!'

'Now, bring uss the ssword, boy,' Aanundus commanded Gawain.

They shot off his hand! I can't do what they want. And I can't not do it. He took a step forward.

And then the sound of Hollë's cackle, gloating softly, 'Glove, glove, glove,' broke the spell of horror clouding his mind.

We have to ask. Why isn't anyone asking? 'Uri,' he squeaked, '*help! Helphelp!*'

I thought you'd never remember, Greyhawk. Run. Take the sword. We'll cover your retreat.

For half a second, Gawain hesitated. He couldn't leave the others defenceless. *Trust me, Greyhawk. Trust us. Go with him, Beloved of the Mighty.* Gawain swivelled and, from the corner of his eye, he glimpsed Retro leap towards Hollë. *Runrunrun.* A ferocious roar sounded behind him. *Faster.* He felt Jed moving at his side. Behind them sounded the whine of bullets and crack of ricocheting gunfire.

21

DON'T LET THEM BE DEAD. Pleasedon'tlet...

Smoke began to billow behind them.

'We need a hidey hole,' Jed panted. '...since we're not gonna be able ta move real fast coz o' that limp o' yours. There's storage rooms but if we cross over the ring...' He stopped talking. 'Gotta keep me big mouth shut. I told the fake Cherry how ta get in, ya know. She musta passed the information straight ta Witchiepoo.'

Gawain wasn't sure how to give Jed the reassurance he needed. *Does he believe he's betrayed his own people for a pretty face?* 'They fooled Uri.'

'Good point.' Jed's sigh of relief was so deep Gawain knew he'd said the right thing. He had a sense Jed would have blamed himself for the rest of his life otherwise. Maybe even shortened it as a result.

Don't let them be dead. Pleasedon'tletthembedead. Hand. A hand in a silver glove. Severed. Like a branch sawn from a tree... Gawain slammed a shutter down on the pictures rising in his mind's eye.

They reached a dead-end. If Jed hadn't winked, Gawain would have been worried. 'What's that?' Gawain could just make out the faintest of luminescent streaks on the rocks.

'Words.' Jed's voice was loud and precise. 'It says: *Speak friend and enter.*'

'Isn't that from *The Lord of The Rings*? The riddle at the entrance to the Mines of Moria?'

'Apt analogy,' Jed commented. 'We're underground and runnin' from some hideous monster like the Balrog. However, we really wanna avoid the Bridge of Doom and the self-sacrificin' Gandalf bit.' He raised a finger to his lips and pulled Gawain backwards. 'Atyewe! Friend!' He raised his voice. 'Atyewe! Friend!'

Right in front of the dead-end, a section of floor slid silently into the wall and just as silently slid back. Gawain gasped. If they'd been standing any closer, they'd have fallen into the darkness below.

Trap, Jed mouthed as he tiptoed back the way they'd come, gesturing Gawain to follow. They'd hardly gone a dozen paces when Retro came hurtling down the tunnel, Angie and Cardea on his back.

Theygotaway, theygotaway! Gawain wanted to cheer. *Maybe there's hope for the others. Theygotaway!*

As Retro skidded to a halt, Angie squealed and fell off. Cardea straightened her burqa so she could see before clambering down.

'Quiet!' Jed's signals were fast and frantic. 'We gotta move quick. Akete-akete.' The lights dimmed so rapidly all Gawain could see was Retro's white hide. A moment later, even that vanished. A touch, feather-light, rested on his hand, then someone—*Cardea?*—grasped his arm and pulled him forwards. The faint hiss of an airlock sliding shut sounded against his ear. 'Stick together,' Jed whispered. 'No talkin'.'

Pleasedon'tletthembedead. A hand in a silver glove. Cut off. Like a branch sawn from a tree... Songs... songs that heal... that heal trauma and abuse and suffering. Gawain could feel himself shaking, the horror rising within. *Gotta stop thinking about Reece and Holly.* As his eyes adjusted to the faint light, he could make out metallic walls polished to a glassy sheen. *We're inside the cyclotron.*

Ten steps later the gleam of silvery smooth walls disappeared and he realised, by the change in temperature, they had crossed over into a new space.

'Arlte.'

The lights flickered on, revealing a small cavern. Gawain moved away from Cardea to look at the long poles leaning against the walls, as well as a folding table in the centre littered with electronic equipment and was hard put to hold back a gasp. 'It's a recording studio!' He noticed the poles were painted with red dots and black lines. *Didgeridoos!* 'Wow!' He couldn't hide his admiration. 'Like, totally *wow!*'

Jed's expression changed from faintly embarrassed to patently thrilled.

Gawain felt vaguely uneasy. *I know his hero is Taliesin's Mantle but he doesn't need my approval.* He cringed inwardly. *So why do I need dad's... and mom's... and Thompson's...*

He blinked. 'Jed, who knows about this place?'

'Nobody. It's secret. *My* secret. Like ya don't want yer dad ta know about yer music, I don't want my mob ta know about mine. If I get found out, then prob'ly I'll get chucked off country...'

Never thought of the military academy as exile, but I guess it's the same as 'off country'. Gawain sighed. 'I don't think this is secret, Jed. This is a very elaborate conspiracy. I think Aanundus knew and that's why he chose me to come. I'm nothing and nobody. But if there's anyone on the face of the planet you'd let in here, it'd be *Taliesin's Mantle.'*

'Don't underrate yerself, Speckly Boy.' Jed held up his hand. 'The sword wasn't activated til ya touched it. And they wanted that glove from Emrys too. I think it's made o' the same stuff as the sword.'

Glove. Sword. Cut off. Like a branch sawn from a tree… STOP! 'They want more than the glove and the sword. They want access to this part of the cyclotron.'

'It isn't part o' the cyclotron.' Jed folded his arms. 'It's just the middle o' the crater. Nuttin' special. An old drill pit from last century when there was geologists here explorin' fer oil and minerals.'

Angie had poked her head into every corner of the small chamber. 'Where's the baby?'

'What baby?' Gawain asked.

'The star-baby what got buried under the basket.'

Gawain put out a hand to fend off Retro, but there was no reaction to Angie's mistake. *Come to think of it, Jed's made some grammatical blunders Retro's ignored. What's up? He's unnaturally quiet.*

'The star-baby isn't here,' Jed said to Angie. 'That's why I'd get chucked off country. The elders'd think I'd of scared it away. Coz me musical style is a shocking violation o' decency.' He turn to Gawain, looking apologetic. 'Ya ain't offended, are ya?'

Shocking violation of decency. Gawain shook his head, realising at once Jed was copying *Taliesin's Mantle.* 'Is Retro sick?'

They all turned to the giant dog. He was hunched against the rocky wall, pawing a collection of small stones together. As soon as he realised he was the object of everyone's attention, he stopped and tried to look innocent. *Which, when you're ghostly white with red-tipped ears and scary as, isn't that easy. Hmm, 'scary as'. Angie's right: gotta stop incomplete comparisons.*

'What are you hiding, Retro?' Angie crept forward but Retro slammed both paws down on top of his rock collection. 'Earth treasures, eh?'

'More precious still,' Cardea said.

Retro growled, his teeth bared into dripping fangs. Gawain ignored him because, as Cardea had spoken, he realised that, if he didn't confront her now, it might be too late. 'What's your supernerd talent, Cardea?'

A long silence followed before she answered. 'I can scry the future.'

'Like a fortune-teller?'

'Nothing like a fortune-teller.' Cardea folded her arms and, even without being able to see her face, Gawain knew she was scowling at him. 'I'm a mathematical savant. I can instantly calculate the probability a particular combination of actions will result in a desired outcome—or one you'd want to avoid.' She glanced sideways at Angie. 'That's why I asked Uri to get the pumpkin smashed. Every branch of the choice-chance tree involving it led to someone dying.' She turned to Jed. 'I didn't know about the doppelgänger, if that's what you're thinking. I just know not to be distracted when making critical decisions.'

Gawain sensed a need to change the subject. 'This is an amazing set-up, Jed. How'd you manage it right under everyone's noses?'

'Wore a loincloth and a bit of ochre and looked feckless. Worked every time.'

'Feckless?' Gawain stared. 'What sorta word is *feckless*? You get it off Heroflix too?'

Jed wrinkled his nose, looking affronted. 'Matter o' fact, it's from the song *StoneSinger* by *Taliesin's Mantle*. Rhymes with *reckless*. Ya musta been truly desperate, Speckly Boy.'

'There's no *feckless* in *StoneSinger*.'

'Ya don't know ya own song?'

'Of course I do. It's *speckless*.'

'Ya're kiddin'.' Jed sniffed. 'Must get me ears checked. I s'pose it makes sense Speckly Boy would think o' speckless.'

'Can anyone get in here?' Cardea asked.

'No way.' Jed was definite. 'Well, okay, not "*no* way". Mebbe it's theoretically possible, but with the songlines movin', it'd be harder 'n ever. This isn't just an old exploratory pit. It's a sealed off-shoot o' the ring, a compartment fer emergencies.'

Pleasedon'tletthembedead. Hand. Like a branch sawn from a tree... STOP! 'What if they used a laser drill?'

'It'll reflect right back and melt the drill.'

'Cold fusion cannon?' Gawain persisted.

'Make the access through the cyclotron unusable. To them and us.'

'Hostages? What about Vasily and Reece and Cerylen?' *Pleasedon'tletthembedead. Hand... STOP!*

Jed's fists clenched.

'After that trick with the doppelgänger?' Cardea asked. 'They'll think twice about that. Besides, remember what Reece said? They need the real Holly. Anyway, Uri's there.'

She can discern choices too. 'What if they threatened some of your mob?' Gawain asked Jed.

'Possible. But takin' any o' my mob from outside the US consulate in Canberra during a protest covered by live social media feed might be the kinda publicity they could do without.' Jed grinned. 'My mob left fer the capital two days ago. And, just before we came in here, I asked Ravi and Jib ta follow 'em and keep 'em safe. I've got tucker down here that'll last ages. So we're not gonna be starved out.'

It's like you were planning for this. Like you knew it was coming.

Almost as if he could see doubt igniting in Gawain's mind, Jed said, 'It's like this. In every generation, we gotta be ready—ready at a moment's notice, in case the songlines shift. Makin' and outfittin' a refuge fer that time is part o' my mob's initiation rite. Who'd of thought *I'd* be the one ta hafta open *my* refuge ta Lion-skin Sky-Eyes?'

Gawain glanced at Retro. *Who'd of thought?* A flash of luminescent red eyes and a twitch of the blood-tipped ears, but no thumping paw or snarling growl at the grammar fail. *What's he guarding under that pile?*

He was distracted by Angie tugging his sleeve. 'But what if mom and dad want to know where we are? What if we're here for weeks and weeks?'

'We can get a message out, if we really need ta.' Jed raised his hand. 'So are we all ready?'

'Ready for what?' Cardea asked.

'Ta make music, what else?'

INTERSTITIAL

VI

THE DOG-BOY WOKE TO WHISPERS, his head throbbing. He winced when he opened his eyes. His hands were bound and he was lying in straw stinking with animal excrement.

Arthur's men, he remembered. He'd reached the white trees of the Wraithwood with their glimmering needles of ice. The ettins had left him, dispersing like smoke. *Did they lead me on, just to betray me?*

Wandering on, he had come to a vast clearing where tree trunks lay fallen chaotically, most of them mantled by thick ice. But there was black wood beneath the white crust. *They're burnt. All burnt.* He turned around, finding nothing but black and white as far as his eye could see. And yes! A single smudge of green.

He had trudged towards it, through the ranks of fallen trees. Had been astonished at how lush and verdant it was. *Enchantment. It has to be magic.* He found himself walking through fields of strawberries the size of his fists and huge clusters of grapes that trailed across the ground in tangled profusion. Not a moment too soon he'd realised the vine-wrapped bushes in front of him were actually treetops. Coming to the edge of a circular pit, he'd stood looking down on a blossoming canopy.

It's a crater. Looking across the treetops he'd seen peaches the size of footballs, cherries the size of apples, apples the size of his head. Another word had floated into his mind: *mutation. I wonder if they're safe to eat.*

Walking around the rim of the crater, he'd found an apple tree growing on the edge and sat beneath its spreading branches.

It had just occurred to him there might be animals to match the plants in size when he was seized from behind. A heavy blow fell on his head and, almost at once, he'd lost consciousness.

Now, as he contemplated the byre, he realised how hopeless it really was. *They'll make a game of killing me. Who'll help me?*

The crude door of the byre was flung open. The dog-boy remembered their names: Cradoc and Illtyd, Arthur's most trusted henchmen. They yanked him to his feet, pulled a stinking tunic over his head and dragged him out the door.

Drunken shouts and roaring laughter—*a mock training session.* A mix of games and weapons practice, it was the best morale boost the high king had ever devised. A word wafted into the dog-boy's mind: tournament, but the word had frills to it this certainly didn't. This was nothing more than another justification for violence and lechery. The dog-boy could hear the taunts of the women, only too glad he didn't much understand. *Oh God, oh help ohhelphelphelp.*

Cradoc and Illtyd dragged him through a mess of mud and rocks and churned up snow.

The dog-boy heard the whoosh of arrows, the twang of bows. He was made to stand, his bare feet on the partially frozen ground, his legs nearly folding under him. *Target practice, they're making me target practice*—he was sure of it even before he shook the hair from his eyes and looked around through the fog of his own breath. Someone threw mud. Someone threw excrement. A rock knocked a wizened crab-apple from off the wand in front of him, and Arthur, with his commanding view of events, jokingly offered the prize to the man who'd thrown the rock. It was a golden chalice.

Unbelievable. A golden chalice for a dog-boy's life.

He looked at Arthur, appalled, and saw that he was in an expansive mood, delighted with the universal approval greeting his latest savagery. The dog-boy looked at the line of very eager archers, and his stomach lurched, his knees buckled. *Everyone will want a go, whether they're good with a bow or not.*

The roar in the place became deafening as Cradoc tied the dog-boy to a pole, while Illtyd plucked the apple from the wand and balanced it on his head. It was scarcely bigger than a cherry. The dog-boy couldn't help it—he shook so uncontrollably the apple fell. Next moment Illtyd had drawn his long knife, and was holding it point upwards beneath the dog-boy's chin. Cradoc, roaring with laughter, mounded mud onto the dog-boy's head, placing the apple carefully in the midst of it.

In remoter parts of himself the dog-boy wanted to face the archers wide-eyed, with fearless disdain. But he didn't. He closed his eyes. There was sweat, there were silent tears. There was mud, there was snow, dribbling down his face. His lips moved soundlessly, beseeching heaven. A moment passed and an arrow whizzed past his ear, nicking it. A wild shout and the apple rolled to the ground. Then Illtyd's dagger again, piercing beneath the dog-boy's chin, twisting a little, drawing blood. Then the apple was back on his head, and a thunderous stamping of feet followed. Mud and blood spattered his neck.

Another arrow came. He heard the heavy thud as it hit the ground behind him, the groan of disapproval, the drumming of feet as the next archer took the last one's place...

Then silence. Utter silence.

The dog-boy opened his eyes.

Who is this?

The man had his harp at his feet, a bow in his hands.

It was the harpist rescued by the Wild Man. *Taliesin.* The name was again a flame in his mind... it belonged to another time...

Taliesin fingered the bowstring, making it sing.

The dog-boy stared at his hands. *He's missing a ringfinger.*

Raising an arrow to his lips, Taliesin whispered to it, tucked it into his jerkin, drew a second arrow from the quiver on his back, then took his stance. Across the length of the courtyard, their eyes locked. The dog-boy, knowing he was about to die, felt peaceful and strangely mesmerised by the harpist's smoky green eyes—eyes that couldn't really be so close as to fill all of his vision.

In that moment, the dog-boy's life flashed before his eyes—and he remembered. Remembered his name. Remembered a sword and a sharva and an alien named Aanundus. Remembered getting shot and fleeing across a desert while laser beams crackled down. And remembered there was something in his hand for the beams to lock onto.

The apple shattered—but Gawain kept his eyes closed, still remembering.

No drumming of feet. No shouts. No applause. Nothing to break the silence until Arthur spoke. Gawain opened his eyes, surprised not so much by Arthur's words—he could barely understand them—but by their unmistakably cold undertone.

He realised Taliesin had won the game—*and saved his life surely?* He didn't dare hope. Gawain watched as the man took out a second arrow and raised an eyebrow at Arthur. Not a word was said, but the look on Arthur's face turned black.

The man threw the bow to the ground, picked up his harp and walked, through the oppressive silence, towards Gawain. *William Tell. That's what's happened. I've got into the legend of William Tell, the Swiss archer who refused to bow to a tyrant and who shot an arrow through an apple on a boy's head.* He wanted to cry. *Oh, Angie, I got to Swizzleland, after all.* He pulled up the thought. *I'm getting hysterical. Arthur was never in Switzerland—was he?*

Gawain looked down on him while Taliesin took out a dagger, sliced through his bonds and steadied him as he slumped. As an archer Taliesin had seemed so tall, so intimidating in the distance but Gawain realised now that he wasn't even as tall as he was, and his eyes were silver-grey, not like green smoke at all.

'I think we've ruined their fun, Gawain.' He winked.

How do you know my name?

'Can you walk?' Taliesin asked.

In a dizzying moment, Gawain recognised the voice of the air: this was the illusionist who'd set Arthur the riddle about what women want most. He was about to nod when a single word rang out. 'Gwalchmai…!'

His head jerked around, and he was astonished when Arthur's woman, Gwynhyvar—*Guinevere*, he realised—inclined her head towards him. Next moment, fierce as a hunting cat, she turned on Arthur and, with a vicious swing, slapped his face. A moment later, she stalked off in a fury, the women of the court tittering after her.

Taliesin's silver-grey secretive eyes turned coal-blue, as he smiled again. 'I was beginning to think it would never happen. Congratulations, Gawain. I think you've just created Camelot.'

22

JED HAD TAKEN CHARGE and, with that, Gawain felt a vast sense of relief. There was, he realised, no point in worrying about Reece, Cerylen and Vasily. If they were safe, there was no reason for concern and, if they weren't safe, there was nothing he could do.

So making music was a good idea. It took everyone's mind off their predicament. Jed gave Angie a pair of clapping sticks and a seed rattle, and Cardea a skin drum. He selected a long hollow tube of wood and handed it to Gawain. 'This is a llpirra if ya wanna practise a bit.'

'I thought that was a didgeridoo.'

'See the flare like a trumpet at the end?' Jed asked. 'That's the difference.'

Gawain put down the sword to take the llpirra and try an experimental blow. A faint whispering burble came out. 'I'm more into the sound engineer bit than the hands-on musical instrument thing.'

'Keep tryin'.'

After ten attempts, Gawain gave up, his lips swollen. 'Sorry, no can do,' he apologised.

Jed was setting the sound levels on his studio equipment. 'Course ya can.' His tone was adamant.

Probably I gotta fulfil some legend about Lion-skin Sky-eyes Fire-head and a llpirra. Gawain took a deep breath and tried again. A rattling echo came from the instrument. Another deeper breath. A full-throated roar rumbled through the pit.

Jed beamed, gave a thumbs-up and began slapping his thigh. 'Catch the rhythm, girls. Match the rhythm.'

Angie clapped her sticks together, Cardea set up a regular beat on the drum. Retro began an eerie wavering croon in time to the pulsing music. Jed picked up a didgeridoo and signalled Gawain to blow the llpirra. He fumbled the cue but the throb of the didgeridoo covered his mistake and together the two instruments created a climatic roar. The sound fell away in subdued waves, the beat of the drum slowed and the clapping sticks faded.

'Well…' Jed's smile was a sunburst of delight. 'Good trial run.' He paused the record button on his equipment. 'So deadly, in fact, I think this band needs a name.'

'This band needs to eat,' Angie muttered.

'Lemme think what's in the pantry.' Jed's brow wrinkled. 'I got witchetty grubs with pickled bush plums.'

Gawain blinked and tried not to react.

Jed burst into laughter. 'Ya should see yer faces.' His laugh degenerated to a splutter. 'Actually, I got a stockpile of beef jerky. And honey drops and granola bars and cans o' spam and spaghetti and meatballs and beetroot and pineapple and even Vitamin D.' He spluttered again. 'And a can-opener.'

'Water?' Cardea asked.

'I gotta atmospheric water generator. Plenty fer drinking. No baths, but.'

Can you end a sentence with 'but'? Still, Retro didn't react. 'Maybe the girls want to check out the stockpile, Jed, while I show you something.'

'Sounds like Secret Men's Business.' Jed reached towards a stack of boxes in the corner and picked up a can-opener. 'Here, girls, check out the food in the pile there while Gawain an' me find a corner ta try an' pretend ya cain't listen in.'

Angie folded her arms. 'Maybe the girls don't wanna check anything. Gawain, it is unchivalrous to keep secrets from family members.'

Jed folded his arms in imitation. 'I don't think ya understand the cultural concept o' Secret Men's Business.'

'I don't think you understand the cultural concept of *family*.'

Jed turned to Gawain. 'Ya sure ya're related, Speckly Boy? She totally lacks any cultural sensitivity. Unlike yerself.'

'She's blood, all right.' Gawain sighed and lifted his arm. Pulling up his shirt, he pinched the nano-jot from the skin under his armpit. 'I guess anyone who saw it thought it was a tracking device someone higher in authority had planted on me.' He held the nano-jot out and placed it on Jed's palm. 'But it's my music. I'd love to collaborate with you on *Galactic Tree*.'

Jed's sudden smile was a curve of unalloyed light.

'I've been thinking, Jed,' Gawain went on. 'Thinking a lot since the singalong at Memory Mountain, about songs. About the nature of music. About songs that heal trauma and abuse and suffering. I don't know how we could do it but I want it to be my life's work.'

Jed punched the air. 'Girls, ya wanna starve, ya can starve.' He waved them towards the stack of boxes. 'But me an' Gawain are gonna be busy fer a while.'

Still Retro didn't react.

Taking the nano-jot to the mixing desk, Jed inserted it into an audio plug. A few bars of music echoed around the chamber, then silence. A throaty whisper followed: '...*help me, Reece... the tree, Reece...*'

Gawain was baffled. 'That's not...' He paused. 'I don't know where that comes from.'

'I know,' Angie said. 'It's like your seashell.'

'What?'

'...*d...help me, Reece... the tree, Reece...*'

'Your seashell,' Angie said. 'It's just the same as when I listened to it.'

'...*do...help me, Reece... the tree, Reece...*'

'What seashell?'

'From your box of earth treasures. Maybe Mister Sharmika has copied all the secrets from your box onto the jot.'

'...*dont help me, Reece... the tree, Reece...*'

'That's kinda conflicting,' Jed said. 'Like a cry for help and a command not to.'

The faint background music rose in a sudden crescendo.

'That's a scryer's nightmare.' Cardea moved closer, listening for the drowned words. 'Equally weighted choices.'

'Not ta be offensive nor nuttin',' Jed remarked. 'But this ain't ya best work, Speckly Boy.'

'This isn't my work at all,' Gawain said. 'Who could have substituted...?'

Cardea stared at him, her expression registering horror. 'Take it out, turn it off—quick!'

Jed yanked the audio plug out and removed the nano-jot. It was stuck to his finger.

Cardea's breathing was heavy and erratic. 'We almost got squeezed into a force-line of single choice.'

Have we fallen into a trap...? Or just avoided it?

'What's that?' Angie pointed to a column of iridescent pastel bubbles cascading towards them. Drifting and falling, they expanded as they wobbled closer.

'Where'd they come from?' Gawain felt an urgent need to retreat. *Maybe a laser drill or a cold fusion cannon can't get in here, but bubbles can.* 'Don't let them touch you!' he barked at Angie as she bent forward. It was too late. The bubble popped.

> *'It's called "fletch". I'll play for winter and you play for summer.'*
> *'What are the rules?'*
> *'That depends on how seriously we are playing. Fletch is played to determine the winner in all sorts of contests. It may decide the fates of princes or kingdoms. Prisoners have gained their freedom through it. And lost their lives, too, of course.'*

'That's Emrys.' Jed sighed in obvious relief. 'The one askin' 'bout the rules. That means they're okay.'

'No, it doesn't.' Cardea's eyes were hooded. 'Those words are not from the present.' She lifted her face. 'They've turned the cyclotron on...'

'Look!' Gawain pointed to the doorway that led into the cyclotron. 'They're squeezing through the seal.'

'Something is wrong...' Cardea's voice was a dull monotone. 'Something they didn't expect. To do with the music we made. We've opened a gateway.'

She's not calculating probabilities. There's no way you could figure that info from mathematics alone. 'How do you know, Cardea?'

There was a hesitant pause. 'I have teleauditory skill.' She sighed and looked, downcast, at the floor. 'That's my secret. I've never told anyone before I can listen to conversations as much as three kilometres away. It helps me calculate probabilities.'

The bubbles moved up to the ceiling, but they were still coming.

'What about this gateway I've opened?' Jed seemed devastated. 'Everything I do goes wrong.'

'It wasn't *you*.' Gawain signalled him to move away from the advancing bubbles.

'They wanted the gateway opened,' Cardea said. 'Just not yet. They need the sword or the glove to negotiate it safely.' She paused, her burqa tilted, obviously listening. 'Something about a tachyon decelerator.'

A bubble drooped down from the ceiling, bursting as it slid over Jed's curls.

'It's an age-old riddle, whose answer would prove you wise enough to retain your kingship. The realm lies in the balance. If you cannot answer wisely, your kingdom is forfeit.'

'If...'

'Yes, if.'

'You delay, Knight of Summer Day. Your riddle?'

'It is the most challenging of all, Winter King—but under the circumstances the choice of difficulty is warranted: What do women want most?'

'I don't recognise 'em,' Jed said.

'I do.' An iron band locked around Gawain's heart. He held up the sword. The compulsion to leave was enormous. 'In a vision. About a dog-boy and King Arthur.' A surge of panic almost overwhelmed him. 'We gotta get outta here. *Now*.'

Cardea nodded. 'We have to be careful not to break the skins of the bubbles. They're different times.'

Skin of time? Hollë mentioned that. Has she done this?

Jed eyed Retro off. 'Ya gonna hafta find ya own way out, boy, coz I've only got a rope ladder at the end.'

Retro scattered the rocks he'd been guarding to reveal his hidden trophy. It was the severed hand in the silver glove. *Pleasedon'tletReecebedead. Songs... that heal...* Gawain realised Retro must have attacked Aanundus and Hollë just to get it. *Maybe that's why they activated the cyclotron—the sword and the glove are so close but also slipping beyond their grasp.* Then it dawned on him. 'Jed, they'll have stormtroopers roaming everywhere topside, waiting for us to appear. Remember the hunting dogs, heat-seeking trackers...'

'But if Cardea can hear three kilometres away, we can avoid them.' Jed picked up the glove. 'Y'know this place has lotsa magnetic and gravitational anomalies. So let's use 'em ta our advantage.'

23

'I THOUGHT YOU SAID THERE was a rope ladder at the end.' Gawain clambered up through a fissure at the end of a tunnel into a small sunlit cavern. He'd struggled to lead the way but Jed had insisted on being last. He wasn't sure he'd be able to seal the studio and block the bubbles from escaping but he was sure no one else could.

'Look around. Ya'll see it.' Jed's voice echoed up past Cardea and Angie still crawling through the tunnel with Retro.

'But there's a stairway.'

'Whaddya mean, a "stairway"?'

Gawain didn't answer. He took a deep breath, allowing the coolness of the cavern to dry his sweat. He held up the sword. *Just in case something wicked comes down the steps.* The stairway curved upward. Light shafted down from far above, giving the steps the look of gold-stippled glass. He went over to it and looked up the stairwell, feeling anxious. 'Uri?' he whispered, hoping against hope. *Please. Be here.*

Nothing. He counted the steps and went back to the tunnel. 'Fourteen steps and then it goes around a corner,' he reported to Jed.

No answer.

He looked down the crevice. Angie and Cardea should be at the top by now. *Where are they?* 'Angie? Cardea?'

No answer.

'Retro?'

No barking reply.

Gawain's anxiety rose several notches. 'Jed?' *Did I take a wrong turn? I must have climbed out too soon or too late. There must be another cave. The one with the rope ladder in.* A prickly sensation crackled over him. Music and fragments of a song drifted down from the top of the stairwell:

> Where is the sword of the summer stars?...
> How was the blade of the cherubim lost?...
> When did their countless sleepless eyes fall,
> away from their hallowed post?

A ripping sound—like a curtain being torn from top to bottom—echoed in the sudden silence following the song. Then a flutter of wings and harpsong voices seemed to come from an immense distance.

'Uri? Uri—are you there?'

He held up the sword, warding against any sudden attack. But it mysteriously left his hands, not dropping to the ground but floating up the stairwell in a strange rising tilt-and-tumble. He lurched for it but missed. It spiralled upwards. He bolted after it, thrusting his uninjured arm out to grasp the hilt but just missing three times. *Get ahead of it.* He scrambled up around the corner, trying to get well above it so he could catch it as it came past.

He was distracted by a shadow moving across the stairwell from side to side, back and forth, back and forth, back and forth... *It's a pendulum. Like an old-fashioned clock.* He surrendered all caution. 'Uri!' he yelled. 'Where are you? Jed! Angie! Retro! Cardea!'

DEA...DEA...DEA... The last syllable reverberated in the stairwell. It was so deafening, he panicked for a moment. Then a memory of Uri talking to Emrys hit him: *I thought you were building a time machine.* He took a shuddering breath. *Could this be it? A time machine built like a clock?*

The thought was absurd enough to calm him down. And as he took a deep breath, the sword floated into his hands and settled there. Exhausted, he dumped himself down on a step. *Pleasedon'tletthembedead. A hand in a silver glove. Sliced off. Like a severed tree branch.* He'd tried not to think of Emrys losing his hand but he started to shake at the memory. *Delayed shock. Gotta be it. And no Jed with his music to distract us.* He looked down the stairwell. *Where is Jed? Where is everyone? Did the bubbles catch them?*

He was about to head back down the steps when a word started to appear below his feet. Multitu...He watched then as gold letters appeared, one by one. Multitudes, they spelled out slowly, multitudes in the valley of decision.

A sudden muffled explosion caused the gold letters to shiver. Looking down, Gawain saw the step become a window. A red emergency light pulsed inside it. Two men in uniform, red stars on their collars, were arguing in a language he couldn't understand. 'Nyet, Arkipov!' one yelled. The gold letters shivered themselves free of the step, spun like autumn leaves around Gawain's head, and spiralled back down into the step to swirl around the men. Abruptly, the window closed, the step went dark.

The shadow of the pendulum was limned with a glow of light and, from behind the moving bob, stepped a huge white doggy shape. It lumbered down the steps towards him. 'Retro!' He was so relieved, he could have kissed the mutt.

But three steps away, it stopped. It wasn't Retro after all. It wasn't even a dog. It was a stag. And it was gazing at Gawain with dark liquid eyes, just like Uri's.

Once upon a time, a harpsong voice said, Innocence and Purity played together for truth. Innocence, of course, did not value truth, because to him it was so common. Purity, on the other hand, valued truth precisely because he'd found it to be so rare. Out of their mutual desire, they combined to give truth form as Truth, and out of their mutual fear, they combined to give form to strength of will as a guardian of Truth.

'How's that supposed to explain anythink?'

Angie! That's Angie's voice. She must be close by.

Ordinarily Innocence went by the name of 'Reece' and Purity called himself 'Tamizel'. The game they played was 'fletch'—they had no idea what they were doing when they agreed to play for truth. Unknowingly, they broke a seal and allowed Truth to take form. It became a tree. And it acquired a guardian.

'A guardian?' Angie sounded dubious.

A stag in a tree in a Wild Wood.

There was a pause, then Angie spoke again. 'Is the stag still with the tree? Or is it with Reece and Tamizel?'

It's always with the Tree.

'Can it be with the tree and Reece and Tamizel at the same time?' Angie persisted.

Three places at once? How would that be possible?

Again a pause. 'Well, it's kinda like this.' Angie's voice had a suspicious edge to it. 'I've thought about it. Every time we first meet one of your friends, they say: "Don't be afraid." And I remembered that's just like what was said to the shepherds watching their flocks by night, all seated on the ground...' A longer pause. 'So was that you, Uri? Were you there?'

The sword, Greyhawk. Protect it. Send it back to the Tree. Send it back to itself.

Uri's talking to me?

'You didn't answer,' Angie said.

Send it back to the Tree... back to itself.

Gawain hesitated. 'I don't know how.' He held the sword higher. *Maybe I'm supposed to drop it through a step. But am I allowing something to take form? Am I breaking another seal?*

The seal is already broken. That's why it's so important to put the sword beyond the reach of Hanundus.

At Uri's words, an image appeared in Gawain's inner eye. It was Jib, silhouetted against the sunset, raising the twisted horn to his mouth.

What have we done? We've moved the songlines. Was that how we broke the seal? He moved up the stairwell, step by slow step, looking for the appearance of golden letters or the opening of a window.

Up and up he went. A hundred steps. Two hundred. He stopped to rest, then went on. Another memory surfaced. *Destroy the sylvan throne. The tree within must be put to the axe.* 'What tree?' he asked, panting. 'The tree of Truth?'

At his words, golden firetongues began to lick along the edges of the sword. *Destroy the sylvan throne. Destroy the sylvan throne.* It became a drumbeat in his mind. *The Tree within must be put to the axe.* 'What tree?'

The Tree of If.

A new voice, patchy and sibilant, flickered across his thoughts.

The Tree of If and If Not. Ssurrender your choicess, Gawain, to your ssuperiorsss, to thosse wisser and more experienced.

Surrender my choices? Gawain sighed at the thought of such freedom. *To give them over would be such a relief...* The sword crackled with flames, almost hissing at him.

Did you just decide, Greyhawk, that freedom comes from giving up choice and being controlled by the choices of others?

You are forbidden to interfere.

Gawain shook his head, trying to clear it. He moved up the stairwell, desperate to see a window. *Send the sword into the past. That's what I choose.* He froze. Ahead of him, three sinuous necks appeared through the gap in the steps. *Kinda like giraffes.* Three green stick-legged horses clambered out and turned to him. *They don't look exactly friendly.* They bounded towards him, their hooves hardly touching the treads. Leaping over him, they got behind him and blew. Their breath was cold and blustery and, out of a dream, Gawain remembered what they were called. *Ettins.*

They blew him into the hole they'd come out of. It was so sudden he had no time to feel fear as he fell.

Fell into darkness.

Through darkness.

The fall was slow—so slow he thought at first that he was floating. He lost the sword as he rotated through a star field. It fell, too, glinting beside him.

He fell past galaxies, past comets, past nebulae like hair floating, past icy planets like white glittering nests.

The sword kept pace with him.

Gawain didn't feel in the least afraid. He was beyond fear. *How can I be falling without reaching bottom?*

Ahead of him was an immense shadow. A Tree. A Tree so huge that he realised its highest branches were actually above him, lost to sight. Beneath him he could see its lower limbs budding with stars. It was growing out of an endless floor of interlocking tiles. Tiles that were moving like a river, some shaped like golden darts, others kite-shaped. Tiles with words—names—on them. They swirled in eddies, or danced, or drifted lazily, or formed into currents rushing headlong across the starscape.

Looking up, the tiny figure of a white stag appeared at the top of the Tree. Effortlessly the stag was leaping down, branch after branch. The shadow of a dragon, dark enough to blot out the stars, hurtled towards the stag. And from the dragon's back an even darker shadow separated itself: a shapeshifting form that alternated between bee and spider and eight-legged horse.

Gawain realised the darker shadow was trying to intercept him. It shook the glittering star fruit, and they plummeted from the tree, as it sped towards him.

A voice like harpsong flowed over his mind: *This is Tau, the Tree of choice. The Tree of If. The Tree that grows in the space between time and eternity as they flow endlessly through each other.*

The dragon attacked the stag. Gawain realised it would be easy to become distracted by the battle. He had to prepare some kind of defence against the beespiderhorse. It was moving far faster than he was. 'Sword,' he begged. 'Don't let yourself be caught.'

With a cry, almost of joy, the sword leapt to his hand and—once again—golden flametongues flickered along its edges. *Can we go faster, sword? Reach the river of tiles first?*

The sword pulled him around, and like an arrow whizzing for an apple on a dog-boy's head, plunged into a vertical dive.

24

TALIESIN'S QUARTERS, TINY AND SNUG, were the warmest place Gawain had been in for months. A fire blazed in the hearth. There was a thick woollen screen covering the single narrow window, and a tapestry hanging from the stone ceiling. It depicted a unicorn, a centaur, a sphinx, a mermaid, and a rooster with a serpent's tail and a blazing eye.

'It's a basilisk,' Taliesin told Gawain without even looking up. 'It has a lethal glance that will turn you to stone. Of course there are many stranger things in heaven and earth than any of these. Though I didn't think I'd need to explain that to someone from the third millennium.'

How do you know where I'm from? And how do you know what I'm thinking? Another thought troubled Gawain—a tenacious thought he hadn't been able to shake, despite its blatant stupidity. *How can you possibly be William Tell?*

'I'm not William Tell, or William of Cloudslee or Earendel or Tyl or Toki or any of a dozen other heroes whose legends I seem to have been creating lately—without any intention on my part, I might add. I'm not even Taliesin, though the king calls me that. My name is Tamizel and I...'

He broke off as the incredulous thought popped into Gawain's mind: *You're Tamizel!?* An image of Holly saying Tamizel's eyes were never the same colour twice and that he called her 'Lady Death' formed in the forefront of Gawain's thoughts. The image shifted to the moment Holly, her eyecup twisting, struggled against the stormtrooper, and Reece collapsed at losing his hand.

Tamizel said nothing. As he got up to tend the fire, Gawain noticed a tremor in his hands.

You said I created Camelot. What did you mean?

'Why can't you talk, Gawain?'

Gawain opened his mouth and a croak came out. *I try, but nothing comes. I think I hit my head.* He recalled falling through a starfield, the sword pulling him down towards the Tree, the battle between the white stag and the dragon, the beespiderhorse hurtling to overtake him. The picture froze—Gawain felt it being seized as Tamizel focused on various parts of the image.

'That's the Storm-Tree of Ruēl I see in your mind. You've been there?'

The Tree of Tau, the Tree of If. The Tree of Choice that grows in the flow between Time and Eternity.

There was silence as they measured each other. 'It's a refuge of delight and wonder,' Tamizel whispered. 'The music of the stars to wake or lull me. Bliss and peace. A place where no dreams drown, where no hope withers or sickens. Still, it was not good to be alone. Not for so long.'

The vision of the Tree in Gawain's mind shifted and the stag came into sharp focus. And then a hidden memory surfaced. Not just the stag. The dragon too. Their battle had brought them to him, just as he reached the river of stars flowing out from under the Tree. On one side the beespiderhorse was stalking him and, just in front of him, the fight between the dragon and the stag halted as they both turned to him.

Usse the ssword ass a key, the dragon said. Open the gate.

'There is no gate,' Gawain answered, drifting along the star-swell.

Sstill hidden, the dragon hissed. Uwriy'el, the boy has the ssword—both passsword and key to the maze. You no longer have the right to keep the gate hidden.

A boy with a sword would certainly have right of access through the Gate to the Tree. But is he a boy? You planted a seed in his palm. A seed, I surmise, from the Fatal Tree. And you want him to go in and merge with the Tree of Life. I question whether he is human any longer.

Nothuman?nothuman?nothuman?Whatdoesthatmean?

You are too late to stop our long-laid play. That was the voice of the beespiderhorse and Gawain's heart contracted in panicked terror.

Greyhawk, you still have a choice. The Tree of If is the Tree of Choice. It's up to you whether this is the last choice you will ever have. The Fatal Tree has been creating a sylvan throne within you. In or out? That is your choice.

You will be condemned to mortality for this, Uwriy'el.

I doubt it, Hu. I have not told him what the choice signifies. I have not revealed what 'in' or 'out' portends.

'I have to make a choice without knowing what the options mean?' Dread flooded him.

In or out, Greyhawk?

In or out, boy?

In or out, Gwalchmai?

In...in...in...in...in...in...in... Everything in his heart wanted to choose *in*. Everything in his mind said *in*. Everything. 'Out,' he chose as he heaved the sword towards the Tree.

The pain of the fragmentation was so intense, the stars went black. 'So it was *you*.' Tamizel's tone was soft and questioning.

Me?

'There is no way out or in to the Tree, unless the Gate-Maze is opened by the sword. There was a moment when it flew in and I was able to use it to get out. And there, waiting for me, just beyond the Gate were Aanundus and Hollë.'

Why did you leave, if it was bliss and peace and all those things?

'I heard *her* voice,' Tamizel breathed.

Gawain knew he meant Holly.

'She was weeping, begging me to help. I didn't realise it was Hollë. Once you'd thrown the sword back to the Tree, Hollë and Aanundus knew that only someone inside the Gate could bring it back out. They couldn't get in. There is a Time Appointed for everything, Gawain, and I knew it wasn't time to leave the Tree. I tried to harden my heart, to close my ears, but the pleas were endless, endless, endless and finally I could bear it no longer. I left the Tree to help her and barely escaped.'

She's here? They're here?

'I haven't seen them. And I'd recognise Lady Death at once. The bee who looks like a spider or an eight-legged horse.'

Oh. Gawain swallowed. *Yes. Unless she's bitten Arthur. Why does he hate me so much? And Camelot—the dream of ages—it can't have been me that created it, not really?*

Tamizel stirred the embers with the poker, and the flames leapt up, accentuating the shifting shadows on the wall. 'Gawain, you're a very kind, decent boy in an unkind age.' His smile was slow and wry. 'Unfortunately for you, that means you're everything that Arthur isn't. Guinevere is smitten with you. Every woman here, if the truth be told, is smitten with you. Their conversation is all Gwalchmai this, Gwalchmai that. Did you see Gwalchmai open the door for me? Did you see Gwalchmai help the orphans? Did you see Gwalchmai carry the swill for the serving girl? And curiously Gwalchmai doesn't kiss and fondle and leap into bed as his just reward. He doesn't go around lifting skirts and grabbing legs and fondling backsides. And what's even more adorable is that Gwalchmai doesn't even know the girls are vying for his attention.'

They giggle at me!

'Because they like you. They're flirting. They're not laughing at you... they just love it when you blush and look at your feet.'

Gawain gulped, blushed and looked at his feet.

'What the age of heroes needs is a decent man, Gawain, and you're it.'

A memory flickered into the forefront of Gawain's thoughts. *Heroes? What the world needs is decent people, making the right decisions for the right reasons.* Gawain could recall a young man, blond and intense, speaking with subdued passion. He groped for a name: *Vasily.*

'It's been wondrous, watching how you have changed people's expectations here. And coming to realise it's not just in the here and now, it's for always. Forever.'

Butbutbut... it's all a mistake. I'm not anything special. I'm not even very nice... He paused, struggling to reframe his thoughts. *Why does Arthur hate me? I need to understand. If what you say about Guinevere is true, then it's no wonder he hates me. But is that it? Is that the only reason?*

'No, it's not the only reason.' Tamizel looked across as the woollen screen on the window banged in a stray breeze and the flames flickered. 'There's far more to it than you being irresistible to women, Gawain.'

Don't say that.

'The real reason Arthur hates you is because he believes you have the knowledge to destroy him.'

Why would he possibly think that?

'It's very hard to explain. The relationships here are so complicated.' Tamizel sat, poking the fire once more. 'Yrien, as I suppose you've realised, is Guinevere's father. Her mother was Yrien's first wife. His second wife is Morgan, Queen of the Picts, who has been in the North since late last year. Morgan is Arthur's half-sister. This makes Yrien both Arthur's father-in-law and his brother-in-law. Hence Arthur has a double claim for hospitality from him. And unfortunately for Yrien, Arthur's made full use of it. So much so in fact that he and his band have strained Yrien's generosity to breaking point.'

He's just sponging off Yrien.

'Correct. Now Yrien's wife, Morgan, has a sister, Morgause, Queen of the Orkneys. She's married to Lot who is the grimmest, most hatchet-faced warrior in all Britain. Famously flame-haired Gwalchmai was their eldest son.'

What's this "was" and why have I got his name?

'I'll get to that part shortly.' Tamizel held up a hand in reassurance. 'As is the custom in this century, Gwalchmai was fostered with close relatives—fostering has all sorts of advantages in this sort of society. It strengthens alliances, it provides for a broader education, it protects against a narrow and provincial outlook in a future king.'

You're not selling it well.

Tamizel ignored him. 'Now Gwalchmai was, of course, Yrien's nephew. But he was also Arthur's nephew. Moreover, because

Arthur's father, Uther Pendragon, was a cousin of Morgause's husband, King Lot of Orkney, then that made Gwalchmai Arthur's cousin as well as his nephew.'

Gawain's head was spinning. He couldn't keep up with who was who, let alone what their relationships were. *What's the bottom line?*

'Arthur has no legitimate son so, whatever way you look at it, his heir-apparent was his cousin and nephew, Gwalchmai. Who, unfortunately for him, was as popular as Arthur is unpopular.'

He killed him?

'No evidence. No body. Gwalchmai simply vanished one day. It had been a tremendous honour for Yrien to be entrusted with the upbringing of the Kingdom's heir-apparent. So, his shame and fear at Gwalchmai's disappearance was overwhelming. He couldn't bring himself to tell King Lot his son was missing. He just lived in hope, praying he'd eventually turn up. Naturally he suspected Arthur of foul play, but had no proof. And then one day, three months after Gwalchmai's disappearance, Yrien was out hunting. He saw a stag—a white stag with seven tines—and Yrien knew, as everyone does, that if he could capture such a magic stag and bring it to bay, it would have to grant him one wish.'

Everyone knows this? Gawain was dubious.

'Of course they do. So Yrien chased the stag a full day, up fell and down dale, over streams and through snowdrifts, leaving his companions far behind him. He ended up crossing the old Roman Wall several times, and then as the sun set, the stag hid in a thicket and flushed out a white fox. Yrien couldn't help it—his horse reared and charged after the fox. But the fox darted into an old rabbit warren and startled a white leveret. The white leveret bounded off, and the horse turned to chase it. Yrien tried to rein it in, but it wouldn't respond. The young rabbit raced to a hole in a tree and out shot a white mouse. The horse reared again, turning to chase the mouse, Yrien unable to stop it.'

Why do I get the really strong impression the white stag and the white fox and the white rabbit and the white mouse are all the same creature?

'You've a suspicious mind, Gawain. Just because it's the stuff of fairytales doesn't mean it's untrue. The mouse finally darted under a large rock and the horse stopped. Night had fallen and, as Yrien looked around him, he realised the rock belonged to the Circle-Of-Stones-Which-Cannot-Be-Numbered. Fearing evil at work, he tried to turn his horse but it wouldn't obey him. Then by the light of a full moon just lipping the eastern horizon, he saw the white mouse again, leaping towards a shadow in the centre of the circle. And so he saw you: a boy half-frozen in the snow. Such a mysterious sight, he said. No tracks in the snow, no footsteps. Just a boy, fallen from the sky. A boy covered in thorns.'

Thorns?

'Mysteriously the thorns weren't sticking into the boy, they were sticking out from under the skin.'

Eerk.

'In or out—that was the question everyone asked you. I don't think it was about the sword. I think it was about the thorn-tree inside you.'

'The Fatal Tree. I shouldn't be alive.'

'Yrien took you straight to the Wild Man and asked him to heal you. That's how I know what happened. Yrien thought you'd been poisoned by witchcraft. The thorns poking out of you and the fact you couldn't speak made him very suspicious. He hoped you were Gwalchmai and that the wish he wanted from the stag had been granted: Gwalchmai's return. You were the miracle he'd prayed for.'

And he never doubted?

'Of course he did, but never enough to alter his resolve. He brought you back to court, put you in his nephew's place, and punished anyone who dared suggest you were not the son of Lot.'

So Yrien does know I'm not Gwalchmai? I'm just a pawn in a game?

Tamizel shook his head. 'He truly believes you are the Mouse sent from heaven to help him thwart Arthur. He's left orders you're to be given whatever you want. Do you think a dog-boy in this land has the freedom you have? An ordinary dog-boy is a slave. Yrien's public face is bleak, but behind closed doors, he collapses laughing. Oh, how his little Mouse makes Arthur look like a brutal profligate fool. He knows Arthur's sponging off him, but there's nothing he can do about it. The laws of hospitality and kinship put him in an impossible position. On the one occasion he hinted that Arthur's men should possibly, maybe, conceivably, just perhaps be subject to the same rationing, what did Arthur do? He proclaimed a High King's Feast! Yrien was livid at first, but to his delight, it simply ended up with Gwalchmai the Silent Hawk being brought to the attention of an even wider, even more admiring audience.'

So you're really saying Arthur wants to kill me because he's jealous of me.

'Not at all, jealousy has nothing whatsoever to do with it. Arthur wants to kill you so his son can inherit the kingdom.'

INTERSTITIAL

VII

VASILY HUGGED HIS KNEES and glared at the locked door. He wondered if they had been left here to die. He wondered if they would be given food and water. At least, in the cooler environment underground, they could go for longer without sustenance. Or maybe just take longer to starve to death. He wasn't sure whether to be depressed or hopeful.

Reece seemed to have guessed the direction of his thinking. 'It could be worse.'

Vasily glanced at the stump where Reece's hand had been. The end was cauterised but it was weeping slightly. It looked painful—but Reece had not made a single complaint about it. His attitude was impressive. Almost Russian in its stoicism. 'True, it could be worse,' Vasily admitted. 'We could be dead already.' He scowled. 'I can see why the bad guys have kept you two alive, but I am not sure what they want with me.'

'That *is* a concern.' Holly's tone was so wry he wondered if she was teasing.

'A bigger concern is the fact they have not taken my laptop. Why would they not do that? Even with the shielding here, I think it will have external access.' Vasily glared at the door once more. 'I am going to risk it. Warn me if someone comes.' He flipped open the top of the laptop as Holly crawled over to sit beside him. As she looked over his shoulder, he typed moon~rose into the password box.

'That's very old-fashioned,' she said.

'An antique computer is, by its very nature, a highly efficient security feature.'

A moment later, the midnight blue petals of Eygul flickered onto the screen. 'I've missed you, Sily,' the rose said. 'Where've you been?'

'Cut it out, Eygul. I am sure you have been busy disobeying me. What have you found?'

'Magnetic and gravitational anomalies…'

Holly rolled her eyes.

'…on an unprecedented scale.'

Reece whistled. 'They're trying to power a time machine. We have to stop them.'

'Stop them?' Vasily said. 'We are not exactly in a position to do so.'

'What if Aanundus or Hollë has already used the time machine?' Holly asked. 'They could control history. Take over time.'

'Exceedingly unlikely,' Eygul sniffed.

'But suppose someone did time-travel,' Holly said. 'How could we find them?'

'The chances are so infinitesimally small as not to warrant consideration. The bad guys can make nefarious plans but implementing them is virtually impossible.'

'*Virtually* impossible?' Holly insisted.

'Humour me, little blue rosey thingie.' Reece held up his cauterised stump. 'I've been wounded. Let's say that, theoretically, someone travelled into the past. How would you locate them?'

'Little blue rosey thingie!' Eygul's sniff was haughty. 'Apart from the inherent difficulty of finding a singularity with an exit as well as an entrance, the problem is that, if a time traveller moves only through time within a space-time continuum, then he'll wind up only in space. This is because the universe isn't a static entity and, if you go back a thousand years in time, the Earth will have regressed a thousand years away in space as well. In other words you will find yourself exploding in the vacuum between the stars, many trillions of kilometres from Eric the Red's longboat. Or wherever you wished to be.'

'Oh.' Vasily hadn't entirely understood Eygul's information, but he'd got the gist of it. And the gist wasn't good. 'But suppose you had a magic sword. That would make a difference, would it not?'

'It's not *magic!*' Holly exclaimed.

Eygul ignored her outburst. 'The properties of magic swords are, by nature, magical. Peculiar. Unusual. However, it is exceedingly doubtful that one of those magical, peculiar or unusual properties would include the ability to whizz a time traveller across the spatial discrepancy to any sort of safety, let alone to Eric's dragonship.'

Vasily refused to be deterred. 'What if the sword could open interstitial doorways?'

'Perhaps. But the conditions for activating *that* sword are so many that it would be easier to teleport through that door over there.' Eygul was scornful.

Vasily leaned back, breathing hard. 'So there is such a sword?'

'Of course,' Eygul said. 'The flaming sword of the cherubim opens a gate between time and eternity and allows access to the Two Trees.'

'Chair rub bin?' Vasily asked.

'Cherubim,' Eygul corrected. 'A cherub is a type of angel. One of the highest ranks. Allegedly higher than thrones, lower than seraphim.'

Vasily was silent.

Reece's gaze met Holly's. 'It must be the same sword. There can't be lots of swords that burn. And it did burst into flames when Gawain touched it.'

'But an *angel's* sword?' Holly sounded dubious. 'Why would an angel need a sword?'

'To guard the gate that leads to the Tree of Life,' Eygul said. 'Once the Two Trees were together. But the Fatal Tree has walked free and now takes up residence wherever it's welcomed. The two must never be rejoined, lest evil become immortal.'

'That's what Aanundus wants!' Reece exclaimed. 'To be deathless. To be able to roam time at will and change what he likes and never be at risk of losing his life.'

Holly's lips formed a thoughtful pout. 'Is the gate guarded by the sword the same as the gate between time and eternity?' she asked Eygul.

'Indubitably. Paradise is in eternity; the fallen world is in time. The borderland between the two is the gate in question. The gate is warded by the sword of the cherubim.'

Several seconds of intense silence followed. 'You want my advice?' Eygul shook virtual dew from its petals. 'Having ascertained the drift of these questions, my recommendation would be to escape, go into hiding and get a new identity. Are you listening, Sily? Are you taking this in? You are my little cabbage, my pet human. I'd hate to lose you. So read my petals. Cherubim are not to be trifled with. Cherubim can kill with a careless look. And you will know when you meet one because clearly there is a protocol in heaven. First contact, first words: *Don't be afraid.*'

Holly held up her hands. 'But he doesn't have wings!'

'What?' Reece looked baffled.

'Uri,' Holly said. 'Remember what he always says when first meeting anyone?'

'So what? I don't believe he's an angel!'

'Good,' Eygul said. 'Forget I said anything, Sily, and for one very simple reason. Angels are messengers but the presence of any of the cherubim indicates a disaster of the highest magnitude.'

'That's his name! Uri Messenger.' Holly's voice had become a subdued whisper.

'What about Mike and Jib and Ravi?' Vasily asked. 'Are their names Messenger too?'

'Ah!' Egyul huffed. 'Nicknames. Not very good ones either, if they're trying to disguise themselves. I should have realised before this. Uriel, Michael, Gabriel, Raphael… So do you want the good news or the bad news?'

'The good news.' That was Reece and he sounded uncertain.

'They're not cherubim.'

'And the bad news?' Vasily asked.

'They're archangels, Sily. So take my advice. Go back to your father's farm in Siberia and take me with you. *Now.*'

'You know I am an orphan.'

'I could fake some identity papers for you.'

'Eygul, you forget, we are stuck. We are in an underground base in Central Australia and the bad guys have us locked up.'

Eygul made a noise—it sounded like a yelp—then curled into a tight bud. 'I never considered the possibility we were caught in the middle between opposing groups of angels. How naïve of me.'

'Do not be such a snivelling coward,' Vasily snapped. 'For once, you are wrong, Eygul. How can you possibly turn religious on me? Angels are mythological creatures. They do not exist. They are a delusion of those who need spiritual comfort.'

'Pity about that,' Reece sighed. 'Because an angel with a miracle would be real handy right about now.'

25

GAWAIN'S BROW FURROWED IN THOUGHT. *Huh? Wait! Back up. Didn't you say before that Arthur doesn't have a son? Isn't that why his nephew is his heir?*

'I said he doesn't have a legitimate son.' Tamizel threw another log on the fire. 'The youngest brother of Gwalchmai, Mordred, is not Lot's son, but Arthur's. Lot has always suspected his wife's unfaithfulness but he's never had proof of it.'

Huh? Back up again. Wasn't Lot's wife one of Arthur's sisters?

'Exactly. Now you see why Arthur hates you? He's terrified you really are Gwalchmai and that you know Mordred is really his son, and he's terrified you're going to use that against him.' Tamizel raked the coals against the sides of the log. 'It would be the end of him, Gawain. Despite the fact that violence and rape are everyday occurrences here, they're not condoned by the common people—and neither is incest. There's no doubt the people would turn against him for good. Already there are murmurings that the endless winter is a punishment because the king has offended heaven in some unknown but terrible way. There were warnings, they say—two lion-lights in the sky, then total darkness. Not to mention the fall of firestones, the elfshot and glass arrows that dropped from the sky and the great waves that drowned the cities of the coastline.'

Lion-lights? Firestones? Elfshot?

'Yes: two comets, one of them Halley's, the darkness of a total solar eclipse, then a rain of meteorites and tektites, a tsunami. There were volcanic eruptions, possibly the result of the meteorite impacts. This is a time of great catastrophe, Gawain: all over the world kingdoms are falling because the people of every land are looking to their rulers and pointing the finger of blame. In China, a portent of fighting skydragons was seen. It was observed here too, but the supporters of the Pendragon were clever enough to claim it as an omen of destiny for Uther's son, Arthur. In China, the Emperor has lost the mandate of heaven—a great dynasty has fallen.'

This is legend.

'No, this is history. History recorded in the trees. It was because of the trees that scientists were first able to convince historians that the records of the winter without end were not fanciful legends but accurate fact. Because the growth rings in the trees said so.'

The trees. Gawain shivered with sudden cold, despite the rising heat from the fire. *In or out? The Tree of Life. The Fatal Tree. Weaving its thorns into a sylvan throne. Is it really gone?*

'The sylvan throne? It sounds like something from my own planet, Dreamfall. Almost like the Coronation Tree. Or one of the Trees of the Year.' Tamizel frowned. 'How could they come here? With Lady Death? With Hollë?' He paused. 'You're right, Gawain. If she has found her way here, she'd go for Arthur. He's weak but he's no fool. He's learned from his father's mistakes. Still, with her backing, he might be willing to risk acknowledging Mordred. He needs some great power behind him—dark or light—or he'll be deposed. And he desperately wants his son on the throne after him. He doesn't want the sword-in-the-stone trick to have to be repeated. It's too unchancy.'

It's a trick?

'Of course it is. Sleight-of-hand, careful conjuring, a few judicious bribes. Very risky business, though, not to be attempted twice. So to ensure Mordred's position, Arthur has to get rid of the sons of Lot by guile and stealth, one by one by one. Then, when only Mordred is left, Arthur can make him his heir without any difficult questions being raised.'

Does Yrien know about Mordred?

'No.'

Does Yrien know about you?

Tamizel shrugged. 'He thinks I come from some magical otherworld; that I'm a denizen of the perilous realm of faery where time stands still. The concept of a spacetime continuum is too hard to explain.'

He's afraid of you.

'True.' Tamizel nodded. 'And it's helped my spectacularly meteoric rise at his court. He hopes I'm enchanter enough to keep Arthur in check. He's about to gift Arthur a round table, just because I suggested it. I'm not exaggerating when I say you've ushered in Camelot, Gawain. Guinevere's told Arthur it's all over between them unless he begins to act with the dignity of a monarch—and he knows she means it.'

I didn't think women had much power in this era.

'Quite the contrary. She's holding an ace: she's Yrien's daughter. And that means Arthur can't feed his troops without her. Four years ago Yrien took heed of the signs in the sky and, realising bad times were coming, sold most of his treasures, stripped his kingdom, taxed his nobles until they bled, and bought grain and wine, salted meat and live cattle, goats, sheep and cows. Now his wealth is restored ten times over, and the nobles who called him a tyrant proclaim him a saviour.'

Why doesn't he become high king?

'He's come to prefer peace to war. In fact, Yrien's troubles started when he called for Arthur's help after his granaries were repeatedly raided. Rationing had begun, and many people felt cheated. When Arthur first came here, he was little better than a mercenary. Still, he'd begun to style himself "Protector of Britain". He'd gathered a band of ambitious men and they all knew a good thing when they saw it. No one ever really knew when Arthur started paying court to Guinevere whether he lusted after her, or her father's storehouses.'

But if Guinevere really is smitten with me—Gawain blushed— *Arthur will kill me anyway.*

'It's undeniable he'll try. Your charming manners do pose a tremendous threat. But don't worry. Jed and I have a plan underway to make sure he never sees you as a rival again.'

Jed? Gawain wasn't sure why but a cold frisson snaked up his spine. A tremendous rush of surprise stampeded through his thoughts. *An underground room with a music studio and a selection of didgeridoos.*

Tamizel clapped his hands. 'I'd forgotten you have to know Jed.' His laughter was chiming and bell-like. 'Haven't you recognised him?'

Recognised him?

'I guess you haven't. Seems he was right when he thought you'd lost your memory. Oh, I'm going to have such fun telling Angie. She kept telling Jed that Gwalchmai couldn't possibly be her brother, no matter how hard he tried to convince her. Not a hope, she said. No female's looked twice in Gawain's direction. Ever.'

Oh yeah? An image of a burqa-clad girl and a petal-light touch on his arm surfaced in Gawain's memory. *Think again, sparrow.*

DOVERYAY, NO PROVERYAY. Vasily scowled at the computer screen. *How can I trust Eygul when it descends into religious mumbo-jumbo? Verification is impossible.*

'Why don't you believe in angels?' Holly asked. 'You didn't hesitate to ask about "magic" swords, after all.'

'Good question,' Eygul piped up. 'I'd like to know too.'

Because I did not mean 'magic'. It was just a figure of speech. 'Stay out of this. Why should I tell you? You are such a conceited cyber-rose.'

The blue petals performed an excellent imitation of a shrug. 'Conceited? Sily, I'm wise to your game. You're just trying to insult me to divert our attention from the rabid inconsistencies in your faith system. You can believe I am the construct of an alien from another planet. And you can believe Reece and Holly have been to Alpha Centauri. But not angels?'

Before Vasily could say a word, Reece raised his good hand in a fist. 'I thought so!'

'Me too!' Holly nodded at him.

'What?' Vasily was baffled.

'Little blue rosey thingie just gave itself away,' Reece said. 'The only way an alien construct could know we'd been to Alpha Centauri is if it's a sharva.'

'Exactly!' Holly nodded. 'Are you Sharmika?'

'Am I Sharmika? What do you think?'

Holly pressed her lips together. 'I think that Tamizel made you to be everything he wasn't. I think that just as you got me to trust you on sight by appearing as a bird, you chose to be a blue rose to get Vasily to trust you on sight.'

'You have a great imagination, *malyshka*. My rule is *doveryay, no proveryay*. I did not trust Eygul *on sight*.'

'Yes, you *did*!' A frenzy of spinning petals tumbled out of the screen and formed into a spindly-legged bird with a silver whirligig atop a multi-coloured cap. Sharmika stepped around the room and cocked its head, inspecting the walls. 'We need a plan.'

Reece's eyes rolled. 'I remember your last plan,' he mumbled. 'Crashing into the wall of the citadel and leaving us to think you were dead!'

'Don't be like that!' Sharmika said. 'It worked to get us in to Aanundus' lair, didn't it?'

Vasily folded his arms. 'I hate to admit this but I do not even know what you are. I have no idea what a sharva is. I have been hoping to figure it out eventually, but I have failed.'

'A sharva,' said Holly, 'is a collection of disconnected fragments of unfinished thoughts.'

'Not to mention,' Sharmika said, 'the odd couple of interrupted musings.'

'Thoughts and musings?' Vasily sounded incredulous.

'All creation originates in thought,' Sharmika said. 'I'm merely a rather nifty exemplar of the process.'

'You said that once before,' Reece murmured.

'Yeah!' Sharmika bounced with glee. 'Just before I convinced you to blow up the tachyon decelerator mesh on Alpha Centauri.'

Vasily butted his head against his knees. 'Angels, aliens. Other planets. What does this mean?'

Sharmika's whirligig began spinning. 'Are you serious?'

'Have you ever known me to be less than serious?' Vasily glowered. 'Angels, aliens, other planets: of course I want to know what it means.'

'So it was a genuine question?'

'I am Russian. I do not ask frivolous questions. And I am not afraid to show my ignorance. Why are you interrogating me about my motives?'

'Because you asked the Grail Question.'

'Grail Question?'

'Yes: *"What does this mean?"* The Grail Question unlocks healing, both for the king and the land.'

Vasily palmed his face. 'First it is mythical angels, now it is mythical history. I cannot believe this.' He shook his head. 'The only thing I want the Grail Question to unlock is answers but that is obviously a hopeless request.'

'Not at all. You've given the password.'

'The password?' Holly asked.

Sharmika waggled its wings. 'Yes! The password is *whatdoesthismean?*'

'Isn't the Grail from the legends of King Arthur?' Reece asked. 'See, I'm named Emrys for Merlin and, once-upon-a-time on Alpha Centauri, I could say to myself, *no, Merlin is not real.* The

Merlin figure is just a nice metaphor for living backwards in time and being trapped in a memory of fear and pain. The essence of what it means to be a "Merlin" is to hold on to grudges and fail to forgive.' He pouted at Holly. 'Right, sis?'

'We wouldn't be here today if you didn't learn to stop being a "Merlin". And dad too.'

"But I'm starting to feel there's more to this than I ever want to know. Like maybe Merlin and Arthur have more to do with this than we realise.'

'Wanna meet him?' the sharva cackled.

'Who?' Holly asked. 'Arthur or Merlin?'

'Both.'

Vasily's pale brows narrowed. 'You *are* serious.' His lips compressed in a thoughtful line. 'You are *really* serious. Really *really* serious. You can take us back in time?' He drew a deep breath. 'You said it would be exceedingly unlikely anyone could travel back in time.'

'Quite true.'

'Then what was all that about Eric's dragonship?'

'I was merely pointing out the problems.' Sharmika's whirligig began to undulate. 'And I did also point out that there is a way to enter the interstitial flow and access the Tree.'

'Something absurd about an angelic sword.'

'Which has time-slipped into the past. With a bit of help from the gravitational and magnetic anomalies around here.'

'The past.' Holly drummed her knees. 'That's how you got here, isn't it?'

'What do you mean?'

'I wondered how Tamizel could send you to us. If he couldn't leave the Storm-Tree, how could you? He did find a way to leave, didn't he? But he didn't get to our time. He's trapped in the past.

That's worse than being trapped in the Tree. Yet the past is where he made you. You've been waiting centuries for us.'

Reece exchanged glances with her. 'How old are you, Sharmika?'

'Quite young by angelic standards. Roughly a millennium and a half.'

'You have come from the Dark Ages?' Vasily asked.

'Don't make it sound like I'm a primitive, ignorant peasant!' In a puff, Sharmika disappeared and a circlet of blue petals fluttered back into the screen. 'It was a most terrible time, I assure you. I was glad to get beyond it. Definitely cataclysmic.' Eygul's petals drooped. 'Cometary debris crashed into the earth and the atmosphere filled with dust, creating a veil over the sun. There were no stars, no moon. No summer either; crops failed and famine stalked the entire globe. In Italy, it was called the "years of the blue sun". In China, strange yellow snow fell and nearly eighty percent of the population died in a single year.' The blue of Eygul's petals paled, as they curled and buckled in some cyber equivalent of frost. 'England became a wasteland. A traveller could cross the entire country and never meet a soul. Every village was deserted. The Vikings believed the fimbulwinter had come—the enchanted winter that heralds the end of the world. To them it was the rule of the frost giants, before whom even the gods themselves bowed.'

'Frost giants!' Vasily sneered.

'How about you consider them as aliens with a physiology that draws heat from the air around them and chills the atmosphere?'

Vasily frowned, his sneer vanishing.

'After the world endured the abnormal winter for three whole years, a greater terror was unleashed on the survivors in Europe.'

'Terror?' Holly asked.

'The prolonged intense cold unlocked a plague virus,' Eygul said. 'By the end of it very few people were left alive. The trauma that birthed the Dark Ages has been engraved deep in mankind's soul. The legends of King Arthur were kindled then. The knights of the Round Table formed their fellowship, Camelot was dreamed into being, courtesy began to replace barbarity. Arthur, when all's said and done, was no more than a petty warlord, and his final battle at Camlann wasn't over any ideal, or even power or land or gold. It was over food.'

Vasily shivered as a vision of Gawain—cold, scarecrow thin, starving—flashed into his mind's eye.

'The tales of Arthur,' Eygul went on, 'finish with the Quest for the Holy Grail. But the Grail Quest was nothing more than the search for an unfailing, bountiful food supply in a winter-locked land.'

Vasily glanced at Holly's face and thought she was envisaging nightmare. He certainly was. 'Relax, *malyshka*. It cannot be true. There is no way Aanundus would risk turning on the machine if there was any chance of sending Gawain and the sword back to the Dark Ages.'

'You think I'm lying?' Eygul demanded fractiously. 'Or mistaken?'

'*Za maal cheevaats*,' Vasily said.

Eygul curled into the velvet blue background of the screen.

'I did not mean it like that,' Vasily said, 'and you know it too.'

With a quiver, a rosebud re-reappeared and revolved a half-circle.

'Don't turn your back on me, you petulant accretion of digital petals.'

'How rude!' Eygul maximised in an instant to full-bloom. 'Next time you tell me to "shut up", farm boy, I will—permanently.'

'Vasily's just trying to stop us worrying,' Holly told Eygul.

Blue petals fluttered. 'You've put your metaphorical finger exactly on the essence of his treachery. He doesn't believe we can get Gawain or Tamizel out of the past without a miracle. And he doesn't believe in them.'

Vasily took Holly's hand. 'Out of the past? A miracle?' He tried to keep all sarcasm out of his tone. 'We will just make one, *malyshka*. We have the technology and we have the talent. We do not need to rely on non-existent angels.' He pulled her to her feet. 'All we need is the opportunity.'

26

GAWAIN WAITED SO LONG for Tamizel on the bench he dozed off, drifting in and out of a restless, dream-ridden sleep. He had been longing to know where Angie was—but there had been no chance for Tamizel to tell him before an urgent shout of 'Taliesin!' had sent him hurrying to attend Yrien.

Gawain's dreams were of Angie. Of being with her in the animal byre, in the keeping of Cradoc and Illtyd. He could hear them whispering outside the wattle walls, planning tortures. Angie was dressed so strangely in red and crowned with gold. She held a book that turned into a fox, and her crown turned to roses. She looked so terrified. Then somehow he knew it wasn't her at all. She was the basilisk staring balefully back at him… and his heart stopped.

The beespiderhorse had become a basilisk. A moment later he was awake, his eyelids jerking open, his heart thudding madly. He didn't move. He stayed rigid, looking up at the tapestry. *Only a dream.* But the whispers continued.

Cradoc and Illtyd again?

No. Gawain soon realised it was the Wild Man. 'Sit down. Ya look terrible, Tamizel. Whaddya need? Food? Drink? Ya shouldn't drive yourself this hard.'

'I'm just tired, Jed. Getting the right resonance of mind to read thoughts is very draining. Particularly when they're Arthur's thoughts. They dart so fast it's hard to follow them.'

Jed? Gawain held his breath. *He's the Wild Man? But... he's old... like twenty-five... how could...*

'Why on earth wouldya wanna read Arthur's thoughts, Tamizel? I'd rather sit in his pigsty.'

'I wanted to know where Excalibur came from, Jed. So I told him I was writing a song about it, and asked him to describe the Lake where he found it floating so miraculously. The story's changed again. What he claims now is a shaft of heavenly light, the music of the spheres, and a woman's arm clothed in white samite, holding the sword aloft for him to take.'

'Don't be so cynical. So he made up a story ta impress the commoners. Don't mean he stole it. Better men than Arthur have created propaganda ta serve their legend.' There was a laugh. 'Better men bein' me naturally. I'm the embodiment of Heroflix's doco series on Merlin the riddlemaster.'

'Jed, it's not the same. You're not harming anyone. But Arthur is. Excalibur is *not* his sword. The Farafolk—my people—called it Mistblade. It was one of our Hallows of Kingship. I thought I recognised it; I dismissed the thought as impossible. Besides the shape's slightly different and the tip's completely changed. It came to us from Hollë, Lady Death. Only now it's occurred to me to wonder how it came to be hers...'

'Ya know, Tamizel, I've always thought ya were someone lost in time, like me, contendin' with mysterious forces we don't understand. This otherworld ya say ya come from, I thought it was just a Many-Coloured Dreaming or mebbe another century with its own customs. But it's not, is it?' Jed's sigh was deep and weary. 'I'm gettin' old. First day I arrived, I didn't think I'd last a week. A year later, I still felt that way. And now years have passed, and I've fitted in. But I still have days when I feel I can't go on.'

It really is Jed. He just got here before I did. And he's been looking after me... just about the whole time. He must have healed my skin of the thorns because I don't remember that time at all.

Gawain heard Jed pour himself a drink. He peeked out through his eyelashes, watching Jed sit with a goblet in his hand, staring into it. At last, he grimaced then sipped a little before speaking. 'So tell me then, how did our illustrious High King get his grubby hands on this sword o' yours?'

'It isn't mine,' Tamizel corrected.

Gawain felt his nearness, secretly, on the edge in his own thoughts, and at once he knew this story was as much for his benefit as it was for Jed's. 'What happened to the sword happened because Arthur was so mightily put out by Yrien's story of chasing a magic stag, and ending up finding Gwalchmai in the middle of Long Meg's circle of stones. Arthur didn't believe a word of it.'

'The story's been embellished a bit with the mouse an' the rabbit, but it seems more or less true.'

'Jed!' Tamizel exclaimed. 'You aren't that gullible. You've learned the language; you've created a legend; you've saved countless lives. You've got to know Gwalchmai looks nothing like Arthur's nephew, except for blue eyes and red hair. His muteness is far too convenient. So, although some people think otherwise, Arthur trusts Yrien about as much as Yrien trusts him. Being not at all. The story of the magic stag simply convinced Arthur the time had finally come to openly challenge his father-in-law.'

'Now that I do believe.'

'But,' Tamizel went on, 'in what I can only think of as an evil prompting, Arthur was persuaded to first check the ring of stones—something no-one else had had the audacity to do. And there he found something Yrien had missed in the darkness of the night and his own fear: a sword, half-protruding from the snow. He realised at once it wasn't any ordinary weapon—and he didn't want anyone else claiming it.'

'But ya had it when ya escaped from Hollë an' Aanundus. How did it get ta the stone circle, when ya were found at the weir?'

'I lost it when I came through the skin of time to this era. And, for whatever reason, the sword seeks Gwalchmai. It went to the place in the land that resonates most strongly of his presence. And because he found it there, Arthur believes it really is Gwalchmai's. But he doesn't want the Pretender claiming it. Hence his concoction of ever more fanciful tales about how he came to possess it.'

'The Pretender?'

'That's how he regards Gwalchmai.'

'I heard a story about ya an' Gwalchmai when I came in. The whole court's buzzin' with it. Ya threatened ta kill Arthur.'

Tamizel sighed. 'I didn't threaten at all. I just hinted that was what the second arrow was for.' He sighed even more deeply. 'I guess now I'm going to have to write the Lay of Excalibur in all its extravagant absurdity as my peace offering to him. He'd have killed me then and there, but for the fact his relationship with Yrien is so shaky nowadays. Doesn't do to kill the raven king's bard, even if you are High King.'

'Ya may be untouchable, Tamizel, but ya shouldn't provoke Arthur. Don't matter what the temptation is. What if he takes his revenge on Gwalchmai instead o' ya, before we can help the kid?'

'You're right, Jed. It was a stupid thing to do. But I was just raging inside. I wanted him to feel afraid. The way he makes others feel afraid.' Then a peal of laughter followed. 'Speaking of those who dominate others, I'm going to enjoy The Goldenhand's discomfiture. Gwalchmai's name really is Gawain. Gawain Aishdene. You were right all along.'

There was silence, complete and total, for almost a minute. Gawain didn't know what to do, so he didn't move. He just caught his breath and held it. At last Jed spoke again. 'It's so sad.' A long exhalation of breath followed. 'He was such a brilliant muso. And I prob'ly haven't protected him enough. Just teased him about bein' a dog-boy.'

Gawain could hardly believe it. He wanted to jump up and protest, *butyoudidprotectme and youdidhealme*, but he couldn't. For the first time he felt guilty and not just frustrated at not being about to speak.

'I s'pose I could find a surgeon fer him. They're not medieval quacks like Heroflix made out.'

'He doesn't need a chirurgeon, Jed. He simply needs to get Mistblade back.'

'Huh? Whatfor? Don't get it.'

'Speech, words, tongue, sword. It's a simple equation really.'

'Tamizel, sometimes ya talk like ya come from another planet.'

'But I do, Jed. I do.' A long sigh followed. 'And I've gleaned enough from Gawain's thoughts to realise another thing you've been right about all along.'

'Me, *right? Again?* Ya don't say. Should I quit while I'm ahead? My track record is gettin' far too impressive.'

'I've got to make a sharva, Jed, whatever it is. Apparently I *have* made a sharva... or maybe two. So I better get to work... I sent one to Holly on Dreamfall and I sent one—which might be the same one—to deliver messages to Gawain. Trying to stop all this from happening. Although the plan was an obvious failure, perhaps it did some good. Who knows?' Tamizel clapped his hands. 'There seems to be a blue rose. And a bird. You wouldn't happen to know what they are made of?'

'No,' Jed admitted. 'But if I had ta guess, I'd say they were prob'ly made o' songs.'

INTERSTITIAL

IX

VASILY FLATTENED THE LID on his laptop as the metal door slid open. Miss Hale, shooting a wary glance backwards over her shoulder, stepped into the room and moved aside. Her back was against the wall, her gun up, as the door shut.

Good spot. Vasily tapped his fingers against his knees. *To see us and to spot anyone coming into the room.*

No one spoke for a full minute. Then she put the gun down. 'Talk.'

No one said anything. Another half minute went by. 'I am not necessarily against you,' she whispered. 'I may be able to help you. But the price is information.'

Doveryay, no proveryay? This is not the time to test it. 'How about you start by gaining our confidence and explaining why the sudden about-turn, dear Witchiepoo?'

'Has anyone ever called you completely impertinent?'

'Believe it or not, *razvaluha*, this is the first time. I have been called many things but never impertinent.'

'I'm trying to help you, *svolach*. Insults are unnecessary.'

Vasily shrugged.

'I find it difficult to believe that you are the diabolically cunning terrorists I've been told,' Miss Hale said. 'Or that, as a hardcore activist group, you have masterminded a takeover of world financial systems and are presently holding various governments to ransom.'

'Reece!' Vasily tutted and looked at the ceiling. 'And you did not tell me! You were going to deprive me of my share, were you not? Keep it from me? I am wounded, truly wounded.' He turned to Miss Hale. 'How much, by the way, are we asking in ransom?'

She ignored him. 'I don't believe most of you knew each other until a few days ago. So, regardless of your genius IQ, I'm doubtful you could form a criminal gang of such calibre so quickly. Especially while you were building air coolers and rigging up communication outlets and heading into town to stock up at a supermarket. Where, for a start, did you find the time?'

'You forgot to mention our bug-squishing program,' Reece said. 'What does your boss happen to say in answer to this question? Or didn't you ask his reptilian highness?'

'He says you ducked in and out of interstitial time.'

'Whoah!' Holly nudged Reece. 'Do you think he actually believes that?'

'That's the issue.' Miss Hale's eyes narrowed as she focussed on Reece. 'He sounded genuine. He said he shot your hand off to stop you opening a time gap and escaping.'

Bad guy gloating? Sounds a bit too clichéd. 'He just volunteered all this information to you?' Vasily tried his best not to sound sceptical.

'Of course not.' Miss Hale sniffed. 'I overheard an argument. That woman who did the Celyren illusion told him how stupid he was to lose the glove. There was a nuclear meltdown of a screaming match while they threw accusations at each other.'

'They've lost it?' Holly asked.

'The dog took it.'

Reece grinned. 'Oh, Retro, you *are* a genius.'

'Well, that changes the power dynamic, doesn't it?' Holly said to him. 'If Gawain's got the sword and Retro's got the glove, then Aanundus and Hollë won't be able to create a tachyon decelerator mesh.'

'I don't think that's their priority.' Miss Hale squatted down, eyeballing each of them in turn. 'Chixiff told the shapechanging woman that everything was going according to plan. *Exactly* according to plan.'

'Chixiff? Who is Chixiff?' Vasily asked.

'You call him Aanundus. Pythagoras Chixiff is the man who shot off Reece's hand. If he is a man.' Miss Hale paused. 'That's my question: is he human?'

Holly glanced at Reece, as if for approval. 'Not last time we met him.'

'And where was that?'

'A small planet called Dreamfall in the Alpha Centauri star cluster.'

'I see.' Miss Hale raised her eyebrows.

'I wouldn't believe us, either,' Reece said.

Miss Hale moved towards the door. 'What's a tachyon decelerator mesh?'

'It's a key to opening the interstices in time.'

'Time travel?'

'I wouldn't believe that, either, if I were you.' Reece shrugged. 'But think about it.'

'Yes, think about it,' Holly repeated. 'You know why Reece applied for this camp. You know we want to access interstitial time by creating the operational heart of a time machine.'

'She does not really think it is possible.' Vasily's chuckle was light and soft. 'She dismissed you both as nutters.'

'Time machine?' Miss Hale breathed. 'If that's true… you'd have the potential to change history. Life and death would be in your hands.'

'You know, the same unnerving thought occurred to me.' Holly's voice turned dreamy. 'I could have the past as my playground… I'd try to make things better, of course, though it's entirely probable they'd end up much worse. At least until I was a little practised at it. But I've had an idea. I've heard there's a revered member of your family tree, Miss Hale. A patriot who gave his life for his country. I could try to save Nathan Hale and see how it worked out. Then, with the power of life and death in my hand, you'd be my first worshipper, Miss Hale, and bow down before me.'

There was a momentary silence. 'You don't strike me as a goddess, Celyren Rhystyllen.'

'You probably won't believe me, but I've actually met a goddess. You have too. Strange to say, she had a name just like mine: Hollë. But she was also called "Lady Death". The only thing that's ever scared me about trying to access interstitial time…' Holly's voice lowered in subdued fear. '…is the possibility of using the power wrongly. Of ending up just like Hollë.'

'Good act. You almost make me believe you.'

Vasily snorted. 'We are adjacent to a cyclotron connected to a massive power grid and you are doubting her word? This is all coincidence?' He glared. 'Let me tell you something, Commander Nathania Hale. As one double agent to another. What the world needs is decent people, making the right decisions for the right reasons. Patriotism is not enough. There is a difference between loyalty and faithfulness, but it seems to have entirely escaped your notice. Do not play god with your choices and flatter yourself it is all for the common good.'

Miss Hale scowled. 'I'll leave the door unlocked when I go.'

'Wait!' Reece called. 'Did Chixie-Dixie-whatever-he's-calling-himself say anything about his plan that was going *exactly* to plan?'

'Only...' Miss Hale hesitated, clearly torn. 'Only that Jedidiah Harris and Gawain Aishdene were together and they were making music.'

Holly palmed the side of her head. 'The sharva said it had told Gawain something important about Jed at Serpent Mound. I bet it was: *don't make music together.*' She turned to her brother. 'Know what, Reece? I don't think this is about *us* at all. Aanundus has set this up to get Gawain and Jed together in the middle of a cyclotron. He has switched it on, hasn't he?'

Miss Hale nodded.

'Sis,' Reece breathed. 'He still needed the sword. Or...' He broke off, staring at the stump on the end of his arm.

'The sword is also, if I'm not mistaken, with Gawain and Jed.' Holly flipped the eyecup aside. 'They've disappeared, haven't they, Miss Hale? You've looked all over and you can't find them.'

She nodded again. 'Where are they?'

'They are perhaps trapped in interstitial time.'

'I doubt they're trapped anywhere,' Miss Hale said. 'Chixiff claimed his scheme was at the very moment of fruition.' She hesitated, then went on. 'Right decisions, right reasons?' Her mouth curved in a wry expression. 'How can anyone ever be sure of either of those, blond boy?' She took a deep breath. 'In case I don't get out of here and you do, report this: Chixiff said the seed he'd planted in Gawain had germinated, grown, and achieved maturity. He spoke as if Gawain had become a tree and he was sending him to join another tree. There's a gateway Gawain has to get through and he needs the sword as his password. Once he's merged with the other tree, he's programmed to come back to Chixiff.'

The door slid open and, raising her gun once more, Miss Hale left. The door hissed shut.

'What tree is growing in Gawain?' Vasily asked.

'Don't know,' Holly said.

Reece frowned. 'When we were on Alpha Centauri, it was always about trees. *Always*. I never could quite figure it out.'

'That is reassuring. Because I cannot figure out what anything means either. Even with the Grail Question to help me.' Vasily tapped the laptop. 'Eygul told me you had been to Alpha Centauri but I did not realise that was a hint I would need an interplanetary passport.'

Holly laughed. 'You think Hale's double-crossing us?'

'Unknown.' Vasily shrugged. 'I hope I gave her sufficient reason to reconsider her unquestioning loyalty to Eyes.'

'She's creepy,' Holly said.

'Nah,' Reece retorted. 'Nothing wrong with her that a personality transfer wouldn't fix. Not like Aanundus.' He eyed the door. 'Let's scram.'

27

TAMIZEL HAD GONE BY THE TIME Gawain woke up. It was a dim, dismal and grey day. Gawain lifted his bleary eyes to the slit in the stone wall that served as a window. The woollen screen had been pulled back. He blinked. *What's the window made of? It's the strangest sort of glass I've ever seen.* He yawned and stood on the bench to peer through the silver-grey sheet. Touching the window, he ran a fingernail over the strange surface.

'Catsilver,' said a voice.

Gawain jumped and turned. *Jed!* He smiled with relief.

'Didn't mean to scare ya, Gawain. Thought ya were wondering what the window's made of. It's called "catsilver" here. Back in the future, it's called mica. Makes excellent insulation.' The smile disappeared. 'I wish I'd been sure sooner ya really were Gawain. I woulda tried harder.'

Gawain raised his hands and waved them rapidly, as if to erase something.

'Nah, Gawain. Ya excusin' me, when I really need forgiveness.'

Gawain stared. There was a sudden hard lump in his throat, at the very same time as he wanted to laugh in frantic desperation.

'I wish I could help ya, Gawain,' Jed said. 'It must be so frustratin'. Tamizel thinks the reason ya can't speak is because o' the sword, but I don't.'

The sword. Speech, words, tongue, sword: a simple equation. For a moment, Gawain could almost see the formula in his mind. Then it was gone.

'I don't,' Jed repeated. 'I think it's the trauma. All those thorns in ya body, pokin' out. Like they'd exploded from the inside.'

I think they did. When I made the choice of 'in' or 'out'. It was about whether I wanted to keep the sylvan throne or not. Gawain patted his arms and face—smooth, thornless. *How did you manage it, Jed?*

'How did the thorns disappear?'

Gawain nodded. *Yes. How did you heal me?*

'I tried everythin'. Just everythin'. Everythin' this age has ta offer and even a few things I 'membered from the future.' Jed sighed. 'Mostly they made it worse. It was terrible seein' ya in so much pain. Then I found I could calm ya a lot by singin'. When I couldn't think o' any more songs, I played music. Made a llpirra. Made a flute. Got a harpist ta play ta ya through the night. Got one of Guinevere's servant girls ta paint ya in healing oil. She sang as she did it. And that's what cured ya. The music and the songs. We brought the breath of the Spirit of heaven down to earth.'

We brought the breath of the Spirit of heaven down to earth. Songs… songs and music… songs that heal trauma and abuse and suffering.

There was a knock at the door. Jed went to open it. A serving girl was there, her face almost as dark in colour as Jed's. Gawain thought it was the girl who warned him about Arthur's troop up on the high fells. *Are you the one sang to me and anointed me with oil?*

Even though he strained to hear what she was saying, he couldn't make out the language.

'Ya'd better get dressed,' Jed said as he closed the door. 'Yrien wants ta see ya as soon as ya're up. He's missed ya these last coupla weeks, y'know.'

Gawain's brow creased in puzzlement. *Yesterday*, he mouthed.

'Yesterday? Gawain, it's been over two weeks since Arthur's men chased ya up the fell.' For a moment Jed seemed bewildered and then it obviously clicked with him. 'Ya've seen the Grail.'

Grail? Gawain mouthed.

'The pit o' plenty, the bowl o' bounty—at this moment in history, the Grail is a real place. Five hundred years from now it'll have acquired a timeless spiritual dimension, and by then it'll have been long forgotten that once upon a time the grail was nuttin' more than a crater—although sure enough a rather special one.' Jed smiled. ''member Tnorala? And Palm Valley?'

Gawain nodded. But he was uncertain.

'Timeless places, just like the Grail.'

I don't think the Grail's a crater. I think it's a song. Isn't it?

'And because it's timeless, it's easy ta lose track o' time in there. Yrien don't even ask anymore when I'll be back. I tell him ta expect me when he sees me. That satisfies him so long as the oats and apples never run short and there's beer and game on his table. As ya've probably guessed, his own supplies have dwindled ta nothing.'

Cradoc, Gawain mouthed. *Illtyd.*

'They caught ya there?' Jed asked.

Gawain nodded.

'That's unfortunate.' Jed seemed pensive. 'Tamizel's illusion maze musta worn thin.' He lapsed into silence. 'I'll hafta get onta him again. He's been busy, then he got distracted constructin' a sharva.'

Gawain, wanting him to explain, mouthed *maze? maze? maze?* until Jed understood.

'The illusion maze is an endless loop. Tamizel made it, so he says, using a simple formula that copied the gate-maze at the Storm-Tree. Let's hope the maze is intact and Cradoc and Illtyd haven't managed to find their way into the garden. It's like a code and they wanna trick us into revealin' it. Remember Aanundus and Hollë finding their way into the ring under Tnorala? Like that.' Jed smiled. 'There's always somethin' ripenin' in the Grail. Out of season, though. Strawberries in December, oats in February, apples in April.' Jed went to a carved box, rummaged through some clothes, then threw Taliesin's best court cloak to Gawain. 'Here, put that on.'

Jed nodded as Gawain swung the mantle around himself. 'Ya actually scrub up quite well, Speckly Boy.'

Gawain glared ferociously, and Jed laughed. 'Can't take a compliment, eh? No good being at Yrien's court then. And no good knowin' Tamizel either. Ya need ta understand compliments in this culture. I'd never have believed it before but praising people in poetry is a deadly worthwhile skill. It not only saved Tamizel's life, it continues ta save lives on a regular basis.' He unbarred the door, urging Gawain to hurry. 'This is such an odd century, Speckly Boy. No matter how bloody the sword is, poetry can conquer it.'

As they entered Yrien's feasting hall, Gawain noticed the new addition straight away—a round table. Yrien and Arthur were laughing together as they inspected the table. Moving closer, Gawain could see artisans painting an elaborate scene at the centre: a hunter chasing a white stag, a fox, a rabbit and a mouse. Gawain glanced at Yrien, astounded by his boldness. *About as subtle as a hit by a lightning bolt. The mouse that changed everything. The mouse that changed the world... He's going to curse the day when he finds out I'm just a jerk from Ohio who got a little lost. A lot lost.*

Yrien grinned as soon as he saw Gawain. 'Gwalchmai! Gwalchmai, dere 'ma, dere 'ma.'

Gawain headed towards him, floundering, as usual, in a rush of strange words spoken much too quickly. At the occasional mention of 'Gwalchmai', he smiled, hoping it was the right reaction. Then an odd fear surfaced. *If this is about the round table, I hope Yrien's not suggesting I join Arthur's bunch of no-hopers. Wait on, in that story about the Green Knight and the beheading game, Sir Gawain was one of Arthur's top knights.*

Gawain became more certain by the second he was being corralled into something unpleasant. He stopped smiling, in case Yrien felt encouraged by it. He risked a glance at Arthur. *It must be the right response. Arthur looked terribly anxious before and now he just seems relieved. After all he wouldn't want me at his round table any more than I want to be there. It'll be Mordred he wants.*

Yrien's tone became increasingly earnest. He put his hand on Gawain's shoulder, looking directly in his eyes, pleading. Gawain returned the look and shook his head with what he hoped was careful, solemn finality. Next moment Yrien sighed, dropped his hand from Gawain's shoulder, and looked away. Gawain kept standing there, not sure whether the audience was over. He was about to back out when, to his immense consternation, both Yrien and Arthur bowed to him.

Uh oh. What have I agreed to? Unnerved, he noticed that Arthur was grinning ferociously. He looked at Yrien, but the raven king was scowling. Gawain, his head reeling, his stomach heaving, knew at once he'd made a very bad mistake. Then Yrien, as if abruptly deciding to make the best of a very bad business, smiled wanly and spoke to him at length.

Finally it was over. With a curt wave, Yrien dismissed Gawain and beckoned Jed forward. *Oh no*, Gawain thought as he backed out of the feasting hall, *what've I done?* He'd had every intention of waiting just outside the hall for Jed but a sense of panic overcame him. As soon as he was out the door and out of sight, he ran for the chapel.

28

WRAPPED IN THE MANTLE, Gawain sat on Tamizel's bench-bed and stared through the catsilver window. He crept in the back way from the chapel and was able to hide as vague shadowy shapes wandered past and shouts echoed across the courtyard. He recognised some voices, though the formless silhouettes visible through the mica remained unfamiliar.

Jed had gone to do Yrien's bidding. Just before he'd left, driving a huge cart with three packhorses tied to each side and half a dozen to the back, he'd shouted in English, 'Gawain, I don't know where ya're hiding but I'm sure ya can hear me. Don't worry 'bout nuttin'. I'll be back as soon as I can. Explain then.' The cart rumbled off.

I wonder how he survived for so many years. I wonder how he became the Wild Man. Made himself into Merlin. For the hundredth time Gawain thought of Tamizel's revelation about Angie being here too. It seemed impossible. In all the time Gawain had been at Yrien's court, he'd never seen anyone remotely resembling his little sister. *Sure, my memory's been faulty up to now, but I'd have recognised Angie.*

Gawain stayed by the window, huddled, listening to the squawking of hens, the squealing of pigs and horses, the occasional clash of steel as Arthur's men indulged in horseplay, the calls of servants as they hurried about their duties. At long last, only animal noises were left.

Must be lunch time. Gawain felt hungry. He got up and wandered around the room, smelling roasting venison, bird pies and baking bread. He tried to distract his stomach by looking at the tapestries. *It's such a strange room.* Then he realised. *It goes back to Roman days. How long ago would that be? That's why everything's such a contrast. Tapestries and a mosaic floor. Carved oak door, marble columns, catsilver windows. Desk ornamented with gold leaf and…*

Gawain stopped.

Desk. He went up to it, felt around the edges and found the catch. *It's not like I'm snooping.* He lifted the lid. *Even if I found anything I wouldn't be able to read it.*

He was wrong.

He fingered the top sheet inside the desk. *Not paper. Not parchment.* He turned it over. There was a poem on the back.

Stone for a pillow
on heaven's shore,
waves lap the sleeper
on eternity's sands,
stars swirl in the ebb
and turn with the tide,
and there! eden's sailors:
angels climbing
a net in the night
bringing their cargo of dreams
from the tree of time's choices.

Perhaps it was because the words were in a language he understood, perhaps it was because he'd seen the Tree and the netted stars, perhaps it was because he'd felt the ebb and surge of time as he'd mounted the stairway of golden glass—he was drawn to the poem.

He read it again, stroking the page as he ended each line. He sensed the pull to enter inside it. It wasn't as intense as the time he'd fallen into the dream of the Tree inside Tamizel's star-glitter eyes but it was strong. And it grew stronger each time he read it again.

He was still looking at it minutes later when a knock sounded at the door. 'Gawain, open up please.' Gawain leapt up at Tamizel's voice, surprised by the elation he felt. He unbarred the door, and stood with a stupid grin on his face. Tamizel swept past him with a sour expression. Gawain felt instant deflation.

Tamizel swung his cloak off and threw it in a corner before noticing the look on Gawain's face. 'Oh, don't mind me. I'm always in a foul mood when I have to deal with the Goldenhand.'

Angie?

'Yes, your darling sister. I often think Angharad Ironfist would be a far more fitting title.'

Can I see her? Where is she?

'In a few days. I've told her you're here, but she takes her peace-weaving very seriously.'

Peace-weaving? Gawain felt more than crest-fallen. He could hardly believe it. *Doesn't she want to see me right away? Aren't I important to her anymore?*

'Peace-weaving is the gentle art of diplomacy,' Tamizel explained. 'And quite contrary to what you might expect, the steel maiden is very good at it—in certain ways at any rate. Not in others, as my foul mood testifies. So don't let it get to you, Gawain. You need to understand that Angie… ahh…' He broke off, noticing the sheet on the desktop. 'Found your poem, did you?'

My poem?

'Yrien's been harassing me for a song about the *Finding of Gwalchmai*. I've got scraps I've been able to use in the construction of a sharva but unfortunately I could never get Yrien's version of it quite right: the stag, the fox, the rabbit, the mouse. Instead I wrote what happened when we first met. When I looked in your eyes and felt your gaze pulling me backwards through the river of time to the Storm-Tree of Ruēl.'

I thought that was you.

Gawain remembered the moment when his gaze had locked on that of the prisoner chained in Yrien's hall. He remembered the climb through the deeps of time and the stars, like glittering fruit, caught in the branches of the Tree that called and called… and the shadow with eight legs falling…

'I should have realised you were a stone-dreamer, a shaper of things invisible, even before I knew your name.'

What's my name got to do with it? Gawain doesn't mean 'stone-dreamer'.

'But Aishdene does.' Tamizel shrugged. 'We all have the power to shape the invisible, but mostly what we shape stays invisible and hence untouchable. Some people though can make the invisible visible and my people, the Farafolk, call those who have the power to make dreams real—both visible *and* touchable—*stone-dreamers*. Our word for it is "ayshden". Even your own language once had a name for the ability. Or rather there will be a word—briefly. Before it changes meaning entirely.'

What's that?

'Fantasy. To make the invisible visible. To give truth form. Not everyone would have seen the golden stairs. Not everyone would have seen the Storm-Tree of Ruēl.'

You mean they're not really there? I imagined them?

'The mind makes sense as it can, Gawain. Which doesn't mean they're not there, just that other people may experience them differently.'

I imagined them.

Tamizel shook his head as he pointed to the tapestry. 'What do you think of my bestiary?'

Imaginary creatures.

'Really? Tell me, what colour is the mermaid?'

Gawain peered at it. *Green. Sea-green.*

'Not blue?' Tamizel inquired.

Gawain nodded.

Tamizel touched the embroidery. 'It hardly looks green to me at all. I'd call it "blue". It's with colours like that, colours that cross thresholds—aquas and turquoises, lavenders, mauves and pinks—that people begin to suspect colours aren't the same for everyone. How do you know for example that what I see as "yellow" is the same as your "yellow"? You don't. But that doesn't make colours imaginary. The mind makes sense as it can—but that doesn't mean your stairs of golden glass or the Storm-Tree don't exist, just that others may experience them differently.'

Yeah. Right.

'What's wrong, Gawain? Something's happened?'

A spillage of incoherent images roiled up in Gawain's mind—round table, white stag, Yrien talking, Arthur smiling, both kings bowing—combined with a sense of barely-restrained fear.

'It's not half as bad as you imagine,' Tamizel said. 'No doubt you realise my illusion protected you that day Arthur hunted you. Unfortunately, in saving your life I threatened him with the only thing he really fears—the loss of his kingdom.' Tamizel almost smiled as he sat down on the bench next to Gawain. 'Of course Arthur's version of the encounter is a considerably different to what you or I might have reported. As he tells it, there was a giant, an ugly, misshapen brute, tall as the clouds, with a club the size of an oak tree.'

Seriously?

'And there Arthur was, passing by the waters of Tarn Wadling, innocently minding his own business, when this evil churl, this monstrous herdsman, threatens to terrorise the entire kingdom unless he can answer a riddle.'

We weren't that scary.

'I didn't think so, either. Apparently Arthur is truly frightened, or else he's using the incident to his advantage. He's sent messengers high and low, looking for someone who can answer the riddle "what do women want?"'

Gawain thought of Angie. *I can tell you exactly what women want.*

'With a sister like yours, you probably can,' Tamizel sighed. 'Still, although it might be obvious to you, no-one else has answered it yet. Love, some say. Wealth, say others. Marriage, sex, commitment, children, happiness, peace, position, power... Anyway Jed and I have decided this is the ideal opportunity to place you out of harm's way.'

I don't like the sound of this.

'It's simple. You need to get married, Gawain.'

The faintest of sounds emerged from the back of Gawain's throat—a strangled squeak.

Tamizel chuckled. 'I must say you're taking this far more calmly than I did when my own betrothal was announced.'

Calmly!? What on earth makes you think I'm calm?... You were betrothed? To Holly?

'No. To the Hollë. To Lady Death.'

I can't get married. No-one gets married at my age.

'They do here, Gawain, even when they're much younger than you. You're more than eligible. You're handsome, you're courteous, you're the heir to the kingdom, and not only that, you don't answer back. What more could a woman want?'

Don't make this into a joke.

'You're also modest and unassuming. So do you want to be trapped into marriage with a girl you've never met because you nodded at the wrong moment?'

That's already happened—hasn't it?

'Gawain, we're trying to help. It's only a matter of time before you find yourself in the middle of an assignation with Guinevere or Elaine or Iseult or Morgan or...'

She's Arthur's sister.

'That wouldn't stop her. How would you defend yourself if she were to claim that you'd led her on? Don't you see, Gawain? They'll trick you and they'll trap you. Even those who claim to love you will use you any way they can to further their ambitions.'

Gawain scowled, breathing heavily. *So who is it you want me to marry?*

'She's called Ragnell. You'll like her, Gawain. She knows who you really are, and she wants to help you.'

Do I have to?

'No, of course not. It's your choice. I know if I were to tell Yrien you've changed your mind, he'd be mightily relieved. What he wants of course is for Guinevere to leave Arthur and marry you. He prays fervently every night for Arthur's death—although he's too good a Christian to actually arrange an accident. Still, he's told me many times you'd make a fine son-in-law.'

Son-in-law!? Guinevere's the last thing I want. Gawain took a deep breath. *What does Arthur think about me getting married?*

'He thinks it's a brilliant solution. It not only gets you out of Guinevere's sights, it gets him out of a tight spot. You see Jed's told him that, because of secret knowledge that's come from the future, he knows that Rags knows the answer to the riddle. And she's agreed to reveal this priceless piece of information, providing Arthur agrees to her penalty—which is, of course, marriage to you.'

Rags? Gawain furrowed his brow, trying to think where he'd heard the name. Was it in a dream? *She's one of servants, right? Is that why she wants to marry me? Can't I just give her some money?*

'It's a nickname—for Ragnell. Which doesn't have anything to do with rags, but with Ragnarok—the twilight of the world's ending.'

The world's ending?

'Don't worry about it. You know it doesn't happen. But that hasn't stopped half the people here being named for the world's ending. Guinevere is named for the great white wave that destroyed the coast.'

There's something you're not telling me, Tamizel, I just know it. There's something else in this for Arthur, isn't there?

'Well, to be honest, Arthur thinks that, because of Ragnell's lowly station, she would never be accepted as Queen. As far as he's concerned, it's just another tiny wedge to edge you out and Mordred in.'

Gawain felt suspicious. *So, just how ugly is she?*

'I didn't say she was ugly but does it matter? We're all shambling skeletons under our skins. Surely it's a person's soul that counts.'

Easy enough for you to say. Holly's a stunner.

'She wasn't when I met her. She gave me hope and I loved her for it. And for her innocence.'

Gawain still didn't feel convinced. *What does this Lady Rags really want from me? I guess she wants the answer to the riddle as well.*

Tamizel grinned. 'And what makes *you* so sure *you* know the right answer?'

I lived with Angie for eight years and my mother for my whole life until a few months ago. I ought to know what women want.

'So what is it, Gawain?'

Their own way.

INTERSTITIAL

X

'BEING THE MOST EXPENDABLE, I believe I should go first.'
Vasily reached the door and put his head out. *No one in sight.*

'What makes you think *you're* the most expendable?' Holly
whispered.

Vasily paused, glanced up the dimly lit corridor, then handed his
laptop to her. He ignored her question in favour of one of his own.
'It is clear Commander Hale wishes us to escape. Her motives...'
He waved his hands up and down. '...are debatable. Much as I have
to admit it is a temptation to run as far and as fast as possible, it
is also likely this might be our one and only chance to shut down
whatever they are doing here. So should we go *in* or *out?*'

Reece sucked in a breath. 'Since you put it that way, I have an
existing track record for smashing up bases occupied by evil aliens.
I'd like it to remain intact. So I vote for *in.*'

'That is the most stupid thing I've heard since the last time
we broke into Aanundus' headquarters.' Holly shot Reece a dark
glance. 'I vote for *in* too, but still I want you to know it's stupid.'

She looked at the stump where Reece's hand should be. 'You need medical attention.'

'I'm doing okay so far, sis.'

Vasily led the way up the shadowy corridor, his steps slow, careful and noiseless. At the first junction he turned right, heading deeper into the complex. He tried each door on the way, but none were open. A light showed through the window in the door in one office, and a conversation could be heard. They ducked down to pass the window and kept on going, checking the doors at every office they passed. Soon almost complete darkness enveloped them. *Cannot risk going any further. Not with Reece needing help.* Vasily was about to turn back when a door handle moved at his touch. *Could be the biggest trap of all.*

With extreme caution, he opened the door. The air was musty. *Good sign.* The darkness was total. He held his hands out, seeking furniture, walls. He found a metal shelf. *Ice-cold. Like the room.* 'I do not think we should turn the lights on,' he whispered.

'Close the door, sis.' Reece was breathing heavily. 'I'm sitting down. It's so hot in here.'

It is freezing. But Vasily didn't say it aloud. *You are in much worse shape than I thought, milord.*

And then there was light. *Not much. Just a faint glow.* Vasily realised Holly had turned the laptop on. He was able to make out their surroundings. There was a computer bank behind a glass partition. *Maybe we have hit the jackpot. This looks like the emergency backup system.* 'Password is moon~rose, if you need it. But you may not. I am supposed to be the only one with access but I have realised sharvas are laws unto themselves.'

'If we could hack in there…' Reece waved his hand towards the glass partition. '…and start up the cyclotron, we might be able to overload the system and put it out of action permanently.'

'But that, dear Reeccce, would mean your friendss sstay trapped in the passt.'

Unbelievable. We did not even get a minute until evil bad guy found us. Every room must be monitored.

A hologram appeared in front of the glass partition. Vasily stared at the yellow eyes, the oily skin and the face with its faint white mottling. He felt repulsed.

Reece heaved an exaggerated sigh. 'I know it's seriously uncool of me to leave them to their fate, Andy Baby, but…' He sighed again. '…I wouldn't trust you as far as I could throw you.' He held his stump up. 'Which, at the moment, is not exactly far.'

'Andy Baby?' The hologram laughed. 'Hollë thinks I sshould jusst kill you and have done with it. But I've endured centuriess of boredom with inferior intellects and I dearly need to keep you for a pet, Reeccce. You never never never fail to amusse me.'

The door opened behind them and light flooded in. Miss Hale was a silhouette in the entrance, her gun up.

'Commander, take the laptop. We have the passsword.' The hologram smiled with malicious amusement. 'Endgame, my chickenss.'

Vasily wanted to thump himself. He'd told Holly how to get access while Aanundus had been listening in. And he'd forgotten about the endless supply of bugs Hale had deployed. Now Eyes could get past the inbuilt self-destruct codes. *It is all about safely getting to the sharva. But even if they do, will it cooperate? No way of telling. It is such a flighty thing.* He turned to Holly. 'Do not give it to Hale.'

Holly folded her arms over it.

The hologram tutted. 'You know the priccce of sstubbornesss, Holly.' A chuckle. 'Bessidess, don't you want to resscue Tamizzel and Gawain and your other friendsss?'

'You said they were in the past,' Reece pointed out.

'Indeed they are. And only you can ssave them.'

Reece snorted. 'You expect me to believe that, Andy Baby? I did not come down in the last meteorite shower.'

'Unfortunately it'ss true. You ssee, I made a misstake.'

'A mistake? *You?*'

'Incredible, my dear Reeccce, but true,' the hologram said. 'You ssee I had the dessign sspecificationss for a tachyon decccelerator—jusst like the prototype you dissarmed and destroyed on Dreamfall. I went back for it when I realissed it was impossssible to reproducce the dessign without the unique metal in the prototype. But tragically, nothing wass left. The prototype had been vaporissed.'

'Tragically.' Reece's voice dripped sarcasm.

'Sso you ssee why I had to bait thiss trap. Without the metal, the dessign is usselesss. I needed the ssword. And I knew Uwriy'el had to be concealing it becausse there was no trace of its pressence. Anywhere.'

'Why did you need Gawain?' Reece asked.

The hologram laughed. 'You don't know, Reeccce? You haven't worked it out?' The laughter stopped. 'Commander, I ordered you to sseize the laptop.'

'I'll destroy it, if you try,' Holly snarled.

Vasily stared, surprised by her bravery. *She cannot do that. But I guess they do not know that.*

'Commander,' the hologram spat. 'Sshoot the blond boy'ss head off.'

Without hesitation, Hale fired.

It was almost point-blank range. Vasily fell back, his forehead spraying with blood.

Holly screamed.

I am dead.

The scream was cut off with a sob.

At least... I think I am dead. Something is dribbling over my face. Surely blood. But perhaps paint. Do not open your eyes. Stay perfectly still.

'Now, Holly,' the hologram said. 'Let'ss sstop playing gamess. I know Reecce'ss glove was made by you from the tip of the ssword. I want the resst of the sswordmetal. The leftoverss ussed in the manufacture.'

Holly was still sobbing. 'There isn't any. I used it all. There isn't any.'

The hologram growled. 'There musst be. It can't all be in the passt, circulating through an endlesss time loop.'

'Not *another* mistake?' Reece sounded remarkably calm for someone who'd just witnessed an execution. 'Andy Baby, how terribly careless of you.'

The hologram snarled at him. 'The tachyon decccelerator can't be sself-exisstent. No. It'ss ssimply that you haven't made it yet, therefore there musst sstill be ssome sswordmetal in this era.'

'You think I'm capable of making that shapeshifting timetwisting mind-control teleportation device? Thanks for the compliment but truly you overrate my talents.'

'Commander!' The hologram's tone had become sharp and aggressive. 'Bring the laptop to me at oncce. And both the twinss.'

'Move!' That was Hale's voice—terse and unyielding.

Vasily could hear Reece and Holly shuffle out the door. He was about to open his eyes when he felt a lick on his forehead. 'Yummy yummy,' said the softest of whispers. 'Tomato sauce. Gourmet, too. She must really like you, Sily.'

It was the sharva.

And it was standing on an assault rifle.

29

'DEADLY.' JED PICKED UP a silk tunic embroidered with a magnificent gold star. 'Whaddya frownin' about? Yrien's showin' off how much he likes ya.'

Gawain glared at him.

'I don't get it. What donchya like about it?'

'He doesn't like that he's fitting into the ancient stories of Sir Gawain of Orkney, knight of the Round Table, like a hand into a glove.' Tamizel tapped his quill while composing a wedding song. 'Take a look at it. That's a pentagram on the front of the tunic.'

Jed glanced at Tamizel, then at Gawain, then back at the five-pointed star. 'I still don't get it.'

'In the stories of the Round Table, the pentagram is Sir Gawain's device.'

'Makes it perfect,' Jed said. 'Don't it?'

Tamizel laid down his quill. 'Think about it, Jed. Is Gawain stepping into destiny or are we pressing fate on him? Are we pushing him onto a pre-determined inescapable path or letting him decide what he thinks is best? Are we force-moulding Gawain Aishdene into Sir Gawain of Orkney—Gwalchmai, the Hawk of May—or are we giving him the freedom to be himself?'

'He doesn't wanna get married.' Jed nodded and held up the tunic again. 'But it's only a star.'

'Jed, you of all people know better than that. It's not *only* a star. It never was and it never will be. It's the ultimate symbol of the conflict between choice and chance, between free will and fate, between determinism and destiny. Of course it will take fourteen hundred years before the truth is discovered. Human beings instinctively make decisions according to a pattern; they follow the mathematics of 'if'—the same mathematics embodied in this star.'

'I think I've got ya figured out at last, Tamizel.' Jed threw the tunic at Gawain. 'Ya're just crazy.' He went towards the catsilver window as the sound of a commotion in the courtyard became louder. 'Looks like they're clearing the yard fer the arrival o' the bridal party.' A moment later there was a shout outside the window. 'I'll go check.' A moment later he was gone.

Gawain shrivelled inside. *If I ran now, where could I go? If only the sharva was here to help…*

'The sharva?' Tamizel looked up, his eyes glowing with sudden delight. 'I've finished one, you know. It might be too rudimentary a creation to survive. So this might just be the prototype for a second or third version. But I'm not sure how to send it to Dreamfall. Or what instructions to give it to avoid Lady Death.'

Lady Death? You mean beespiderhorsethingie that calls itself Hollë?

'Yes. I realise I have to have created a viable sharva. There was one that sacrificed itself to provide a distraction when I left the Storm-Tree and Hollë and Aanundus were waiting.' He paused. 'It wasn't that either Hollë or Aanundus were fooled by the distraction, it was that the sharva's sacrifice broke the mind control luring me. I don't know why—since it's necessary to program the sharva for self-preservation not self-sacrifice.' He looked down, his breath becoming ragged and uneven.

'This may not make any sense, Gawain, but I grew up knowing I'd been born in a shroud. Knowing that Lady Death had claimed me before I'd so much as opened my eyes for the first time. I grew up believing the highest destiny I could attain was to be written into the Music of Death. To become one of the Lady's chosen. Even after I came to hope in Ruēl of the Wounded Hand, I still believed the Farafolk were bound to Lady Death by cords of motherhood. I was her child and I was to die her lover, and it never occurred to me it was all a lie—that written into the fabric of our very existence is the Sign of the Wounded Hand, the emblem of both free will and destiny.' Tamizel sighed. 'You're a child of the far future, Gawain, where truth is no longer valued. Where only information is. "Is it true?" means nothing. The important question in your century is: "Is it real? Is it relevant? Is it fun?" I laughed at Reece once about something he thought—"whatever reality really is." But it was hypocritical of me, because I couldn't have told him myself what reality really is.'

But you can now, can't you?

'Reality is that which does not cease to exist when you stop believing in it.'

Gawain blinked. *You mean God?*

The commotion outside the window began to sound like loud turmoil. Gawain's nervousness increased. He held up the tunic. *It's not a star. It's a brand.*

'No one can force you.'

It's not a real marriage, is it? Like not with vows that mean anything... Yelling from outside interrupted him. Gawain recognised the voice, if not the words. *Angie!*

'Of course.' Tamizel's laugh was light and soft. 'You didn't think we'd let you marry without Angie being here, did you?'

Seconds later there was a pounding at the door and even before Tamizel opened it, Angie swept in followed by Jed. 'Gawain, you haven't changed a bit!' She hugged him. 'Oh, big brother, you have no idea how much I've missed you.'

Gawain realised it had been stupid not to have anticipated the vision in his arms. Angie was no longer eight, but eighteen, with wavy tresses of corn-gold hair, skin like milk, a mouth like a rosebud, and gentian blue eyes. The only thing still recognisable was the golden glove on her right arm, although it too had metamorphosed— embroidery decorated its length and pearls encrusted its rim.

Angie held him at arm's length, inspecting him. 'Cat got your tongue, Gawain?'

'Angie, we told ya he can't talk.' Jed sounded both anxious and protective.

'Sure you did. But talking never was Gawain's strong point. He might just have carried silence a little too far.'

Gawain shook his head, almost unable to comprehend the change. *How long have you been here? Where have you been?*

'He wants to know how long you've been here and where you've come from,' Tamizel said.

'Oh, about ten years come Christmas. And I've been at Avalon, or at least I am now. The time vortex had a bit of a scatter effect and dropped me and Jed in different places. Fortunately, I arrived in that red silk firebird costume—remember from Halloween?— looking like a distressed daughter of the nobility. Also fortunately, I picked up the language rapidly. Anyway, I've been staying at Avalon ever since I was forced to tell Rory that, no matter how ardent his passion was, he couldn't just click his fingers and have me.'

Avalon? Rory?

'He wants to know…'Tamizel began.

'I can tell what he wants to know.'With an irritated gesture and a look to quench fires, Angie cut Tamizel short. 'Avalon's between the Walls. Hadrian's Wall and the Antonine Wall, you know: it's the old Roman province that used to be called Valentia. Now it's Avalon. There's a glass hill with an old Roman fort that's all mine.' She grinned at Gawain. 'Remember Emrys had a castle of his own? Well, now I've got one too! As for who Rory is—he's Arawn, King of the Northern Picts. And he's ultra-cute. Retro likes him, so that tells you how okay he is. But he's already got a wife and well, you know how it is.' Her voice dropped to a confidential whisper. 'I don't want to have to share. Or play second fiddle for that matter.'

You can have more than one wife in this century?

'Hey, I've just had a great idea.' Angie was almost shouting in her sudden enthusiasm. 'You can honeymoon at Avalon. It'll be fantastic—we can catch up on everything then.'

What? Why not catch up on everything now?

'I know what you're thinking Gawain,' Angie said. 'But you're getting married and you really need to get ready.'

Angie spotted the blue tunic and picked it up. 'This is it, I suppose. So c'mon, put it on.'

Less than a minute later, Gawain was not only dressed, but glaring at Tamizel's raised eyebrow. *I'm not giving in about the shirt. It's just you don't know Angie.*

Tamizel winked. *Oh but I do*, he mouthed.

A moment later, Angie grabbed Jed's arm. 'Come on, Wild Man. This is a big day for you too… stop looking like you're off to a funeral, not to a wedding.' Next moment she'd swung Gawain around and was heading out of the room with him arm-in-arm. 'Let's get you hitched, then we can be off, out of here. I've never liked Carlisle—every time I come, I feel like I'm about to be trampled by a thousand Roman ghosts marching down the street.'

'Slow down, Angie,' Tamizel called, lagging behind. 'I haven't finished Gawain's wedding song yet.'

Angie glanced over her shoulder. 'Oh, Tamizel honey,' she said at her most provoking, 'everyone will be far too drunk to care what you're singing. Just make it up as you go.'

30

THE DRUNKEN REVELRY REMINDED Gawain of the night Tamizel had been fished out of the salmon-weir, looking just as foreign as he'd sounded. He looked around the hall feeling nauseated. Arthur's troop had already forgotten their new-found manners and courtesies. They snuffled and grunted like greedy pigs. Every so often one of them would yell 'oink oink' before vomiting into gales of laughter.

Gawain was forced to admit there wasn't much fighting: no knives drawn; no arguing over who best deserved the hero's portion. Then again this was Yrien's banquet, not Arthur's, and right now the raven king was offering some sort of long and complicated toast to the happy couple. But nobody seemed to be listening.

It seemed to Gawain as if the wedding had happened to someone else; he'd gone through the motions in a daze. He recalled the ceremony itself, as if he'd been an observer in Yrien's chapel. The monks had chanted, incense hazed the air, a bishop in white-and-gold with a staff even taller than his mitre had presided, and, of course, the heavily veiled bride had stood by his side. He'd spent the entire ceremony staring at the spiral of the bishop's staff, thinking 'if'.

If only...

When it came time to exchange rings, he'd glanced up momentarily from the tiny dark hand lying in his palm only to see Arthur's grinning face. He knew for certain at that moment this was the real deal. Yes, for better or worse, richer or poorer, he really was being married.

Tamizel's wedding song lilted down from a balcony, accompanied by harp and flute. He couldn't understand most of it but there were a few lines in third-millennial English:

> *Turn your eyes away from me.*
> *I cannot bear the love I see.*

He'd focussed again on the bishop's staff and felt considerable relief. Taking deep slow breaths, he sensed that the hand resting in his was quivering slightly and realised his bride was just as frightened as he was. He was desperate for Tamizel's help, but the bard was strolling around, strumming his harp. Angie wasn't available either—she was by Yrien's side, amusing him with ceaseless prattle.

The bride had said not a word, but had sat unmoving under her lace veil. The only glimpse that Gawain had had of her was of wrinkles and warts, a squint and black teeth. It was well into the morning hours, but much too soon as far as Gawain was concerned, when the moment he'd been dreading arrived. Unfortunately the ground hadn't opened up and swallowed him. Neither had the sky fallen on his head and crushed him. Arthur's men grabbed him and lifted him above their greasy heads, then jostled and cursed and guffawed their way to the bridal chamber.

Yrien said something incomprehensibly solemn to Gawain as they set him down in the doorway, and then he was pushed inside and the door was locked behind him. Gawain stood then looking at the tiny lace-clad figure sitting on the edge of the bed, a feeling of such utter helplessness overwhelming him that he sensed himself beginning to faint. *I hope she doesn't expect me to kiss her. Or anything. Especially the anything.*

After several seconds, the woman lifted her veil. Her hair was greasy and matted, great warts covered her nose and chin, the wrinkles of her face and neck were like furrows, her brow was a cavernous overhang, her black teeth barely visible behind puckered lips. 'Hello, Gawain. Remember me?'

Gawain, astounded that she spoke twenty-first century English, shook his head. The woman began peeling the warts off her nose then, rubbing the wrinkles off her forehead, ripping away the overhanging brow. 'Not up to Hollywood's standards, of course, but enough of an orc woman to fool that lot outside.'

Gawain blinked, finally recognising the voice. *Cardea! Not Ragnell?* The flicker of unease he felt was overwhelmed by a tidal wave of thankfulness so strong he had to sit down to stop himself from fainting. *That's what you look like under the burqa!* She had a bird-like grace accentuated by obvious hesitancy. He could tell she was watching his reaction intently.

But Gawain was so delighted to see her, he drew a question mark in the air as she pulled off the last vestiges of gum.

'How did I get here? Is that it? Or: why am I wearing this uglifying mask?'

Gawain nodded.

'It's for Arthur,' Cardea said. 'He's been making out you're under an enchantment, so we thought we'd turn the tables on him. As for how I got here—oh, it was just so long ago. With Angie and

Jed. But we got scattered.' She glanced at him, her smile uncertain and shy.

Gawain waved his hands, trying to ask another question.

Cardea frowned. 'You want to know where Uri is?'

Gawain shrugged, drew another question mark in the air then put up splayed hands trying to explain 'stag' without words.

'In the Tree?' Cardea asked. 'Tamizel's Storm-Tree?'

Not what I was trying to say, but right enough. Gawain sat down on the bed, tucking his boots up. He patted the spot next to him. *Talk to me,* he mouthed at Cardea. *Explain what's happened.*

'Talk to you?' Cardea kept her gaze down. 'You can't be so starved for company you want to put up with my inane chatter?'

Gawain nodded firmly. *Please,* he mouthed.

'Well…' Cardea settled down beside him, her gaze still directed to the floor. 'We thought you were ahead of us, in the crevice. Jed wanted to go back when he realised that you weren't in the cave with the rope. But then the bubbles came… and when one of them touched Reece's glove, well, it was like being sucked into a vacuum cleaner full of stardust…'

Gawain relaxed, his eyelids fluttered and, with Cardea's soft voice in his ear, he began to drift off. He jerked up with a start as the door burst open and a party of wild dancers began snaking through the room. 'Oink, oink,' they grunted. 'Oink, oink.'

Cardea burst into tears. Gawain, shaking off the beginnings of sleep, instinctively put his arm around her. Then, angry with repressed fear, he kicked the nearest dancer. It was a dark-haired boy Gawain had never seen before, and his fall caused the entire line of drunken dancers to land in disarray. Cardea jumped up and shouted at the sprawled heap. The only word Gawain could make out in her storm of protest was 'Mordred'. He looked where she was pointing and it dawned on him that the dark-haired boy he'd kicked was Arthur's son.

Mordred laughed at Cardea.

'Oink, oink,' the dancers chanted. 'Oink, oink.'

Gawain grabbed hold of Cardea's hand, swung her away from the bed and, stepping over several prone bodies, ran towards Taliesin's quarters. 'Oink, oink,' followed them down the hallway and across the courtyard. He arrived just as Tamizel was leaving.

'There you both are.' Tamizel was hoisting his harp over his shoulder. 'I'll be back shortly. Make yourselves at home.' He turned and placed a chased silver box in Gawain's hands. 'A wedding gift.' He smiled. 'One of my finest poems… and a sharva. Maybe two.'

Gawain blocked Tamizel's exit. *I need to know something.* He grabbed hold of the bard's arm. *I won't let you go until you tell me.*

'What is it?'

What does 'oink, oink' mean?

'It's a compliment, Gawain. The court believes you to be Gawain of Orkney, the land of 'orc', of pigs. From the same word that 'ork' comes, so does 'pork'. It's a way of congratulating you.'

Oh, really?

'I'll be back soon,' Tamizel said. 'Angie's with Yrien. Why don't you join them for breakfast?'

Gawain just wanted to be alone. In the distance he could still hear 'oink, oink,' followed by gales of laughter. *Congratulating me?* He didn't believe it. *Orkney might be the land of pigs but I can tell the difference between congratulations and ridicule any day.*

He glanced at Cardea, remembering her disfiguring makeup. *They're mocking me because she's the Oink Maiden—they're snickering at her. The pigman of Orkney marrying Lady Ragnell, the pigwoman of Wadling, I'll bet that's what Arthur's saying. That's why none of them fought for the hero's portion—it was all part of the joke.*

Something cold and savage rose within Gawain and he found it difficult to banish the violence in his thoughts. He went to Tamizel's desk, found quill and parchment and began to write.

Dear fellow-swineherd,

Next time I want to huff and puff and blow their sty down, please remind me they can't help it — they're just ignorant little piggies.

Long before Gawain had finished, Cardea was laughing. The tears in her eyes had been replaced by a sparkle and she bent to kiss him lightly on the forehead.

In that moment, Gawain felt a shadow on his soul. He became aware of three terrible things: he knew that he'd been right about the ridicule, he knew that Cardea was hurt heart-deep anytime someone mocked her and lastly, but most importantly, he knew that she'd been in love with him for a long time.

I hardly know her. He was alarmed. *I've never given her more than crumbs of kindness.* He felt the butterfly kiss on his hairline, saw the smile in Cardea's eyes and wanted to run for his life.

Then, as swiftly as the lovelight had appeared, it was masked. 'Tamizel's going to be upset. You've ruined that nib.'

Gawain didn't know what to do. Needing an immediate distraction, he mimed spooning food to his mouth.

'You're hungry?' Cardea asked. 'Let's raid Yrien's larder.'

Off they went to find the kitchen and came back with bread and meat, cheese and apples. 'What else?' Cardea asked, as Gawain began miming again. 'Oh, you'd like coffee?' She pummelled him playfully on the side of the arm. 'Not for a thousand years.'

Gawain gave an exaggerated sigh and broke off some cheese. Angie, all ermine collar and floating green silk, sailed in as he was taking his first bite. 'Where've you two been?'

'The bridal suite became a public thoroughfare, so we left.'

Angie rolled her eyes at Cardea. 'Get changed, you,' she said to Gawain. 'Yrien wants to make sure his little darling hasn't been eaten by the ogress.'

Gawain bared his teeth, but capitulated and went to find Tamizel's court cloak. As he did, he noticed Angie pull Cardea to the door. Straining, he could just make out his sister's whip-cold whisper. 'Don't bother denying it—it's written all over you. You're an idiot. There's no future in loving Gawain.'

'He doesn't need to know how I feel.'

'The only person you're going to hurt is yourself.'

Gawain clumped his way across the floor, making sure his approach was loud and obvious. Both Angie and Cardea were smiling as he reached the door. Angie immediately linked her golden-clad arm with his, then marched him off.

Yrien was plainly delighted to see him and just as plainly astonished by Cardea's transformation. She might not be a stunningly fair damsel, but she wasn't the hag he'd clearly expected. Gawain didn't have a clue what Angie was saying, but he recognised the wheedling tone from way back. She must have got what she wanted, because she bestowed a dazzling smile in Yrien's direction and blew him a train of kisses. 'Right-o,' she said to Gawain. 'It's off to Avalon we go.'

I wish people would stop ordering my life for me. It would've been nice to be given the choice.

He glowered at Angie, but she poked her tongue at him. 'In a bad mood, are we, diddums?'

I'm not your baby brother. Fuming, he found Cardea gazing far too steadily at him.

Don't, he mouthed. *Leave me alone.*

Without a word, she turned away.

Angie took Gawain's arm. 'Anything you want to pack, pet?'

She's become like mom. An obnoxious sixth century socialite. How terrifying.

'No?' Angie inquired when he didn't answer. 'Then let's make ourselves scarce before Yrien changes his mind.'

31

THE PATTERNED SILVER BOX WAS EMPTY. No sharva. No poem. But the words of Tamizel's wedding song echoed like a refrain in Gawain's mind. *Turn your eyes away from me, I cannot bear the love I see.* Although he was standing right beside Cardea as she loaded a packhorse, Gawain had managed to ignore her veiled presence for five uncomfortable minutes.

Angie just finished helping her secure the pannier when Tamizel appeared. Her lips formed a rosebud pout. 'Where've you been? You know I hate it when I don't get to say goodbye to you.'

'I've been going and coming—coming and going,' Tamizel said with a wink. 'Helping Jed contribute to the legend of Merlin—appearing and disappearing at whim and will.' His eyebrows rose at the provisions piled in the panniers.

'We're going to Avalon,' Angie said, before he asked any questions. 'Gawain and Cardea are on their honeymoon. I talked Yrien into it. He thinks it's a novel concept. It might even catch on, in his opinion.' She sighed. 'You know, Tamizel sweetie, if you could just tear yourself away from the court for a few days, you could come with us.'

Tamizel didn't appear to hear her. 'Are you okay, Gawain? Is everything fine?'

Gawain realised Tamizel must have noticed his stiff, ramrod-straight figure. He made an effort to relax. Turning he smiled and nodded, then went back to the packhorse. Too late he remembered Tamizel could read thoughts.

'Turn your eyes away from me?' Tamizel touched Gawain's shoulder in obvious concern. 'Ahh,' he whispered, finishing the line under his breath. '*I cannot bear the love I see.* I didn't mean it to be prophetic.'

Gawain glared at him in anger. *You and Jed should have realised how vulnerable Cardea is when you thought up this idiot plan.*

He saw Tamizel tense, then glance at Cardea. Her gaze was glued to the ground.

'Well...' Tamizel said after a moment. 'Let's be off.'

Angie stared at him, incredulous. 'You're coming?'

'If you've an objection, I'm sure Yrien will be happy I've changed my mind.'

'No, no.' Angie clapped her hands, clearly transported with delight.

Gawain turned on her in surprise. *So you're keen on Tamizel, sparrow. And no amount of tantrum-throwing is going to get him, is it?* The meaning of some of Tamizel's comments dawned on him. *At least Cardea can take a hint right away. Angie wouldn't be deterred by an outright rebuff. It's probably because he's such a challenge.*

Gawain felt sorry for Tamizel, pursued without pause, without mercy, by the Goldenhand. No wonder he'd called her 'Ironfist'.

Tamizel patted the packhorse. 'Mind if I take this one, Gawain? We need to get you riding lessons as soon as possible.'

Go right ahead. Do I get a pony? Or the litter? He was surprised when Tamizel handed him a leather scabbard, decorated with intricate knotwork. The weight of the scabbard indicated there was a sword inside.

'Shhh…' Tamizel breathed. 'Don't say a word.'

Behind him, Gawain could hear the clucking of chickens and cackling of geese as the servants chased them through the courtyard. And the distant squeal of the pigs. 'Oink, oink,' one of the serving girls chanted as she passed by.

'Ignore it,' Tamizel said.

Gawain glared at the girl, then on impulse reached out to Cardea and grabbed her hand. Her veil was just transparent enough for him to see her shocked surprise. *Friends,* he mouthed.

Tears welled in her eyes. Gawain looked away, only to notice Guinevere gazing at them from a doorway. The expression on her face was inscrutable, the light in her eyes unreadable. Something about her stance made Gawain acutely uncomfortable. He was still holding Cardea's hand so he raised it to his lips and planted a lingering kiss.

Her half-snatch backwards almost spoiled the effect of a romantic gesture. Then she straightened. Out of the corner of her eye, she must have seen Guinevere. She folded his hand in hers and held it up to her veil.

'Hey, lovebirds,' Angie said, 'don't overdo it.' She frowned. 'Where's Jed?'

'Just getting Retro,' Tamizel said. 'Now that Arawn's got some ghostwhite hunting dogs, guess who wants to breed some, just the same?'

Angie sighed. 'Camelot, indeed,' she murmured. Then she brightened. 'Actually, I really kinda like it. If it wasn't for the plumbing, I think I prefer it to twenty-first century Ohio.'

Of course you do. Gawain felt more than a touch cynical about his sister. He helped Cardea mount her pony as Jed appeared so they could finally set off. *You'd never get your own way there nearly as much as you do here.*

INTERSTITIAL

XI

VASILY WIPED HIS FOREHEAD and tasted the red gunk on his fingers. *It really is tomato sauce. Hale must have known Mr Creepy would order one of us killed. She is playing a very dangerous game if she thinks she can deceive him for very long.* He picked up the assault rifle. *But I guess she does not expect to do it for very long—just long enough.*

The sharva was in the doorway, one wing beckoning him out, its propeller cap fluttering in a soundless whirl. He'd have loved to ask it questions but didn't dare speak. He tip-toed into the corridor, into the intense darkness. The sharva had a faint glow. He followed its luminescent outline as the shimmering whirligig bobbed along. Minutes passed in silence and, when the sharva stopped, he realised that he recognised the area. It had brought him to the outer door. He shook his head, trying to get the sharva to understand. It kept judding its beak towards the codepad, and he kept shaking his head. *We have to save Reece and Holly.* Realising the sharva simply didn't understand, he turned away from the door, back towards the darkness. *Have to go it alone.*

He felt a beak pulling on his shirt. *Psst!* The sharva leaned close to his ear. Its whisper was so low he almost couldn't hear it. 'To make a quick getaway, it's wise to have the outer door open.'

Oh. Right. Forward planning. He paused. *What was the code Jed used?* Vasily realised he had to risk a question. 'Is this not a genetic lock?'

'It's been altered,' the sharva whispered. 'So the stormtroopers have access. It's now the same as their tunnels. Just a simple number sequence based on the date.'

'American dating system or Russian dating system?' he breathed.

'Australian. They think it's not as easy to crack.'

Seriously? Are they morons? 'Is it November yet?' *I hope Australian dating is the same as Russian.*

The sharva's whirligig fluttered as it nodded. 'The first.'

Vasily lowered the assault rifle as he tapped 0111 into the codepad. There was no shrieking alarm—just a faint hiss from the outer door. With a nod of approval, the sharva left the entrance and trotted back into the tunnels. Its wingtips started to glow and its whirligig shimmered as it led the way. It seemed to know where it was going. Vasily kept the assault rifle up and ready as they went. The darkness seemed interminable. At last, a distant buzz could be heard. Then a faint light. Then voices.

The sharva slowed as they reached a partly open door. Its glow faded and the sharva itself began to vanish, becoming transparent. Only the very top of its whirligig remained, the blades turning bright blue and re-forming into a cluster of petals. 'Eygul,' Vasily breathed. The petals floated towards him, desaturating in colour and tucking themselves behind his ear.

Vasily wasn't sure what the purpose of the change was, but it gave him confidence as he backed himself against the wall and began to listen to the conversation inside. He recognised Hollë's voice at once. 'I believe the little stains, Aanundus,' she said. 'If there's any swordmetal left, they don't know where it is.'

So Ms Scary is here as well as Mr Creepy.

'There'ss a chancce ssome sswordmetal wass losst here when the ssongss unlocked the time portal. You ssaw the way the boy wielded the blade. Amateur.' Aanundus' voice had a sinister rasp. 'Or the curssed dog might have losst a thread of the glove. We don't need much. And it hass to be here. As I ssaid, the tachyon decelerator cannot be sself-existent.'

'But since it can disguise itself, how do you plan to find it? We don't have much time. Although Uwriy'el has been recalled from active duty, his replacement will surely be on the way.'

Aanundus gave a gravelly chuckle. 'We have all the time in the world. If only we usse it well. If… if… if…' The laughter became tinged with a sinister edge. 'Reecce, fire up the ccyclotron for uss, won't you, pet?'

'At once, sir.'

What? Vasily was sickened by Reece's servile tone. *He has been brainwashed. Creepy dragonman has taken control of his mind.* Vasily tightened his grip on the assault rifle. *How do I avoid that?*

'If there'ss any sswordmetal in the viccinity,' Aanundus said, 'we'll be able to detect it from the vibrationss oncce it's activated by the ccyclotron.'

That might be my chance. As soon as they go looking for the metal, I will make my move to rescue Reece and Holly.

'Cyclotron at ten percent power.' That was Holly's voice.

Good. At least they are together.

A minute went by before she spoke again. 'Cyclotron at twenty percent power.'

Vasily felt a tingle behind his ear.

Another minute went by. Two minutes. Three. Vasily found himself tensing. The tingle behind his ear had turned to a prickle.

'Cyclotron at thirty percent power,' came Holly's voice.

Vasily's ear started to flap and it became harder to hear the conversation in the room. Hollë was speaking again, but he couldn't make it out. As his ear lobe settled into a steady—and alarming—vibration, he heard a few muffled syllables: '…lotron… ty… cent…'

A moment later, a sting so severe—like a needle piercing his ear lobe—caused him to gasp in pain. Before he had a chance to recover, Aanundus' arm had snaked around the door, grabbed his assault rifle, flung it aside with a clatter and wrenched him into the room.

'Sorry.' He heaved a sigh as he met Reece's gaze. 'No Cossacks to the rescue, after all.' His ear was burning. *How have I just got an earring? Out of nowhere.*

Aanundus spun him around and gazed into his eyes. A mesmeric whorl, a Tree of thorns, hung with dark stars, tumbled in front of him. *So… he is trying to spellbind me?* 'You think now that Uwriy'el is no longer protecting us that your hypnotic trance will work?' *Did I just say that?* Vasily's laugh was cold and spine-chilling. *Whoah! I am sounding more venomous than Mr Creepy himself.*

Aanundus' reptilian eyes narrowed. Behind him, Vasily spotted Miss Hale, back to the wall. 'Don't try and be a hero,' she sneered. 'The world doesn't need any more superstars.'

Whose side is she on? 'You are right.' Vasily looked her straight in the eyes. 'It needs decent people, remember, making the right decisions for the right reasons.'

She raised her gun and he couldn't tell whether it was pointed at Aanundus or at himself. 'Who are you?' she demanded.

What's she playing at? 'A very good question, princess.' He smacked his lips in a kiss. *What the insanity am I doing?*

'Who are you, blond boy?' she asked again.

'I am a fragment of a dream, the remnant of a vision, the remains of a song.' *Where is this coming from?* 'I can make and unmake myself by the power of the Trees, the energy of its sword-leaves, the spirit of the door that divides time from eternity.' *Something has taken over my vocal cords.* 'The one who created me had spent so long in the Tree that he did not realise part of it had fused with him. Just as the Fatal Tree merged with the once-golden angel, Hu Gadarn, transforming him into the thorn-demon, Aanundus.'

'Sso, ssharva, you are the tachyon deccelerator.' Aanundus seemed pleased with the knowledge.

Sharva? That would be right. Used to be behind *my ear, now in my ear.* 'Sharva? Hardly.' Vasily found himself laughing without any conscious volition. 'Hardly. I am triviality itself compared to such a magisterial and complex entity. Tachyons travel backwards in time, you know. Do I look like I am doing that?'

As Vasily finished, he registered the faint click of a trigger being depressed but, before he could react, Aanundus had swung him around, using him as a human shield. 'Fire away,' Aanundus sneered at Miss Hale. 'Your little boyfriend here doessn't mind ssacrificing himself.'

Miss Hale was clearly reluctant. 'Sorry, blond boy,' she said. 'I can't leave him alive.'

She fired, but her warning gave Vasily just enough time to duck his head. He felt Aanundus lose his grip ever so slightly. Twisting around, he realised Aanundus had caught the bullet between his teeth. He spat it out and roared with mocking laughter.

'No one betrayss me.' He smashed Vasily aside and darted forward to grab Miss Hale by the throat.

At the same moment as her scream was choked off, a line of bullets smashed into Aanundus from behind. There, in the entrance, assault rifle blazing, was Ms Gunn. As Aanundus slumped to the floor, she kept up the barrage.

'The outside door was open.' She looked around. 'So I invited myself in.' She hoisted the assault rifle. 'You need a decent housekeeper around here. Someone left this just lying on the ground.'

'Thanks, Meg,' Miss Hale croaked, raising her gun and emptying it—this time at Hollë. But Lady Death was too fast. Flitting through a series of transformations—horse, spider, bee— she whizzed into an airduct.

Ms Gunn eyed Aanundus on the floor. 'Is it dead?'

'Good question. The bullets in that rifle were never intended to kill a human being, but I don't know. It's a virulent herbicide mix. I'll find something to tie him up just in case.'

'Handcuffs would be good,' Ms Gunn said.

'Watch him.' Miss Hale nodded. 'I'll get them.'

Ms Gunn flicked a glance at Vasily as Miss Hale left. 'Nice earring,' she complimented. 'Why's it blinking? Holiday lights? Or red alert?'

32

'BRINGING THEIR CARGO of dreams from the tree of time's choices...'

Gawain felt his eyelids constantly drooping as Tamizel's soft strumming brought him to the edge of sleep. But he'd jerked awake when Retro flicked up his red-tipped ears and howled as the harp song finished.

'Sad,' Tamizel said, 'very sad. The most appreciative member of my audience is a dumb mutt.' Gawain, harnessed behind him in the open litter, leaned over to thump Tamizel on the back. Tamizel's long cloak swirled up tiny ice clumps as he turned to deal with the attack. But instead of retaliating, he visibly checked himself and laughed at Gawain's fierce expression. 'Oh, I didn't mean you, Hawk of May—I meant this treasured hound of the Kingdom of Britain. He's the only one of us welcome anywhere. Every petty king in this land thinks he's a special breed of luck dog.'

Retro raised his head higher and began mincing along.

'No, no…' Angie looked down from her bejewelled pony. 'You'll give him a swelled head, you'll create a monster.'

Cardea grinned at Retro's gait. 'You show 'em, boy. They have no sense of your true worth.' Retro woofed at her.

Angie, producing her most winning smile, reached out to touch Tamizel's arm. 'I know Yrien will want you back right away, but you could contribute more to the legend of Merlin, you know, by disappearing for a few months.' She squeezed his arm. 'There's plenty of room at Avalon.'

'I don't think you understand this contribution to the legend of Merlin at all.'

'Haven't you told them?' Jed cantered up on his white stag.

'I was hoping for a solution first.'

'There's a problem?' Angie asked.

Jed nodded. 'Back in the twenty-first century, I watched a lotta documentary series. So ya gotta realise this is the most catastrophic period fer thousands o' years. It's the end o' the world—at least as this generation knows it. It's so unimaginably disastrous that people in later ages will dismiss the record o' this time as exaggerated legend.'

'I know this.' Angie sighed and pulled down her chaplet of flowers. 'We're at the start of the Dark Ages.'

Tamizel nodded. 'And the preternatural winter that ushered them in is ending. Summer is finally coming.' He paused, sighing.

'But prolonged cold activates certain viruses,' Jed went on, 'and this has been the longest deepest cold in thousands o' years. There's a plague coming—it'll emerge outta Africa.'

'It will be called the Plague of Justinian after the present Byzantine Emperor,' Tamizel said. 'We've got a year or two before it reaches here. We must be ready.'

'How?' Angie was incredulous. 'Are we going to barricade ourselves? Against a virus?'

Exactly. Gawain understood Angie's reservations perfectly. Against a plague virus?

'We're going west,' Tamizel said.

'But that's ocean,' Angie said.

Gawain felt his face light up. He tapped Tamizel on the shoulder. *America,* he mouthed.

Tamizel nodded. 'Yes, America, Gawain. Ohio, if you wish. We can't take everyone, but we can take quite a few. We can take anyone who wants to come from Yrien's lands. That's why Jed and I disappear from time to time, why both of us contribute so much to the legend of Merlin—we're looking for someone to build a ship.'

Angie clapped her hands. 'We're going to discover America before it was discovered!'

'There are countless stories,' Jed said, 'o' sailors reachin' America before Christopher Columbus did: Vikings, Brendan the Navigator, Prince Madoc. And they're just the better known ones. All we need is the right kind o' ship. We heard o' an Irishman with boats but turns out they're a bit flimsy. We're lookin' fer somethin' large and sturdy.'

'You've been to Ireland?' Angie exclaimed.

Jed and Tamizel both nodded.

'And you didn't take me?'

'It wasn't a shopping expedition.' Jed's voice was stern. 'It was serious negotiations fer an ocean-going vessel. The monk tried ta convince us his coracles were just what we needed, but we didn't buy his assurances. Even though history'll prove us wrong.' His brows came together and he scowled at Tamizel. 'Next time, lemme do the talkin', silvertongue. You gave far too much away. There wasn't even the tiniest thought in Brendan's head o' the west until ya put it there.'

Angie's face puckered in disgust. 'There's even less plumbing in America than here.'

Jed glared at her. 'I think it'd be very good fer ya, Angie Goldenhand, little chickadee.' He patted her pony's rump. 'Very good: ya might stop acting like a spoiled princess and hopefully a little—just a little—o' yer brother's genuine humility might rub off on ya.'

INTERSTITIAL

XII

VASILY KNEW HIS SMILE was wan and uncertain. 'I don't know why it's blinking. I didn't have an earring five minutes ago.'

'Suits you,' Ms Gunn commented. 'Gives you a pirate look.' She moved to help Reece. 'You okay, Emrys?'

'Not sure.' Reece sounded groggy.

'Medical help is on its way.' Ms Gunn squatted next to his seat as Miss Hale arrived back with the handcuffs. 'Just hang in there. I've called your parents as well as the Flying Doctor.'

'Cyclotron at seventy percent power.'

Ms Gunn turned at the sound of Holly's voice. Vasily realised there was a console tucked around a hidden corner. He was moving to her side when she called out, 'Reece, I can't get the cyclotron to switch off.'

'I'm com—' Reece began, getting up.

Vasily spun on his heel and cut Reece off. 'Stay right where you are, milord. I'll wheel you round to her.' *I do not like the way he is perspiring. It is not Siberia here but it is not a sweat lodge either.* Grabbing the back of Reece's chair, Vasily pushed him around to the hidden console.

Reece looked up at him. 'Cute earring. Didn't notice it before. You get it when we were in Alice Springs?'

'I think the sharva's trying to disguise itself.' Vasily refused to admit how painful it was. 'Aanundus thought it was a tachyon decelerator.'

Reece peered at the ring. 'He could be right.' He nudged Holly as his chair reached her. 'Hey, sis. Look at Vasily's ear.'

Holly's gaze locked on the earring. 'It's not as strong as before… the desire to possess it, I mean, to have it all for yourself, so your every wish can come true. Even the darkest.'

'Not as strong,' Reece agreed. 'But still there. And see—the scrollwork, the spiral patterns—the same.'

'What is a tachyon decelerator again?' Vasily asked. 'I know you told Hale but I forget.' *Actually, more like I cannot think with this pain in my ear.*

'It's the operational heart of a time machine. It opens the interstitial gaps in the space-time continuum to enable access to other periods of time and locations in space…'

'And…' Holly said, '…we think it allows you to avoid something called a "wheeltrap". But we don't know what that is.' She turned to the console as it beeped. 'Cyclotron at eighty percent power.'

'Tried cascading the switches?' Reece asked her.

A cry echoed from behind them. Vasily swivelled, pushing Reece back as a wild sheet of flame hit the ceiling. *Whattheblazing…*

Miss Hale was on the ground, Aanundus astride her body. A torrent of fire poured from his mouth. He raised his bound hands to the ceiling and snapped the cuffs like twigs.

Ms Gunn fired the assault rifle—but, even as she did, Aanundus was changing. Metal scales filmed across his arms, his face distorted into a silver snout, his legs shortened and a lashing armour-plated tail appeared.

Herbicide? Nyet. Not this time. He has changed from a tree to a dragon. Adrenaline rushed through Vasily's body. *Fire extinguisher?* It wasn't much of an idea but he didn't have a better one. He ran... like lightning. But his speed wasn't enough.

The dragon whipped around, catching him in a clawed fist before he reached the door. With a malicious snarl, it ripped away his earring.

Then it was gone. Through the doorway it charged, and up the tunnel—further into the darkness.

Vasily's ear was excruciating. He took a deep breath. 'Now might be a good time to leave.'

'We have to stop the cyclotron,' Reece called.

'There's no time...' Miss Hale clambered to her feet, unsteady and hurt. 'Meg,' she ordered. 'You get the children out. I'm going after Aanundus.'

'You are *not*,' Vasily said. 'You are coming with us. You could not take Mr Creepy out when you were in one piece. What makes you think you can do it now?'

'You lead the way out, blond boy,' she said. 'That's an order from the President of the United States by whose authority I am issuing this command.'

'An order from the President himself?' Vasily tried to keep the scorn out of his voice as he looked her up and down. She was in such a bad way she was using the wall for support. 'Obviously you did not get the memo, princess. I am Russian.'

'She's limping.' Ms Gunn nodded towards Miss Hale as she wheeled Reece around the corner on his chair. 'Help her, Vasily. I'll bring Emrys and Cerylen out.'

The darkness was intense.

'Arlte!' Vasily called, hoping that he'd remembered Jed's word correctly. To his relief, the lights came on. Still it was slow going, partly because Miss Hale was leaning so heavily on him for support and partly because, when they moved too fast, Reece's chair slid into the walls and smashed his knees.

They were almost at the exit when a song began. It echoed through the tunnels, building in crescendo. Vasily felt the thrumming in his blood, *calling... calling...*

'Hollë,' said Reece. 'We need to resist it...'

How? Calling... calling...

'Yes.' Holly agreed with him. 'Lady Death. It's like the song she made on Dreamfall. To summon her children to protect her.'

Yes, it's a summoning. Vasily felt Miss Hale begin to struggle with him, trying to turn back. That, more than anything, gave him the strength of will to resist.

'It's not the same, sis. It's different. Sounds more like something Gawain or Jed would cook up.' He gasped. 'That's what Aanundus meant. When I asked him why he needed Gawain and Jed. It's gotta be for their songs. There must be something about the frequency or the rhythm that opens the gap into interstitial time.'

'They still need the sword, Reece.'

He gasped again. 'Or some of it. Empowered by the cyclotron. The earring. I'll bet it's the last remaining bit of swordmetal left in this time... and the sharva was hiding it.'

They reached the door. Vasily shoved it open. Searing light blinded him for a moment before he was able to guide Miss Hale out.

'What're they trying to do?' Ms Gunn asked as she pushed Reece's chair through the exit.

'Open the gate between time and eternity. Maybe try to use the tachyon decelerator as a kind of beacon to take them back in time to wherever the sword is. Once they have it, they'll try to go to the Tree. I'm not sure, but that's my guess.'

'This crevice is too narrow for the chair,' Ms Gunn said. 'Do you think you can help your brother, Cerylen, while I lock the door?'

33

FOUR DAYS HAD PASSED since they'd left for the north. *If I'd known how far Avalon was, I'd have insisted on tents.* Gawain wondered how much longer until their overnight stop. *Why do we have to keep travelling out of our way to find abbeys?*

A strange glow appeared on the western horizon: the colours of sunset merged into a soft glimmering of red, yellow and green. The resulting iridescent mist cloaked the hills in unearthly light.

'What's that?' Cardea asked.

Gawain held up his hands, gesturing his uncertainty. The rainbow mist rose higher, painting out the stars. Retro barked.

Jed shushed him. 'Reminds me o' them colours the night we went to Kurrkalnga for the singalong.'

Retro growled.

'*Those* colours,' Angie corrected.

'Mebbe we should head in the opposite direction.'

'Don't be a fraidy cat, Jed,' Angie laughed. 'We'll soon be safe in the monastery.'

The rainbow glow became more intense—like an emerald and ruby curtain threaded with flickering electrical charges. 'It's just an aurora,' Tamizel said.

But Gawain knew it wasn't. He knew Jed was right. A picture appeared in his mind's eye—a long-ago memory surfacing in a frisson of warmth. He was barefoot, walking in darkness through desert sand, weaving his way through a crowd swaying in worship. One musical note began to open wide, to bloom and flower in the firelight—a living thing twirling with grief and dancing with joy, all entwined. It rose in the air, towards a lighted cross. Kissing the light, it went up, up, up in its centuries-long journey of healing.

'We should hurry.' Jed's voice was urgent.

No. No. No. Gawain scrambled off the litter as the others began to turn their horses. *We have to heal the land.* The moment he thought it, he knew it was true. *Jed, that's why Uri protected us right up until we started making music. It's why he didn't prevent Aanundus from sending us into the past. We've got an assignment here.*

'What on earth are you doing, pet?' Angie glared down at him from atop her pony. 'Get on that litter.'

Pet!? Gawain balled his fists. *Make me.* He bared his teeth. *Just. Make. Me.*

Tamizel turned back, his voice coaxing. 'Gawain, now's not the time to be stubborn.'

Swirls of mist began to gather in the gloom. Gawain relaxed as three pale green snouts and long-limbed legs blew towards them. *They're on my side. They always have been.* He raised his head to direct a thought straight at Tamizel. *Ettins.*

He was surprised when Tamizel spun around, looking stunned. 'Ettii? Here?'

'What are they?' Angie asked. 'They look like ghost horses.'

'Night mares,' Jed said.

'No.' Tamizel sounded puzzled. 'They're from Dreamfall. They are helpers in times of trouble and very sensitive to the sort of crisis that splinters worlds. But I don't understand how they could possibly be here—they are native to another planet in another star system, not to another country in another continent.' The Ettii blew towards them, gusting in flurries, tumbling over each other. 'They shouldn't be here.'

Gawain started trudging towards them. *They want us to follow them.*

'You're right, Gawain.' Tamizel nodded. 'They want us to follow them.'

'I don't like it. I'm not going.' Angie pulled her pony around. 'The monastery can't be far.'

She's not making my mind up for me. Gawain gestured to Cardea as he strode on. *Come with me,* he mouthed. *They're friends.*

She turned at once, Tamizel following after her. Jed, with a deep sigh, came trotting up to Gawain. 'Hop on behind me.'

Gawain shook his head.

'I won't turn back,' Jed said. 'I just don't want ya ta freeze yer feet.'

'Stop!' Angie commanded. 'You're all going the wrong way.'

Gawain just kept going, ignoring Jed and following the misty Ettii. After a minute, he heard Retro woof. The bells on Angie's pony jangled as she cantered after them. The Ettii led them to a valley ringed by dark pines, deep in snow and shadow. The strange light seemed to come from a hidden lake.

Gawain directed another thought at Tamizel. *Tell Jed we have to sing. Like at Kurrkalnga, at Memory Mountain. Healing the land. Singing not just to the boy struck by thorns but to the whole thorn-wounded world.*

'Jed,' Tamizel began, 'Gawain says—'

'I think I know,' Jed interrupted. 'Healing fer the land. We hafta bind up the wounds o' this age through song. We have ta bring heaven ta earth, and open the stairway so angels can descend ta help us create the symphony.' He paused, as if listening to something beyond the world. 'And we hafta open a passage ta Dreamfall so the Ettii can take the sword back so it can become a treasure of the Farafolk.'

'Ahhh...' Tamizel breathed. 'Of course. Of course.' He flicked his fingers. 'But still one problem. If we open that door on the stairway of time, we cannot guarantee which angels will find us first. We may give away our time and location to Aanundus or Hollë.'

It's worth the risk.

'Gawain thinks it's worth the risk,' Tamizel reported.

Jed raised an eyebrow. 'You would, Sky-Eyes Lion-Skin, you would.' He took a deep breath. 'Okay, let's make that Star-Tree at the heart o' time shake in its little booties.'

INTERSTITIAL

XIII

VASILY HAD STAGGERED less than a dozen steps, Miss Hale leaning on his shoulder, when they were surrounded by stormtroopers. *Must have heat-sensitive detectors. Our body heat would have registered as soon as the door opened.*

He was relieved when he didn't have to make any explanations.

'Make sure all entrances and exits are sealed,' Miss Hale ordered at once. Her voice was husky and uneven. 'Then retreat immediately. We need to be as far as possible from here when this place blows.'

Hey, what about warning the local inhabitants?

'I don't think it'll explode,' Reece said. Both Holly and Ms Gunn had an arm around him, holding him up. 'Aanundus wants to use the energy, not waste it.'

'Agent McKenzie,' Miss Hale called. 'Where's the ATV?'

'Destroyed, ma'am. There's a helicopter arriving in less than a minute, though.'

'Then pick the boy up and carry him to the landing pad.'

'No!' Vasily snapped as McKenzie stepped forward. 'Your boss is in much worse condition than milord Rhystyllen. Carry her instead.'

'Blonde boy!' Miss Hale's voice was sharp and snarky. 'You are starting to become very very annoying.'

'What a compliment, princess. I am touched.' He shrugged. 'McKenzie, use some initiative and assess the relative critical condition of Hale and Lord Rhystyllen yourself.'

McKenzie looked like a creature whose eyes have been caught in the headlights. His head didn't move but his eyes swivelled from one to the other. He picked up Miss Hale while growling at another stormtrooper: 'Carry the boy and follow me.'

Vasily watched one of the troopers swing back his weapon and lift Reece in one smooth move. A curtain of light drifted down from the high reaches of the sky. *Same as the other night. Like the rainbow serpent light at Memory Mountain. Must be something Aanundus and Hollë are doing with the cyclotron. Wonder if it is about fine-tuning the position. And would the fine-tuning be for time or space? Or both?*

'Whatever they're doing,' Holly said to him, pointing at the slithering light, 'we can't stop it. I only hope Gawain and Angie and Jed and Cardea got out before they turned it on. And Retro.'

Vasily took hold of her elbow and led her after the two agents carrying Miss Hale and Reece. Flanking them front and behind were the rest of the stormtroopers. 'Do you think they are stuck in the past as Aanundus said?'

'Maybe that's true, maybe not.' Holly's sigh was deep and anxious. 'He's likely to have been lying just to get us to cooperate.'

They were following the agents through the rocky terrain when a spear of rainbow light plunged to the desert floor right in front of them. It swirled with tendrils of red, green and yellow—like a spiral staircase ascending and descending from heaven to earth.

They stopped. Stared. Waited.

'It is a portal.' Vasily knew it without being told.

'Careful,' Holly breathed. 'The last time we experienced anything like this at close quarters we wound up on another planet.'

'I do not think this goes to another planet.' Vasily wasn't sure why, but he was aware with a deep knowing that the portal wasn't intended to transmit matter through space. *Or, only as much space as it would take you to connect up, as the sharva had said, with Eric's dragonship. Or wherever else it was you wanted to be. The portal is primarily meant to give access to time.* 'I think it is a passageway back in time.'

'Or possibly forward?' Holly asked.

'Or possibly forward,' he agreed.

'Look!' Holly grabbed his arm so suddenly he thought it was about to be wrenched off. 'There's something in it… it's a box!'

34

THE LIGHT FROM THE HIDDEN LAKE swirled into a shimmering rainbow column. Yellow, green and red steps appeared in it—a spiral stairway flowing in and out of an escalating cascade. The dark pines ringing the valley were reflected from the water. The Ettins were tattered tongues of white mist, fragmenting and reforming as they tumbled around the pillar.

Gawain watched Angie ride past him as he stopped to gaze at the flickering column.

'A rainbow stile.' She raised an eyebrow as her pony reached the edge of the water. 'With a step up to it so impossibly high only a giant could reach it.'

'Stile and step?' Jed said. 'Ya need ya eyes checked, Goldenhand. It's a fence, a ginormous fence, with a rainbow gateway.'

'It's a bridge,' Cardea said, 'with a toll-gate. The pylons are rainbow-coloured, not the gate.'

It's a column. With a rainbow door in it.

'A tree with branches forming a rainbow canopy—there's a ladder this end.' Tamizel nodded to himself. 'Whatever it really is, it must be on the very limits of comprehension or we wouldn't describe it so differently. Our minds are making the best sense they can of what we're experiencing.'

We're all seeing it as the brink of another place. Maybe another realm...or dimension...

'Or planet?' Tamizel asked. 'Is this some sort of transportation device? Perhaps this is how the Ettii got here. They seem to want to go in...'

We need to open it for them.

'That might be true. But how?'

The sword in the scabbard? It is Excalibur, isn't it? Mistblade?

Tamizel puffed out his cheeks. 'Gawain thinks this is a doorway to another place. And the sword opens it.'

'Why aren't we going to the monastery?' Angie's voice was waspish. 'This is dangerous.'

'We could test Gawain's theory,' Jed suggested, ignoring her. 'But before risking the sword, mebbe we should try somethin' else. Just ta see if it opens by itself.'

Gawain looked around, noticing the silver box that had been Tamizel's wedding gift. He hefted it and threw it at the pillar. It was sucked straight in.

'The sharva!' Tamizel was aghast. 'Did you take it out?'

But wasn't the box empty? Gawain stared, horrified, as the rainbow steps ascended and descended around it.

He heard a far-far-far-distant voice. 'There's something in it... it's a box!'

'Holly?' Tamizel dismounted in a leap. 'Holly, is that you?' His face lit up with a glow of wonder.

'Tamizel?' Holly's voice seemed to echo along an immense tunnel.

'Holly?' Tamizel's face glowed. 'Where are you? Are you in the Storm-Tree?'

Gawain stared at Tamizel, realising Angie had never stood a chance.

'No, we're outside the Bluff. Aanundus and Hollë are powering up the cyclotron.'

'They're ten years in the past,' Angie exclaimed. 'They're back when we made music in Tnorala.'

'No, chickadee,' Jed said. 'They're fifteen centuries in the future.'

'Reece, it's Tamizel...' Holly's voice became clearer, as if some distortion had been removed. '...and he's sent us the box that we found the tachyon decelerator in. But I can't see how to get to it.'

'Don't try.' Jed and Tamizel both yelled together.

Gawain stepped towards the litter and picked up the scabbard. With great caution he unsheathed the sword, hoping it wouldn't burst into flames. But he could see leaping tongues of fire before it was halfway out. The blaze died as soon as he handed it over to Tamizel.

'What did you tell me, Jed?' His eyes half-closed, Tamizel traced the scrollwork.

'It's gotta go with the ettins ta that Dreamfall Dreaming ya talk about. Ta become a treasure o' the Farafolk. They're here ta collect it.'

Gawain realised Jed's insight was true. The ettins had somehow followed him through time to retrieve the sword. *If it goes back to Dreamfall now, it will enter an endless time loop that puts it beyond the reach of Aanundus forever.* As he thought of Aanundus, his hand began to ache—a phantom pain from a thorn-seed long gone but so sudden and intense he knew it was a warning. Aanundus is coming.

Tamizel whirled. 'Are you sure?'

Gawain held up his hand. The palm was throbbing. *He's very near.*

'We must go. Aanundus is coming.' Tamizel stroked the scrollwork for the last time and strode into the lake. He slipped the sword under the water where the rainbow column met the surface. The ettins dived down to it and, blowing it upwards with their ghostly snouts, sent it sailing up the stairway. Gawain saw its bright glittering tumble and knew it was rising through a host of welcoming stars.

'Reece, I can see my sword! Reece, the Ettii are back... they're here! Caroon and Glyffy are here!' Holly's voice was full of thrilled excitement. And then confusion. '...no, they're gone...'

Gawain blinked away tears, surprised at the loss he felt. *It wasn't really my sword*, he reminded himself. *I shouldn't feel grief at its going.* He realised as he wiped his eyes on his sleeve that the door in the rainbow column was wide open. The sword had indeed been the key.

Retro set up a howl as he leaped towards the door. He vanished.

'Retro!' A distant scream of joy and wild woofing echoed from the far side of the door. Reece could be heard exclaiming, 'Down, boy! Down! Don't knock us over! Stop slobbering, you silly mutt.'

It took Gawain a full second to realise what it meant. *The rainbow column is a time portal. It will take us home.*

Angie was already ahead of him. She was at the door before he could move. 'Someone hoist me up on this stile,' she commanded.

Jed and Tamizel were at her side straight away. Tamizel cupped his hands for her to step up and be lifted higher. It wasn't enough. Gawain couldn't see the stile but he could see the door closing. He noticed a handle shaped like a wheel he hadn't seen before. She needed to turn it before she could get through. But even standing on Jed's shoulders she wasn't tall enough to reach it.

'The wheel*trap*.' Holly's voice was distorted again. 'Care*ful... wheel*trap.'

Angie clambered down from Jed's shoulders. Tamizel threw his mantle to one side and took a flying leap, trying to kick the door open. But he bounced back as if the door had repelled him in mid-air.

Sing. We need to sing it open. Gawain took hold of Cardea's hands and turned them as if rotating a wheel. *Sing*, he mouthed at her. *We. Have. To. Sing. It. Open. Itneedshealingtoo.* He didn't recognise the tune she began to hum. She dropped his hands. Moving towards the door, she pushed Tamizel and Jed aside, and reached for the wheel. Gawain saw it shudder in her grasp but she was able to hold it.

Jed began to sing with her, floating ancient words on the melody she was humming. It was incomprehensible but Gawain knew it didn't matter. The wheel itself understood. *The Grail that heals the land and mends its splintered vision isn't a bowl of plenty. It's a song.*

'Go through.' Cardea strained at the wheel. 'Quickly. Keep singing.'

Jed's voice became huskier as he reached out a hand to Angie and together they sidled, one by one, through the door.

There were jubilant shouts as they reached the other side. 'Angie!' It was Reece's voice. 'Is that you? You're... older, chickadee. Beautifuller.'

Retro's instant growl echoed through the passage of years.

'Just testing, boy,' Reece laughed. 'Just wanted to be sure you haven't lost your finest talent!'

'Jed! Welcome back.' A new voice. Gawain strained to remember. *Vasily... from Russia.*

Cardea nodded at him. 'Gawain, you now.' She smiled as he ducked past her and her voice dropped to a whisper. 'Be safe... love.'

The ripple of light as he walked through the rainbow door parted like a curtain. He stood at its edge, holding it to one side. He was able to look forward and see a massive helicopter landing in the desert and to look back and see the snow-ringed pool and the dark overshadowing pines. Tamizel was coming through the door towards him. Holly, her face radiant with unalloyed happiness, stretched her hand out through the parted curtain to welcome him.

Come on, Cardea. He beckoned her forward—into the future.

Tamizel walked past him into shouts of wild joy. 'We'll have the biggest party ever!' Reece was yelling. Retro was barking in ecstacy at all the happiness.

Come on, Cardea.

Something was wrong. He knew it by the look on her face. *What's up?* he mouthed. He dropped the curtain of light and went back to the door.

'The wheel's spring-loaded.' Her eyes had a frantic glaze. 'I can't hold it open and go through the door at the same time.'

She's trapped.

He saw her lips tremble, the fine muscles around her face quiver. Her arms were shaking—the wheel was too strong. She needed someone to hold the wheel for her, but it couldn't be done from the inside.

He tried to think of something to help.

Tears sparked in her eyes. She stared at him as if etching the memory of his face on her mind forever and blew him a kiss. He felt it, a living thing as light as a petal, as it sped towards him. It landed on his brow. With a gleaming flash it took form as a butterfly and sat on his temple.

No. No. No. There's got to be a way. I won't leave you behind.

If... He struggled to speak. 'If...' The word was an explosion in his mind. He saw himself back at the Tree, at the edge of the river of stars that flowed between time and eternity. Trapped between the dragon and the spider, he watched the white stag moving closer. And he saw what, in his terror, he had missed before. Each hoofprint of the stag was shaping universes: sweeping galaxies into shimmering spirals, twisting the turrets of seashells into order, enfolding fragrance into budding roses, awakening the dawn with birdsong and rubylight. *In or out?* It was a choice. *Just as 'if' is a choice. And unless every 'if' is a choice of love, the universe is meaningless. Unless choice and chance intersect in love, I will never be anything more than a random aggregate of atoms travelling together.*

'If...' he repeated.

Cardea's sudden smile was a sunburst of light in the midst of flowing tears. 'Oh, Gawain, I hoped so much your voice would come back. I prayed...'

'If... if...' The words came one by one. *Love isn't mushy feelings. It's a choice to care for another person whatever the cost. It's a frightening power. It's the power to change the world.* 'If... I... hold... you... as... you... let... the... wheel... go... I... can... catch... you.'

She shook her head. 'I'll be crushed.'

He reached his arms around her. The weight of the silence surrounding them was immense. The universe itself seemed to be holding its breath. He felt the butterfly flap against his temple and, in that moment, he was swaddled, enfolded, caressed by a dozen beating wings. 'We... have... to... try.'

'You'll be crushed too.'

'I'm willing... to risk... it.'

'I'm not willing for you to do that. Let me go.' Cardea stifled a sob.

'No.'

'Let me go.'

And he almost did. The sudden spike of pain in his hand was so intense he jerked without thinking.

'I haven't asked for your pity.' Cardea's face was so close to his. Her eyes were fire-stoked. But he wasn't fooled. She was trying to make herself angry so she could force him to let go.

And then he saw the dragon. Skimming over the trees it landed, with a sizzle, in the pool. Its towering hulk blotted out the star-frosted sky. 'The ssword, It wass here. Reccently. Where have you hidden it?'

Gawain knew they were out of time. Cardea had to let go of the wheel. Unless she did, the dragon would enter the doorway— and flit back to their own time. Or perhaps not. Perhaps it had the ability to dart across the timeways where it chose.

'Where have you hidden it?'

And then, with a thunderous jolt, an eight-legged horse dropped out of the sky beside the dragon. It was Hollë.

'He's here,' she said. 'My betrothed.' The horse pawed at Tamizel's cloak that had been discarded on the ground. The dragon lifted it in a delicate claw.

'Taliesin's mantle,' Gawain said. 'He doesn't need it anymore.'

The dragon roared. 'Where iss he?'

Gawain didn't answer. He watched as the horse opened its mouth revealing dripping spider fangs and as the dragon flicked the mantle over him, laughing with contempt. 'Let go, Cardea,' he begged. 'Let go.'

She shook her head. 'Not unless you do. I won't have you die for me…' Her words broke off in a scream as the spiderhorse spat a sticky shroud of poison to envelop them both. She lost her grip as the dragon's tail lashed her at the same moment.

The last thing Gawain knew was a violent slam as the wheeltrap activated, crushing him in a pressure lock. The door exploded around him.

35

VASILY WATCHED AS MISS HALE was lifted into the helicopter on a stretcher held by paramedics. The doctor on board directed her straight to a life support unit. 'I'm holding blond boy hostage,' she yelled as she was wheeled away. 'Just to make sure you supernerds all behave yourselves. The power you have at your disposal is a temptation.'

'As if we are the ones with a temptation problem,' Vasily said. 'When you are well, we can discuss loyalty and faithfulness.'

With effort Miss Hale produced a grimace. 'If I didn't already understand the difference, I'd never have left the rifle for you.'

'Thought so,' said Vasily. 'That is three.'

'Three what?' Reece asked.

'Three times she has saved me. Okay, it is a package deal and she is saving you lot too. Still I can only conclude, since we know she is not acting out of the goodness of her heart, that Witchiepoo loves me.'

'Dream on, blond boy.' The door to the life support unit closed.

Reece bent his head close to Vasily. 'Tell Jed to come see me, then distract this mob as best you can, willya?'

Vasily nodded and went to talk to Jed. *Did not Reece realise he was already working hard at distractions? Bantering with Hale and trying to raise the gloom to ground level, not subterranean. Getting the stormtroopers to focus on him and not anyone else.*

Jed was comforting Angie—both of them looked so much older, he felt awkward at approaching them. Only hours ago they'd been his closest friends and now they were strangers. Only hours ago they'd been young and idealistic and now they had a brittle cynicism he didn't like. It reminded him too much of himself.

Angie was weeping. Retro's head was in her lap and he was gazing up at her with sympathetic eyes.

'Milord Rhystyllyn wants to see you.' Vasily pushed Jed aside and sat next to Angie. 'I will stay with the Goldenhand.' He understood her grief. Everyone had been so excited, so busy concentrating on the reunion of Holly and Tamizel, none of them had noticed Gawain and Cardea's plight until too late. By the time Angie realised they were trouble and had run back towards the rippling rainbow, nothing could be done. An explosion ripped through the air, hurling her back onto the desert floor.

The colours were gone. The coiling rainbow dissipated in a flash. The spear from heaven vanished.

If they are alive, they are trapped in the past. Vasily had the sinking feeling Gawain and Cardea would be better off dead. *Trapped with a dragon and a spiderhorse. Who are no doubt vengeful beyond imagining.*

He watched as Reece spoke with Jed and was then hoisted into the helicopter. Jed waved and then wandered around to the far side of the massive machine.

Vasily let out a scream, jumped up and beat the ground. 'Something tried to bite me!' He had the attention of every stormtrooper in sight and no doubt most of those who were out of sight. 'Arrghh!' *Best I can do. Hope it is enough.*

Once the wounded were securely loaded, the stormtroopers came back for Vasily and conducted him, along with Holly and Angie, to the helicopter. Even Retro got the full escort treatment. Only Jed was missing. A thorough search was conducted but he'd vanished into his own country. Vasily wasn't sure he'd managed to get away until the helicopter lifted off.

He sighed, his gaze moving from Holly with Tamizel's arm around her to Angie's limp form. She'd been sedated. He sighed again. He didn't like thinking about the questions she wouldn't be able to answer when she finally woke up.

Epilogue

A LIBRARY FLOATED amongst the stars and around the Tree. A rooster perched on its topmost shelf. It wasn't a happy rooster.

'No sympathy,' the library sang, pages rippling. 'You should have left the arena when the butterfly took form. Kisses don't turn into butterflies in the low-dimensional worlds. You've been around— you're not some dewy-eyed cherub who doesn't know the drill.'

The rooster's beady eyes narrowed. 'Uwriy'el got to be a stag in a Wild Wood on a gameboard when the last seal was broken.'

'Was that Uwriy'el's choice?' The books and scrolls in the library shuffled around, reordering themselves. 'What do you think you are manifesting, Gabriy'el?'

'Don't know,' the rooster said. 'Some shaken-and-stirred cocktail of honour, bravery and sacrifice. But it's such an unusual feeling, I can't be sure. It's like weight, when you first experience it on entering the material cosmos.'

'You are Courage,' the library sang.

With a flash, a scroll appeared, mid-space. It rotated slowly, looking over the library's new ordering.

'Uwriy'el has returned,' the library sang in multi-part harmony. 'Let us rejoice in union, reunion and communion.'

The Uwriy'el scroll sang, breathing harpsong and wingbeats along the starwinds. 'If... if.'

When the song of choice ended, Uwriy'el asked, 'What's happened to Gabriy'el? Why's he a rooster?'

'Caught in the crossfire between love and fear,' the library sang. 'Shot through with honour and sacrifice, taken form as a Rooster of Courage.'

'What about you, Uwriy'el?' the rooster asked. 'Our assignments do not permit us to interfere in humanity's movements of choice and chance. No exceptions, no excuses. So what's the word on your status?'

'It was never brought up. The Wounded Hand and I discussed how painful love is.'

The library, for once, was silent. The song of the spheres was stilled.

The rooster spoke. 'I don't understand, Uwriy'el. Did you rebel? Or not? Did you manipulate free will? Or not?'

The silence continued until the Miyka'el scroll spoke. 'A new paradox: until now, faithfulness and loyalty have been one and the same for us. It has not been possible for us to separate them-only for the sons and daughters of men. We misunderstood the test. It was not just for Nathania Hale.'

'Perhaps,' said the Uwriy'el, 'it was never for her. Just as the test of the sword was not for Gawain.'

'One test, two tests...' The rooster inspected itself critically. 'Why am I asking you all about this form when I can ask the Wounded Hand?' In a flash, it was gone.

Uwriy'el's sigh fluttered the starwinds. 'They should have all got back. Especially Gawain.'

'Especially Gawain,' the library said. 'His scroll speaks of an appointed time and place in the final war between the courtiers of heaven and the spawn of air and darkness. That scroll was erased when he became the song.'

'If I'd waited...' Harpsong and wingbeats resumed in Uwriy'el's voice. 'If...'

If... All along the songlines of the universe, the music of the spheres resonated to the singularity: stars continued to wheel in the spiral dance, seashells to grow in their curving logarithmic whorls, flowers and ferns to unfold, the helix of life to renew the dream of tomorrow.

'If,' harmonised the library, singing new form into the future. 'If...'

Five Years
Later

JED EMERGED FROM THE PRIVATE JET to find Reece waiting for him. He kicked a battered suitcase down onto the tarmac and parked a didgeridoo on the steps.

'Long time no see, buddy!' Reece called up at him. 'Welcome to Wales!'

Jed brought a stash of musical instruments to the doorway. A llpirra, a pair of seed rattles, a drum-stack and two clapping sticks. He was hard put to keep a neutral expression on his face so he muttered, 'Nice job,' and stared at the artificial hand a team of the world's best cybersurgeons had created for Reece. 'I thought the others'd be here.'

'They're in the village.' Reece picked up the suitcase and the drum-stack. 'We'll go up to the castle together.' He threw Jed a sidelong glance. 'What's this all about, buddy? Not like you to ask for anything. Ever. You never make demands, unlike my secretary. I had to threaten to fire her to get her here, Jed. The Goldenhand is seriously unimpressed at having to interrupt her social whirl.'

Jed followed Reece to a luxury limosine parked just beyond the terminal fence. Reece helped him load the baggage, then turned, twirling his keys on one metal finger. 'Spit it out, Jed.'

'Yer'll know soon enough.'

'Not good enough.' Reece leaned against the limosine, palming the keys and folding his arms. 'Why here? If you wanted a meeting in Sydney or even London, I'd understand. But Wales? I don't even know if my castle is currently habitable, so I've booked us some rooms in the village.' He unfolded his arms. 'What're all the instruments for?'

'Ta make music, what else?' Jed risked a smile. 'Ya know, Reece, what the best thing about ya is?'

'What?' With a suspicious glare, Reece put his metal hand on his hip.

'Ya got such an uncommon surname.'

'What?'

'Yep. Yer the most findable o' us all. Is Retro here?'

'Back in the village. He wouldn't stop barking. Tried to drag us all to the castle before you got here. Vasily and Tamizel both had to hold him down. That's why I came alone to pick you up.'

'Gone crazy, has he?' Jed couldn't stop a smile creasing his face. 'Let's go. Straight ta the castle. I imagine Retro has herded them there by now.'

'What's up, Jed?'

'We're havin' that long-delayed reunion, aren't we?' Jed flexed an eyebrow. 'Back at Tnorala, ya said we should have the biggest party o' all time but we never did. Okay, the interrogators from Eyes kinda put a dent in those plans. But still it's been five years and I kinda got tired o' waitin' fer action on that front.' He jumped into the passenger seat.

Reece eased down behind the wheel, clearly unsettled. 'Is this because you haven't forgiven me for giving you the codes to permanently disable the cyclotron? Nothing's really been the same between us since.'

'Nah, I'm all good with that.'

The car's silence as it moved off was eerie. 'You're hiding something.'

They turned from the main road to a narrow country lane. 'How'd ya figure that?'

'It's my emerging supertalent.'

They drove in silence for five minutes. The lane merged with a long sweeping driveway leading up to stone gates. Jed could see Retro leaping around Holly and Tamizel. Angie and Vasily were there too. *Who's that hangin' on Vasily's arm?* It took a moment to recognise Miss Hale, without her mirror glasses. Jed chuckled. *Cradle-snatching. Still, surprised it took so long.*

He was out of the limo the moment it stopped, hugging Holly and Angie and everyone else in sight. Retro barked and raced in circles around them as the joy of the reunion eased aches in Jed's heart he hadn't known were there. 'Calm down, boy,' he commanded. 'I know what ya want, but we gotta keep the surprise fer just two minutes more.'

At once, Retro became meek and submissive.

Jed threw his arms open wide. 'Lords and ladies, gentlepersons, princesses, Russian farm boys and aliens, no doubt y'all are wonderin' why I've called ya here today.' He clapped his palms together above his head. 'Reece, open the gates so I can tell youse all a story.'

Reece glared but did as ordered. Retro trotted through the gates, Jed following close behind. 'My story starts three days ago. I was uploadin' a soundtrack ta freeweb when a review caught me eye. The moment I saw it I said ta meself, "I'm gonna kill 'em.

I'm trackin' 'em down an' they're gonna pay fer this impersonation. Nobody gets away with identity-theft like this.'"

He paused. The silence was broken only by the crunch of footsteps on the gravel path.

'On freeweb, y'know, it's all about the interaction. So I click through ta the music an' I realise this faker scum is there in real time, answerin' questions. I'm about ta let loose with a blast when I notice somethin' strange in the review. Lemme read it ta ya.' Jed pulled a phone from his pocket. '"It's been a long hard drought fer fans o' *Taliesin's Mantle*,"' he read. '"But after five years, the mysterious band has re-emerged with an all-new album, hammerin' with pyrotechnic tone shapes."'

Angie's golden fist was balled. 'You don't get to kill 'em, Jed. You line up behind me.'

'Lemme finish. "The feel is vintage TM, melded with a radical re-imagined sound. In the song suite—*Time-Killer, Eyecup Closeup, Goldenhand and Deadly Jed*—there are..."'

Vasily gasped and Angie screamed. Holly clenched Tamizel's arm in shock and Miss Hale's mouth dropped open.

'Who'd know those names?' Reece asked. 'It's impossible...'

'Exactly my reaction,' Jed interrupted, slipping the phone back into his pocket. 'So I message this guy and ask how he got outta the wheeltrap.'

Angie was visibly shaking.

'And he says: Hollë spat a sticky shroud, an' he an' Cardea got covered in it. It protected them when the dragontail lashed them through the doorway just a fraction o' a nanosecond before Aanundus an' Hollë got crushed by the wheeltrap. The dragon an' the spider are imprisoned forever in the gap between one second an' the next.'

'Where are they?' Angie cried. 'Gawain and Cardea?'

'So…' Reece's eyes were wide. 'When I gave you the code to cripple the cyclotron, I not only locked Aanundus and Hollë in the interstice but fused two moments. It'd be like killing time.' His breathing became ragged. 'Uri always said I would. I thought he was joking.'

'Where are they?' Angie repeated.

'They nearly died when the dragontail flicked them into a timespin. They traversed the centuries—cradled in song—until they manifested into the wilds of twenty-first century Britain. Just a coupla months ago. As they healed, they walked the land, makin' songlines, creatin' the canticle o' the Grail.' Jed paused dramatically. 'They thought you'd be at yer castle, Reece.'

'*Here?*' Angie dashed up the path.

The castle door swung open and two thin figures stepped out, arms wrapped around each other.

Only Reece held back, keeping pace with Jed as everyone else rushed, laughing and hollering, towards the distant, waving couple.

'The biggest party of all time?'

'Yer department, Milord Time-Killer, not mine. Just bring it on.' He grinned. 'Me an' me friends'll all be there.'

Acknowledgments

Thank you, thank you, thank you:

Rose
Melissa
Adele
Rosemary
Jenny
Nola
Rebekah
Ray
Chaim

Notes

Each book in *The Battle of the Trees* series is designed using numerical literary style. *Merlin's Wood* is 77,777 words long, and so is *Taliesin's Mantle*. This is an ancient arithmetic symbol of armour and is also emblematic of an awakening kiss. In addition, the chapters in this book are either multiples of 111 or 1111, or else proportioned according to the golden ratio—another symbolic number, one of freewill and choice.

I hope you didn't notice these features at all. I tried to make the numerical underlay as invisible as possible.

The musical themes are as follows:

Bura Fera ('Boss Pharaoh'), a nineteenth century African-American tune kept alive in the indigenous communities of Australia: chapters 5, 6, 7, 8, 10, 12, 13, 14, 15, 18, 20, 21, 22, 34.

The Golden Willow Tree, a traditional American folk song telling the tale of a ship: prelude, chapters 1, 2, 3, 4, 9, 32.

Llwyn Onn (The Ash Grove), a Welsh folk song hundreds of years old: chapters 23, 24, 25, 26, 27, 28, 29, 31, 33, and Coda.

Hati Memuji (The Heart Praises), an Indonesian folk song extolling the beauty of the land: chapters 11, 19, 30.

Beriozka (The Birch Tree), a very old Russian folk song: chapters 17, 18, 35.

Be Thou My Vision, an old Irish hymn based on a poem written in the sixth century: chapter 16 and Epilogue.

Anne

THE BATTLE OF THE TREES
MERLIN'S WOOD
ANNE HAMILTON

Reece has always ignored Gran's wild stories about the Welsh castle he'll one day inherit. He isn't interested in his namesake, Merlin the enchanter-who-lives-backwards-in-time either. Fairytales, no. Facts, yes. Nerdy research into time travel, definitely.

Fortunately his sister Holly has paid more attention to Gran's otherworldly ramblings. When the twins are caught in a mysterious explosion and catapulted onto an interplanetary spacecraft, they'll need to know what it means to live backwards in time.

Just for starters.

MERLIN'S WOOD, the first volume in the *Battle of the Trees* series, is numerically styled at 77,777 words. Award-winning finalist, YA fiction, **Selah Awards** 2018, and Silver Medallist, **Literary Classics International Book Awards** 2018.

'What's to stop me killing you and taking the Powers?' The giant raised the sword. 'All I see is a dwarf, a pony and seven children, none of whom is even remotely capable of resisting the might of Uller Princekiller.'

For centuries, the knights, dwarves, giants and sages of Auberon-Zamberg have been intent on a single quest. They're all searching for 'The King Who Guards the Gate'. Prophecy speaks of him as one of seven protectors who will defeat the armies of night and overcome the Dark Sleeper.

The last thing anyone expects is that these seven protectors are ordinary children.

DAYSTAR: THE DAYS ARE NUMBERED is numerically styled at 77,777 words. DAYSTAR was a finalist in the **CALEB Awards** 2018 and winner of a Notable Book citation in **Children's Book Council of Australia Awards** 2018.

Love, faith and the theory of relativity.

MANY-COLOURED REALM is a children's and YA fantasy in numerical literary style—a rigorous mathematical design underpins the text. The prologue is 1111 words, the book 111,111 words and the blurb 111.

It's got 1 nice girl, 2 bad boys, 3 tortuous tasks and 4 strange ambassadors. After that, it's hard to keep count. Dozens of elves, hundreds of goblins and legions of demons all converge on the colourless goblin realm for the king's birthday party. Robby and Chris enter a world where time is relative—can they name the king and rescue Stephen before they're all trapped? (Yes, this too is 111 words.)

Award-winning finalist in **International Book Awards** 2011.

Lightning Source UK Ltd.
Milton Keynes UK
UKHW040743020123
414708UK00001B/155